HA EL McH                                      PhD in Social
Sc nces, and                              te of Medical
Et ics. She   e author of almost a hundred published articles and books,
and won the British Medical Association Book of the Year Award in 2002.
*Right to Die*, shortlisted for the Popular Medicine prize, was highly com-
mended in the BMA 2008 Medical Book Awards. *Saving Sebastian* is her
seventh published novel set in the world of medical ethics.

### Praise for Saving Sebastian

'Problems in medical ethics are not just for doctors but for everyone. Hazel
McHaffie has found a way to bring them before a wide public. You are gripped
from the very beginning, but as you turn the pages, you are compelled to think
about the issues. It is an excellent formula.' *Baroness Mary Warnock*

### Praise for Remember Remember

'This moving book will resonate with anyone who has 'lost' a loved one
through the living death of Alzheimer's.' *Sir Cliff Richard*

'...McHaffie raises emotional and ethical issues: the use of electronic tagging
devices; the funding for Alzheimer's medication; balancing caring for a close
relative and one's own needs; and questions around the end of life... not as
theoretical 'thin' cases, as are so often used in teaching in medical ethics, but
within the richly characterised world of the novel.' *Professor Tony Hope*

'...*an amazing insight into the thought process of someone with dementia... a
gripping and heartfelt narrative.' Journal of Dementia Care*

'Extremely moving and touching. This novel, I'm sure, will resonate deeply
with family members and carers trying to cope with this most distressing
condition. Recommended.' *The Bookbag*

### Praise for Right to Die

'This heart-rending book about a young journalist who has all to live for but
is dying from Motor Neurone Disease, is written with a rare understanding of
the conflicts and horrors of such a death. Those who read it will understand
why the law needs to be changed to allow assisted dying as an option for those
whose quality of life has disintegrated...' *Lord Joffe*

'This is an immensely sensitive and thoughtful book. It tackles in raw and
compelling detail the deterioration caused by degenerative disease, while
at the same time exploring the ethical issues surrounding assisted dying.
The characters are real and attractive; their pain almost tangible. This is an
astonishingly authentic-feeling insight with a highly articulate and intelligent
central character.' *Professor Sheila McLean*

By the same author:

*Right to Die*, Luath Press, 2008
*Remember Remember*, Luath Press, 2010

# Saving Sebastian

HAZEL McHAFFIE

**Luath** Press Limited

EDINBURGH

www.luath.co.uk

First published 2012

ISBN: 978-1-906817-87-9

The author's right to be identified as author of this book
under the Copyright, Designs and Patents Act 1988 has been asserted.

The publisher acknowledges subsidy from

towards the publication of this volume

The paper used in this book is recyclable. It is made from
low chlorine pulps produced in a low energy, low emissions manner
from renewable forests.

Printed by Bell & Bain Ltd., Glasgow

Typeset in 10.5 point Sabon

# Acknowledgements

This has without doubt been the most taxing subject I've tackled to date. The science behind creating a saviour sibling is so complex that I was in danger of drowning when Dr Sue Pickering came to my rescue. Her knowledge is immense, her experience and wisdom reassuring. She answered all my questions with patience and clarity and I owe her a huge debt.

In spite of running a busy reproductive centre, Dr Clement Tay and his team gave me fantastic insights into life in this rarefied world. I left overawed by their skill and sensitivity and with a much better awareness of what it feels like to sit trembling in anticipation in such a very special clinic.

My long-time friend Dr Ian Laing put me in touch with these impressive people.

Rev Norman MacRae checked the dialogue where Nigerian inflexions and patterns of speech were used, and I'm grateful for his thorough attention to detail.

Thanks go to the Luath team for bringing another book to fruition, especially to my editor, Jennie Renton, for helping me to tighten the text and excise extraneous adverbial phrases with her usual incisive advice.

As ever my family were an ongoing support. Jonathan and Rosalyn read early manuscripts with enthusiasm and encouragement. David cast an eagle eye over the final text and removed typographical errors and inconsistencies. My preoccupation with the dilemmas relating to saviour siblings threatened to spoil the honeymoon phase of his retirement, but he learned to adapt to the demands of my working life, and drank many solitary cups of coffee in the garden without complaint.

I thank them all most sincerely.

# PROLOGUE

THE CHILD DIDN'T STIR as his mother eased the door of the cubicle shut and tiptoed away. Outside in the hospital car park the drizzle felt cool on Yasmeen's cheeks, hiding the tears she'd been holding back all evening.

It was still light for the drive home. As she let herself into the house, her husband looked up with an anxious frown. 'How's Sebastian?' The refrain of their lives.

'The IV line blocked.' Yasmeen sighed wearily. 'Again. The transfusion didn't finish until 7. Bassy looked so...' her voice trailed away. The doctors seemed confident that her four-year-old son was on the mend again, but with each crisis he moved closer to that day when nothing would bring him back from the precipice. 'He was fretting. I couldn't come away until he was fast asleep,' was all she said.

The staff had urged her to go home and get some rest after four days and nights in the ward. But she'd been reluctant. There'd been something about the way Sebastian's eyes had kept darting towards her, his reluctance to go to sleep...

Karim broke into her anxious thoughts. 'Meena.'

The tone of his voice made her turn with fear in her heart. 'Mmm?'

He held out the letter.

'Our appointment. From The Pemberton.'

Sebastian woke drenched in sweat. 'Mummy,' he whimpered. 'Mu-u-mmy.'

The nurse took his pulse and temperature then rolled the

child onto his side. She recoiled. A livid rash covered his back.

Not again. How much more could this poor kid take? If she had her way, they'd just stop all the treatment, cuddle him, let him slip away in peace.

But the parents had other ideas.

# I

'VENISON! OH DEAR. I do wish I could overcome my ridiculous prejudice against killing such beautiful creatures.' Angela's comment squealed into a lull in the conversation.

Justin shot a glance at his wife. He recognised the momentary clench of her jaw, but her voice was even.

'There's a vegetable curry coming for you, Angela. Hopefully no form of life left in it. Lindy, help yourself to potatoes. Nudge Justin for more wine, Colin.'

Justin reached for the bottle, ignoring the warning from his phone. Not until everyone's glass was refilled did he slip from the room, leaving a muttered pretext hanging in the air.

'Blaydon-Green speaking.'

'It's Anton. Labour Ward. Sorry to call you at this hour.'

'No problem. What's up?'

'Candice Opakanjo. She's five centimetres dilated. Good contractions every four minutes. You said you wanted to be informed.'

'Right. Thanks. Any problems?'

'Not so far. She's had pethidine. Tracings are good. For all three.'

'OK. I'll come in, as soon as I can decently get away.' Just give me time to taste the venison.

Helen looked up with a resigned expression as he came back into the dining room. He sent her an apologetic shrug, holding up ten fingers in a semaphore she knew only too well.

He was partial to all forms of game but venison topped his list, and this particular dish was a new one. The aromatic marinade of juniper berries, peppercorns and red wine had worked its magic. Ten minutes extended to fifteen… to twenty. The least he could do when Helen had pounded, basted and seasoned to produce this perfection.

But babies care nothing for consultants' domestic commitments.

'Sorry, folks. I'm afraid I'm going to have to leave you. Special delivery.'

'Sounds like the Royal Mail,' Colin laughed.

Justin stooped to drop a kiss on Helen's head, inhaling her light aura of sandalwood.

'Masterclass venison. Bless you. Save me some cheesecake?'

'That depends.'

Candice Opakanjo was breathing her way noisily through a contraction when he entered the delivery room thirty minutes later. Five pairs of eyes checked him in. He nodded in the direction of the paediatrician already in attendance, but his gaze homed in on the man at the head end of the bed. Samuel's face registered the pain of his wife's crushing grip on his hand.

Beside the bed the monitor spelled out the seismic activity of labour; good healthy tracings. These babies seemed to have read the right books.

The pain receded and Candice looked up at him. 'This is it, then. No going back.'

'The moment you've been waiting for.'

'For all these years. Thanks. Thanks for everything.'

'Our pleasure. You're the one doing all the hard work.'

He smiled at Samuel, perspiring in the heat and emotion of impending fatherhood.

'How's it going, Samuel?'

'Fine, thanks. Just be glad when it's safely over.'

'You and me both!' Candice said. 'Yeeooow. Here it comes again.'

Justin watched the huge ebony abdomen grow tense as she huffed and blew the next contraction through its course. The midwife's hand massaged the aching back, a curious art he'd never really understood.

'Well, these little people seem determined today's the day,' he said when Candice stopped squirming long enough to take a gulp of iced water.

'Please God,' Samuel muttered under his breath.

'Or tomorrow,' Justin amended. 'Will your hands survive to see another day, Samuel?'

'I'll never be able to play the cello again!' Samuel pulled a mournful face.

They exchanged a grin. It was a joke shared in those long-ago months when emotion had threatened to overwhelm this complex man. Unlike Justin, Samuel had never even held a cello, far less mastered the art of playing one.

Justin observed Candice through three more contractions, then, satisfied that all was normal, he went in search of caffeine. He'd need a crutch to survive the night. Drinking the instant Fair Trade coffee they stocked in Labour Ward he felt a pang of regret. 9.55pm. His dinner guests would be savouring a superior blend at this very minute.

He sighed. Loyalty had to be a two-way street. After sharing all the disappointments, having assisted with the conception, he'd be mad to miss the celebration.

3.20am. From his vantage point beside Candice he could see the waiting name bands. Opakanjo Twin 1 – two labels. Opakanjo Twin 2 – two labels.

'It's a... boy!'

The first band was fastened to a quivering wrist. Twin 1.

The midwife held the child up for the new parents to see the defining genitals, his body sagging against her hand as if already wearied by the burden of independent existence.

A perfect arc of urine sprayed the sheet.

'A fine lad he is too,' Justin laughed. 'Congratulations.'

The midwife laid the boy down on his mother's chest and Candice's hands closed protectively around him.

'Hello, little man. Orlando? Yes, Poppa?'

'Orlando still sounds good to me.'

'Orlando Samuel,' Candice murmured, stroking the child's head.

A fuzz of tight black curls, huge dark eyes, broad nose, pouting lips – the baby was the very image of his father.

'Orlando. Wow. Very Shakespearean. So what's the next one going to be?' the midwife asked.

'Valentino if it's a boy. Destiny if it's a girl.'

'Fabulous names. And if it had been two girls?'

'Destiny and Venus.'

'Ahh. Gorgeous.'

A hush fell over the room.

The midwife kept her hand lightly on the swollen abdomen waiting for the first tremor. Only Candice could afford the luxury of a doze.

Justin watched her closely. For a woman of thirty-eight it had been a taxing pregnancy, and an exhausting labour. Even for an ex-long distance runner. Intervention might yet be necessary.

The midwife reached across to realign the remaining name bands. Opakanjo Twin 2.

'Here we go again!'

Orlando was thrust into the hands of the paediatrician. Candice, eyes bloodshot, voice hoarse, gathered every shred of stamina for this final rally.

After the tension of a slow first delivery the second baby seemed to shoot out.

Silence.

Then, quietly, 'And it's a... girl.'

He sneaked a look at Candice. Her skin glistening with sweat, her face puffed up with the strain of the last eighteen hours, she had eyes only for her husband.

'Destiny,' she breathed. 'Destiny Grace. Orlando and Destiny. One of each.'

'Perfect.' Samuel leaned across to kiss her.

Destiny's shrill cries filled the room.

The midwife deftly wrapped the child in a warm towel and handed the bundle to her mother. 'There we go.'

Justin sensed rather than saw Candice freeze. But it was Samuel who broke the silence, his eyes searching the doctor's face.

'Do they sometimes... go darker?'

Justin could only shake his head.

As if in slow motion, Candice unwrapped the towel to look at her daughter. Destiny lay pale against the swollen black breasts, her tongue nuzzling her mother's nipple. Her snuffling ceased as she settled into the rhythm of sucking.

Candice drew the towel back over her baby, leaving no more than the dark hair visible.

Six pairs of eyes watched her in silence.

# 2

TWO HOURS OF FITFUL SLEEP on the narrow bed in the resident's room were all Justin was able to muster. Not nearly enough for what lay ahead.

It was a relief to find the staff room empty. He chose his position with care, slightly removed from the main body of chairs but not too distant.

Coffee mugs and crisp packets littered the table, magazines and tissues lay where they'd been tossed, the daily cleaning scourge postponed to allow them to rake over events leading up to the birth of an unexpected baby. Justin stared at the debris. Was it only yesterday he'd cared about high cholesterol and appearances? The light-shade hung at its usual crazy angle, like the sword of Damocles. He hitched the collar of the white coat away from his neck and watched his colleagues filter in.

The inspector at the Human Fertilisation and Embryology Authority, had been sympathetic. 'Damn bad luck, Justin.'

The Pemberton Centre for Reproductive Medicine prided itself on its transparency and its open dealing with the governing authority. Not like some fertility units where the HFEA were the enemy, where nobody ever made a mistake, nothing ever went wrong. They were the ones the HFEA worried about. Working with material a fraction of the size of a pinhead there was always the potential for error. If Justin had declared no breaches of procedure they'd be closing his centre down right now, suspending treatment, dragging away computers, tearing through records. But they knew they could trust him. The Pemberton had reported its quota of accidents, human and mechanical. Nothing to be gained by adding to the distress of all the couples they were currently treating.

Only this time it wasn't a question of the temperature of one of the freezers rising overnight, ruining its contents, or the wrong embryos being thawed out, or a precious dish dropped. No, this amounted to the actual birth of the wrong baby. She existed. She was in a cot beside the woman who gave birth to her. She had a name. A brother.

'Carry on as usual, Justin. We'll do our best to make this investigation as low key as possible. Factor us in for about a week. I'll need to rearrange my appointments and get one of my colleagues to come up with me. And for the technical questions, Jarman – Professor Alan Jarman. Know him? Heads up the London Lucifer Centre. Sound man.'

Now Justin faced his colleagues at the sharp end of all this scrutiny.

'Here's the scenario. We have one black mum; we have one black dad. Most of you will know the Opakanjos. They've been coming to us for years. Their last IVF cycle was successful and last night they had twins at 37 weeks. One black male babe, one mixed-race female babe. The HFEA have been informed. Scott, as senior embryologist, will be liaising for us. He'll be speaking to all of you to see where we went wrong. Anything so far, Scott?'

Dr Scott Martindale, in pristine lab scrubs and white clogs, lowered his head to the papers on his lap. Six foot four in his socks, not an inch of spare flesh on his bones, he was looking positively gaunt today, hair scraped back as if he'd just stepped out of the shower, his face a study in angles, deep vertical gouges elongating the sharp nose and long chin. Curiously though, Justin observed, his rimless spectacles were filthy.

He'd always been something of an enigma, Scott – 'Great Scott' to the team – low on people-skills, high on ambition. A driven man as far as his own research was concerned, passionate even, but quickly bored by routine. He'd be so frustrated by the slog of an inquiry.

'I've extracted the relevant dates and figures,' he said in his soft Highland accent.

More riffling through the file.

As everyone waited for him to continue, Justin found himself mesmerised by those spidery fingers. He wanted to send sympathetic vibes to his colleagues but no one was looking in his direction. They were ranged in two camps. At one end, the lab staff. Centre stage the two embryologists: Scott, crouched like a suspicious schoolboy, his file shielded from sneaking glances; Nina, perched on a stool behind him, one foot flicking up and down, the insole of her clog thumping against her heel with each beat. Up, down. Up, down. Up, down. Her ankle beneath the scrub trousers was still brown from her holiday on a South African game reserve. Elephants and wildebeest had seemed an unlikely choice for someone so shy and domesticated.

A supporting cast of their laboratory colleagues ranged alongside: Emma, Zubin and Raisa. But... no Jack. Curious.

Still puzzling, Justin scanned the other end, the clinical team. The nurses, Amy, Elka, Glenys, Rita, Surata, Claire, Astrid and Marelda. The doctors slightly behind them, one step removed from the emotion. Leonie and Zhen meeting his gaze without flinching, too junior to take any real responsibility here. The senior medics, Campbell, Gavriella and Kristen, lounging in their chairs, inscrutable, almost nonchalant.

Justin knew better. This catastrophe had implications for them all, individually and collectively; for the very viability of the whole outfit.

'The paperwork looks straightforward,' Scott said finally.

'Clear track right through?' Justin asked.

'Seems to be.'

'How many others on the day of harvesting?'

'Seven. That's Readington, Lander, Carling, Dixon, Abernethy, Garnock and... Habgood.'

'Remind me, how many non-white Caucasians?' Justin said.

'The mother in the Landers case. She's Asian.'

'And Mr Garnock has some Indian blood, doesn't he?'

Gavriella chipped in.

There was a murmur of assent from the nurses.

'None of them Afro-Caribbean though?' Justin clarified.

'No.'

'Any irregularities with anybody?'

'Not that I can see.'

The door inched open and the longest-serving lab technician, Jack Fitzpatrick, let his apology precede him. Justin waited for him to sit down before continuing.

'Right. How many successful fertilisations on that date?'

'Six.'

'Hmmm. High. So that's seven batches of eggs, seven sperm samples.'

Scott grunted assent, running a fingernail down his list.

'Two days later we've got six batches of embryos.'

'That's correct.'

'And on the day of the Opakanjo replacement, how many did we transfer?'

'Of the original seven? Four others besides the Opakanjos.'

'Who were they?'

'Carling, Abernethy, Habgood and Readington.'

'Ahhh. The Readingtons delivered several weeks ago, didn't they?' A bad memory that one.

'Aye. Male infant. Prem. Lived five days,' Scott read. A statement. Nothing to indicate the pain behind that outcome.

'And Marcus Habgood was white.'

'Definitely,' Scott confirmed.

'And the Dixons?' This time it was a genuine question; Justin couldn't remember hearing about them.

Scott's finger tracked along the columns. 'Lost theirs at eighteen weeks.'

'How many embryos do they have left?'

'Two.'

'Still frozen?'

'I think. Aye. There it is.'

'Which leaves?' Justin asked.

'Carling and Abernethy. The Abernethys had a girl last week. In Special Care. Traumatic delivery. Severe birth apnoea.'

'But white presumably?'

'Yes,' Dr Kristen Blackwell said, her voice heavy with emotion. 'She was white.'

Justin remembered Kristen's distress. How she'd wept with frustration and pain at the waste of a hard-earned life thrown away. A healthy term-baby damaged beyond repair during a protracted delivery because of the mother's insistence that everything be 'natural'. He'd told her, 'You can't afford to take it so personally, not in this game.' But sometimes you just did, and anyway, better a tear or two than Scott's robotic detachment when it came to the tragedy of infertility.

'So, only one pregnancy left from that batch.'

'The Carlings,' Scott said brusquely. Emotion always unnerved him.

'Twins, as I recall?'

'That's right,' Scott confirmed. 'Due any day.'

'Plus we have frozen embryos from how many of the original seven?'

Scott scrutinised his figures. 'Five.'

'Including the Opakanjos?'

'No. We only got two good embryos from them. Put them both back.'

'And no black or brown infants born to white parents?'

'Not so far.'

'Which means,' Justin scanned his team, 'we hold our breath till the Carling twins arrive.'

Holding breath was the least of it. The scenario was unravelling in all their eyes: the meticulous checking of every movement. Their own internal search; then the heavy brigade from the HFEA bulldozing all over their territory. Deciding whom to recall, who required an apology, whose certainty to erode, whose trust to destroy. Playing shipwreck with real lives.

No one wanted to be the hand that precipitated this landslide.

Justin was gentle. 'Scott will be talking to you individually. Mistakes happen. If you can shed any light, don't hesitate to come forward. The sooner we can clear this up, the sooner we can return to normal.'

Watching them file out in silence, he wondered if any of them had realised the implications for him as Clinical Director. No, their own futures filled the whole screen right now. He sighed. Only eleven days ago these very same people were celebrating.

It had been a tough year: the constant struggle to justify the service to NHS managers; too many couples waiting to be treated; too few embryologists; dwindling numbers of sperm donors; pressure to take on more and more private patients. The unexpected surge in their fertility rates had been a boost to morale. The team took the credit to their united selves, thumbing their noses at the tight-fisted finance department. Even Scott, normally too preoccupied with his own projects to engage in the clinic's real life battles, even he deigned to join them at the local hostelry.

They raised a toast to the good news travelling.

Eleven days ago nobody conceived of *this* word travelling.

# 3

IT WAS COOL inside the Posybowl. Everything was wide open – the shop, the florists' van, the back door. And empty.

Natalie inhaled the scent of freesias and stephanotis, eucalyptus and lilies, merging with a hint of damp moss. This florist was good. Beautiful colour combinations, unusual shapes, clever use of pampas and variegated leaves. She swithered between two arrangements. Stargazer lilies or Casablancas?

'Hey, Earth to Ruthie! Hello-o!' The delivery-man's words carried easily. Natalie could see his green overalls leaning on the doorpost of the back room.

The disembodied female voice was barely audible. 'Look, Arthur, I'm already miles behind schedule. If I'm to get home this side of midnight I really *must* get on.'

'OK, OK. Can't a body be friendly round here? A bloke has to take a break sometimes. It's all right for you safely in here, but it's chaos outside, what with temporary traffic lights in the High Street, and the bypass gridlocked. Eight miles an hour, that's what we was doing this morning. Eight bloody miles an hour.'

Natalie heard the sigh above the creak of a foot moving another rung up the stepladder. 'I'll be down in a minute.'

'But don't you reckon it's odd? About those kiddies,' he persisted. 'One black and one brown.'

Ruth's voice came more clearly, 'How come?'

'Don't ask me. I only deliver the flowers, not the babies.'

'Well, I've met the grandmother and she's coal black. She was in here earlier in the week. Proud as punch she was. And the dad's been in a couple of times. He's black too.'

'So's the young Mrs Opakanjo. So I guess that makes them all black, barring the one kiddie.'

'Arthur, is this a wind-up?'

'No. Honest.'

'So how d'you know – about the babies?'

'Seen them meself. They was lying there in their wee baskets, side by side, when I rolled up with that spiky thing you do – you know, orange and blue.'

'Strelitzias.'

'That's the one. And she got me to carry it right into the house. That's how I seen those little piccaninnies. So, what d'you reckon?'

'Don't ask me. Ahhh! *There* they are!'

Two boxes of florists' wire dropped to the ground. The aluminium creaked as the legs descended the ladder and a head of bright honey-blonde curls appeared, framing a freckled face. Ruth picked up the boxes, dragging her tabard down with her free hand. Even from a distance Natalie could see Arthur's eyes were appreciative.

'Well, as me dear old Gran used to say, I smell a bit of hanky panky in there somewhere.'

The girl strode over to the work counter and plonked the boxes of wires down with a thump.

'You'll smell more than a bit of hanky panky if you don't get this afternoon's order into that van of yours in four minutes flat. You haven't even *started* moving them to the Conference Centre! I did not slave since the crack of dawn to have this lot' – the wave of her hand took in a row of purple and cream hand-ties – 'wilting in my shop. So get your butt out of here before I stick these wires somewhere the sun don't shine.'

Arthur moved away from the doorpost but made no move as yet to pick up the flowers.

'No team spirit, that's your trouble. I bring you news to brighten your little isolation cell here, and all I get is insults. You'll rue the day when I retire and there's nobody to fill you in on the gossip.'

'The way you're going it'll be the sack long before your pension.' Ruth pulled an oblong of oasis towards her and clamped it into a plastic container. 'There's gossip and there's gossip. We aren't paid to speculate about the private lives of our customers. The Opakanjos and their friends have spent a fortune in here and I don't intend to pry into what's no concern of mine.'

'Spoilsport,' grumbled Arthur, but he stooped to pick up the first of the arrangements.

Natalie lingered just out of sight until Arthur had driven off and Ruth had returned to creating a foil of green foliage. She moved to the shop front selecting chrysanthemums, roses, gerberas, so absorbed in her task that she was startled when Natalie stepped forward.

'Oh, I'm so sorry. I do hope you haven't been waiting long.'

'Not at all! I've been trying to decide between these bouquets. You're really very good.'

'Thank you.'

On an impulse Natalie rejected both the lilies and chose instead a flamboyant crimson and white arrangement wrapped in red cellophane.

'I'm sure, being in their locality... do you know the Opakanjo family? They've just had twins?'

'Yes, indeed. I've done several lots of flowers for them.'

'And has anyone chosen this particular bouquet?'

'Not that I can remember.'

'Then I'll take it. It's perfect.'

When she reappeared ten minutes later Ruth looked up from a sea of yellow and bronze and tipped her head enquiringly.

'Something wrong?'

'Oh no! It's... well, I've done the silliest thing. I don't seem to have brought the Opakanjos' address with me. Must be in my other bag. Would you mind terribly?'

Ruth put down her secateurs and wiped her hands on her tabard.

The order book was dog-eared and stained. Her fingers were

still damp. Natalie held her breath.

'Ahhh. Here we are! Opakanjo. 47 Hill Drive.'

'Thank you *so* much.'

Natalie walked briskly away from the shop. In a quiet cul-de-sac she took out her mobile phone and dialled her boss.

'*Evening News*. Sandra Lifton speaking.'

'Sandra, hi. It's me, Natalie.'

'How're things?'

'Listen, I've just overheard something. Some story about mixed-race twins... No, I don't know that... Worth a little sniff around?... Yes, yes! Discretion's my middle name. OK. I'll keep you posted.'

She had the rest of the day to follow her nose.

# 4

JACK OPENED ONE EYE. Only 6.30. Another thirty minutes before the alarm would drag him out of slumber. He drifted gently.

'You awake?' Patsy's whisper reached into the privacy of his dream.

'Half.'

'Can I ask you something? Hypothetically speaking.'

'Bit early in the morning for hypotheticals, isn't it?'

'Shut up. And you can stop *that*, Jack Fitzpatrick, *right now*! I'm serious.'

'Oh, so am I. So. Am. I.'

'I'll get up and that'll be that,' she warned, flouncing across to her own side of the bed.

'OK. I'm listening.'

'You know about genes and fertilisation and everything, right?'

'Well, basically, yeah – not all the really technical stuff though.'

'So, can a black woman have a nearly white kid?'

'If the dad's white she could.'

'But if the dad's black too?'

Jack took his time, dissecting each word before he let it escape. Patsy had a habit of quoting him ages after the original conversation.

'If they aren't black through and through, she could,' he said. 'Maybe if they both have a white relative in a previous generation, something like that. I don't know about the colour genes – if one of them's recessive or not.'

He dropped his head to kiss the bump in her collar-bone where it hadn't set quite straight when she'd fallen out of a tree, a snotty little kid competing for the respect of her much older cousins. She didn't jerk away so he moved up to her neck. This time she swotted him to the side and he subsided onto his own pillow.

'They *look* totally black. I mean straight-out-of-Africa-black. Both of them,' she said.

He froze. 'Hey! What's this all about? Thought you said it was hypothetical.'

'Well, one of our doctors, he's got this couple on his list and they're black Africans and... Listen, this is in confidence, right?'

'Right. Cross your heart and hope to die.' He traced a cross over her heart so swiftly she had no chance to react.

'These patients in our surgery, they've just had twins, only one's black and one's kind of light brown. I mean, how can that happen?'

He whistled, he hoped convincingly. 'No kidding?'

'No kidding. So?'

'Mother been fooling around maybe?' he said, praying for forgiveness. 'I read somewhere some woman conceived twice at the same time – by two different men. Playing away as well as at home. She had twins. Nobody would've known except they were both the spitting image of their dads.'

'Straight up?'

'Scout's honour.'

Patsy was silent for a long time. He half-lifted his head to look at her but she was lost in thought.

'I don't think this mum's like that. I mean, they've been doing the whole IVF thing for yonks.'

'So?'

'Well, if you go to all that trouble.'

'Doesn't mean she's Mother Theresa. Maybe she got fed up waiting. Maybe *she's* fine herself. Fertile, I mean. Maybe it's *him* that's got the problem. Say she secretly has a fling with somebody else. A white bloke. Only she gets pregnant by him same time the IVF works.'

She turned slowly. Jack stared into the flecked hazel irises.

'That possible?'

'*I* don't know.' His eyes slid down to her parted lips, her long neck, the thin blue veins threading down to her breasts. 'I'm only a jobbing lab technician, not a PhD in genetics! I guess it's *possible.*'

She was silent so long that Jack began to suspect she had dozed off again. He sneaked a sideways glance. No, she was very much awake. When she spoke it was as if she were trying words on for size.

'Do you – people like you, I mean – the technicians and everything – do you get to handle the eggs and things and the embryos?'

'Well, nobody actually *handles* them.'

'Tsccch!' Her elbow was sharp in his ribs. 'You know what I mean. Carrying them on dishes or in syringes or whatever you do?'

'Sometimes. Why?'

'So – could they get muddled up?'

'The technicians?'

'No, idiot. The eggs.'

'I guess it's *possible,*' Jack said. 'But this stuff is regulated like you wouldn't believe. Everything gets checked and double-checked, everything's charted and labelled and signed for. I can't see a mistake happening.'

'So you'd think it was the mother having a bit on the side?'

'More likely than a lab error, I'd say.' Suddenly Jack knew an urge to adopt Catholicism. The need for absolution was visceral.

'You wouldn't imagine something like that happening, would you? I mean getting caught out like that. So obvious.'

'It'd teach you not to fool around ever again, I guess.'

'I feel sorry for the dad. Imagine what he thinks whenever he looks at that kiddie. Or when anybody else sees it.'

'You're wasting your talents. You should be writing detective stories, instead of being a doctors' receptionist,' he said lightly, inching closer. 'Patsy Graham, the novelist. Sounds nifty, don't you think?'

'Now you *are* kidding!'

'You're skinny enough to fit onto the jacket flap anyway.'

'For the last time, Jack, I am *not* skinny!'

'You should hear what my old ma says.'

'Huhhh!' disposed of that threat.

He closed his eyes and feigned sleep.

After a while he said casually, 'What does the doc in your surgery think?'

'About me becoming an author? No idea. I haven't asked him.'

'Touché,' he grinned at her. 'About that coffee kid?'

'How should I know?'

'Doesn't he write things in the notes?'

'Course. But *we* don't see it. We have *our* code of practice too, y'know. It's not only your infertility place that has rules and regulations.'

'Uuueww! Who rattled your cage?' Jack propped himself up on one elbow and watched her brow furrow in annoyance.

'Nobody. And don't be such a moron. I wish I'd never mentioned it.'

'You premenstrual or something?'

'Trust you!' and with that she threw back the duvet, grabbed her clothes and stomped off to the bathroom.

Jack watched her pert exit and then lay back down again slowly, warning flags flapping across his field of vision. Ominous ones.

He was still pondering her questions when he arrived at The Pemberton Centre. All the team were in today, both clinical and lab staff. By nine o'clock the waiting room was seething.

The staff exchanged banter as they passed each other. 'It's a madhouse out there.' 'Battery farming comes to mind.' 'Remind me why I turned my back on accountancy.'

But once into the routines of lab work, Jack's mind had space to roam. The rows of tubes, the pipettes, the dishes, the medium – he knew where everything was, what everything did. The repetition had a rhythm and security all of its own. Troubling thoughts began to recede. He hissed tunes between his teeth; sizzing, Patsy called it. She hated it with a passion.

When he could take a break he started on his daily dose of Sudoku. He was soon absorbed and it took time for the polished shoes standing to the right of his clogs to register. Had to be the boss, Dr Justin Blaydon-Green.

'Are you all right, Jack?' The quirked eyebrow and the glint of his glasses made Justin look slightly myopic.

After a glance up, Jack swallowed a mouthful of coffee. 'Yeah. I'm fine. Thanks.'

When Justin still didn't move Jack half-turned in his seat as if anxious to get on with relaxing. 'Something wrong, Doc?'

'I don't know. That's what I'm wondering.'

'Sorry?'

'You're not exactly your usual perky self. I was wondering if there's a problem.'

'Just thinking. I guess there's always a first time, huh? *Thinking is the most unhealthy thing in the world, and people die of it just as they die of any other diseases.*' It was a struggle making the smile fit his face. The smokescreen of Wilde's wit seemed oddly transparent today.

'Well, it looks like thinking isn't good for *your* health!'

'*Fortunately, in England at any rate, thinking is not catching.* For England read Scotland.' This time the smirk came more readily.

He scribbled a '3' into the top right-hand Sudoku box and tracked down to the next square without his brain engaging with his hand.

'Care to share your thinking?' Justin said.

Jack flicked the end of his biro in and out three times in quick succession before speaking.

'Well, I reckon Mr Opakanjo's feeling pretty scunnered, right this minute.'

'Ri-ight.' The hard look bored into him. 'Because?'

Jack gave up. Keeping his voice low, and watching somewhere east of Justin's face for his reaction, he blurted it out. 'People are talking. I heard it myself yesterday.'

Justin sank down onto the chair opposite.

'Well, it was always going to happen, Jack. Eventually. Although I'd hoped for a bit more time. But hey ho! Moses' mother couldn't keep him hidden either and I guess she had more reason than most to try.'

Jack's heart seemed to be fluttering too close to his larynx, seriously affecting the steadiness of his voice, but he looked straight at Justin.

'Was it us? Was it our mistake?'

'I can't think of any other explanation.' Justin was leaning forward now, looking at the neat rows of numbers, but it felt like he was crawling inside Jack's head. 'Can you?'

'The lady? She might have been playing away. If you get my drift.'

'You've seen what these treatments are like. I can't imagine any woman feeling like having an affair when she's going through harvesting and transfer. Can you?'

'Not if you say not.'

'It's technically possible, but practically unlikely.'

'OK, but…'

'But?'

Jack gulped twice. 'Well, I was reading that some animals have chimeric sperm.'

Justin stared at him in amazement.

'Were you indeed? And what do you know about chimeric sperm?'

'Well, this paper I was reading, it said some creatures – like marmosets – they can have babies with the DNA of the father's twin. Even though the twin hasn't been anywhere near the mother.'

'And you're thinking?'

'Could Mr Opakanjo have funny sperm? Chimeric.'

'To the best of my knowledge humans don't have chimeric sperm.'

'I guess not.'

Silence.

'Still thinking, Jack?'

'Still thinking.'

'Let me know if your thinking takes you somewhere I should know about.'

'Sure thing.'

For the rest of the morning Jack's mind played with the questions.

It dawned on him that he had no idea what Justin was thinking. His own speculation had been drowning out all other sound.

# 5

SAMUEL WAS STARING down into the matching Moses baskets. His back was towards Candice but she knew he'd sensed her presence. He didn't turn, didn't speak. She tasted the bile of irritation. She made herself search for the man she'd fallen in love with all those years ago.

She'd been bouncing on the running track, limbering up before a long distance race, well aware of her magnificent body, the power perhaps more than the beauty. Her coach had told her: 'This one's in the bag, kid,' and his confidence had given her a glow of satisfaction. All those gruelling hours of training were paying off.

She was concentrating on pseudo-starts when the unknown black man hoved into view, trailing a white-line machine. Something about the discrepancy in size and colour had made her giggle. She didn't intend any ridicule, it was nothing more than the tension she always felt before a race, but he'd heard her; his face told her that. She took a step... at that precise moment the official roared at them to take their positions on the starting blocks.

Perhaps it was her conscience weighing her down, or maybe she'd lost focus – whatever, she'd come fourth in the heat, out of the race before it became any kind of a challenge. After her coach had finished with her she slunk away to a bench out of view, and that's how the nameless white-line man, squeaking his marking machine back to base, found her, all blotched and defeated.

If the positions had been reversed she knew she would have

felt a fall from grace was exactly the punishment for a conceited bitch who cared nothing for other people's feelings, but young Samuel Opakanjo had been cast in a very different mould. He hung around, sympathised, put this one hiccup in her career into perspective, made silly jokes until she couldn't help but smile. By the time they left that hidden spot and she faced the world as it existed after her shame, her self-esteem was on the way to recovery.

He didn't tell her until their fifth date that he was a university student augmenting his meagre allowance with casual labour. By that time she wouldn't have cared where he came in the pecking order.

Not once since had he ever alluded to that first encounter, but Candice had never forgotten it. Time and again she'd seen the same integrity. Like a stick of Blackpool rock; whatever you did, the essential core of authenticity remained. It was hard sometimes not to resent a man whose moral plumbline showed up her own uncertain standards, but his devotion and pride in her achievements somehow neutralised her volatility. Slowly, gradually, she learned to trust. It took time. You couldn't overnight shake off the inheritance of childhood: blazing rows, a stormy separation, an acrimonious divorce.

Nowadays though, since the twins, everything was different. His passivity and tolerance irked her increasingly. Why did he never retaliate? Why did he just take whatever she threw at him, no matter how mean and unreasonable she was?

Her eyes took in his sheer size; the bulk of a man who packed a frightening punch in the gym, who'd been first choice in the local tug of war every year. She noticed the hunched shoulders, the bowed head above the uneven hairline – the same hairline she used to trace with her finger, teasing him that it showed he had a crooked sense of humour, back in those far-off days when life smiled.

Here in this small room, he was like a slave chained to the galley, forced to row against the tide, for an overseer who was at once fickle and domineering. She knew a sudden desire to release him, send him away, before the damage became irreversible.

It was his boss's fault for granting him protracted leave. In the early days she'd have given anything for extended homecomings, but the repeated absences had taken their toll. Onshore leave wasn't the honeymoon her friends imagined. Adjusting was hard work. Both ways. Especially when he was at sea at her most fertile times. When there was no one around to share her monthly disappointment.

He'd told her only this morning: he'd been given another two weeks off work. Full stop. There was no 'Would you like?' 'What d'you think?' Couldn't he see how much she needed her own space?

The words when they came slammed their way through all her mental preparation.

'I can't go back until we've decided.'

She gritted her teeth.

'I don't see what we've got to lose,' Samuel said.

'Destiny. That's what.'

He turned to face her. She saw something in his eyes she didn't want to name. She looked away.

'They wouldn't do that. They wouldn't take her away,' he said.

'You can't promise that. You don't know.' She heard her voice rising and forced herself to stop.

'They *wouldn't*. You have all the claims. You carried her all those months. You gave birth to her. They *couldn't* take her away.'

'So, why d'you need tests, then?'

She watched him rehearsing his reasons. It had become habitual, this caution, doctoring sentences, tiptoeing around her emotions.

'Well, what about the real parents – the biological ones, I mean? This was their embryo. Maybe it was partly yours or partly mine, but it's somebody else's too. It's not wholly ours. It's their genes too. Maybe they haven't got any kids at all. Maybe they won't ever have any. They went through all the hell we went through to produce this embryo, then somebody else gets the kid. Don't they at least have a right to know?'

'But why? For what purpose?'

'Well, I'm sorry, but *I'd* want to know if I'd had a kid.'

'What good would it do?'

'I'd feel better if they at least knew they'd created it, and it was being brought up properly.'

'She's not an "it". She's a "she",' Candice bit back.

'I was being non-specific.'

'Hmm! Well, to be *very* specific, suppose we had the DNA test, this other person, this *stranger*, this couple, are told and they want to be part of Destiny's life. Or to bring her up themselves? What would you say to that?'

'What would I say?' Samuel mused. 'I... I wouldn't want them to take her away.'

'You sure about that?' It was a quick slice at his defences. Uncalled for. But instinctive.

'Of course I'm sure.'

She shrugged.

'It's about fairness,' Samuel said, as if all the energy had been hammered out of him.

'Really? Or is it because you're suspicious?'

'No.'

'Or worried what people will think?'

He gave her a hard look, opened his mouth, closed it, and walked out of the room without another word.

There was suddenly no outlet for her pent-up emotions. What was it with men? Why were they genetically incapable of reading signals? Why didn't he fight back? Couldn't he see how he drove her to say things she instantly regretted? Things that hovered unresolved until the next time words broke into the silences that inhabited their days.

Her mother had warned her, 'If you marry an Aquarius he won't fight. He'll walk away. Anything for peace.' She'd pitied her mother her impoverished understanding. This was *Samuel*. Of course he wouldn't fight; he loved her. Neither would she; she loved him. And she'd had enough of fighting to last her a lifetime.

But he *had* walked away. Many times.

She sighed. Because this tension wasn't new; it couldn't all be laid at Destiny's door. At first it was the infertility. She'd blamed the hormones, the waiting, the loss of control, the whole stressful business. 'As soon as I'm pregnant...'

Then she *was* pregnant! Wonderfu. Except it wasn't. Because it was twins; twice the hormonal upset, double the anxiety. OK, just 'hang on in there till the babies are safely here. Then we'll be fine again'. She knew they would.

And then there was Destiny.

Everything had conspired to grind them deeper into this habit.

She didn't know who to dislike more in this moment – Samuel or herself.

Later, uncomfortably engorged with milk, Candice stood staring down at the sleeping twins.

The room was a mess. Stains, clutter, the remnants of snacks; everywhere evidence of her neglect. She stooped to gather up the soiled garments discarded at bath-time – two tiny cardigans, two sleep-suits, two milky bibs, a sheet sticky with vomit.

Destiny was sleeping so quietly Candice checked she was breathing. The baby screwed up her eyes and yawned. Candice dropped a kiss onto the downy cheek.

'Oh, baby,' she whispered. 'It's not Poppa's fault. Just you make sure you don't grow into an old crosspatch like me, all scratchy and horrid.'

She sighed. Hadn't she vowed not to be like her own mother? And daily now she recognised the carbon copy; same glowering looks, same cutting asides.

There had been no cessation of hostilities after her father finally moved out when she was fifteen; there was simply a change of whipping boy. Now Candice's younger brother took the flak. Jordan had been labelled from the age of two: a 'slow developer', a boy with 'learning difficulties'. His problems became the trigger for tantrums and maternal spite that would have brought the social services down on them – had her behaviour been visible. But Blossom Solomon was Mrs Respectability outside her own four walls. People looked with admiration and pity at this stoical single mother bringing up a difficult teenager who still couldn't travel on a bus alone, who couldn't tell the time, who refused to go to clubs or into respite care.

And then Jordan was killed, aged twenty, falling down a mine-shaft on the moors behind their home. A merciful release, they whispered. But how terrible for his grief-stricken mother – seeing it happen, summoning the emergency services, watching while they pulled up his mangled body.

Only Candice knew how much her mother had resented Jordan. And she kept her suspicions to herself.

Now she was free to leave the parental home. For good. Her days as comforter, as lightning conductor, were over. She moved four hundred miles away and immersed herself in her work as a physiotherapist, and in her first love, sport. She scrubbed her memory slate clean. She was Candice Solomon, a stand-alone individual, a new creation.

Or was she?

Candice lifted her head and stared at her reflection in the mirror. What had she inherited? Her eyes strayed back to the sleeping child. What if... ? Perhaps it would be a mercy if her genes had not been passed on to another female baby.

She stroked the soft cheek. The pouting lips turned towards her finger, tongue exploratory even in sleep.

'Would you be better off with another mummy...?' She couldn't go there.

Destiny began to whimper. It was all the excuse Candice needed to hug her close. She inhaled the smell of babyness, felt the panting breaths against her neck. Her hold tightened.

'I can't,' she whispered. 'I *can't* let you go. You're mine. You belong to me.'

The snuffling grew more urgent. Destiny licked the skin of her face, searching. The milk surged before she could unbutton her shirt and draw out her aching breast. The sight of her black nipple against Destiny's pale lips made her shiver, but the baby knew no doubt.

'Oh baby, baby, what will you think when Mummy comes to collect you from school? When the other children say cruel things? Will you wish you were in a white family? Is that what you would choose, sweetheart? Will you hate me for keeping you?'

A tear splashed onto the pumping cheek. Candice wiped it away with her thumb.

'I'm just so, so tired. So tired.'

As if he smelled his own deprivation, Orlando woke, and his demands raced from nought to sixty in two seconds flat. Before she could move, Samuel was there, lifting him, changing him, passing him across, clean and comfortable.

The wrinkled fingers, the strong smell of steeping fluid, told her Samuel had been sluicing the nappies. She wanted to thank him for his support. She didn't. There it was again; that malfunctioning valve between intention and action. As soon as mother and twins were happily synchronised Samuel returned to the washing without a word being exchanged. He left her to simmer until coffee time.

'Doughnuts today,' he announced as if the rest of the morning had never happened. 'You deserve a treat.' And talk moved onto the news that three suicide bombers had attacked in Afghanistan, fourteen innocent lives had been forfeited, two of them babies.

What were *her* cares in the face of tragedy of those proportions?

Sadly, today, in this house, they were a thousand times bigger.

# 6

UNTIL NOW CANDICE had always deferred to her consultant, Dr Blaydon-Green. She liked him, she respected him. He had a wealth of experience – not only of obstetrics and fertility, but of life, its tragedy as well as its comedy. And he knew her. Inside out, you could say!

But on this one point she was adamant: she wanted their next meeting to be at The Pemberton Centre, as every other time.

An hour before they were due to leave, Lily-May, the receptionist, rang.

'Would you mind coming to the back entrance this time, Mr Opakanjo? Instead of taking first left off the main road, go third left. Follow the road round to the signpost and go sharp left again. You'll see a grey door on your right with a reinforced glass window in it. The car park's on the right. Ignore the signs that say, "Staff Only". Call up on the intercom at the grey door and we'll let you in. Take the lift to the second floor. You'll come out right opposite reception. Any problems, give me a ring.'

No reason given. But there were always road works somewhere. Good of the staff to let them know.

The misgivings started the minute she saw the familiar row of blue chairs. The old disappointment, stress and tension mocked her stupidity.

Wreathed in smiles, Lily-May came out from behind the desk to crouch beside the twins, cooing.

'I'm afraid Dr Blaydon-Green's been held up. But that gives

38

me a chance to admire these beautiful babies.'

No specifics. But they understood. It was the price of dedication.

Candice tried to immerse herself in the Mary Higgins Clark novel she'd started the day before. It was one of the few bonuses of her new life; even during the long night-feeds she could find solace in fiction. She read novels she'd never even heard of before, air-headed beauties falling in love with seriously rich heroes, and for a time her own problems would recede.

But here in this clinic today the words might as well have been ancient Greek. Samuel was hidden behind the *Guardian*; a much more sensible choice. Why hadn't she thought of that? A crossword, codewords, anything would have been better.

Thirty minutes passed without a syllable being exchanged. No sound except the rustle of the paper, an occasional grunt from one of the twins.

Another couple took their seats, directly opposite. Candice allowed herself a swift glance, a half-smile, before dropping her eyes back to the safety of her book. They were smartly dressed, Asian. And they too sat in silence.

But now the atmosphere seemed charged with a different kind of tension. Oh for an invisibility cloak to throw over her babies. *Babies? Here?*

A second couple joined them. More apologies from Lily-May.

Regret turned into annoyance. Dr Blaydon-Green should have known, he should have overruled her, insisted somewhere else would be more appropriate. Samuel should have known, he should have insisted.

The second couple spoke occasionally in heavily accented whispers, barely intelligible. The rustle of sweet papers, the scent of mint, the rasp of a stiletto repeatedly scuffed against the coarse carpet, somehow injected a hint of normality into the room.

Candice glanced across to the feet opposite her. Perfectly-creased black trousers set off rows of bright beads on the open sandals. Pearl pink toe- and fingernails echoed the rose-pink of the embroidered tunic. A row of bangles lay half hidden in the sleeve. And the face... the woman was stunning.

A surge of pure envy coursed through Candice's veins. She stole another glance. The dark eyes smiled. Candice looked away. Absurd to feel such jealousy. The car-seats full of baby were at *her* feet not those of this gorgeous stranger. The rest was down-payment for a dream fulfilled. The moment passed.

Her eyes wandered to the other side. Bare mottled legs, miniscule red straps, sharp three-inch heels. They seemed too frivolous for the solemn business of IVF, of ICSI, of embryo transfer.

A phone rang. The measured tread of the receptionist's serviceable shoes broke the silence.

'I'm terribly sorry to keep you all waiting. Dr Blaydon-Green really wants to see you all himself, but I'm afraid he'll be about another twenty minutes. Would you like to go for a coffee or a breath of fresh air, maybe, and Mr and Mrs Opakanjo, if you could come back in, say, fifteen minutes? I really can't apologise enough. I know you've all got appointment times but this is a genuine emergency. He'll do his best to be here as soon as possible.'

Orlando, woken by the sudden noise, started to whimper. Candice snatched him up. He nuzzled for a moment – only a moment – and then with a single breath cranked up the volume.

'He needs to be fed,' she whispered to Samuel. 'I'll just stay here. Could you bring me a coffee?'

Even the sound of the baby's gulping seemed to eclipse the thud of four pairs of receding footsteps. Why, oh why hadn't the Asian lady gone with them? Orlando would drink in his mother's mood; they'd have yet another fretful afternoon. Fizzy milk, the health visitor called it. 'Stay calm; the babies will detect your stress.' Candice kept her head bent towards Orlando.

'He's beautiful,' the woman said softly.

'Thank you. I'm sorry.'

'What's his name?' 'How old is he?' 'Is he a good feeder?'

'Does he sleep well?' 'How do you manage with two of them?' The questions kept coming and Candice felt her reserve melting in the face of such genuine interest.

Destiny startled awake and let out a wail. Candice half-stooped, Orlando was dislodged, the twin crescendos mounted. Suddenly the stranger was there, lifting Destiny, deftly tipping her over her shoulder, not waiting for consent to her 'May I?'

'Thank you. I'm so sorry.' Candice mumbled.

Emotions churned. This stranger's hands – her Destiny-coloured hands – were those of an expert. The baby's eyes closed, only an occasional empty sucking breaking the peace. She seemed so at home nestling there on the foreign shoulder.

'You're... a natural,' Candice said, her throat clenching on the words.

'Oh, I've had two of my own. And I simply adore babies.'

Candice stared directly at the other woman.

She laughed. 'Karim and I aren't infertile; we just need a specific baby.'

'Oh. I'm sorry.'

'Please, don't apologise, it sounds crazy, I know. By the way, my name's Yasmeen. Yasmeen Zair.'

'I'm Candice. Candice Opakanjo. I'm sorry. We used to come here. For IVF. I just assumed. You don't need to explain.'

'I don't mind. It's not a secret.' Something changed in her expression, her voice sliding into a lower register. 'We have a little boy, Sebastian. He's four and a bit, and he's got a blood disorder. He needs daily treatment and he won't live to be an adult if he doesn't get stem cells from a matched donor. He's got an older sister who's fine, perfectly healthy, but not the same tissue type. So we need a baby who's a match. That's why we're here. Goodness! I've made it sound so simple. But of course, it's not. We don't know yet if it's even possible.'

Candice stared, tears blurring her vision. 'I can't imagine... how do you cope?'

'When it happens you don't have much choice. But actually, Sebastian is how we cope. He's so brave, in spite of all the treatment and everything.'

At that moment Karim and Samuel rounded the corner bearing four steaming coffees, the Nigerian dwarfing his companion.

'Not right now, Karim,' Yasmeen said, waving the hot drink away from the baby in her arms. But no sooner were the words uttered than Destiny was encased in big black hands, lifted from her shoulder and buckled back into her car-seat with no more than a brief, 'Thanks. I'll take her. I'm sorry.'

'Thank you *so* much.' Candice was torn between annoyance and gratitude.

'A pleasure,' Yasmeen smiled.

Samuel swung Destiny to and fro until Candice felt seasick herself.

It was at this moment that the other couple appeared, bearing not only hot drinks but carriers of snack food. Candice glanced up. The girl, all flashing thighs, bleached hair and sulky mouth, was only one step in front of her escort, but it was her skimpy floral cotton skirt, her bare midriff, that demanded all the attention. Her companion's square face wore an expression of apologetic concern.

'I need to get oot this place,' the girl began in a thick Scottish accent. Her eyes fell on Destiny. She bent to peer more closely. 'They both belong to yous? Twins, eh?'

'Yes.' Candice dug her toes further into her shoes – Marks and Spencer's glove-shoes, bought to accommodate her swollen feet, to bear the burden of twins. So dowdy against the skimpy styles of the other two women.

'Was it IVF?'

'Yes.'

'How come they're different?'

'*Des*!' the boy hissed.

'We aren't sure.'

'You having it an' all?' It was Yasmeen's turn for scrutiny.

'We don't know yet.'

'How long've you got?'

'*Des*! I'm sorry!' The boy gave a despairing look.

Yasmeen smiled at him before turning back to Des. 'Well, it's rather different for us. We have two children already.'

'How come you're here, then?'

'Our little boy is sick. We need another baby to save his life.'

'Eh?'

Something stronger than good manners compelled Candice to stare as Yasmeen outlined Sebastian's problem to an open-mouthed Desirée ('real name's Doreen but everybody calls me Desirée. Des for short.'). Her prurient curiosity was somehow mesmerising.

'Blooming heck!' Desirée breathed finally. 'Do they *let* you do that?'

'We hope so. But this is our first consultation with the doctor here.'

'I thought you had to have what they give you. Me and Luke's got four bairns froze. Getting two put in the day. Maybe *we* can choose what we get an' all.'

Luke snorted, flicking an imaginary cigarette. 'Don't expect we've got any little Einsteins in our batch, Des.'

'But maybes we could get my blue eyes and things.'

'Things?' He was looking at her with an expression in his own smoke-grey eyes that made Candice avert her gaze.

'Aye, well. We'll see.'

Rescue came in the guise of the receptionist.

'Mr and Mrs Opakanjo? Sorry to keep you waiting. Dr Blaydon-Green is ready for you now. Would you come this way, please?'

Candice threw Yasmeen a quiet, 'Good luck.'

'You, too. Nice to meet you.' Yasmeen's smile was wide and generous. 'And thanks for the cuddle. They're lovely babies. You must be very proud of them.'

The second they were out of sight, Desirée's voice pierced the silence. 'Weird that, huh? Twins, only... D'you think...?'

The Opakanjos followed Lily-May's generous hips as she led them down the main corridor decorated with assorted photos of babies: studio portraits, holiday snapshots, family groups. The Pemberton's success stories. Would they want to add mixed-race twins to this gallery?

Lily-May stood to one side at the open door. 'Do go in. Lovely to see you again in happier circumstances.'

The door closed behind them. Even the consulting room seemed somehow different from the last time they'd seen it.

Candice looked across at the one man who knew the full story. Now that she was a mother, he too seemed different. Much older. Greyer.

She pushed the babies in front of her by way of reassurance.

# 7

JUSTIN KNEW HE wasn't in the right frame of mind for this consultation. He absolutely was not.

His thoughts were still upstairs. Caroline Chambers was weeping; her husband was pacing the corridor unable to face her. Nothing the staff could say reached either of them. Their four-month-old fetus lay still and purple in a dish in the sluice. Their last hope. The bed was drenched with blood, the room heavy with a misery you could reach out and touch.

He was unpardonably late starting this clinic but could offer no explanation beyond a trite, 'I'm so sorry; we had a medical emergency.' It sounded so feeble. Rather like the GP he'd known once who arrived late every day, rushing in past the waiting patients clutching his medical bag, as if he'd been up all night saving lives: nobody believed it, but everybody colluded with the fiction.

Today's crisis was all too real but etiquette prevented him from defending himself. Blood staining his clothes, or the sound of grief, would have added weight to his words, but as usual he was crease-resistant and outwardly unmarked.

What a day! Doomed from the start.

Usually the jungle drums alerted him, but this time there had been no warning. The first he'd known of trouble ahead was when he turned the car into the main gates.

There they were. Five skull-masks, placards, clenched fists punching the air. There was no way of knowing if they were the real career activists, but he wasn't taking any chances. He stayed within the protection of his car, windows and doors locked, creeping up to the main door where he did an abrupt left and roared off round to the other entrance, leaving them standing. If only...

If only he hadn't left earlier than scheduled to fit in two egg collections before clinic started.

If only he'd listened for his mobile instead of to Radio 4; maybe then he'd have known to take the back route in the first place. Although it wouldn't have stopped them being there.

Even after all these years, the hostility unsettled him. *'Baby killer.' 'Frankenstein.' 'Playing God.' 'Adulterer.' 'Battery farmer.'* Nothing he hadn't heard before, but today, with the whole future of the clinic in jeopardy, the taunts caught him on the raw.

Were these demonstrators old acquaintances, passions rekindled by the whiff of error? Possibly. But there must be at least one new hand on the block, an artistic hand, because the placards were more striking, more professional, than last time. The dramatic red blotches looked so much more like real blood. He sneaked a proper look from behind the blinds once he'd reached safety. Yes, graphic stuff.

Mercifully only two patients (still two too many) got snared in their judgemental web. But they were reduced to tears; riddled with uncertainties themselves now. It wasn't Lily-May's fault, she wasn't able to contact them to warn them.

As if that wasn't enough, that reporter, the Wyatt woman, had been sniffing around again, hell-bent on winkling something out of someone.

He sighed. There would always be a minority who objected to what he did. No, the real mystery was why Candice had insisted on coming to the clinic for their appointment. He'd offered her alternatives, but she'd been adamant. Why?

He watched now as Candice and Samuel settled the twins.

'How are things?' he said. Without weighting.

'Fine,' they told him.

Were they? Were they really? Something didn't feel right.

Stealth and secrecy were part of the fabric of Justin's working life. People could have a myriad reasons for seeking anonymity in the business of reproduction. But not the Opakanjos. They'd been so open from the outset. Not for them whispered identification; no whisking them to the back waiting area to escape notice. Nothing to hide, nothing to fear.

He'd warmed to them from the start. Though a giant of a man, Samuel had a beguiling gentleness about him, and his ability to joke and laugh even through the most undignified of procedures endeared him to the team. He lifted everyone's spirits. And his exaggerated brand of a Nigerian accent just added to the attraction. He inspired confidence: he'd make a brilliant dad.

Candice too was impressive. She'd enter the room fizzing with vigour; not just the physical kind, the culmination of years of training and discipline on the running tracks of Europe, but a kind of inner strength and energy. And her deep throaty laugh had been the amen to Samuel's banter.

As a couple they'd hung together like an acorn in a cup; the kind of relationship everyone dreamed of for the babies they helped to create. But now? the longer he watched the more his unease grew. Samuel and Candice sat in the two chairs facing his, not touching, avoiding his eyes.

A surge of annoyance towards the HFEA's regulations caught him off-guard. They ought to dirty their hands in the mess of real-life disaster before they turned up their noses at the unpleasant smell of a mistake. Visions of protracted legal wrangling muscled their way into his mind. He thrust them to one side. This was the Opakanjos' tragedy; The Pemberton's concerns were secondary.

It could just be hormones. Sleep deprivation. Babies. They changed couples.

He went through the motions, taking his time admiring the twins, talking in generalities, normal, everyday parenting questions. Their answers were polite, but without enthusiasm.

'Did you know a lady from the *Evening News* came?' Candice said suddenly.

Something in the region of his diaphragm plummeted. '"Came" as in?'

'To our house.'

He searched for the right tone. 'I'm sorry about that.'

'Not long after we got home.'

'D'you know how she found out?'

'No idea. She came with flowers.'

'And did you talk to her?'

'Certainly not! Why would I? It's none of her business. It's nobody's business except ours.'

'Right. Sorry.'

'I told her there was nothing to tell. Nothing. Full stop.'

Justin looked at Candice, his mind in a turmoil. Was she for real? A lesser woman would have milked the situation for thousands, achieved martyrdom status, crippled the hospital. Not Candice Opakanjo.

No embellishing. No self-pity. No indignation. Just 'Nothing to tell.'

Why wasn't she looking for compensation? For an apology? At least for medical confirmation of her integrity in all of this? It didn't feel right.

And Samuel? Why was he staring somewhere above Justin's head, saying nothing?

This was the stuff of his nightmares: carrying a couple through the minefield of treatment only to wonder, too late, if the price had been too high. It happened. He just hadn't expected it in this case. But then, nobody had factored in such a colossal mistake.

It was time to inch carefully into the dilemma they faced.

'Have you thought any more about having Destiny tested to establish her DNA?'

'Could you go over again what you think happened?' Samuel said quietly.

Justin's words clattered out like plastic letters from a child's first reading set. He outlined the lab procedures, the tight regulations. *Was he being too defensive?*

He told them that they suspected an error at the point of fertilisation. *Had he said too much?*

The team were checking everything minutely. *Would the Opakanjos expect to know every detail?*

The HFEA were involved. Everybody taking it very seriously indeed. *Was he compounding their alarm?*

Lawyers were involved to establish the rights and interests, the law and the boundaries, the consequences and entitlements. *Was this a cue to sue?*

'And if you had Destiny's DNA it would confirm who her real parents were, right?' Samuel was merely setting out the cards.

'Yes.'

'But you need our consent for that.' There was not so much as a demi-semi-quaver of the old music in Candice's voice.

'Exactly.'

Samuel, sitting at a distance from his wife, made no attempt to touch either her or the babies as he started to speak. His very immobility was eloquent. But he left Justin in no doubt: he personally wanted the evidence. It was categorical. It crossed Justin's mind that perhaps it was Samuel who had the most to lose here.

Candice sat upright, Destiny over one shoulder, patting the sleeping child, rocking to and fro.

'And you, Candice? How do you feel about what Samuel says?'

Her own case seemed every bit as persuasive for all it was succinct and delivered in a flat impassive voice. Destiny, whatever her genetic origins, was hers. No test, no supposed right, would persuade her to relinquish her baby.

Looking from one to the other Justin felt an overwhelming sense of sadness. Destiny was threatening the very love that had craved this fulfilment in the first place. He felt himself being sucked out into the very fringes of his professional responsibility. Battles were his currency. He'd fight against biological clocks, against nature's anomalies, against the cruelties of disease and malformation; for funding; for clinical judgement to supersede administrative constraints. He would happily do another thirty years of active service if necessary. But he could not, must not, be seduced into family war-zones.

'This is obviously an extremely difficult situation for you. I'm wondering, would it help to talk with someone impartial. A counsellor, perhaps?' he ventured. 'You've met Josephine Vine. She's very good. Very discreet. Or we could ask somebody not connected with The Pemberton in any way, if you'd prefer.'

Two sets of inscrutable black eyes stared back at him. Both were considering his suggestion – alone.

Samuel was the first to speak. 'I'm willing.'

Candice was a beat behind him; too quick to be a response to what he had said. 'I don't see what purpose it would serve. We're talking to *you*.'

'Well, I've been closely involved in the process,' Justin said. 'You might think I'm trying to cover something up – I'm *not* incidentally, but I could be. Or maybe you don't like to say what you really think because you're reluctant to imply criticism of the care you received in my centre. Someone outside of the clinical team might be able to help you find some kind of resolution.'

'It wouldn't do any harm to try.' Samuel was still not looking at Candice.

'It would be a waste of time, as far as I'm concerned.' Candice continued patting Destiny's back. 'I've got enough else to do looking after these two. Nobody can change what happened. What's done is done. There's no point in raking it over.'

'That's just it. It *isn't* done,' Samuel interjected. 'An answer's all I'm asking for. What went wrong?'

'An answer that tells you it's OK not to love her?'

Samuel's eyes went wide as if Candice had slapped him. 'No!'

'Or that says someone else has more right to her?'

'No.'

Justin's fingers toyed with a paperclip until it snapped in two. He tossed it in the direction of the bin. It fell short.

'I just think,' Samuel insisted, 'that we should have the full facts. Destiny will want to know herself – when she's older.'

'And I want her to know how much she was loved from the outset.'

The silence stretched beyond them all.

'What about from your point of view, Dr Blaydon-Green?' Samuel asked. 'If it was an error in your lab, don't you need to make sure it doesn't happen again?'

'Yes, we have to look into how this happened. As will the HFEA. But *our* interests mustn't sway your decision.'

'And is it possible... might you find... our... our embryo somewhere in your lab?'

'I simply don't know what we'll find at the moment. But we shall certainly inform you if we find out anything relative to your own situation – insofar as you wish to be told, that is.'

By the end of the consultation Justin felt utterly drained. Neither side had given so much as a millimetre. His greatest advance was their tentative promise to consider talking to Josephine. Consider. That was as far as it went.

Justin felt a wave of annoyance. Scott Martindale was dragging his heels on this one.

He'd never been an easy colleague. And his stony silences were legendary – when he didn't want to state an opinion; when he disapproved; when he simply didn't care. Justin had always found him disconcerting, but the brilliance of the man, his undoubted skill as an embryologist, had been a major compensation for his poor communication skills.

Only this time Justin really needed him to share his thinking. And exercise some diplomacy. Instead Scott had barely concealed his irritation at the interruptions from the HFEA inspectors, and all he'd divulged was that the interviews with staff were progressing, No loopholes in the standard procedures thus far. But there *had* to be a flaw somewhere. If two embryos had been given to one black couple and one of them turned out to be coffee-coloured, was there a missing black gamete lurking somewhere? Was it wrongly marked? Where was the bombshell at this very moment?

OK, the stored embryos could be biopsied; it only took one cell to do a basic DNA test. But what if they needed to do full profiles? destroy hard-won embryos?

And what if this scandal involved couples who had no uncontaminated frozen embryos left? They'd be offered a free cycle of treatment, but would they want to stay with a team who had compounded their problems?

What about all the publicity? the wasted resources? The future of The Pemberton?

News was seeping out. Jack had heard it. And that reporter, she must have picked up something from somebody, somewhere. It was only a matter of time.

Where *was* the flaw? When did it happen? No one was in the clear. Because labels could be swapped. Tubes, lids, dishes could be interchanged. Without trace. Without a signature. Innocent mistakes. It wasn't necessarily down to the person who officially signed the paper.

The very presence of the HFEA hung a luminous question mark over the whole practice of every single person in the centre. And some of them were taking it hard. He'd had a bruising encounter already with two of the nurses coming to see him together for moral support. Destiny Opakanjo should be with her biological mother, they had insisted, whoever that is. Genetic ties are stronger than those of pregnancy and birth. Would he assure them that would happen? He couldn't, of course; even if he'd felt as strongly as they did, he couldn't.

# 8

DEEP WITHIN THE bowels of the animal research lab, Scott's mice scuttled around in their ultra-clean wood shavings, feeding, eliminating, copulating.

His every fibre longed to be down there now, talking to them, stroking their gleaming coats, examining their girth, their skin, checking gestations, side effects. These prize rodents held the key to his success. Instead here he was, glued to the computer screen, shoulders aching, a migraine threatening, awash with caffeine and resentment. Out of the corner of his eye he was all too aware of the inspector's head bent over the clinic records, heavy-rimmed glasses trained on columns of data. An interloper in a polyester tie and brown suede shoes.

Scott leaned back in his chair, swivelling to and fro, staring at the spreadsheet. Bald facts.

Justin – aspirated Candice's eggs, handed them to Nina
Nina – stored them
Emma – received Samuel's semen, handed it to Scott
Scott – cleaned the sperm
Scott – carried out the fertilisation process; witnessed by Jack
Nina – took the embryos out of incubation
Justin – received them (via Astrid) and transferred them into Candice.
Nothing incriminating.

It had been hectic in the lab that day. He remembered wondering… Samuel's sperm count was not exciting but it was adequate.

Perhaps… In the nick of time he'd remembered. He *had*. He *had*! He remembered remembering. This one was black. He remembered picking up the pipette again. Drawing up the pure Nigerian semen… Jack Fitzpatrick needling him. Injecting.

It had to be a genuine mistake. Cruel irony really. But it had to be.

Every single member of the team had been on duty at some point during that critical period. Almost all of them *could* have been involved in the mix-up.

Scott seethed at the waste of his precious time. He still had to prepare teaching material for tomorrow's fourth-year tutorial. The editor of *Human Reproduction* expected his revisions by the end of that week. A paper for the international conference in Montreal next month required data to be added, new data that would make the headlines – still to be extracted data, from the pregnant mice he should be monitoring.

Science was his first love, a single-track, unwavering love since he was eleven years old. Things like financial constraints, the human face of infertility, internal inquiries, they weren't for him. They were for the economists, or the folk at the soft end of medicine, the Blaydon-Greens of this life. He'd steadfastly refused to get embroiled and yet, here he was up to his neck in the treacle of the Opakanjos' mess, his mind, that should be free to soar, bogged down in trivia.

He was under no illusions. His science could save this place. His mouse data had the potential to put The Pemberton Centre for Reproductive Medicine on the world map. Their IVF rates were already up – due in no small measure to his own input. A scientific coup now could bring the research funds flooding in, put them up there with the big guns. Why on earth didn't Justin draw a line under this mistake, or at least free *him* up to concentrate on the trail-blazing work? But the director was like a man on a mission. Absolutely insistent: this inquiry took precedence. If a black embryo was at this moment in the wrong place he *had* to be aware of its existence. Not to mention the 'bigger lessons that needed to be learned'.

To be fair, Justin wasn't shirking the ultimate responsibility. As he said, the buck stopped with him. But he needed a bit of steel up his backbone. Stick two fingers up to the CEO. And the HFEA. But would he? No! Not Mr Meticulous. Which meant Scott, as head of the lab, had to be involved.

And now they were going for the next level of approval, ISO accreditation, things were going to get a whole lot more demanding. New licenses for increasingly challenging problems meant more rigorous auditing.

Justin had been pretty spooked on the day the twins were born. Scott had been surprised by his candour.

'How many other mistakes have we missed?' Justin had said, turning a stub of pencil over and over between his fingers. 'Less obvious ones.'

'Oh, come *on*,' Scott protested. 'We're bogged down in regulations. We can't *breathe* without everything being recorded in triplicate!'

'On the face of it, yes, it's watertight. But we're all over-worked, sometimes demoralised. The processes become pretty automatic. How careful are we *really* when we double-check things? Could you swear you always, without fail, check thoroughly when someone hands you something?' Scott shrugged. 'Well, *I* couldn't. And we pass things to Emma or Jack or Raisa or whoever. We have to trust them to put the right label on, the right lid on the right base, to store it in the right place or whatever. I mean, I don't take every egg and move it without taking my eye off it for a second. Once it's inside the lab I have absolutely no control over anything that happens to it. I rely on you lot to do the right thing at every stage. I have to accept that it's the right embryo coming out a couple of days later when I re-place it. And even you people who *are* allowed into the lab, you don't sit there round the clock guarding one individual set of gametes until the embryos are put back inside the mum. We simply can't and don't have that kind of set-up. Any one of us can make a mistake. We're all fallible.'

'Maybe,' Scott conceded. 'But we've all been trained to get it right. We *have* to trust each other.'

'Exactly.' Justin was staring down at his twisting fingers. 'Until something like this happens. There's no getting away from the fact that we're always only a misspelt name, a wrong label, a changed consonant, away from trouble.' He paused. Then sighed. 'You know, my old mentor, Prof Vertbauer, used to say, "*Only motherhood is a fact: fatherhood is a matter of opinion.*" He'd turn in his grave if he saw what we see today. It's not only fatherhood that's questionable!'

Since that day, even Scott had become aware of how strained Justin had been looking. The embryologist might be doing the groundwork but it was the director who was fielding the flak. And to make matters worse, some newspaper reporter was known to be lurking somewhere close. Neither of them wanted to be making front page headlines.

But Scott knew it was more than bad publicity that was concerning Justin. He cared, he really cared, for the couples he dealt with – got far too involved, in Scott's judgement. Most people in his position handed the pregnant couple over to their obstetric colleagues and lost contact. Not Justin. He even went to some of the deliveries. Madman!

And it showed now, with this Opakanjo case. It was one thing for the staff to be under suspicion, he said, but it was the family who were out there facing the real music. And of course, he was right on that. It was a cruel world out there. There'd be snide comments, innuendos.

If the Opakanjos had been leaping up and down demanding answers, threatening legal action, Scott knew he'd take this whole tedious exercise of tracking their gametes more seriously himself. But there again, the atmosphere in the centre would be even more intolerable. It was bad enough as it was.

Scott grimaced at the memory. Take that pest, Zubin – not long in off the boat and here he was, wanting the same rights as true-blue genuine British citizens. Plus he thought he had some God-given right to get in on the act – as if Scott's statement wasn't good enough. Bloody immigrants!

The guy'd got off to a bad start, sidling up behind Scott when he was trawling through the records early on.

'What the hell d'you think you're playing at, creeping up on me like that?' he shouted, flicking off the screen.

'Sorry. Didn't mean to startle you. But, look, everybody knows you're working on the inquiry. I saw the names.'

'Well, let me tell you something for nothing, Zubin Para-mesh. Here we do not consider it good form to sneak up on somebody doing confidential work. You'll have your moment of fame when the report's written.' He wagged his finger. 'And I'd be wary of acting like the guilty party if I were you.'

Back came Zubin, more plucky than wise. 'I'm not guilty of anything, but I think I'm entitled to see where I come into this. Besides, a fresh pair of eyes.'

A step too far.

'Listen, Paramesh.' Scott drew himself up to his full height, towering over the tiny lab technician. 'If there's any hint of a suggestion of wrongdoing, *I'm* going to be the one to sniff it out,' he said, drumming on his chest for emphasis. 'You just get back to what we pay you for.'

Zubin turned away with something incredibly close to insolence.

'Finding people hanging about where they shouldn't be, only makes me more suspicious.' Scott's words hissed in the direction of his retreating back.

Remembering, Scott sank back into his chair with a barely suppressed shudder. It was tricky enough juggling all these balls without anyone else looking over his shoulder.

Emma had presented a different problem.

He'd found her in tears late one evening struggling with tables that simply refused to stabilise on her computer.

'I *hate* this new software. My old package l-let me do this. It never crashed j-just when you got it right.'

'Leave it,' he said briskly. 'Try again tomorrow. It's far too late to be working on this stuff. It'll all slot into place when you come to it fresh tomorrow.'

'I'll never s-sleep if I leave it in this mess.'

'Look, you're tired out. That's how mistakes are made. Go home.'

She froze. 'Mis... Are you suggesting...?'

'I'm not suggesting anything. I'm simply telling you to go home.'

'But you think it was me – I was too tired, I made that mistake.' She was actually backing away as she spoke.

'Now you're being paranoid. I'm not saying who made the mistake until I'm absolutely sure. Maybe you did, maybe you didn't. All I'm doing is strongly recommending you don't hang around here in this state now.'

'But *you're* still here. *You're* still working.'

'Emma. I'll pretend I didn't hear that.'

He'd cut off her apologies midstream. 'Look, there's no comparison. I'm having to spend so much time tracking down stuff for this damned inquiry, I haven't got time for my research. And nobody else can do that for me. The only way I can get anything done is to stay on when it's quiet and there are no interruptions. So off you trot. It'll all seem better in the morning. Get Jack to have a look. Good *night*, Emma!'

She'd rushed from the room, holding her hand over her mouth, leaving her screen still covered in figures.

A cursory glance at them and he'd switched the machine off – without saving the work.

Word must have spread. He'd had far less interruptions and even dared occasionally to work on his analysis during clinic hours. This was lead-article material in the raw. It lifted his spirits as nothing else could.

## 9

NEW COUPLES ALWAYS presented a challenge. You needed sharp antennae and the insight of a psychic to see between and behind what they divulged. Starting off with a jaded perspective before he even heard their story wasn't good news, but he couldn't seem to shake this horrible sense of depression. The demonstrators had abandoned their protest, the Opakanjos had taken their babies away with their differences, but their issues remained hung around his neck like garlands of weights.

He took a deep breath and called for the next couple. 'Mr and Mrs Zair.'

The letter from the GP gave no indication that he might expect a vision of loveliness to glide into his consulting room. Yasmeen was easily five foot ten inches tall with a figure his wife would describe as 'to die for'. Impeccably groomed. Confident and friendly. Cut-glass English accent. There was absolutely nothing about her that betrayed her tragedy.

And she was the main spokesperson. He had no reason to drag his eyes away from her.

Karim hovered close. Protective? Possessive?

The photographs Yasmeen laid on his desk would wrench at the stoniest heart. Shahira and Sebastian. Both exquisite replicas of their mother. It flashed across his mind: did Karim ever doubt his parenthood as Samuel had been forced to do? Where were his more rugged features, his stocky build, in these sharply chis-elled little faces, these lithe childish bodies? Odd really. Samuel *should* have been the one with the absolute confidence that comes from assisted reproduction. Justin took his time admiring the children. Strange to think that behind those serene smiles was knowledge borne out of suffering. Sebastian's beauty and courage had to be a powerful weapon in the fight for his survival.

'You do realise that there is as yet no test we can do to detect Diamond Blackfan's in the embryos, don't you?'

'Yes. Sebastian's doctors told us that.' Yasmeen was like a fabulous leopard caught in the beam of a searchlight. Wary, curious even, but fearless.

'And in your case, though it's not an inherited disorder, there's something like a one-in-fifty chance of another child having it.'

'They told us that, too. Yes.'

'So *even if* we agree to select a matched embryo we should need to wait about six months after the birth to be sure the new baby didn't have it too.'

'Nobody wants to bring another child with the same condition into the world, least of all us, but it's our only hope.' Her tone was final.

'You will also know, I'm sure, that no treatment with stem cells, no matter how perfect the match, comes with a hundred per cent guarantee of success.'

'We aren't looking for guarantees. We simply want the chance to try.' She made it seem so modest.

'I appreciate that you've given this a great deal of thought, but I have to check. You do understand the costs of this line of action?'

'In terms of the procedures I shall have to undergo, you mean?'

'That's one factor. Yes.'

'I've read up on what's involved. The ovarian stimulation and everything. And the success rates according to age, and this hospital's statistics.'

Justin glanced down at her age.

'Mmm. Below thirty-five years of age there's about a forty per cent chance of a pregnancy. Above forty there's only a five per cent chance. Time isn't on our side, I'm afraid.'

She shrugged.

'I know. Our GP has been very helpful. And thorough!' she smiled. 'And the doctors who look after Sebastian. I'm prepared for the physical unpleasantnesses. And for the psychological consequences, aren't I, Karim?'

He reached across to cover her hand with his, the lines around his eyes deeply etched. 'I don't doubt it for a moment, darling.'

'And you, Mr Zair?'

'I'm behind her one hundred per cent.'

'And the costs for the donor child. You've considered that?' Justin let his glance flicker between them.

She nodded. 'Of course, we hope it will just mean the painless collection of cord blood. But if it's more – well, we know that Shahira would do anything, *anything,* for her brother, if she could. And we feel sure another brother or sister would too. What I'm not so clear about is, what about the risks to the embryo? Firstly of doing the test. And then afterwards.'

'To be honest, we aren't actually sure if there is, or is not, a risk to the embryo of extracting a couple of cells to test for compatibility. We *think* the risk is minimal and it's certainly not part of our plan to treat a sick sibling by bringing new suffering into being. But this science is in its infancy. And as for longer-term risks – well, how do you measure the emotional/psychological risks? It depends on so many other factors. All I can say is that *as far as we can tell* there's only a tiny risk to the embryo from what we do in the selection process.'

The Zairs exchanged a look.

'Have you also thought,' Justin said, 'about the consequences if it fails? If Sebastian dies despite having this saviour sibling.'

'If it's God's will, it will work,' Karim answered quietly. 'We are both prepared to go through with this if it will give our son a chance. We can only do what's in our power. The rest we leave to Him.'

Justin managed to fight back several rejoinders. Instead he

looked from one to the other with what he hoped they'd interpret as genuine concern. He leaned towards them.

'I'm afraid there are some people who are implacably opposed to this kind of action. And if word gets out, they will not be above giving you a very hard time.' He paused to let this filter through. 'Are you prepared for that?'

'For Sebastian's sake, we will be.' Yasmeen's conviction was palpable.

'And we've decided to be perfectly honest if anyone asks us,' Karim added. 'We know this is right for our family. If other people have prejudices, that's their problem. If they adopt a hard line, we can only appeal to their understanding and compassion, explain, our son is precious; this is his only real chance.'

'And I'm sure you'd be very eloquent in doing so,' Justin said warmly. 'But taking such a stand comes with a price. I don't want you going into this blindly. We would do our utmost to protect your privacy and confidentiality, but these things have a way of getting out. And if you yourselves decide to talk about it openly, the news is bound to reach those who will milk the story. You'll be seen as fair game, I'm afraid. It comes with the territory. And I say this with some feeling. We're subject to this kind of thing all the time. And it can be very disturbing, even frightening. Feelings run very high when it comes to embryos – especially destroying them.'

For the first time a shadow clouded Yasmeen's face.

'Ah, that's one part of this we do feel sad about. Can we talk about that?'

'By all means.'

'We don't like to think of embryos being destroyed, even those in the very early stages. And we don't like the idea of abortion. But we can't keep having children on the off-chance that one of them might be a compatible donor for Sebastian. So it seems to us, our best option is to go for selecting a matched embryo. Which means the other embryos will have to be disposed of. But then they'd never have come into existence at all if Sebastian hadn't needed help, would they? Does this make sense?'

'Perfect sense.'

'Are we being too naive,' Karim said, 'in thinking people might be less critical if we explain why it's necessary? We have to do this, anyway – for Sebastian's sake, but we don't want to *invite* trouble.'

'I'm not sure about "naive". But feelings do run very high on this issue. Not all causes are based on logic and reason.'

'You're meaning fanatics?'

'And protestors. I wish I could be more reassuring. Losing a child is a terrible prospect. I would put such a life far above that of a guinea pig or an eight-cell embryo. But sadly not everyone shares my priorities. I don't want to add to the burden of your situation, but I wouldn't be doing my job if I didn't check things out thoroughly with you, I hope you can understand that.'

Their acceptance gave him the courage to press on.

'I'd like to pick up on something you suggested earlier, Mr Zair. You're contemplating creating a life for a specific purpose; a child who wouldn't have existed at all if Sebastian hadn't needed help. It's obvious you love your two existing children very much, but what of this as-yet-unknown one?'

'We have love enough for all the children,' Yasmeen said softly.

'But you're choosing to have this one for an unusual reason,' Justin persisted, hating the necessity. 'To put it crudely, it's a kind of spare-part factory. How will you feel about him or her if Sebastian's life can't be saved? Or, in years to come, how would you react if Sebastian needs bone marrow or a kidney maybe, and the younger child refuses?'

'We have talked about that specifically,' Karim said. 'And we've read a few things about that side of it.'

'*My Sister's Keeper*, perchance?' Justin shot in with a crooked smile.

'The novel? The world and his wife seem to know about that!' Karim smiled. 'But those parents are nothing like us. And I hope those children are not like ours either. No. I wasn't actually thinking about fiction. We've read things that actual, real-life parents have posted on the internet. People motivated by love for their children. That's what drives them to go down this route of having embryo selection or a saviour sibling. Yasmeen and I would love the next child every bit as much as our other two, irrespective of the outcome.'

'I *know* we would.' Yasmeen's conviction was absolute.

'And if the next child had Diamond Blackfan's as well? D'you think you could stand the strain of that?'

'We can't possibly know that in advance,' Karim answered. 'But we have faced this possibility, and we still think we have to take that risk. For Sebastian.'

Justin sent up a prayer of thanks for Josephine. As a trained psychologist and counsellor she would read the signs better than he could. Later she would ask all the questions he knew had to be pursued, allowing him now to concentrate on the procedures, the chances, the facts, the statistics – his own area of expertise. Some of the tension eased from his shoulders.

Only when they were leaving did he remember Destiny Opakanjo. Had they seen her in the waiting room? Did they wonder? Were they simply sparing him their doubts? He took what solace he could from their apparent trust. They'd stayed, hadn't they? They'd sought his help.

In spite of the immensity of the questions this case raised he was buoyed up by the new energy surging through him. He was ready to fight again. For Yasmeen. For Sebastian. For that saviour sibling.

# 10

JUSTIN HARDLY DARED ask Lily-May for any more favours. She had already covered for his absence, excusing the delays, soothing waiting patients, circumventing trouble with the demonstrators. But she made no comment when he requested a few minutes to dictate his report about the Zair family before she ushered in the next couple.

After twelve years as his receptionist, Lily-May wore her familiarity with assurance. Consultant and director he might be, but if he infringed her idea of what was 'right and proper', he was left in no doubt. When it came to Joe Public, however, she could be relied on to be courteous and non-judgemental. 'You just never know what sad lives they're living at home,' she explained to all new recruits.

Empathy borne out of experience. A dependent relative, serious illness, a long period of homelessness due to subsidence, the loss of her teenage son from a heroin overdose – through them all Lily-May had retained an impressive courage and tolerance.

As Justin dictated he stared unseeingly out of the window. He saw again Yasmeen's fluid walk, her smile, her confidence.

He was suddenly jolted into the present. Another girl, dressed from head to toe in black, entered his line of vision. Slight beneath the hooded coat, she moved with agility and deliberation, but with an occasional alert pause as if listening for predators. There was something oddly familiar in the hesitation. She stooped to pick up a lone placard lying abandoned on the grass, the crimson paint glinting as she lifted it.

He sighed. How black and white the issues were for these campaigners, so different from the shades of grey he saw. When it came to the life of a child like Sebastian, Justin was half way to saying yes before he even met the parents, because the loss of a child was one of the few things in medicine he could not let himself imagine, the worst of all calamities. He'd been obsessively protective of his daughters from infancy. Bobby, Lexie and Kate laughed at him now, but his anxiety eclipsed their ridicule.

The girl with the placard reached the gate and turned for a moment. She seemed to be looking his way, though her face was hidden inside her hood. She raised one hand in a salute to someone he couldn't see, and tilted her banner, like a standard dipping in tribute. Then she was gone.

He made himself concentrate on the task of dictating his notes on the Zair case. At least now that the HFEA allowed for embryo selection in such cases, they wouldn't be compelled to try their luck abroad, where the safeguards could be less rigorous.

Justin snapped off the dictaphone. There. He'd made the case for saving Sebastian. His own team would be sure to back him. They saw the suffering at first hand, in every case the pain had a name. But would the arguments be strong enough to convince the HFEA? Please God.

First task, assemble his experts. Then get the Clinical Ethics Committee on side. And who knew which way they'd jump? Their distance from the coalface could provide useful perspective, and Ray Brookes at least could be relied on to get to the kernel of the matter and dispense wisdom. But some of them could be downright cussed at times. Emeritus Professor Margaret Beuly forever raising philosophical objections in terms no one else could fathom. Or Barbara Down, the lay person on the committee, couching everything in question form so as not to betray either ignorance or opinion. Jennifer Ruskin would ask: *What guarantees can you give that you'll get enough stem cells from the cord blood? What are the chances of the saviour sibling needing to give other tissue, other organs at a later date? What are the long-term statistics for this procedure?* – knowing there were no meaningful statistics available. She thought these probes made her look smart; nobody told her otherwise. The Rev Alex Steinbrook would talk about the sanctity of life as if he had a direct line to the Almighty. The chairman, Ian Hollinghurst, a consultant orthopaedic surgeon with a PhD in the ethics of xenotransplantation, would corner Justin after the meeting, grump about the others, and pretend a support he had a habit of withholding when it counted.

How would they respond to Sebastian's need? And the publicity it might generate.

And how would the CEO, Carruthers, react? Probably baulk at the cost as usual, without deigning to attend a meeting.

Justin pushed the dictaphone to the back of his desk and stretched. One more couple and then he must get hold of Scott Martindale. Surely he had some news by now.

LILY-MAY DESERVED A MEDAL. Justin hadn't realised whom she'd been left to pacify.

This was his fourth encounter with Desirée Wanless and Luke Simmonds. Each time he'd agonised over what kind of life a child would have in this family, and ended up riddled with doubt. He'd have laid odds on Luke not being the type to hang around past the first flood of hormonal tears, but the lad had attended every clinic visit; comforting Desirée in his embarrassed way when Justin gave them the news about her irretrievably damaged fallopian tubes; injecting her hormones himself because she was 'too squeamish for that sort of thing'; holding her hand while her eggs were extracted at the last visit; coming today to witness their embryos being transferred into her womb.

He sighed. Who really understood the chemistry between two people? He'd been wrong twice already today. It was a grave responsibility, intervening with nature, especially since infertility imposed a huge strain on any relationship.

'Nobody's perfect, Justin. Good enough has to do. Just good enough.' His old mentor, Kurt Vertbauer's words echoed in his head.

Even so, Desirée proceeded to take his breath away.

'Those folk you just saw, they're looking for a specific kid, right?'

'Och, you dinnae have to worry about confidences. The woman says it herself. Straight out.'

'Can me and Luke choose? Can we have just girls put in? With blonde hair and blue eyes, so they look like me.'

68

'How come they get to choose and we dinnae? Is it money?'

'But you could keep the others and we'll still have them if it all goes pear-shaped. It's no like we're saying kill them off or nothing.'

How he regretted the time he had lingered with Caroline Chalmers. And the Zair's candour.

Desirée was draped in green towels, her legs up in the lithotomy stirrups, and Justin was on the point of introducing two of her embryos, when she suddenly clenched her buttocks and lifted her head to say, 'You are sure these are *my* bairns? I dinnae want no black ones growing inside me.'

He had a sensation of the room contracting. Cheque books, journalists, Max Clifford, flashed through his mind. But here, now, he could only calmly continue, assisting in the creation of what he predicted would be a dysfunctional family.

'*A child is a gift not a commodity.*' Kurt Vertbauer was so right.

These embryos seemed uncomfortably close to being commodities.

No one knew where Scott Martindale was. Justin could only leave a message and return to the pile of paperwork his secretary had left for his attention. By 7.30pm Scott had still not put in an appearance, but Justin was beyond useful productivity. Helen would have left for orchestra practice, so at least she wouldn't be infected by his melancholy.

For once he drove the car right into the garage instead of leaving it on the drive. It would be a shorter distance to carry the three boxes of books from the boot to his study. One of the bulbs had gone and the back of the garage was dark, but as he stooped to lift the first box, a splash of crimson caught his eye. He straightened up. Yes, something red was glinting between the stack of garden chairs and the coiled hose. It looked wet and shiny. Curious.

The hose slipped from his hand with a crash as he saw what it concealed.

He forced himself to carry the boxes into the house one by one. It was too early to jump to conclusions.

'Bobby,' he called up the stairs. '*Bobby*!'

He found her lying on her bed, eyes shut, her body pulsing to the rhythm blasting through her earphones, a spindly teenager who only yesterday was a toddler with an adorable lisp and a penchant for mustard sandwiches.

She looked so vulnerable – pale skinned, dark hair cropped close to her head, two small numbers short of a shave. She looked rebellious – a row of graded silver hoops in one ear, a single black stud on the other side, dark maroon nail polish. She looked so normal – midriff bare between tight jeans and skimpy T-shirt.

She reached for the CD player but not finding the button, opened one eye. Instantly she was upright, radiating currents of indignation.

'For goodness' sake, Dad! You scared me half to death. What are you *doing*?' She folded her arms around her skinny frame, wrapping her privacy close.

'I knocked, but you didn't hear me.'

'What's so urgent you couldn't wait till I came down?' She got tangled in her earphone leads and looked away to release herself.

'Have you been out this afternoon?' he enquired.

'Yep. Why?'

'May I ask where you went?'

'Just around.'

'Around where, exactly?'

'I didn't know I had to report everything nowadays. I'm not a kid, in case you hadn't noticed.'

'That rather depends on what you were doing.'

'Well, if you *must* know, I was with Melanie Cruse.'

'And did she come with you to the hospital?'

A dull flush crept along Bobby's neck.

'Is that a yes or a no?' Justin held her gaze.

She shook her head.

'It was you, wasn't it?'

She nodded. 'I didn't know if you could see me or not.'

'The penny dropped when I saw the placard in the garage.'

'I'm taking it back tomorrow.'

'"Back"?'

'I tried today, but he wasn't in. I'll ring first thing. Promise.'

'And who might "he" be?'

'I didn't know where else to put it. You don't usually go into the garage.' She made it into an accusation.

'Bobby. I think we need to go back to the beginning here.'

'I haven't done anything wrong,' she flared.

'I'm not accusing you of anything. I simply want to know how an anti-abortion placard comes to be lying in my garage.'

Unexpectedly she grinned. 'Nice touch, huh?'

'Hmm. Under other circumstances I might appreciate the weird humour in that fact, but not at this precise moment.'

'Oh, come on, Dad, lighten up!'

'Listen, today I've had patients reduced to tears because of demonstrators. And that's only the tip of the iceberg. You know about the bricks, and bombs, and people in fear of their lives. I didn't think a daughter of mine would get involved in that sort of stuff.'

'*They* don't do those kinds of things. They promised me. They *don't*.' Her eyes were blazing but he couldn't tell with what.

'You *know* the people who demonstrated at the centre today?' Justin's world had just developed an ice-cap.

'No. Only Melanie's brother – he's there sometimes when I go over to their house. But he never even *speaks* to me usually.'

'And he was one of the demonstrators?'

'Today he was. He's never done it before, though.'

'And how old is Melanie's brother?'

'Don't know. Twenty maybe. He's at uni anyway.'

'And what precisely is his objection to fertility treatment?'

'*I* don't know!'

'So he doesn't speak to you, you have no idea what he thinks,

71

but you're willing to follow his example.'

'I didn't follow him anywhere. I hardly know the guy.'

'So, what is his placard doing in my garage?'

'It's not his. They just asked me to get it.'

'Oh well, that explains everything!'

Bobby rammed her hands on her hips, elbows jutting through her black sleeves.

'Look. I went over to Melanie's, right? Dan was there. He said, "You're the kid whose old man works at the fertility place, aren't you?" I couldn't say I *wasn't*, could I? Everybody knows. So he said would I do something just for a laugh. I said, "That depends." He said, "Well, seeing it's on your way, will you go and get a picture? We left it behind this morning." He wanted me to take it back to his mate in Afferton Crescent. It was only when I got there I saw what it was. I didn't like it, but I was there, so it seemed silly just to leave it. I wondered about coming to see you first, but you don't like us disturbing you at work. Then I saw you looking out the window, and I gave you a wave, but you didn't wave back. I thought you didn't see me. Anyway, I didn't want anybody else to catch me with that thing so I lugged it off to Afferton Crescent. But when I got there this bloke wasn't in. I couldn't leave it lying in the street, you never know who might see it.'

He held her gaze, wondering if this was the truth. It sounded plausible, but she could be a consummate actress these days, this emergent adult Bobby.

'So at what point,' he said sweetly, 'did you find out that they were just having a little harmless fun and they don't do cruel things to people?'

'When I phoned Melanie, and Dan told me.'

'I don't follow.'

'Well, when the guy at Afferton Crescent wasn't in, I phoned Melanie and she put Dan on, and he said bring it here meantime. He knew I was pretty mad, I told him straight. He said his mates were only into peaceful demos. Because babies can't speak for themselves...' Her voice petered out.

Before his watchful eyes she became the girl he had the power to console. He was back on familiar territory. But first a few hard truths. In spite of her entreaties, he was adamant on one point: Dan Cruse would be seeing him in the flesh before the week was out. Too bad if that sounded the death-knell on his daughter's romantic aspirations.

On the way downstairs the irony of his position struck him. He might be the one with a criminal record if the HFEA found him accountable for the Opakanjo cock-up. What would the girls make of *that* claim to fame? He grimaced. This was one time when the CEO wouldn't be posturing as license-holder. Oh, Carruthers was perfectly happy to take all the glory going, thanks, and he liked to remind Justin that he held the power to remove him from office if he stepped too far out of line, but he'd most definitely be skulking behind the door when the muck hit the fan; '*You're the clinical lead, Justin.*' Ergo, it's your head on the block. The pompous ass would be the first to point out he hadn't even met the Opakanjos, never mind dabbled with their gametes.

Oh Bobby – if you only knew!

Pity Helen was out tonight. He could do with a confidante.

What a rock she was. How many other wives would have tolerated his passion for this work? Who else would have understood his disappointment when treatments failed, when hopes had to be dashed, when the law clipped his wings? It helped that she breathed the same atmosphere, of course. And her appointment as poet-in-residence within the Trust meant she saw the trauma as well as the miracles, on a daily basis, but she interpreted it, not through science, treatments and cures, but through art. She gave feelings a voice.

Yes, she'd understand today's turmoil.

But Helen returned with a headache that sent her straight to bed, so there was no sharing the load tonight.

## 12

YASMEEN WATCHED THE CHILDREN from the doorway.

'Now, you go to hospital while I cook the dinner.' Shahira, at her most brisk and practical.

Sebastian, busy settling his comforter, Humphrey, in front of an array of cups and saucers laden with plastic fried eggs and sausages, cauliflower and bananas, hesitated. He glanced at the Wendy house that doubled as Tinkerbell Ward, and pretended not to have heard.

'Bassy! Go on! Off you go. Now! You don't want to *die*, do you?'

Yasmeen expected him to dissolve into tears, but he stood his ground, fists clenched around Humphrey and the teapot.

'OK! Die then! See if I care.' Shahira stomped into Tinkerbell Ward herself.

Sebastian gave Humphrey a fierce hug, then sidled into the hospital, his obedience more poignant than weeping.

Taking refuge in the kitchen, Yasmeen stared out at the starlings jostling for pre-eminence on the bird table, next door's cat crouched below them. Her mind returned to the November morning that would haunt her for the rest of her days. The consultant's mouth framing the words beneath his clipped brown moustache, his Mickey Mouse bow-tie jarring with his verdict.

*Diamond Blackfan's Anaemia.*

DIAMOND BLACKFAN'S ANAEMIA.

**DIAMOND BLACKFAN'S ANAEMIA.**

The diagnosis was like a stun gun, and the after-shock reverberated down through the months that followed, every ache, every bleed, every fever, adding momentum to the prognosis. Along with hope, other consolations drifted out of her reach; her legal career, her art classes, her travel plans. Lifelines severed. She shivered, remembering another day: 21 July that same year.

She'd been with a friend, Simone, enjoying a couple of hours of innocent fun at a fair in the Borders. They'd won teddy key-rings on the hoopla stall, taken photos of each other poking heads out of rude cut-out figures, shared a giant stick of candy floss, the keen wind blowing the froth against their cheeks.

It was Simone's idea to pay fifty pence for a palm reading. Newly divorced, she lapped up the news that she would soon meet a tall stranger who would whisk her to foreign parts. Yasmeen had entered the tent still smiling broadly at her friend's reaction. She didn't believe for a second that 'Gypsy Moll' had powers, but the money went to the local children's hospice, and where was the harm in it? There were the usual reassurances about new opportunities, the chance of untold riches. When the woman's tone sank to a confidential murmur she'd leaned in to humour her.

'I see a large black cloud. It's hanging over someone dear to you. Only your love will keep them safe.'

She'd almost snatched her hand away.

Simone had scoffed. 'It doesn't mean a thing! Everybody has hard times. And that silly old fraudster knows they do.'

Karim had looked at her in astonishment.

'Meena! Don't tell me you give credence to some local hair-dresser's wife dressed up in dangly earrings in a darkened tent, muttering mumbo-jumbo over a paperweight!'

Her rational self told her they were right; her emotional self watched her children with haunted eyes. And then four months later came that fateful diagnosis of a life-limiting blood disorder.

'Beep beep. Beep beep. Mummy! Beep beep.'

'Oh sorry, darling. I didn't hear you coming.'

Shahira manoeuvred the cardboard box through the doorway

and out into the utility room with much huffing and grunting.

'You have to stay there, Bassy,' she said, slapping her hand twice on the top. 'And keep quiet, OK? Remember, you're dead.'

She stood poised ready to quell an uprising, but when none materialised she walked in a solemn procession of one back into the living room and, closing the door between the cemetery and the festivities, she proceeded to host an extravagant wake to which she had invited every toy she could lay her hands on.

Yasmeen folded back the flaps of the box. The dark eyes that met hers were unafraid, and a whispered offer of a biscuit was enough to make Sebastian forget his sister's instructions and leave his coffin without a backward glance.

'Hey, Bassy! Dead people don't eat biscuits. Do they, Mummy?' Shahira, wandering back to check on her victim, oozed indignation.

'Shahira, Sebastian can't sit in a box all day.'

'Can I have a biscuit as well?'

'Not if you ask like that.'

'Please may I have a biscuit?'

'Only if you promise to be nicer to your brother.'

Shahira's mane of blue-black hair glinted as she nodded, but once the first bite of the biscuit was in her mouth, she qualified her response. 'Do I have to be nice to him all the time just 'cos he's going to die?'

'Shahira!'

'Polly at school says so.'

'Polly doesn't know what she's talking about.'

'Her mum told her, and she's a doctor.'

'Well, she may be a doctor but she knows nothing whatever about our family.'

'So is God going to make Sebastian dead?'

'I don't want to die, Mummy,' Sebastian wailed. 'Granny Dita's going to take me to Disneyland.'

'Disneyland? Wowwee! What a lucky boy you are! I've never been to Disneyland.'

'You can come too,' he said, wrapping his arms around Yasmeen. 'And Daddy. And Shahira.'

'Wowwee!' was all she could manage.

When she could, she turned to Shahira.

'Eat your biscuit, young lady, and I'll be back in a minute. Sebastian, come into the living room, poppet. You can watch a video and I'll bring you a banana milkshake.'

Shahira turned the full power of her almost-black eyes on her mother as she re-entered the kitchen.

'You can't stop God, Mummy, if He wants Bassy dead. God's bigger than you *and* Daddy.'

'Yes, but God has given us clever doctors to help people like Bassy. They're going to do everything they can to make him better.'

'How?'

'Well, they're going to try to help Daddy and me have a baby who's a lot like Bassy. Then they'll give Bassy good blood from the baby so he isn't poorly any more.'

'Oh, that's not fair.'

'Why not?'

'Because it hurts. Bassy says so.'

'No, Shahira, the baby won't feel anything. Remember the cord coming out of a baby's tummy, that feeds it inside its mummy? The doctors only have to let the blood drip out of that. It doesn't hurt at all.'

'And how do they get the blood into Bassy? Will it hurt him?'

'Through a tube. Like the blood transfusions. It doesn't hurt. It just runs in down the tube.'

'Like Poppa Zair?'

'Yes. Like Poppa Zair.'

'And will Bassy have a tube for peeing too, like Poppa Zair?'

'I don't expect so. He'll be able to wee normally.'

Shahira gave this thought.

'Poppa Zair died.'

'Yes, he did, but he was very old.'

'When I grow up I'm going to be a doctor like Polly's mum and then I'll get to put lots of tubes into people. And I'll make Bassy better.'

'That'll be nice, sweetheart. But you could help him feel better right now. You don't have to wait until you're grown up.'

'How?'

'Play happy games. It's hard enough for Bassy having to have medicines and transfusions and everything. You don't have to *play* hospitals as well.'

Shahira said nothing.

'And it's probably best if you don't play being dead, either.'

'It's only *pretend*, Mummy. We're only *practising*.'

Perdita's question sounded tentative. 'So, what did the consultant say?'

'He can't say yes on his own, he needs to talk to other people first,' Yasmin replied.

Perdita's look was eloquent.

'I know, Mother. More delays. But we don't have many choices here. I haven't got *time* to have six more pregnancies. Especially not if any more end in miscarriages.'

She felt her stomach knot. It had only been twelve weeks old, but it had been her baby. And she had already endowed it with a passport out of this nightmare.

Perdita laid a hand on her arm but said nothing.

Yasmeen swallowed hard. 'Besides, even if we went down that path there's no guarantee of a match.' She straightened her shoulders. 'I have to say, it was really good talking to the counsellor. Josephine. She understands the emotions as well as the practical stuff. We could ask her anything.'

'I'm glad they're there for you.' Perdita's face said something different.

Yasmeen bit back a retort. It was nobody's fault. Nobody *could* get it right. There *was* no right.

'It's easier for them. They're one step removed.'

Perdita took a sip of her green tea. 'Are you sure, Yasmeen?'

Yasmeen hesitated. Was this a burden to share? Especially with someone whose own eyes were full of sorrow.

'I wish you would talk to me. I only want to help you.'

'I know, Mother,' Yasmeen sighed. 'All right, I'll be honest with you, I do have qualms. That doesn't mean I'm going to change my mind. But there are parts of this whole thing that...'

Perdita waited for her to continue.

'If it was a straightforward case of IVF. It wouldn't be so bad. But once they've created the embryos, then they have to choose... and it feels like condemning little Shahiras to death simply because they aren't Sebastians.'

Perdita closed her eyes against the idea.

'But they were saying today, you shouldn't look at it that way. These embryos, they're only a few cells. Nothing recognisably human.'

'Right.'

'They wouldn't have existed at all if we hadn't needed a saviour sibling. That's all very well, but they *do* exist, and it feels as if we're making them sit an exam. If they don't pass they die – even though it's not their fault they aren't *exactly* what we want.' Yasmeen heard the heaviness in her voice. 'I wish there was some other way. But we can't just let Bassy die. We *can't*! And we can't have eight more babies. The birthday presents would bankrupt you!' The smile didn't reach her eyes.

Perdita reached out to touch her daughter's hand. 'You know I'll be there for you, whatever you decide.'

'Thanks, Mum. And thanks for not trying to talk us out of this.'

'It's a hard enough decision without other people interfering.'

'Doesn't stop them trying though!'

'I don't think they mean to be cruel. People are scared of serious illness. They say superficial things without really thinking.'

'Maybe.'

It didn't lessen the hurt.

*'It's like making a child for spare parts.'*

'*Designing a kid by numbers.*'

'*The stuff of science fiction.*'

Her mother's anxious face swam back into focus. It struck her, maybe Perdita too had to face these same barbs. She felt a rush of affection and gratitude.

'What would I do without you? Pia's been brilliant, too, you know.' Yasmeen deliberately made her tone more robust.

'I'm glad to hear it – but not surprised. You two are so close. Pia's always looked up to her big sister!'

'She often surprises *me*, actually. Although she hasn't had children of her own, she seems to know what it feels like to love them more than anything else in the world.'

'Well, she adores your children. She was devastated when Bassy got his diagnosis.'

Yasmeen grinned. 'D'you know what she said – when we first heard about Bassy needing a matched donor?'

'Remind me.'

'"Maybe *I'll* go for IVF anyway, clone the embryos, and then I'll have a ready supply of donors if anything goes wrong."'

'If Pia ever does marry I think her husband will have a hard time controlling her!'

'Does it bother you that she turned down the man you chose for her?'

'Not now. She had her reasons.'

'Meaning?'

'I think Pia wants a marriage like yours. But she is not you. And Soroush was not Karim. It couldn't be the same.'

'I hope she finds someone right for her. She'd make a brilliant mother.'

'*I* only hope she doesn't decide to dispense with a husband and go for children on her own.'

Yasmeen stared at her mother. 'Is she thinking of doing that?'

'Oh, not that I know of. But she is so, I don't know, *modern* in her thinking.'

'The idea never entered my head.'

'And please don't put it into hers!' Perdita sighed. 'How

things change. There will soon be no mystery to life. In my day we'd never even *heard* of genes and everything. And we certainly never *talked* about them!'

Yasmeen had to laugh. 'I wouldn't want us to go back to *that.*'

'Well, even though most of the business of having babies was beyond my comprehension, I can still remember the feeling of awe holding you in my arms for the first time. To think I had created something so perfect, inside me. Just *how* you'd grown I didn't need to know. Maybe young mothers today want all the whys and wherefores, but don't you think we've lost something of the magic?'

'If they hadn't developed these things to the extent that they have, there wouldn't be *anything* we could do for Bassy. But I know what you mean. Who knows what decisions the next generation will have to make? It's scary stuff.'

Perdita smiled. 'We are so proud of you – your father and me – and Pia, too.'

Yasmeen looked at her enquiringly.

'You've coped with all this so well. And it's made you softer, more compassionate, wiser.'

'Well, if I am, that's thanks to Karim. He's been an absolute rock. He keeps me going when I start crumbling.'

'He's a good man.'

'You chose well, Mother.'

This frank talk with her mother unsettled Yasmeen more than she cared to admit. She spent the next hour scouring the oven with a ferocity that left her exhausted as well as spattered. Afterwards she rewarded herself with a hot soak in a bath laced with minerals from the Dead Sea and acacia oil, which restored her to something more like her usual equilibrium.

But her mother's doubts continued to compound her own.

## 13

SAMUEL'S FACE WAS THUNDEROUS as he flung the newspaper down on the coffee table with a snort.

'Look at *that*!'

He was so controlled these days that Candice felt a wave of panic rising up in her throat. She glanced across without getting up; the twins at feeding time were a force to be reckoned with.

One look was enough.

MIXED TWINS. *Black couple give birth to one black, one brown baby.*

The facts were almost correct, the speculation damning.

Who were these '*friends of the parents*', '*neighbours*', who had betrayed them? Who was the '*spokesperson for the fertility unit at the centre of this row*' who denied the possibility of malpractice or negligence? How much deeper would this reporter dig?

She pushed the paper away, and her eyes went to the children who had caused this furore. She held them closer. At least there were no names. Samuel hunched in the chair, glowering.

'It'll die down. It'll pass,' she said, without colour.

'And what will you do when the gutter-press find us, and camp in our front garden? You're a virtual prisoner already!'

'I certainly won't be giving them a comment, that's for sh...'

A sudden hammering on the door cut her off mid-sentence. They stared at each other. Surely not already, not before they'd agreed a strategy.

Candice watched Samuel leave the room with fear in her heart. The door clicked shut behind him. She bunched her old cardigan closer around the babies as if at any moment flashing cameras would violate their private space.

But the stampede came from a single pair of feet. Without so much as a greeting at the door, her mother-in-law erupted into the room, her traditional Nigerian dress a splash of colour amidst all their careful neutrality.

'Dis has got to stop!' she announced. No apology. No preamble. No ceremony.

'This what, Momma?' Samuel was actually wringing his hands as he hovered nervously behind her. Candice was appalled by the trace of mimicry in his accent too.

'Dis!' Aurora spat out, stabbing a red fingernail at the paper she carried.

'It's nothing to do with us. We didn't tell them,' Samuel protested.

'Even de girl in de flower shop, she know! She say she *sorry*! Dis girl dat I do not know!'

'What did *you* say?' Candice's voice shook.

'I say... I say...'

'Yes? You said?'

'Oh, I am so excited when de babies born. It is two, I tell her. Boy *and* girl. It is good. Perfect. She know I am excited. I am so proud.' Aurora closed her eyes reliving the memory. Then they flew open and her whole expression disintegrated. 'And now *disss*.' Again the rap of nails on newspaper.

Without a word Candice heaved herself up off the sofa. In principle she swept out of the room with dignity and eloquence; in reality she lumbered upstairs with two babies still attached to her breasts. It was more of a retreat than a statement.

She sank down onto the bed.

Samuel's mother had made no secret of her own preferred choice of a mate for her son, and since her husband's death, she had not hesitated to put her criticisms of Candice into words. She would pounce on a stray cobweb, an empty milk carton, a stained towel, a single sock, as evidence of wifely incompetence. She scorned Candice's athletic prowess, and constantly bemoaned her own fate tied to substandard Britain.

Once, at that time when her hormones were being excessively stimulated, Candice had dared to retort: 'Why don't you go back to Nigeria then? What's stopping you?'

Aurora had bridled in astonishment. 'You ask dis? Of *me*? I am a momma. One day I will be *grand*momma. I *must* be here.'

Maybe there was something to be said for infertility after all, Candice had thought.

And then Aurora's ailing father moved to Scotland. She took him into her home and lavished all her thwarted grandparental yearning onto him. Aurora alone was a force to be reckoned with; but she and her father together would make a champion bull falter.

Absolute silence followed Candice's departure.

Then the indignant voice came to her clearly. 'But we never, NEVER had white people in our family! *Never.*'

Samuel's voice was less distinct but Candice knew it so well she could decipher most of the blurred connections. 'You can't blame Candice. It's not her fault.'

'No? Who do I blame den?'

'I don't know. I...'

'So, you have white blood in *you* now?'

'No, of course not.'

'Well, den. It must be she.'

'No, Momma. There are things – things you don't know.'

'Dis child, she is not, is she my granddaughter?'

'Listen, Momma. Please. Sit down. *Please.*'

Candice knew from the ebbing and flowing of sound that Aurora was continuing to pace, ignoring his request.

'I said, you must not marry dis woman, Samuel. I told you. But you would not listen. Oh no! I know she not good for you. Momma, she know dese t'ings. And now you see, I am right. But I *read* it in de *newspaper*! First she do not give you a child. Now she go wid anoder man, she give you a child dat is not yours. Oh, Samuel, why you not...?'

'No, Momma! *Listen*!'

Silence. Candice could picture Aurora staring at her son as if he had struck her. Never in all his thirty-nine years had he ever raised his voice to her – until today.

'You do not know the facts, Momma,' he said eventually, without apology.

'De facts? Is it not enough you have a white man's child in dis house?'

'We – Candice and I – she didn't... We had to go to a fertility hospital.'

Candice's lungs refused to ventilate.

'We couldn't have babies the normal way. We had IVF. The twins – were made that way. There must have... been a mistake. At the hospital.'

In the silence that followed she could feel Aurora wading through generations of prejudice and superstition.

'You? My son An *Opakanjo*? You?'

'It was the only way.'

'Opakanjos, dey always make babies. Fine, beautiful, *black* babies.'

'But for us, it didn't... It was the only way.'

'No! It is *never* de way! Never. To do *such* t'ings? *Naaaah.* And now you see what come of such folly. Well, de blame, den, it is yours. *Yours*, Samuel. You let... you agree *Paahh-hh.* I cannot even say it!'

Her disgust, her incredulity, slid into every crevice of their home.

'Momma.' The appeal in his voice stopped Candice in the very process of lifting Destiny to her shoulder. 'I'm begging you. Candice, she is not well. You must not...'

'Not well? *Not well?* Of course she not well! No momma can be well wid such t'ings done to her.'

'No, not because of the treatment. Now, with all the stress. The babies. Momma, please.'

Candice held her breath.

'Please, you must not upset her.'

'*I*? *I* upset her? It is not *I*, it is dat… dat child dat upset her! Of course she is upset. *I* am upset! And *I* do not nurse such a t'ing to my bosom.'

'She is so tired, so…' His voice sank so low Candice missed what he said next. But Aurora's strident tones easily cut across him anyway.

'Hah! You see? Like I say,' she declared. 'You must not agree to dese terrible t'ings and…' Her sentence trailed away.

'She needs… I don't know how to help her.' His voice dropped. 'I shall have to go back to work and…'

'Babies are tiring.' Aurora's tone was softer this time. 'One baby is tiring. Two? Two is exhausting. It will be better when dere is only one. When he does not feed at de bosom.'

'No, Momma. It's not that kind of tiredness.'

Candice was stunned. He had noticed? He knew? In all these weeks he'd simply accepted her sharp tone, her silences. He'd quietly picked up responsibilities he'd never tackled before. He'd bought her flowers, cooked her favourite fish dishes, got up in the night to bring a hungry baby to her, picked up the clutter she'd dropped. All without appearing to notice her depressed state.

Her mind slid back. To the look in his eyes when she'd entered the room, the compliments, the way he touched her as if he would never tire of the sensation, the pride he packed into any introduction of 'my wife'. Had she killed all that? Was it her fault? But it took two to tango. And she was simply too tired.

A sudden ring at the doorbell made her shrink back into the pillows, rocking her babies, willing them not to take exception to this second intrusion.

'Hello, sir.' The voice sounded vaguely familiar. 'Only me.' It was cheerful at least. 'Arthur from the Posybowl, at your service.' Ahhh. Of course. 'Hope I didn't wake the little ones. Getting to be a regular flower shop in your front room, eh? Very nice too. Want me to carry them in for you? Tricky to balance these kind.'

'I'll manage, thanks,' Samuel said above the rustle of cellophane.

'There you go, then. Just make sure the bottom sits nice and snug on the table, otherwise you'll be christening your furniture as well as your bairns! Doing all right, then, are they?'

'Very well, thank you.'

'Jolly good. Bye then.' Harmless. On their side. Candice let out her breath slowly.

This time Samuel closed the door behind him and she could hear nothing of the conversation that followed Arthur's interruption. She laid the sated children down in their cots, and climbed wearily back onto the bed. Exhaustion closed around her like a lumpy eiderdown.

When she eventually surfaced, Aurora had gone.

Samuel was at the sink peeling vegetables. She walked up behind him and slid her arms around his waist, leaning her head against his broad back. It took time to swallow the tears.

He stood still as if checking the boundaries of dreams, and then he placed his hands over hers.

'Thank you,' she said softly.

'For what?'

'For understanding.'

Before he could respond she drew away, busying herself putting things away.

'I want to help, Candice. But don't you think… perhaps you should go back to the doctor?'

'I just need sleep.'

The water in the hand-tie was seeping slowly from the base onto the carpet. She lifted the mass of pale pink lilies, roses and chrysanthemums in their froth of gypsophila into a bowl and placed it in the centre of the table. The serrated edges of the pampas fronds nicked her fingers and she withdrew her hand sharply, sucking the spots of blood.

Was it an omen?

# 14

DAN CRUSE WAS not the person Justin expected.

His lanky fair hair hung in clumps onto his shoulders. Thick lenses gave the impression of a mole peering out of a fox's den. He seemed tangled in a persistent growth spurt that took him by surprise whenever he moved.

Justin introduced himself and Dan took his hand in a firm grasp before inviting him into the house.

The alpha male with attitude Justin had anticipated lounged across the sofa with his booted feet on the coffee table. Justin quirked an eyebrow at Dan.

'This is Reuben. Reuben Fox.'

'From Afferton Crescent?' Justin said.

The hint of a startle confirmed it.

'Hello. My name's Justin Blaydon-Green.'

Reuben made no effort to observe the usual civilities. Could this be the kind of creature who had the power to stir teenage girls to anarchy? The thought hurtled Justin into action. He turned to Dan.

'I believe you were at the hospital yesterday with a number of other demonstrators?'

Dan nodded.

'And you left a placard behind?'

'Ahh.'

'Which you asked my daughter to retrieve later in the day.'

'She didn't have to.' Dan shrugged.

'No, she didn't. But as I understand it, she was unaware of the nature of this placard.'

Another shrug.

'Have you any idea of what we actually do at the clinic?'

'Torture animals and slaughter babies,' Reuben drawled.

'Dan?'

'Like Reuben says.'

'Both accusations are absolutely untrue.'

'Yeah, right. You would say that,' Reuben's sneered.

'Mr Fox,' Justin said, meeting the insolent gaze, 'were you also at the demonstration?'

'Nope. Small fry. But these guys've got to start somewhere.'

'Start what, exactly?'

'Fighting back. Defending the rights of innocent creatures.'

'Does that include violence?'

'If necessary.'

'Isn't there something rather strange about saving a guinea pig and harming a human being?'

'People can speak for themselves. Animals can't.'

Justin swung round to face the ill-prepared Dan. 'Is it animal testing *you* object to, Dan, or…'

'Animals, babies – it's all the same to me. Innocent creatures.'

It had all the hallmarks of a lesson learned by rote, but somehow lacking genuine conviction. Or was that his imagination?

'I take it you're a vegetarian?'

'Vegan.'

'And you don't wear leather?'

'Nope.'

'And if you became ill you wouldn't have medicines that were tested on animals?'

'Not me.'

'And you'd know which ones were so tested, would you?'

'I'd find out.'

'From your Intensive Care bed, yes?'

'I'd find out for him,' Reuben chipped in.

'Or you might ask my daughter,' Justin ventured.

Reuben swung his boots off the table and Justin knew a

moment of fear as the solid mass of young, fit muscle walked towards him, but Reuben was only tracking down his jacket which lay in a black leather puddle by the door. The metal studs chattered together as he rummaged until he found an oblong of gum.

As he passed Justin he growled, 'You may have brainwashed your kid into thinking you're in charge of life and death, but now she's old enough to make up her own mind.'

He draped himself back over the sofa, the gum squelching against his teeth. Justin transferred his attention to Dan.

'The reason I'm here is because I care, not only about my daughter and the company she keeps, but about the innocent lives you imagine are in danger. And I care about you. You're young. The direction you take now will affect where you go and where you end up. I could have rung your parents, but I reckoned you'd want to deal with this yourself. Look, there's a lot of stuff talked about cruelty to animals and needless waste of life in fertility clinics, but most of it's based on imagination and prejudice rather than fact. I came to ask you two things.' Dan's pale blue eyes flickered to Reuben, and then back to his inquisitor.

'First, what is it you're fighting for? Have you got the facts? Causes can get out of hand – even good causes. Do you *really* value human lives and human happiness? If so, what about those who get caught in the crossfire? People were hurt yesterday, Dan. Couples who come to our clinic are already coping with huge dilemmas you can't even imagine. Some of them were shaking with terror. The last thing they needed was a group of strangers chanting, and waving placards, questioning the things they're going through. And that was what *you* call a *peaceful* protest. *They* didn't know you were "peaceful". It didn't *feel* very peaceful from where they were standing.' He paused. 'And more than that, things can easily get out of hand, people get maimed, killed even. Is violence ever justified for the causes you're campaigning for? Is it?'

Dan had the grace to look sheepish but the courage to keep his head high. Justin noticed he didn't look at Reuben, who, curiously, said nothing.

'And the second thing is, please don't involve my daughter in this. Contrary to your friend's belief, she has *not* been brainwashed. She has ideas of her own. But she's still a schoolgirl, and it's my job to protect her from getting into situations she can't handle. Incidentally, she didn't want me to come here today, she wanted to handle it herself. She only gave me the bare bones of the story because I found the placard in my garage. But I insisted on coming. You see, I *know* how things can escalate, and I do not want an innocent person hauled off to jail for no other reason than that she happens to be in the wrong place at the wrong time. And I'd be sorry to see that happen to you too, Dan. I'm not saying you shouldn't fight for what you believe in. But be aware, be very aware, of where ideological fervour can lead. Beware of the fundamentalists, the extremists who've lost perspective. And be aware too, of how easy it is to erode your own sensibilities once you start excusing threats and violence.'

He stopped.

Silence.

'I'm sorry,' Dan said quietly. 'I didn't mean to get her into trouble.'

'I didn't think you did. And I accept your apology. Just you stay out of trouble yourself, Dan.'

A slow handclap made them both turn.

'Yeah. Yeah. Yeah. Mr Nice Guy. All things bright and beautiful.' Reuben wasn't slouching now; he was wired, his grey-green eyes glittering. 'You may be fooling Dan, but you don't fool me, Doctor whatever-your-bloody-name-is. "Erode your sensibilities", my eye! It's *your* sensibilities you should be worried about. You think because you've recited some stupid Hippocratic oath, you can do just what the hell you like. A few thank you cards from patients, your name in the BMJ, and you think the world's a better place because of you. But these kids you make, how do *they* feel when they find out that, for every one of them, a whole bucket-load of others died? What would the punters think if they saw you lot dredging up those frozen embryos that've sat around for ten years waiting to start growing again – saw you *destroying* them? Little people – human beings – that never asked to be made in the first place.'

His cold anger held real menace.

'These women that creep along to your filthy centre, what gives them the *right* to have a kid? Children aren't bits of junk on a market stall, there for anybody that wants them. They're human souls. Not possessions.'

'I agree with much of what you say,' Justin said.

'No, you don't,' Reuben cut in. 'And you needn't waste your psychological tactics on me, Mr Smart Ass.'

'Did you paint the placards, Reuben?' It was a long shot but Justin had just noticed colour on the sole of his boot.

'What if I did?'

'You're wasting your talents. They're really good. Powerful. I noticed a new hand straight away. Are you a trained artist?'

'What if I am?'

'I'd like to see some of your work. Have you exhibited?'

Reuben shrugged.

'Have you ever thought of translating your opinions into art? You could send out a terrific message in that form. Other people would pass the word on from their walls.'

Just then the front door opened. The two young men froze.

'Don't worry,' Justin murmured. 'I'm leaving.'

Reuben lounged back on the sofa. Dan hovered alongside Justin, eyes on the door. High-heeled footsteps tripped along to the kitchen. Justin's soft-soled shoes were soundless on the laminate floor. Not until he was safely striding down the road to his own house did Justin unclench his fists and wipe the beads of sweat from the crevices of his palms.

Bobby was incandescent.

'How *could you*, Dad? How *could you*?'

'Because I've seen what these protests can lead to. That's how. And there is no way I'm standing by while my own daughter gets dragged into something as dangerous as this.'

'I wasn't *dragged* into anything. What d'you think it makes me look like, you steam-rollering in and fighting my battles?'

'Is it important what Dan Cruse thinks of you?'

'Yes. No.'

'Or Reuben Fox?'

'No, not them *specifically* – whoever Reuben Fox is – but *anybody* who gets to hear about it. I... oh, can't you see? I'm *seventeen*! I'll be away from home next year. It was only a stupid *placard*.'

By the time Justin had finished outlining the evolutionary history of the common placard, his truculent daughter had also evolved. It was time to hold out an olive branch.

'I'm sorry, darling, if I've ruined your credibility with Melanie's brother and his militant buddy. But if it's any consolation I told them you didn't want me to get involved.'

'You said that?'

'I did. And anyway,' he grinned at her, 'somehow I doubt very much if either of those gentlemen will be reporting anything of our little tête-à-tête today. They couldn't get me out of the way fast enough when Mrs Cruse came home!'

'You didn't tell *her*?' Bobby wailed.

'No. I left without her even seeing me.'

'Thank God for that! I do *not* want to be responsible for getting Melanie's brother into trouble.'

'Au contraire. I rather think you might have been instrumental in getting him *out* of trouble,' Justin said wryly.

'Oh, did you give them what for?' Something sparkled behind her eyes.

'Let's just say that I believe, for an old codger, I gave them pause for thought. They weren't exactly crowing when I left.'

'I can believe that!' she said with feeling. 'But you know, Pops, it's maddening when you're so... so *reasonable*! When you trot out all these arguments and facts and you are so *calm*. Sometimes I just want to be angry about something.'

'I know, sweetie. And it's OK to rant at home. But out there, in the big old world, you need to be sure of your ground if you're going to have a rant. It does your credibility no good at all if you go off at half-cock.'

'And did Dan? Go off at half-cock?'

'Well, I guess I didn't give him much space to prove himself in the oratory stakes. It was pretty obvious that he was on borrowed ground.'

'How d'you mean?'

'Dancing to somebody else's tune.'

'So, the other guy? Was he calling the shots?'

'Maybe. He's a much more dangerous animal anyway. Definitely not somebody Dan should be spending too much time with.' He gave a short laugh. 'Actually, just as Reuben was gathering a nice head of steam I recommended he concentrate on his art. Told him he had real talent.'

'Did you?'

'I did. And it's true. That placard was powerful stuff.'

'I didn't take much notice.' She shrugged. 'Well, I didn't want to get caught with something like that.'

There was a long pause.

'Miss Taylor says it's the third stage of emancipation.'

'What is? Good art?'

'No, silly. Fighting for animal rights.'

'How does she work that one out?'

'Well, we've had slaves, then women. Now it's animals.'

'Do they teach that at your school?' He was a sparrow sensing a hawk.

'Oh, no. But she got us to debate the animal rights question in our moral philosophy class a while back.'

'Well, bully for Miss Taylor.'

'She says thinking only of the cruelty-to-animals angle, or the killing of babies, can mess up your mind.'

'She's right on that,' he confirmed with feeling. 'That's what leads to vicious behaviour – hate mail, arson, explosives, even murder.'

Her mind was clearly far away.

'Does it bother you what I do for a living, Bobby?'

'Nope. But then, I know what you're really like.'

He could only hope this was the reassurance he thought it was.

Long after she'd gone to apply her un-messed-up mind to French vocabulary, Justin pondered the danger of Reuben Fox and his ilk.

If they only knew the agonising that went into decisions about real-life tragedies. Would they be less quick to judge? Probably not. Their world was more monochrome, more polarised. Justin shivered. If Reuben sniffed a hint of the waste of life Justin was contemplating in order to create a saviour sibling for one sick four-year-old, he would stock-pile ammunition for World War III. If he knew the number of lives potentially damaged by the mistake that resulted in Destiny Opakanjo, he'd be marching with thousands to Downing Street at least, if not to Strasbourg.

It would only take one person – one Desirée Wanless – to sell her waiting-room gossip. Crazy really. Medicine was aeons away from creating designer babies; still at a debatable stage with preventing incurable diseases, nowhere near choosing aesthetic extras. Indeed, the vast majority of the population stood more accused by selecting their mates, than he did in helping the Zair family.

Choosing a mate... Ahhh. It looked as if he could relax on that score at least. Bobby seemed in no danger as far as Messrs Cruse or Fox were concerned. Nor did she appear to be on the path to becoming an activist herself. She was, however, honing the requisite talents for life – compassion, logical argument, determination, intellectual integrity, drive, articulation. He must have a chat with this Miss Taylor next parents' evening.

He could only hope that Yasmeen Zair had acquired the same skills. If she didn't let her indiscretion jeopardise her chances, she could be The Pemberton's best ally.

Calm he might be on the outside, but Justin knew both his digestion and his sleep would suffer if he didn't get rid of the internal tension somehow. He channelled his energy into mowing the lawns, tying back climbing plants and clearing weeds until darkness drove him indoors. An hour and a half with Dvořák, struggling to master the fingering for his Cello Concerto in B minor, was exactly the challenge he needed before bedtime, and gradually the mellow beauty of the music seeped into his being.

# 15

AS SOON AS she saw the article in the paper, Yasmeen knew. The pieces slotted together.

A growing sense of unease plagued her. How was Candice coping? Had she got family and friends to shield her from the press?

There were six Opakanjos in the directory. By the time Karim came home from work, she had rehearsed every possible variation of her opening gambit, but she still hadn't persuaded herself that even lifting the phone was the right thing to do.

Karim was to the point. 'If they've any sense, every one of them'll deny even knowing her. *I* know your intentions are honourable, but they won't.'

'You're probably right.'

The idea died. The troubled thoughts persisted.

Two nights later she was back on the horns of that same dilemma. This time the points were sharper.

'By the way, you know that couple we met in the clinic?' Karim said, eyes on the pile of essays he was marking. 'The ones with the twins.'

'Yes.'

'Well, one of the kids in my fifth-year class lives in the same town as them.'

'How d'you know that?'

'I was talking about genetic inheritance today. So I used a couple of examples – including that one from the papers. Afterwards this girl came to tell me she knew the family by sight.'

'And this all came about in a *biology* lesson?' Yasmeen looked at him hard.

'Scout's honour.'

'Biology lessons obviously aren't what they were in my day.'

He grinned. 'I doubt any of the lessons in my school bear any resemblance to your experience at Cheltenham's finest.'

'The only wonder is we learned anything about the human body. Our Miss Fish was a true blue prude.'

'And it certainly wasn't *de rigeur* to use *newspapers* to augment the standard texts, I'll bet.'

Yasmeen gave a theatrical shudder. 'I doubt Marjorie H. Fish would have even touched such a filthy object! But I'm interested in why *you* did.'

'Because it makes the subject real. Shows they aren't theoretical issues, they're part of real life.'

'Hmm. How would you like teachers using us and Sebastian as an example?'

He gave it some thought. 'If they stuck to the facts, sensitively and appropriately, why not?'

'I'd need to think about it.'

He shrugged.

'So this girl came – of her own accord – to tell you about knowing the Opakanjos?'

'She didn't say their name, but there surely can't be two families in this part of the world with this particular story.'

'So?'

He flashed her an odd look, and then turned to watch his hand doodling on the back of an envelope.

'This girl in my biology class lives in a town south of the school on the main A-road to Edinburgh. I checked and only one of the Opakanjos listed in the directory lives in that area.'

'You are a very decent honourable man, Karim Zair.'

'But not as decent as Miss Fish!'

It was Samuel who answered the phone. He was understandably cautious. He asked the right questions, got the right answers.

Only when he was perfectly sure of her identity did he offer any information: Candice was already in bed, exhausted. Yasmeen left her number anyway; but it felt odd being treated with such suspicion. Did she really want to pursue this? Well, it was done now. Maybe that was the end of it. She'd tried.

The call she didn't expect came that same evening. Brief but definite. Please come. Friday afternoon any good? Of course. She'd make sure it was.

Sebastian permitting.

Two days later Yasmeen found herself outside 57 Hill Drive, a bouquet of lilies in one hand, a pork and apple casserole in the other. Vertical blinds deadened every window. Her resolve faltered. It was 57, wasn't it? It was Friday?

She rang once more.

Her eyes strayed over the front garden. In her mind Yasmeen loosened up the symmetrical design, added some height and structure, introduced contrast and shape, a touch of romanticism. She was already choosing a twisted hazel to complement the dwarf pine, and a purple-leaved heuchera for richness when she felt the scrutiny and turned.

The door opened. There was no one in sight but it was clear she was intended to step inside. The door closed swiftly behind her.

An aroma of baby vomit hung around Candice, stains marked both shoulders, her skirt, her slippers. The thick black hair, which had been braided and beaded so artistically, stood in an unkempt fuzz. Nappies and baby clothes, newspapers and coffee mugs littered the living room. Huge bouquets of flowers decayed in their vases, the smell mixing with the odour of damp washing and yesterday's vegetables.

'Candice, it's lovely to see you again.'

Candice gestured for Yasmeen to sit down. 'Would you like a drink?' A sleepwalker on auto-pilot.

'I'd love to make you one.'

By the time she reappeared with the drinks Candice was

slumped back in her chair, eyes closed, a trickle of silent tears sliding down her cheek. Yasmeen let her cry before despatching her to bed, with a promise to listen for the twins.

Yasmeen peeped into the second bedroom. Orlando lay spreadeagled on his back, arms thrown out, his breathing punctuated with grunting snores. Destiny curled low down in her cot, so still that Yasmeen found herself placing a hand beneath the pert little nose to check that she was still breathing. Their room was immaculate; the children themselves spotless. She crept out, praying there would be no imminent demands for food.

By the time she detected the first whimper from Orlando, she had established some order in the kitchen, and the first machine-load of nappies and towels was flapping in the breeze. The baby stared up at her with fearless dark eyes as she carried him, talked to him, played with him, content for now to have her within sight as she dusted and tidied. Destiny, wakening forty minutes later, was much less sure of this stranger, but placed beside her brother on a rug on the floor, she too quietened.

Yasmeen was kneeling beside them when Candice dragged herself into the room, bleary eyed. Her gesture swept the fresh flowers, the tidy room.

'Thank you. You're very kind.'

'It's nothing. I'm only sorry I didn't know before.'

The stare came from a thousand miles away. 'Why would you?'

'I should have thought. Twins. It's a lot of work. It was only when...' In the nick of time she stopped herself. 'I'm so sorry.'

Candice seemed to fold in on herself.

'But now I'm here, you must let me help. Washing, ironing. A few meals.'

'You've got your own family.'

'Shahira is at school and my mother will help with Sebastian. I won't intrude. I can do things like the laundry and cooking at my place. Bring it back when it's done.'

'But you hardly know me.'

'Well, I'd like to get to know you better.'

'I ought to be more organised.'

'Babies are hard work. Breast-feeding one takes the stuffing out of you, never mind two. You need all the rest you can get.'

'Samuel tries.'

'If he's anything like my husband, he won't *see* what needs to be done.'

A smile flitted across the wan features.

'Men are just wired differently,' Yasmeen said lightly.

She changed both children deftly and handed them over to their mother. Candice visibly relaxed once they had latched on and started gulping down her milk.

'You look as if you've been doing this for ever,' Yasmeen murmured.

'It feels like a lifetime.'

Yasmeen nodded.

'I'm afraid I'll have to run now, Candice. My mother's got Sebastian but I have to collect him for his evening treatment. I'll be back in a few days with these gorgeous baby clothes. Monday OK?'

Candice nodded as Yasmeen stuffed the washing into carrier bags.

'I'll ring four times to let you know I'm friend, not foe!'


Yasmeen discovered an unexpected delight in hanging the tiny garments on the line, ironing the sheets, the vests, the dresses. Her hands lingered on the soft new fabrics; her mind dreamed dreams.

She had given away all her baby things as Sebastian outgrew them; her family now complete, glad to get the space back that had been filled with the pram, pushchair, highchair, cot. But at the last minute she'd tucked away the jacket her mother had crocheted for the day Sebastian came out of hospital, a seven pound three ounce bundle of contentment. Until she was smoothing Orlando's blue cardigan she'd forgotten that moment of weakness. She sneaked a quick look, holding the garment up against her cheek, inhaling its scent. Her memory slid to those early days and nights at home. The delight, the pride. The perpetual tiredness, the isolation.

And now she was five years older. She'd be into her forties this time around if – *when* – they had another baby. She turned sideways looking at herself in the mirror, her hand flat on her tummy. She pictured it round and full.

The bathroom door clicked. She pushed the jacket back out of sight and closed the drawer with a snap.

# 16

THE HEADLINE IN the *News* caught Scott's eye as he strode down the supermarket aisle to pick up his usual ready-meals after work. Cooking was for restaurant chefs and people without careers. The marvel of stainless steel and electronic wizardry he called his kitchen had been inherited, along with the minimalist décor and the two en-suite shower rooms. He had no use for ninety per cent of it.

Weird, really, that he should see the headline at all. As far as he was concerned, the *News* was best relegated to cat litter and fish-and-chip shops. He was an *Observer* man himself. But today the words leapt out to grab him by the throat.

*MIXED TWINS. Black couple give birth...*

He tossed the newspaper onto the kitchen table and tore away the film on his chicken provençal – did an accent make this travesty more acceptable? He set the microwave dial, and ripped open a bag of continental leaves, a token nod in the direction of the health nannies. He sliced two vine tomatoes. Now there he *was* fussy. Tomatoes had to taste of sun and vitamins; to smell like his grandfather after a morning pollinating the plants in his greenhouse. Beetroot was another favourite. Of course it tasted better freshly dug and home cooked, but if it was a toss-up between reading the latest medical journal or cleaning a juice-speckled hob and work-surface, the journal won every time. He sliced open the tight plastic without spilling a drop. His entire meal would be over within thirty minutes.

It was his colleague, Nina, who'd introduced him to seeded

bread – only hers had been homemade. He couldn't resist slicing the crust off a lazy man's substitute and eating it while he pottered about. The fruity white Italian wine someone had brought him, thinking they were in for a gourmet supper, tasted pallid, but it served the purpose.

A first skim of the paper looked promising. Nothing to identify the family or the leak. He read it again, this time looking between the lines as well as at each separate word. This Natalie Wyatt was persistent, you had to grant her that. Her instincts were good. Even in the face of 'no comment' she could speculate pretty accurately for a non-medical investigator. Nothing to identify the Opakanjos unless you knew them, but more than she could have obtained by fair means. *Somebody* had talked.

Hard to believe Samuel Opakanjo *wasn't* talking. He must realise the potential in this, and if he was any kind of a man he'd want some form of retribution.

Scott let his shoulders relax. Being the key internal linkman for the HFEA investigation had its compensations. He'd trawled down those columns so many times he knew there was nothing to incriminate anyone directly. Nothing. That meant any claim of negligence or malpractice would sit outside the director's door. Default setting. It wasn't a comfortable thought; Justin was a decent bloke. But he stood tall with the HFEA, maybe he'd survive intact.

It was he, Scott, who seemed to be public enemy number one. The girls would fall silent as soon as he approached. He hadn't been invited to the Prince and Feathers last Thursday to celebrate the arrival of Zhen's third kid. Jack, who could normally be relied on for a touch of dry humour to lighten the atmosphere, was doing his job minus the bonhomie, minus the sizzling. Scott would give a lot to hear that infernal sizzling back in the lab.

And the meeting with Justin... Scott glowered into his wine at the memory.

He'd spent hours analysing the recorded facts, but when he'd made his initial written report, all Justin had said was, 'I don't like it, Scott. Too squeaky clean. A mistake has been made. So, where is it?'

Scott was supposed to be implementing an even more rigorous audit, but to hell with that. His research looked set to take the scientific world by storm; why should he throw away two years of meticulous work?

Like he'd told Jack: 'Keep your head down and get on with your work. If we all do that, eventually it'll just die down.'

He could see from Jack's face that somebody had come up behind him.

'This isn't some schoolboy prank to be overlooked.' Justin's privileged voice that no one had ever heard raised. 'It can't "just die down". Where is that black gamete?'

Jack had sidled away with a sheepish look that said he wished he hadn't been part of this scene. The whole damn place felt claustrophobic, even down amongst the animals where he used to be assured of solitude. He'd found Phyllis lurking there one morning, when everyone thought he was at a scientific meeting in Glasgow. Phyllis, who they said had a hot line to somebody in the HFEA.

And Nina – plodding, unambitious Nina. Even she was twitchy. He seriously resented having *her* watching *him* while he was clarifying sperm or handling pipettes. The nerve. He was her senior by two years. He knew what he was doing.

But he'd got his own back the other evening. Well, she deserved it.

She was crouched over her computer formulating tables. Scott could see the outline, not the detail, as he approached.

'Scott! What on earth are you doing sneaking up on me?' she exploded.

'Only wondering what you're up to at this hour,' he said mildly, spinning it out while he scanned her figures.

'What d'you *think* I'm doing?' She pushed a buff folder across the bench; a box of paperclips spewed chattering metal everywhere.

'I don't know. You tell me. I'm just checking. Nobody's above suspicion. And you've been working late a lot this past fortnight.'

'This past fortnight? You have to be kidding! I've been working late this past *four years!*'

'On your own?'

'Of course on my own. Since when did I need a minder?'

'People are wondering, that's all.'

'People? What people?'

'People.'

'D'you mean Justin? Are you saying he's sent you to spy on me?'

He shrugged noncommittally.

'Well, I don't believe it. He wouldn't. If he had issues with my work he'd talk to me himself.' She glared at Scott, daring him to deny it. 'And none of the technicians gives a toss about me working late. What on earth would anyone suspect me of? There's no secret about what I'm doing. I'm not muddling up embryos. I'm not creating a monster in a petrie dish. I'm not falsifying records. I'm not screwing up families.'

'Most people know what *I'm* working on, but who really knows exactly what I do down there in the zoo?'

Nina hated the in-house slang for the animal labs. He knew that.

'Look, back off, Scott. OK, somebody fouled up with those black embryos. They may not even be aware they made a mistake. You said yourself, there's no record of an error. But for heaven's sake, it doesn't mean there's major scientific fraud going on here.'

'It could be symptomatic.'

'Of what?'

'Sloppiness.'

She actually snorted. 'Listen, I don't know what's got into you lately, but I can't be doing with it. I have analysis to do, so I'll thank you to get out of my hair and let me get on.'

'Your lack of co-operation is duly noted.'

She stared at him as if he'd just backed his Land Rover into her Ferrari.

Justin was not his usual benign self.

'What's going on, Scott? I've been getting complaints. And your full report, why's it taking so long?'

'I'm onto something, actually. More a hunch than evidence, but I don't want to point a finger until I'm sure.'

'Fair enough, but why the heavy hand? You'll end up with no staff left if you keep going like this. I'm talking about a good team here.'

'So, what are they complaining about?' Scott interrupted sharply.

'Insinuations. Intrusion. I mean, what possessed you to phone Raisa when she was off sick? And Nina. She's one of the best up-and-coming embryologists we've had here in years. I've never known her get rattled, but you've done something to annoy her. What's going on?'

'It's all part of a longer-term strategy,' Scott said carefully.

'Well, ease off, will you? If you can't handle things better than this...'

'Did these people all come to complain to you in person?' Scott interrupted.

'No. I called a meeting the day before yesterday to find out what was going on. You can feel the atmosphere as soon as you open the door. I can't have this, Scott. So back off. And I need some sort of a result – verbal will do – by the end of this week.'

Good. The cracks were appearing. Someone somewhere knew something and he was going to be the first to find out about it.

# 17

JACK WAS SHOVELLING cereal into his mouth when Patsy groped her way into the kitchen, minus her lenses. It was 6.15am – not her best time. She was the owl, he the lark, in this household.

'Whatever time did you crawl in at?' she slurred, yawning expansively.

'Round about 2ish, I guess.'

'One of these days that door'll be locked so you can't get in at these crazy hours and ruin me beauty sleep.'

'You hardly stirred!' Jack protested.

'Hardly is too much. I need eight hours – uninterrupted.'

'So that's why you're as crumpled as yesterday's clothes,' he teased, his eyes skimming the smooth satin of her negligee.

'Not funny. I heard you come to bed. I wasn't in the mood for your nonsense.'

She dumped herself down at the table cradling a mug of black tea, strong enough to dye a pullover. She reached out to turn his wrist and peer at his watch.

'And you're up early.'

'Couldn't sleep.' He crunched with deliberation through a fresh mouthful of bran flakes.

'Yuck, that stuff stinks. Like a compost heap,' she said, wrinkling her nose.

'Hefty chunk of my five-a-day though. Beats your white toast.'

It was one of their points of difference. In spite of working in a doctors' surgery, seeing disease up close and personal, she had remarkably little respect for her diet. Probably came from being wafer thin, Jack suspected. Mars bars and Kettle crisps didn't show on her. Whereas he, well, he'd lost his old man at forty-five – never out of the chippie; heart attack bang in the middle of football match at Meadowbank. Jack wasn't about to give his genetic inheritance a helping hand. His dad was why he wouldn't go for the 'marriage lark'. He didn't want to make Patsy a widow.

'Where were you anyway?' she asked.

'At work.'

She clicked her tongue. 'I know that hospital's your second home, but till 2 o'clock? What kept you?'

'Strange goings on in the middle of the night up at the madhouse,' he intoned in a graveyard voice. 'You'll never guess.'

'The Pemberton's been taken over by a poltergeist.' Her sparkle was returning as she warmed to her theme.

'Nope.'

'Don't tell me your boss has taken up satanism.' She crossed herself.

'Nope. Better than that.'

'You slowly opened the door of the animal lab, where you found' – she dropped her voice and leaned closer – 'six of the mice turning into footmen. Looking handsome in their powdered wigs and scarlet and gold livery, they leapt onto a golden coach and sped off to collect Cinderella. She was so ravishing in her white dress and silver cape that the dashing young prince couldn't bear to let her go. The clock had already started to chime midnight when she finally appeared. Gallant to a man, the footmen drove the horses at a fierce gallop but at the last bend the coach overturned and they all flew out of their seats and landed head first on the road. Cinderella ran for home and got there just as her ballgown turned back to rags. The police found six tiny carcasses strewn across the grass verge, and a squashed pumpkin in the gutter. Now the country's finest vets are closeted with Scotland Yard's top detectives piecing together the last hours of The Pemberton six.' All this with vivid changes of expression. 'And you're about to speed off to the rescue this morning to buy six more identical specimens to save the reputation of your scientists.'

He grinned. 'Patsy Graham, your talents are wasted on "We have a 4.15 slot on Thursday, Mrs Brown."'

She flushed a soft pink much like the flimsy garment she was hugging around herself.

'OK, Mr Secretive, tell your Aunty Patsy all about it!' She propped her chin on her hands and opens her hazel eyes wide.

He sketched the scene for her and the battle he'd witnessed. 'Talk about prima donnas!'

'Aren't prima donnas female?' she said, rubbing one eye.

'Well, anyway.'

'You surprise me, I must admit. The doctors in our surgery wouldn't argue in front of *us*.'

'Oh, they didn't know I was there.'

'How come?'

'I was in the next room. They couldn't see me.'

'They'd have seen the light on.'

'Didn't put it on.'

She stared at him.

'Let me get this right. You went to the centre. At night. Didn't put the light on and listened in to a private row – yeah?'

'More or less.'

Patsy sat totally still. A rare occurrence that.

'Look, something doesn't stack up here. What were *you* up to, Jack?'

'Looking at stuff.'

'Looking. At stuff. I guess that makes it all crystal clear, your Honour.'

Jack swithered. He'd known her for three years, lived with her for twenty-three months and three weeks, but...

'Listen, Patsy, if I tell you, will you promise not to breathe a word of it to a living soul?'

'Cross my heart and hope to die.'

He couldn't take the risk. 'Nah. You're better off not

knowing. What you don't know you can't blab.'

'Jack Fitzpatrick!'

Still he hesitated.

'Well?'

'Look, something happened in our lab. Let's just say, somebody made a mistake. But nobody knows who. Our senior scientist can't find where it went wrong.'

'Right.'

'So we're all under suspicion.'

'You too?'

'I said everybody. Last time I looked I was a body.'

'No need to get narky,' she sniffed. 'So this has got something to do with what you were looking for last night?'

'Sort of.'

She waited.

'I reckon,' he said, weighing his words one by one, 'somebody's covering up something for somebody. So I thought, why don't I have a wee look-see myself?'

'And?'

'And what?'

'*Did* you find anything?'

'I told you. Nina was already there when I arrived. I thought, she'll go soon and I'll have the place to myself. So I stayed there in the dark, waiting. But then in comes Scott. Blimey! It was like Picadilly Circus!'

Patsy grinned. 'Now who's being a drama queen?'

'Yes, but why does he sneak in like that? He scares Nina half to death. And that's when she turns on him, all guns blazing.'

'So you chickened out and came home.'

'Hey, less of the chicken. I waited as long as I reasonably could. But they still hadn't come out at 1.40 so I reckoned I'd better call it a day.'

A frown lined her forehead. 'You still haven't told me, what did you expect to find?'

'I don't know. I just wanted to have a squint at that report. See if I could maybe spot anything fishy. I mean, it can't be right.'

'This mistake – it wouldn't have anything to do with those twins, would it?'

'Don't push your luck, Patsy. You know I can't give you chapter and verse. Shouldn't have told you this much probably, but hey ho! I've got to live with you.'

'Well, I'll tell you this for nothing, Jack,' she sniffed. 'There's no way *I'd* go to that clinic of yours!'

'Oh, come on, Patsy. This is the first hoo-hah I've heard about in all my years there.'

'That you've *heard* about. But how many other mistakes might there have been? What else is being covered up? No, just make sure *I* don't get carted off to your place.'

Patsy realised what she'd just said and a dull flush spread from her ears down beyond her cleavage.

'Curses! Look at the time!' Jack leapt to his feet and bundled his dish and mug into the dishwasher. 'Must fly. Last thing I need today is a rocket from Dr High-and-Mighty Martindale!'

He dropped a kiss somewhere in the region of her tannin-scented mouth and grabbed his rucksack. 'Expect me when you see me.'

It was an anti-climax. Scott wasn't in. Emma said he'd gone off to a conference in Birmingham, for two days. First Jack had heard of it. Nina was in the lab by 8.15 as per usual. No battle scars that he could see. Maybe she'd done away with Scott!

Jack's late night caught up with him at around 11.30, so he indulged in a remedial dose of caffeine, then snatched forty winks at lunch-time. When he came to, Justin was in the staff room two chairs along from him, reading some thick journal or other, chomping on a Braeburn apple and cheese.

He grinned as Jack staggered upright. 'Heavy night?'

'Yeah. Sorry, Boss.'

'Hope it was worth it.'

'Well, you know.'

'Everything all right, Jack?'

'Fine, thanks.'

'Still thinking?'

'Still thinking.'

'It's a funny thing, but I could have sworn I saw somebody riding your bike away from here just before 2 this morning.'

'Why would anybody want to take my old rust heap for a spin in the wee small hours, Boss?'

Justin nodded and resumed his reading. The edges of the bite marks in his apple were already turning brown.

Jack made himself another strong coffee.

'Jack, would you say you're up to speed with the research going on in this department?'

'I probably know pretty much what's what.'

'Good. I like to think you do too.'

Another long pause while he finished his apple.

'Keep thinking, Jack. And remember, my door's open.'

'Thanks.'

Time for a sharp exit.

## 18

YASMEEN PROPPED THE laundry basket on one hip, and pressed the bell. Four times.

Silence.

She watched a delivery lorry manoeuvre into a tight parking space outside the house opposite, holding her breath, waiting for the crunch of a snagged wing mirror, the scrape of metal on metal. She rang again, leaving her finger on the bell for the fourth ring this time, hoping it didn't spell irritation.

Silence.

She opened the letterbox. 'Candice! It's only me, the washer-woman! Can you let me in?'

There was a shuffle inside and the door opened a crack.

One look at her was enough. 'You need bed – lots of it!'

Candice slept for five hours, stirring only when Yasmeen presented the twins for a feed. She looked no better when she eventually lurched into the living room, her steel-wool hair on end as if an electric current had jolted her awake.

Competing demands tore at Yasmeen's resolve. What if Sebastian... her mother...

'Candice, what time does Samuel get home?'

'Next month.'

'Sorry?'

'He's away.'

'Away? How long for?'

Candice's brain seemed to be struggling to locate time and place. 'Another three weeks. Four, maybe. I'm not sure.'

'Is it work? Or?'

'He's on the rig. For two months.'

'Is there somebody else? Family? Neighbour? Anyone?'

A blank expression, the tiniest shake of the head, was all the response she could elicit. How could anyone withdraw from life to this extent without notice?

'Does Samuel know how bad you feel?'

'I wanted him to go back.'

What other misery did this flat voice conceal?

It was almost 4pm when Yasmeen eventually dared to leave Candice.

Far from missing her, Sebastian clamoured to stay with Granny Dita for longer. He was standing aloft in a spectacular construction of coffee table, chairs, sheets and tablecloths, a solid mahogany barometer and an antique map sacrificed on the altar of his nautical needs. Completely unaware of the price of his grandmother's dedication, he peered out of the one eye not bound by a scarf, brandishing his cardboard cutlass, and consigned his enemy to the deep. Perdita created impressive waves in the ocean of Persian rug.

The pirate turned, spied Yasmeen and let out a wail.

'Mu-um-my! You *can't* come yet! Granny Dita hasn't escaped for the *foo-ood.*'

'Ahh. Well, far be it from me to come between a man and his stomach.' Yasmeen cowered away. 'I'll just hide here on this desert island.' She wrapped herself in the full-length curtains and swished the fabric, moaning wind through the palm trees.

Her mother sidled out to the kitchen, returning almost instantly with two pillowcases bulging with goodies, and proceeded to row vigorously across the water.

'Come on up the ladder, you bad old man,' Sebastian bellowed. 'And mind you don't drop the treasure.'

Once on board the hapless captive reached into the first sack and presented him with a coconut cookie.

'Now, Captain Jake, sir, I beg you, sit down for this fine feast lest the storm send you head first into this boiling sea.' The whole edifice creaked ominously as she spoke.

Captain Jake hunkered down inside the legs of a chair, one fist clenched around the nearest upright, and crammed the cookie into his mouth.

'Now, Captain, some fine wine?'

Perdita paid no heed to the juice slopping over her tapestry cloth as well as her own sleeve, but once he had vanished inside the metal tankard she seized her advantage.

'Ahoy there! Here's an island hoving into view. And there – shiver me timbers, there's the chief of the ocean police himself. Come aboard, sir. Come aboard. Here is the dastardly villain!' She flung her arm out to point at Sebastian. 'Haul him off to jail.'

Yasmeen effected the capture and bundled her son and his diminishing blood count into his duffle coat amidst loud protests.

'We must go, honey. Daddy and Shahira will be home from piano practice and they'll be wanting their tea.'

'And Granddad will be hungry, too,' Perdita added swiftly.

Sebastian's brow furrowed at this mutiny in the ranks, but the inducement of more cookies to take home to share with Shahira softened the betrayal.

'Say goodbye and thank you to Granny Dita.'

His grandmother pretended to be scared to death of his proximity and he giggled as she fought against his hug.

They left wreathed in laughter.


Not until both children were safely asleep did Yasmeen offload her anxieties about Candice.

Karim shot her a strange look.

'Don't you think you're getting in over your head with this one?'

'You should see her, Karim. She's like a zombie. And she's responsible for these two babies. Most of the time on her own.'

'Maybe. But you've got more than enough on your own plate with Sebastian.'

'It's only until she gets on her feet. It's such hard work having two.'

'And what if *we* have two? You'll be exhausted before you start.'

She was shocked into silence. Two? She'd be lucky to get one.

'It happens,' he said. 'And at our age they're likely to implant more than one, aren't they? If you're serious about this, you should be resting now, while you can. Building yourself up.'

'I can't leave Candice in the lurch. It wouldn't be fair.'

'Doesn't she have family? Or friends? Can't social services help?'

'His mother is local but Candice doesn't get on with her.'

'She's not your responsibility.'

'You wouldn't say that if you saw her now,' Yasmeen said, willing him to understand. 'She's so... overwhelmed.'

'Doesn't she have people calling – to check she's coping? Health visitors, district nurses? Somebody.'

'Apparently not. Well, she doesn't see them, if they do come.'

There was a long silence. She stole a sidelong look at him.

'I'm serious, Meena. Nobody else but you can have a baby for Bassy. We'll need to get on with it as soon as we get the green light, and you have to be fighting fit to give it a chance.'

'I know. You're right. I'll try to ease out of it.'

He was very still, a strange expression in his eyes.

'What? Why are you looking at me like that?'

'Are you sure about this?'

'I've said I'll try. But I can't simply desert her.'

'No. Not that. Are you sure about trying for a baby?'

She couldn't answer him immediately. Thoughts jostled and tugged in every direction.

'We have to, Karim,' she said eventually. 'Bassy's top priority.'

'Not what I asked. Are you sure for *you*?'

'I'm not sure what you're asking.'

'You always said you wanted two. You wanted to get back to work when the children were old enough. Bassy's changed all that. Another child would change it more.'

'I know. But I'd give up my career altogether if it would save Bassy. You know I would.'

'I know you *would* do it. But how will you feel inside?'

'I've changed,' she said softly. 'Shahira and Bassy have changed me. I'd do anything for them. Gladly. What does a silly career matter?'

Karim's look held a world of sadness.

'I would!' she protested. 'They mean everything to me.'

He nodded. The long pause was unnerving. 'I only hope the price isn't too high.'

'You're scaring me now. I thought we agreed. I thought you wanted this too.'

'I want the best for our family. I thought the best was a baby for Bassy. But sometimes, I don't know, I wonder if it's asking too much of you.'

She moved across to where he was sitting, meeting his gaze directly. 'Just think, how fantastic it will be seeing Bassy strong and well again. Anything's worth that. Anything.'

She dropped down beside him and he slipped an arm around her shoulders. For a long time they were silent, Karim stroking the hair back from her face with gentle fingers. She closed her eyes, savouring the moment.

'You're the light of my life, Meena. I so much want you to be happy.'

'I *am*! In spite of everything, I *am*.'

'Don't let's jeopardise what we have.'

Something cold wrapped tentacles around her heart. 'Are you saying...?' She couldn't utter the words.

'I don't know. But sometimes I wonder what it will mean for us – for the whole family.'

She buried her face in his chest and wrapped her arms around him. 'We'll be all right. We will.'

# 19

FOUR HOURS UNTIL the interview.

The bread-and-butter stuff had always irked Natalie: reporting local functions, dredging up anniversaries, interviewing would-be celebrities – like this afternoon's home-grown poet who somebody upstairs thought might be another Pam Ayres. Had they even *read* her drivel? Bo-ring. *Nothing* like Pam Ayres!

She wanted adrenaline. Risk. She idly trawled down through her files.

*Opakanjo.* It jumped out at her. Unfinished business. A kid still out there, a tawny cuckoo in a black nest. Whose cuckoo? How safe was the nest?

She had nearly four hours.

She wasn't expecting somebody to be ahead of her in the queue. Already on the inside too, hanging out clothes in the back garden. Skinnier than Mrs Opakanjo, paler.

Natalie watched her bending, straightening, shaking, pegging. Like a dancer, lithe and graceful. The woman turned. Natalie did a double take. Wow! What a beauty. Front-page photograph material. *Now* we're talking! What was her connection? What was *her* story?

Did these people know you could see right through their all-in-one rooms? The woman was flitting around picking things up, dusting, vacuuming. Didn't look like your average cleaning lady, though. She answered the door within seconds, pulling it almost shut behind her. Natalie backed away.

'I'm sorry,' the woman said, 'but I don't want my friend woken.' You didn't get those vowels from the back streets of Baghdad!

'Ahh. I do hope I didn't disturb her. She must be exhausted.'

'She is. Can I help at all?'

'My name's Natalie Wyatt. I'm from the *Evening News*.' There, it was all above board.

The woman didn't even flinch, she simply waited.

'I spoke to Mrs Opakanjo a few weeks ago. I was wondering if there'd been any further developments.'

'I'm sorry. I really don't think she'll want to talk to anyone right now.'

'Of course, I understand, Mrs...?'

The eyes were wary. 'What is it exactly you want?'

'Perhaps you could tell me? I was just wondering if the Opakanjos have made any decision yet about the baby. Perhaps you could...'

Yasmeen froze. Natalie knew she'd blown it.

'May I ask you to leave. My friend does *not* want to be disturbed.'

'Oh please, I had no intention of disturbing anyone. It's entirely up to Mrs Opakanjo whether or not she wants to talk to me. Here's my card. I'm willing to come back when she's ready to tell her side of the story.'

The Posybowl had had a facelift. The dark green paintwork framed a magnificent window display of orchids and spider chrysanthemums, dusky-pink merging into burgundy; Natalie's favourite colours. She paused to relish the balance of shape and colour before re-entering that cool interior. Ruth was leaning on the desk, the phone to her ear, but she acknowledged Natalie's presence with a nod.

'Certainly. We'll get that delivered tomorrow morning, Mr Ferdinand. Thank you for calling.'

She scribbled a note in the order book.

'Can I help you?'

'Hello, again. I was wondering if you had such a thing as a single orchid flower in one of those little specimen pots.' Natalie held her fingers two inches apart. 'I know you get them in for Mother's Day.'

'No, sorry. Not single blooms. We do have sprays though. They start at £8.50 a stalk for those green cymbidiums. The bigger ones over there are £12.95.'

'For *one stalk*?'

'They last weeks.' It was more a statement than a defence.

'I was looking for something a little more modest than that.'

'Does it have to be orchids?' Ruth's eyes were already darting round the shop.

'What else d'you suggest?'

'Is it for something special?' Ruth tilted her head on one side and the light from the fluorescent strip above her glinted on her fair curls.

'It's for somebody who's recently become a grandmother. So nothing big and flashy, but I'm looking for mature, unusual.'

'What about an anthurium? They're exotic and they last ages. Maybe with a spray of grass.'

'Could you show me?'

Ruth presented a series of choices, with a loop of greenery turning the elegant into the friendly, a contrasting colour adding warmth to the impersonal. Natalie couldn't help but be impressed, envious even.

'That's *per*fect!' Two stems of stephanotis were tweaked into place as a final touch.

Ruth moved back to her work counter and expertly shredded ribbon to create a cascade of white fronds, complementing the embossed cellophane sleeve.

'Brilliant. And exactly right. Now, I wonder, do you by any chance have a box, or something that I can carry this in? I'd hate it to be spoiled in transit.'

'I might have one out the back. We had a special delivery in yesterday and I haven't got round to flattening the boxes for recycling yet. I'll only be a mo.'

'Take your time,' Natalie called after her.

The delivery book was already open. She flicked back to page 27. Yes. There it was: Customer – Mrs A Opakanjo. Lingate Street. Number 167. She scribbled it on the back of a With Sympathy card and it was in her pocket by the time Ruth returned. The spray looked even better nestled in navy tissue paper.

Natalie pictured her boss's face as she read another invoice for flowers.

Aurora Opakanjo's sheer size and presence were impressive. Her black turban was tasselled with crimson silk, swirls of flame colours flowed over her black dress, the fabric enfolding her like a second skin as she wove her arms into a knot beneath her generous bosom. Brightly painted toenails adorned the feet planted wide apart beneath her. With slow deliberation she sized up her caller.

Natalie, a pygmy at five foot four in her loafers, proffered Ruth's beautiful creation.

'You bring flowers? For me?' The woman looked doubtfully from the floral tribute to Natalie and back again.

'It's only a little token. I've just been to your daughter-in-law's and seeing how the experience is affecting her, I thought I'd pop along with a few flowers for you too. To show, well, you know.'

'Ahhh. You know, you know.' The deep African cadences seemed to spring straight from a powerful opera.

'Yes.' Natalie let out a long sigh. 'It must be *such* a difficult time for you. All of you.'

'It is,' Aurora closed her eyes, 'a nightmare.'

'I can understand.'

'If she does not accept, not'ing can make dese t'ings better.'

'Indeed.'

'You say you come from Candice…?' She was staring straight at Natalie. The façade began to develop hairline cracks.

'She was resting actually, so I didn't get to see her *in person* this time. But her friend told me...'

'Friend? What friend is dis?'

'A lady who's been helping Candice. Washing, cleaning. Things like that.'

'T'ings grandmommas do. If it was only Orlando. Ahhh, how happy I would be to do dese t'ings. How happy. If only she would see.' The ample flesh trembled beneath the weight of her sigh. 'But some oder man's child in her home?' She shuddered. 'No! Now I can not come.'

'Mrs Opakanjo, I don't want to intrude but, perhaps, we might go inside? To speak in private?'

'Yes, yes. It is best.'

'My name is Natalie.' She let it drift by Aurora as she passed her. 'Natalie Wyatt.' Then, very quietly once her back was turned, '*Evening News.*'

The scent of stephanotis reached her as Mrs Opakanjo moved. Mercifully Ruth would never know the rough way her exotic flowers were abandoned on the first available chair.

A seat was not offered; Natalie dared not take one. Poised for flight, she was aware that this big grievance of a woman was between her and the door.

'So. She send you to beg for her. But no! You must see. Dis child, she is not my grandchild. She is not my son's child. All dese years I look forward to de day my son give me his child; *his* child. And now dis! Everyt'ing, it is spoiled.'

Natalie nodded sympathetically.

'You see! *You* know dis. Why does *she* not see it also?' A sudden fit of dry coughing prevented her saying more.

'Can I get you a glass of water?'

Aurora shook her head, clutching a tissue to her mouth. The coughing stopped.

'It is not'ing. It is cosmetic only, my doctor say. All is well when dis trouble is ended.'

Natalie nodded. 'What would *you* like to see happen next?'

'Dis child – it must go to de real parents. My son, he will be a real fader to his own son. I will be grandmomma. *Proper* grandmomma. Like my momma was for my Samuel.'

'And your son? This must be Samuel.' Natalie moved across to the portrait of a young graduate on the mantelpiece. 'What a very handsome young man.'

'Dat is my Samuel. Any momma be proud of my Samuel.'

'Indeed. A happy day.' She let the memory soften the edges of the maternal frustration. 'And what does Samuel do?'

'Engineer. Very good engineer. Wid a fine brain. A fine degree.'

'And what does he think about this whole business?'

'He does not know *what* he wants.' Anger, confusion, sadness, struggled for pre-eminence. 'She make him do t'ings no Opakanjo ever did. Better he stay at sea. One day I hope he find peace. But no, dere is no peace while she make him do such t'ings. One day he will come back to his momma. He will see his momma was right. She know dese t'ings. She know always. She is his momma.'

Natalie dared not ask.

'Mrs Opakanjo, do you know why the baby was born the way she is?'

'Do I know? Do I *know*? Of course I know. Candice, she do t'ings – t'ings nobody ought to do.' The tassels on her turban shivered.

Then her eyes dilated and she seemed somehow to shrink before Natalie's eyes. There was a click and then the sound of a door closing.

A huge black man with a halo of tight grey curls, leaning on a walking stick, nevertheless filled the doorway with his presence. He hesitated.

'Aurora. You no goin introduce your poppa? Where your manners gone, girl?'

'Poppa, you home early. Dis is surprise. Dis is my fader.'

'Pleased to meet you, sir.' No bombshell dropped. 'I'm Natalie Wyatt. I work for the *Evening News*.'

To call the moment electric would be to seriously undervalue the effect of her revelation. The giant turned to his daughter with a ferocity more at home behind a bayonet.

'Aurora! You leave your senses in da field? You talk wid *she*? You? Ma own flesh and blood?'

'Poppa. I didn't know.' This once fearsome mountain of female flesh was actually quivering. 'I...'

'Young lady!' her father roared, turning to Natalie. 'How you get in ma house?'

'Mrs Opakanjo invited me in. She's been very kind.'

'Aurora. Is dis da truth? You invite dis lady in?'

'Yes, Poppa, but I did not know who...' She faded away as lamely as her excuse.

'Young lady! You tell ma girl where you from? Or you not tell?'

'Yes, sir. I did say. But in fairness I'm not sure she heard me.'

'Now! Please! You leave. I not talk wid da press. My daughter, she not talk wid da press. Not in *ma* house. *Nobody* talk wid da press!'

He swept his arm towards the door.

As she shot past him it flashed through Natalie's mind that no one at the paper even knew where she was. The door slammed behind her and she heard the deep bass voice rumbling. She would not be Aurora for a million pounds plus a lifetime's contract with *The Times*.

Maybe safe and boring had something going for it after all.

# 20

HE WAS IN DEEP STOOSH this time; Patsy was emphatically not amused.

'We *agreed*. You promised.'

'In your dreams!'

'You did, Jack. You absolutely did.'

'Well, I know for a fact it's not in my diary.'

'Since when did I need to write our personal arrangements in your diary? You're not a flipping consultant brain surgeon! It's only a trip to a furniture shop. On a Saturday morning. When you're supposed to be at home.'

'It doesn't have to be this minute, *today*, does it?' He tried a more wheedling tone. 'I'll come. I *will* come. Only not this morning. I really do have to go to work.'

'Work! It's all work, work, work these days. Anybody'd think you were indispensable.'

'No illusions in that direction. The cemetery's full of indispensable people. How about we go this afternoon? I should get what I have to do done by say... 2. We could go after that.'

'I know you. Once you get to the lab you'll forget all about the time.'

'Promise. On my honour as a gentleman and a scholar.'

'Well, that lets *you* off the hook, then.'

'On my honour as a scoundrel and a couch potato.'

'Swear?'

'I swear by all you hold sacred.'

'What? What do you swear? I know you, you'll have some way of wriggling out of it.'

'I swear I shall do my utmost to be here to collect you at 2 o'clock, pm, to go to look at leather sofas.'

'2pm *today*!'

'2pm today.' Said with clerical gravity.

'Huhh. No doubt you're this very second adding some little qualifying words inside your head.'

'Oh ye of little faith.'

'I'm warning you, Jack. You don't show up at 2 o'clock and I swear I'll go on me own, and I'll buy whichever one I like, to hang with what it costs.'

'I'd better scoot then. See you by 2.' He blew her a kiss.

It was good, being alone. The reassuring familiarity of the cooling machines, life humming inside, unseen. The peace.

He did a quick recce. Once he got immersed in his work it was always a shock somebody appearing unannounced, somebody else in search of solitude, somebody else wanting to get ahead with the work. No one. A good start. But you could never be sure it would last.

He slid the files and papers out, taking the utmost care. No point in advertising his presence. He carried them carefully to the workbench, buying himself bargaining time, just in case.

The record was methodical, explicit.

*Opakanjo. F: Samuel M: Candice.*

He double-checked his own initials first. Even though he knew what he knew.

*JF. JF.* Yes, there he was. Witnessing Scott doing the fertilisation. Only a witness. It wasn't *his* hand labelling, storing, taking out of refrigeration. Not for the Opakanjos. Of course he *could* have messed with their embryos – deliberately and knowingly; but not recorded it. Except he knew he hadn't.

He tracked back up to another set of initials. *JB-G.* Yes, the boss was the one up to his neck in this bog. Chief action man. Harvest *and* implantation. Only trouble was, Jack would trust Justin Blaydon-Green with his life. *And* the lives of all these would-be babies.

*NMcE*. Nice girl, Nina McEllery. Down to earth, quiet, no airs and graces. And a sport; didn't mind a bit of teasing. OK, hers was the hand that received Candice's eggs, that took those Opakanjo embryos out of incubation. Was it her mistake? Well, she'd have no reason to cock things up on purpose, that was for sure. It'd be a genuine error if it was her. And Scott wouldn't cover for her.

He held the page up to the light. Nothing scratched out, nothing altered that he could see.

Next.

*SM*. Scott Martindale. Great Scott. Thinks he's topcat, but nobody else shares his opinion. Going places, never mind who he tramples on. So what was his role in this little debacle? Present on each occasion. Fair enough. Admitting to actually doing the fertilisation. OK. So, could he have guffed up? Yes. Oh yes! Would he have *deliberately* messed with these embryos? Shouldn't think so. The guy might be a smug git but Jack couldn't see him as a total scumbag. Ambitious, maybe; unethical, no.

He checked the patient record against the master file. Hold on a minute... He skimmed down the column front to back. Back to front. Same column. Same initials. *SM. SM. SM. SM.* This guy signed off pretty much all the fertilisations.

So? He was the senior embryologist. It was what he did. Creepy crawlies squiggled along Jack's spine. He lost track of time staring at that column. He shook himself. Been watching too many sci-fi films. And there was he telling Patsy *she* was into fantasy-land!

Next.

*EG*. Emma. The day she came he'd told her, with initials like that she absolutely had to set an example. Nice kid, people person, easy on the eye. Bit of a ditherer, but heart in the right place. Got her troubles back at home but didn't wear them like a trophy.

Nobody else in those particular columns. But he knew, and they knew, all the lab staff hung around the place. It always came back to that. *Anybody* could have mucked things up. You don't have to sign for that.

He restored the documents to the drawer. It was only then he thought of rubber gloves. Damn it! He wasn't aware he was sizzing.

He was back in the house by 1.45.

Patsy was wearing a fuchsia-pink outfit, skirt barely skimming her knickers – *before* she tried out sofas. Oscar Wilde came into his head: *She wore far too much rouge last night, and not quite enough clothes. That is always a sign of despair in a woman.* Only there was nothing despairing about Patsy. He was the one fearing she'd leave him behind.

'New clothes?' he hazarded.

'Ish.'

'They'll be whistling all down the High Street.'

'Not with you there they won't.' But he could see she liked the comment.

Something was still niggling. Probably why they ended up with a square-cushioned sofa, too deep for her, too shallow for him, stupid colour that didn't go with anything they owned. So slippery he slid off it as soon as he leaned back. Not the kind of thing you could snooze on.

But Patsy was twinkling. Pretty as a picture in her pink.

And he lived to fight another day.

Monday morning. It felt like somebody had died.

Emma Gordon had vanished. No explanation, no goodbye. Just not there. All her things gone. A junior lab technician wiped off the board.

Justin's door was shut. What had happened to his open-door policy? Another cornerstone dislodged in this earthquake. Jack knocked anyway.

'Come in.'

He poked his head half round the door, poised for a rapid retreat. 'Any chance of a word, Boss?'

'By all means, Jack. Come in. Take a seat.'

Justin swivelled his chair so he was facing his visitor.

'And what can I do for you?'

'It's Emma. None of my business, I know, but any chance you know why she's gone?' There was a sudden change in Justin – the human equivalent of ears pricked. 'I'm not fishing, Doc. Only I wouldn't want her losing out on a reference.'

'D'you know something I should know, Jack?'

'Not sure what you know already.'

'Did I know she was unhappy here, for example?'

'Something like that.'

'I do, since I spoke to her this morning. I didn't last week, I'm sorry to say. I take it you did?'

Jack pursed his lips, nodded a few times, watching him.

'Easy for them to talk to me. I'm just there, working alongside.' He dismissed his advantage with a shrug. 'They don't need me for references.'

'Do I know why she was unhappy?' Justin asked, holding his gaze. 'No, I confess I don't. Care to enlighten me?'

'I can't say why she upped and left, but I do know one thing. She didn't hit it off with... everybody, Emma. Sweet kid, mind, but sensitive. Took things to heart. Not the best at standing up for herself.'

'You think maybe she was being bullied?' Said all soft and tranquil like that it didn't fit Jack's idea of bullying.

'Maybe. Sort of.'

Jack had a nasty feeling he'd pushed it too far this time. A sick feeling started somewhere around his waistband. Even when he wriggled up straighter it was still there, like indigestion, the kind that made him think of his dad's heart attack.

When Justin eventually spoke it came out so middle-of-the-road Jack figured he'd put an awful lot of energy into pitching it right. Which meant he was probably mad inside.

'We have some very clever people working here, Jack. Top notch. They're working under extreme pressure. Doing a very responsible job, and doing it well. Sometimes maybe they forget what it's like for everybody else in this kind of environment;

having to work to high expectations. They aren't always the best team players.'

'Maybe.'

'We all handle stress differently. Some of us have thicker skins than others.'

'Right.'

'And there's a *lot* of pressure on the scientists. Sometimes maybe they take their frustration out on junior staff. It's not only what you see in the lab. These guys are responsible for keeping the money coming in, getting the grant applications out on time, reports finished to deadlines. Monitoring the success rates, worrying about the patients. It's tough.'

'Sure.'

'But you still think Emma had a raw deal, right?'

'The poor kid worried herself sick that she might have been the one who guffed up. But I don't think she was. Dead conscientious, Emma.'

'Guffed what up?'

'The mix-up. You know. The Opakanjo babies.'

There it was again – ears pricked, very still.

'Somebody suggested she did?'

'It really upset her, that – anybody implying it was her fault. She says she did check. But now she thinks people don't believe her. She's young, doesn't need to have her confidence knocked by a comment like that. Specially when there's no proof.'

'I agree. Nobody needs that little lot laid at their door. I'm sorry. I didn't know that had been suggested.' Justin turned his wedding ring round and round, then dragged his eyes back to Jack. 'You think that's why she went?'

'Wouldn't surprise me. Partly that anyway.'

'Only partly?'

'Well, the new software was a headache too.'

'Oh?'

'She needed a wee hand now and then.'

'I know they rely on you. And I'm grateful.'

'Anybody'd do the same. I've been around the block a few

more times, that's all. And I didn't want to see the kid losing out. She's a good little worker, she'd have got there. If she'd had the peace to get on in her own way.'

'I'll bear that in mind if she asks for a reference. But for the record, nobody's ever complained about her to me.'

'Sorry if I overstepped the mark, then. But seeing somebody blamed unfairly, sticks in my throat.'

'Fair enough. I appreciate your coming to see me, Jack.'

Jack opened his mouth to tell him… and shut it again.

Not yet.

# 21

YASMEEN SLICED THE ONIONS with ferocity. Why did things have to be so complicated? Karim's words had found a mark. But she *had* cut back on what she was doing for Candice. And she *was* working on her own health. She dropped the onions into the hot oil and began chopping the peppers and mushrooms.

5.45. Karim was due home from school any minute. But he had to be back by 7 to stage-manage a production of *The Pirates of Penzance* – although by his account of the histrionics to date, it was more likely to resemble a pantomime.

It was one of those days. Three phonecalls. The meal only half ready. Shahira in her room sulking because she couldn't go to her friend, Alice's. But Sebastian *had* to take precedence. His paleness and lethargy were the reason Yasmeen had cancelled a visit to Candice – and was now hovering somewhere between taking up nail-biting and dialling 999.

On top of that, there'd been no word of how her father had fared at the hospital. He was very old school, reluctant to mention anything remotely intimate, so all she knew was it had to do with the 'waterworks department'.

She gave herself a mental shake. Karim was right – she had to back away from other people's problems. The Opakanjos would survive.

Karim's first question was, 'How's our little soldier?'

'Listless. Quiet. Nothing definite. No fever. No pains.'

He popped his head round the sitting room door and she watched him observing his son engrossed in a DVD. She turned back to the stir-fry and tossed the vegetables this way and that, the pungent aroma prickling her eyes.

'Where's Shahira?'

'Upstairs in her room, probably phoning Childline.'

His feet thudded on the stairs and resentment settled like a weight in her stomach.

'Please let me come back as a man,' she muttered.

The mushrooms turned from raw white to honey gold.

'Meal's ready!'

Sebastian was seated at the table, forlorn in his apathy, before Karim entered the dining room with Shahira in tow.

'Mummy, Shahira has something to say to you.' Karim's tone reminded her that he could control a classroom of hormonal adolescents.

Shahira squirmed, half hidden behind his legs. 'Sorry, Mummy.'

'Thank you. Now, let's eat,' Yasmeen said, serving the rice.

'Well done, Shahira.' Karim's voice was low and warm, and Yasmeen saw the child sidle closer to her father, eyes down.

She rummaged in the stir-fry for the things Sebastian liked, knowing her efforts were wasted. It was a strained and protracted meal and Karim had long gone by the time the children had picked their way to compromise. No time to express her appreciation of his support. Visions of fatal crashes, impending widowhood, an eternity of regret, overlaid her earlier forebodings.

Shahira had forgiven her by the time she'd read the bedtime story and kissed her goodnight, but anxiety surged back with a vengeance as she stood staring down at her son, hollow-eyed against the pillow. What if?

She could not endure this pain for a second time. She absolutely could *not*.

Karim flopped down on the sofa, hours later, with a huge sigh.

'Praise be, that's over!'

'And how did it go?' she asked, smiling at his expression.

'A nightmare behind the scenes, well enough to please doting parents on the other side of the curtain. Remind me not to come within fifty miles of the drama group next year.'

'You'd miss your annual dose of manic depression.'

'Like banging my head against a wall, you mean?' He grinned and leaned back wearily. She noted new tension lines around his mouth.

'And what about you? Bassy OK?' he asked, his look suddenly intense.

'Asleep before I'd finished the story.'

'But you're still worried?'

'I'm always worried about him,' she said too sharply.

'I mean *especially*, today.'

'I don't know. If he's no better in the morning, I think I'll call Dr Douglas.'

He nodded. 'Good idea. I'll pop up and check on him.'

His report seemed to deny her reality. 'Sleeping like a baby.'

He dropped back onto the sofa, pulling a cushion behind his head, and closed his eyes.

She felt the first tear slide down her cheek. Then another. That was the thing with tears. You could bottle them up successfully most of the time. But give them the tiniest opening and next thing you'd got an unstoppable flood on your hands.

It was such a rare occurrence Karim was nonplussed. 'Hey, what's up?'

Struggling back to some semblance of control took time. It was much later that the conversation came round to Candice.

'She's so depressed, Karim. She rang today and she thinks she's worthless, letting everyone down. She even said maybe Destiny *should* go to her real parents. Maybe *both* the twins would be better off without her.'

'Sounds like she needs professional help.'

'I think so too. I've tried to encourage her to talk to her health visitor. Her GP maybe. *Some*body. She definitely needs help. I'm so worried about her, in that state, alone in the house with two babies.'

'I can understand, but, Meena, I've never seen you in such a state before.'

'I feel so bad about letting her down today.'

'You *had* to be here. Bassy comes first. You have to hand this over to somebody else, sweetheart.'

'I'll have to, if Bassy needs me.'

He turned to look straight into her eyes. '*If* Bassy needs you? *If?*'

'It's so easy to say "don't" to somebody else.'

'Sometimes you need saving from yourself,' Karim said quietly. 'And I wouldn't be much of a husband if I didn't say something, now, would I?'

This time she simply dissolved.

Karim cradled her in his arms. 'You, young lady, are completely overwrought.'

'I'm so afraid for Bassy, Karim.'

'Mm?'

'Seeing him like this, can he wait that long? I'm not getting any younger. And what if...?' She couldn't say it.

'They always said there were no guarantees. We can only do what's in our power.'

'I can't do it again. I simply can't face going through all this again.'

'All what exactly?' She felt his sudden tension.

'Having another child – like Bassy.'

'So are you saying...?'

'I don't know. I don't know any more.'

He waited in silence, stroking her hair softly.

'If Bassy... we wouldn't need to.' It was too dreadful a prospect to consolidate out loud.

'Is he more ill than you're telling me?' Karim's fingers were still now.

'No. But every time I can't help thinking, what if, this time?'

'I know. Me too. It's only natural.'

'Only now, it's not only that. It's: what if we've already started on the road to creating a donor baby and *then*...?'

'We can only do what feels right now. Nobody knows what lies ahead.'

'But imagine!'

'Don't, Meena!' Karim sounded sharper than he intended and he gave her a swift hug to compensate. 'Don't torture yourself. Imagining the worst isn't helping anyone. Least of all Bassy.'

She seemed to shrink in his arms.

'You're exhausted,' he said. 'Let's leave it for now. This is no time to be making major decisions.'

'It's not just today.' The words came out devoid of emotion. 'And it's not going to be better tomorrow. Or the next day. Or the day after that.'

'But you might be in a better frame of mind to think it through sensibly, tomorrow, or the next day, or the day after that.'

'How come the first time I get upset about it my frame of mind is called into question? From where I stand, I think I've got every reason to be upset. And despairing. And seriously doubtful.'

'Of course. I'm not meaning to belittle your anxieties. But what with your father, and Bassy, and Candice, today's not a good day. You're too upset to think straight.'

'I'm not on top of anything these days.'

'Listen to Mrs Superwoman! Give yourself a break.'

'I'm just so scared, Karim,' she whispered.

'I know, sweetheart. I know. It *is* scary.'

'What if we go ahead and the next one has it too? We'd have brought more suffering into the world – for nothing. And even if he or she doesn't have Diamond Blackfan's... What if they have something else wrong?'

'Now, hold *on*! You could say that about every child.'

'But we've already brought Bassy's suffering into the world. That's more than enough.'

'That's today talking. We brought Shahira into the world too and she's fine – apart from the odd temper tantrum! We all want the best life possible for our children. But who's to say what that is? There's no guarantee that because a child is free from a particular disease he'll have a better life.'

'But it's not like we're taking what comes naturally. We're choosing. *And* choosing for the sake of somebody else.'

'Someone who might die. I know.'

'Who are we to make such a colossal decision? What do *we* know?'

'We know that Bassy needs our help. And that we're the ones to decide how to help him. Nobody else can make the decision for us.'

'No, that's not what I'm talking about. Let's say we have three embryos to select from. All matches for Bassy. A, B and C.'

'Lucky us!'

'OK. Say we choose A. He might have Diamond Blackfan's. Or he might go on to develop some other terrible disease. If we choose B he might not have any of those problems but he might be seriously depressed, or be a wayward kid who puts terrible stress on all the family. And if we choose C – well, you see what I mean? We are *choosing* and it'll be our fault if we get it wrong. We'll have given our baby a hard life.'

'I see where you're coming from. But surely, that's not the way it works, is it? I mean, *we* wouldn't choose which one, if there was more than one suitable match, would we? *They* would select it, not us, and they'd select the best one in terms of what it looks like at that stage of development. The healthiest. I think, anyway.'

'Maybe. Yes, you're probably right.'

'And anyway, even if we *had* to choose, well, let's say we chose A, he'll become A – no, let's give him a name. Let's say Imran. If we choose Imran he'll be Imran. He won't be B or C – Aakash having a worse life, or Gurpreet having a worse life. He'll be Imran having the only life available to him. Aakash might well have other problems in life, like you say. Gurpreet might be a model normal child. But they'd only be *themselves*, not Imran having a better life.'

'I see what you're saying, but say there were four other embryos that didn't match Bassy. And they were all perfect, no problems of any kind. You'd want to have the child that had the best life for *himself* not the one that gave Bassy a chance but made his own life a nightmare, wouldn't you?'

'If you could predict such a thing, yes, I'm sure we all would.'

'So?'

'Well, it seems to me, if you spend all your time thinking what a future life might be like for these imagined offspring, you're in danger of worrying yourself silly for nothing. And missing out on what life is like here and now for our *actual* children.'

'You are such a rock, Karim. I'm sorry I've been so cross tonight. It's only that...'

'You're in the thick of it all the time, but it's not that I don't care, Meena. I just don't let my anxiety show.'

'I'm so glad *you* don't go away to the rigs. I need you here to keep me sane.'

Not until they were in bed did she return to the subject that still plagued her.

'Karim?'

'Uhmm?'

'You asleep?'

'Not while you have any say in it!'

'These embryos – the ones we don't use – is it wrong not bringing them into existence, d'you think?'

'Heavens, Meena, you sure do know how to put a chap off his sleep! I do *not* want a dozen extra kids, thank you very much! And I didn't think you were keen to live in a shoe either.'

'But are we denying them marvellous fulfilling lives if we don't nurture them all?'

He flopped over to face her. 'Who's to say they'd have wonderful fulfilling lives? They might all have gross personality disorders brought about by having a neurotic mother!'

'And a heartless brute of a father!'

He pulled her close and in the shared smothered laughter the doubts receded.

# 22

SCOTT WORKED METHODICALLY. He'd carried out this task countless times, but for every case he felt a certain sense of ownership. He held in his hands one of the essential component parts of a human being: the XY part. Exactly what he did, cleaning and preparing these sperm, was partly instrumental in deciding who that future person would become. Where else could you find that kind of power, that degree of control?

At this precise moment he was alone in the lab, just for what? – half an hour, three-quarters tops. It was the way he liked it. His colleagues weren't so sure.

His predecessor, Dr Angus McCormack, had led with the rulebook in his right hand and a monitor in his left, but the team had loved him for all that. Every last one of them dropped his name into conversation with reverence and respect. The fact that he was only thirty-five when he went to meet his Maker helped; early death gives special poignancy. They still talked of the day he told them the diagnosis, how the bone cancer stole his film-star looks, then his energy, then his life. It was hard work for Scott dragging through his footprints.

Gradually, though, he'd begun to loosen McCormack's boundaries. And the statistics gave him leverage. The centre had become much more successful in recent years, and success bred success. Increasing the workload meant streamlining the procedures.

Of course, there was no latitude when it came to the key stages of the process. The protocol was unequivocal: two witnesses, two signatures, everything recorded, subject to scrutiny.

Full stop. The HFEA demanded it. The centre's very licence depended on conforming.

But outside of those rigid requirements Scott decreed commonsense and efficiency should prevail. And solitude suited him. 'I like to give the job my undivided attention. Some people are looking for tomfool chatter. Not me. Too distracting. I like silence when I'm working. Concentrate on the job.'

The sooner he completed his clinical commitments, the sooner he could get back to his research, and get the results he needed. And what better way to achieve his ambition: his own lab, a professorial chair – freedom to lead a team of scientists down his chosen route.

He frowned. It had been a shock last night, finding two mice dead; two out of sixteen. They weren't supposed to die. The girls looking after the animals were good, no question about that, no blame attached to them, but they weren't trained to see what he saw. None of them knew exactly what he was injecting into his mice. They only knew he was the most assiduous researcher they'd ever worked with, popping in at all hours.

So why two deaths, as soon as his attention was sidetracked? Maybe if he hadn't been fencing with Justin's paranoia he'd have seen warning symptoms and circumvented disaster.

He made a note: *Track down early papers.* There weren't many scientists in the world creating chimeras; he knew them all by name. Maybe one of them had published something. If not, a quick call to Seamus Rush might not come amiss. Soul of discretion, Seamus, and he owed Scott a favour too.

The old thrill of being out there with the pioneers surged through him. Who needed sex, who needed recognition, who needed holidays, when you could know the ecstasy of scientific breakthrough? The frisson of danger only added to the heights. A very real danger it had been too, when he'd started down this route, back when the creation of animal-human embryos was strictly forbidden. Now the governing bodies permitted it – for research purposes only. Even so it was still wrapped up in layers of restrictions but, fair enough, when it came to creating life, the concerns of the public had to be heard.

Reporting his latest interim discovery would be some small compensation for the delays of the last couple of weeks. Getting this stuff out into the scientific world represented a major step forward. Other researchers who spoke his language would dissect it, analyse the challenges and difficulties, and advance their own solutions. Worry about the general populace came later, once you tried to move the results into a therapeutic context.

The only snag was this damned clinical inquiry; it only needed a hint of suspicion anywhere for the HFEA spies to start teeming all over his activities like termites with magnifying glasses.

As if drawn by Pavlov's bell, Jack wandered in at the exact moment Scott needed a witness. His hackles rose. What kind of antennae did this technician have? OK, he'd been best buddies with Angus bloody McCormack, but it wasn't Scott's fault the guy died young. There was no call to mind-read in that annoying way Jack had.

He said nothing. They both signed. Jack wandered down to the end of the lab bench and Scott heard the unmistakable sound of suppressed sizzing. He gritted his teeth. It was down to the sperm now. Nothing more he could do. He was free.

The afternoon multi-disciplinary meeting presented Scott with an unexpected window of hope. It was usual practice for a registrar to present the cases for everyone to comment on, but today Justin himself took the helm for the last one. Tricky situation with a family wanting a saviour sibling for a kid with Diamond Blackfan's. Too controversial to delegate, Justin reckoned.

Scott recognised the signs. This guy cared; he personally wanted to help Sebastian Zair. He'd even brought along a photograph of the kid, a little stunner, guaranteed to tug at everyone's heartstrings. But the team hadn't looked into the eyes of Sebastian's mother, and they were still smarting over the

Opakanjo business, surely *somebody* would have qualms. A little opposition, just the thing to divert Justin's attention away from the twin mix-up. There was nothing they could do to change the reality of Destiny's birth; but there was all to play for with Sebastian. Yes, this decoy might yet work to Scott's advantage.

The questions came thick and fast. Justin fielded them with the energy of a man on a mission. He had a case to win.

Excellent.

## 23

THERE WERE EIGHT people in the room, and it was no surprise to see the CEO wasn't one of them. Some licence holder he was!

Justin knew all except one of the people around the table, but, aside from his own departmental colleagues, Scott, Josephine and specialist nurse Elka Erickson, he had no way of predicting their reactions to the case he was presenting.

Rob Tyson was a clinical scientist trained in genetics, sane and likeable. And one of Rob's own kiddies had cystic fibrosis. He'd once told Justin in confidence that if she hadn't been their third child, he and Margot would have gone for pre-implantation genetic haplotyping to eliminate the possibility of another one with the same disease – if such a thing had been available.

Gwilym Haig, their head geneticist, could be a bit of a performer at times, but in the depths of his Welsh verbosity there was considerable wisdom. And he'd be toned down by the no-nonsense approach of Blythe Cunningham. In the face of her experience as a practising clinical geneticist there would be less scope for his posturing. And Blythe was so accustomed to handling distraught patients that Justin knew he could depend on her for a word fitly spoken if the emotions threatened to get out of hand.

The real unknown was Ajit Madhar, a cyto-geneticist – a chromosome man. Justin had an innate respect for these chaps who knew so much about exactly where faults were to be found in the complex structure of everyone's DNA. He could only hope this specific expert had enough compassionate genes on his own helix to want to help right nature's mishaps. They definitely needed him on side. Ajit was a slight man with a flare of a birthmark on his forehead. Justin wondered if he ever told kids he was Harry Potter's uncle.

The meeting called to order, Justin launched straight into the facts. It took a mere ninety minutes to reach unanimity. The team had the science, they had the expertise, they had the skills and the facilities, they believed in the cause.

Everyone agreed to scrutinise the treatment licence forms as a matter of priority so that they could be submitted to the HFEA without delay. The clock was against Yasmeen Zair. Meticulous attention to detail was called for. But within those four walls they told each other, they were quietly confident. The Pemberton's track record with the HFEA would surely stand them in good stead.

The local ethics committee was another prospect altogether. Ironic really. Justin was under no obligation to consult them; the HFEA licence was sufficient. But trust and transparency were part of good practice.

Although the science was way outside this committee's sphere of expertise, they had already sent back Justin's first proposal with questions about the targeting of chromosomes and the probability of success, and whether the team's combined skills were adequate for such a task. Seek expert advice, they 'advised strongly'. What were these weasels on about? Did they imagine these ideas had simply been plucked out of thin air? The Pemberton team *were* the experts! Communication lines with other such teams were red-hot.

Justin was requested to appear before them in person.

The chairman, Randolph Gutterman, a benevolent paediatrician retired now some four years, invited Justin to outline his case in 'everyday language'. Justin couldn't resist a quirked eyebrow. Everyday? Dr Gutterman smiled ruefully. 'Well, as close as you can get to something we'll all understand.'

'I ask myself three questions,' Justin said in his best expert-witness voice. 'What *can* we do? What *will* we be able to do in the foreseeable future – let's say, five to ten years? And what *should* we do?'

It was hard to know how to pitch remarks to cater for everything between a reader in medical ethics and the wife of a banker, a geriatrician and a man of the cloth. Was he hitting anyone's target?

'The fundamental principle I work to with all new therapeutic procedures is to determine in advance whether or not the probable benefits outweigh the risks. So let's start with the facts.'

He built up a case, block by block, knowing that this committee had no viable scientific ammunition capable of undermining his careful edifice, but knowing too that they had other weapons which could wreck his hopes. Emotion and moral scruple had an uncomfortable habit of creeping through the cracks between the facts.

The banker's wife brought up the old chestnut of designer babies. It was easily dealt with. The ethicist talked learnedly of the competing interests and duties, but gave nothing away as to his position.

Having established that his team had the resources to carry out this procedure, Justin was free to move into territory more familiar to them: the impact on the family. But before he could flesh out his own points the clergyman, Vince Garfield, launched into an impassioned speech about a family in his congregation who had lost a child to leukaemia, and the devastating effect on the siblings as well as the parents. Everyone wore that 'poor-family' look they reserved for moving tales. No one wanted to be seen to be lacking in compassion.

Justin capitalised with a graphic picture of Yasmeen Zair, the devoted mother touched by tragedy. Of Karim. Of Shahira. And of Sebastian himself, his life of pain and uncertainty. The committee's fear of adverse publicity slid off the scale of importance, mere froth and semantics.

The banker's wife spoiled the moment with a question about the costs to the Trust.

Justin kept his voice even. 'Against the costs of IVF plus pre-implantation genetic diagnosis, we have to set the cost of caring for a child with a life-threatening illness for however long this little boy may have. Pray God, many years.'

The chairman didn't give anyone an opportunity to mention that IVF might be needed several times. 'And from what you say, the sooner this mother goes through this procedure the better the chances of it succeeding. Thank you again, Dr Blaydon-Green. We'll be in touch.'

The house was silent by the time Justin arrived home. Helen had left him a brief note.

> *Taken B to station. L and K at music lessons. Please ring*
> *Faith. Dinner in oven. Should be back to eat with you.*
> *Love, H xx*

The kitchen exuded the fragrance of baking cheese and roasting potatoes. He couldn't resist a peep. Whatever it was was oozing cholesterol onto the racks below. He slid a baking tray under it to catch the drips.

His sister, Faith, had big news. Her son had become the father of twins, making her a grandmother and Justin a great uncle, a month ahead of schedule. She was so excited. Normal natural happiness, normal natural reproduction. Continuation of the family line. It was all so reassuring.

But Sebastian's plight dominated his thoughts that night, and his sleep was threadbare.

# 24

NATALIE GROPED FOR the alarm clock, knocking it half under the bed. She groaned as she left the warmth of the quilt to stun the offending sound.

Yesterday flooded back.

'Cut the waffle, woman – maybe this, maybe that,' Adam Leishman had roared. 'I don't pay you to sit around waiting for something to hit you between the eyes. Get off your backside and *find* the bloody story. Get out there. Get people talking. Get the dirt before the signature's dry on the IVF form. *If* there's a story *tell it* before every other newspaper's run with it. And just you make damn sure you don't bugger it up!'

She lingered in the shower, searching for inspiration.

An hour later she rejected the tailored trousers she'd laid out the night before, and pulled on casual khaki, vivid pink lipstick and fake eyelashes. Added a bandana and sunglasses.

She locked her front door, drove for half an hour and then became a runner minding her own business on the anonymous streets of a perfectly ordinary Scottish town.

The Opakanjo house was silent, bedroom blinds on both sides still closed.

As Natalie jogged slowly past, she almost collided with a laundry basket.

'I'm so sorry,' she panted. 'Oh dear, I hope I haven't done any damage to all your careful work.'

The other woman – *that* other woman – patted the pile of clothes and smiled. 'No harm done.'

'Are you going far? Can I help you carry some of this stuff?

You look laden.'

'No, I'm fine, thanks. I'm only going to this house.'

'Well, apologies again.'

Natalie jogged away.

After a short tussle with her conscience she doubled back and leaned against a lamppost as if recovering from runner's cramp, just in time to see the woman being admitted to the house by an unseen presence.

Now what?

Silence. No movement anywhere.

She stayed put.

A door clicked. A sheet was thrown over the washing line. It billowed in the breeze. A pair of brown hands pegged it securely. Another sheet followed.

Natalie shot around to the back. It was impossible to see anything without peering through the slats, so she leaned her two hands against the fence and bent as if regaining her breath.

'...that's why I had to come early.' No mistaking that polished accent.

'Poor little mite. But you shouldn't have come here. We can manage.'

'I thought if I could just collect the next load, I could be getting on with the ironing at the same time as looking after Bassy. But I can't stay long. Karim has to be at school for first break.'

'You are so kind. I don't know what I'd have done without you these past few weeks.'

'Oh, it's nothing. I'm just glad you're getting back on your feet. They say the first year's the worst with twins, so here's hoping, eh?'

'Just as long as we've still *got* twins in a year's time.'

'You will, I'm sure you will.'

'They slept...'

The voices were lost as the door shut behind them.

Should she wait until the Asian woman left? It would be before first break at school.

'I'll see you at 4.30ish then.' The voice carried clearly. 'By the swings.'

Natalie raced round to the side of the house until she could see the front door through the fencing. What luck it was on a corner; she could cover all bases herself.

'Great. And it'll do the twins good to be in the fresh air.'

'If Bassy isn't up to it, I'll give you a ring.'

'OK. See you later.'

Natalie watched the black Audi glide away from the curb. A plot was hatching in her mind. Two birds, one stone. That'll show you, Leishman!

But which park? It had to be within walking distance for a woman pushing twins.

Time for a reconnoitre.

At 4.30 that afternoon a very pregnant young woman waddled through the memorial park, the shriek of small children echoing round her. She kept the visor of her cap pulled low and her gait shouted discomfort. Occasionally she paused, arching her back or holding her side.

A few feet from a parkbench, she sank to her knees on the grass, wriggled into a semi-recumbent position, and took out a magazine to read.

'When does Samuel get back this time?' The voice was unmistakable.

'Next Friday.'

Candice's deeper tones carried well. Good position.

Natalie fidgeted until her newly-acquired bump was more evenly balanced, took out her notepad and pencil, slipped them inside her magazine, and scribbled a few words.

'And how long will he be home for?'

'Three weeks.'

'So you'll be all right if I don't…'

'Oh, absolutely. We'll be fine. You concentrate on Sebastian. Bless him.'

Natalie glanced up in time to see both women looking at the

boy asleep in the pushchair.

'He should be chasing around screaming with these other children. Begging to be pushed higher and higher until he can see into heaven – like Shahira at this age.'

'Are you any further on with... you know?'

'Apparently, we should know next week.'

'And d'you think?'

'I daren't let myself think one way or the other. Dr Blaydon-Green was cautious, but if anyone can persuade the authorities, he will.'

'He's so nice, isn't he?'

'Yes. And he puts so much time and effort into these applications. Apparently there's loads of paperwork.'

Candice let out a sigh. 'It's a crazy world. Anyone can see this is an extreme situation. It's obvious you only want what's best for your kids. I mean, what's to question?'

'Well, you know us – me. But society in general doesn't. I might be wanting a particular kind of baby for some quite frivolous reason. They have to be careful, and go through procedures, and make sure nobody's going too far and risking too much.'

'I suppose.' Another long sigh. 'You're a lot more understanding than I would be. I'd be leaping up and down, protesting about the injustice.'

'I don't think so. Look how patient you've been over all this business with Destiny.'

'Not inside, I haven't! But in any case, it's different. The quieter *we* can be, the more likely it'll die down, and we can start being a normal family.'

'Does it still feel that tentative?'

'Sometimes. When I think about what might happen if it all got out.'

'Poor you. You've got enough on your plate looking after the babies without all that.'

'And the longer it goes on the worse it would be if somebody else got to take Destiny away. I couldn't *bear* it.'

'I'm sure that won't happen.'

'That's what Samuel says. But what if *we*'d been trying for years to have a baby, and found out that somebody else had a child that was half ours?'

'I see what you mean.'

'They really want us to do the DNA thing. So *they* know. But if we do, how can we *then* not say anything to the real parents? If we don't do the test she's ours. Nobody can prove any different.'

'It's a tough one.'

'So's yours.'

'Yes. But in a different kind of way.'

'I still think there shouldn't be any doubt in your case. You're trying to save Sebastian's life. You can't get a purer motive than that, surely.'

'Maybe you should go and plead my cause, Candice.'

The two women laughed together.

'Besides,' Candice said, 'anybody who's had IVF knows you don't go down that path for kicks.'

'Says she in a heartfelt kind of way!'

'Well, you know.'

'You're meant to be encouraging me, not scaring me.'

'Oh, it's worth every minute. I'd do the same all over again, even knowing what I know about what the treatment does to you.'

'Would you, Candice? Even given what happened?'

There was a long pause. Natalie sneaked a look from under her visor. Candice was staring at the sleeping twins.

'Even given what happened,' she said so softly Natalie couldn't be sure she'd heard correctly.

Though she waited until they left, Natalie heard no more of interest to her story. After an hour of reclining with a pillow stuffed inside her trousers, she was glad to stand up again. In the nick of time she remembered to waddle to the gate.

Back in her office next morning, once more the smartly dressed reporter, she skimmed through her notes before lifting the phone.

'Dr Blaydon-Green, please.'

'Who shall I say is calling?'

'Natalie Wyatt.'

She drummed her fingers on the writing block as she waited.

'Dr Blaydon-Green speaking.'

Phew. Surprise number one.

'Dr Blaydon-Green. How are you?'

'I'm fine, thank you, Ms Wyatt. How may I help you?'

'I've received some information that seems to be in the public interest, but I wanted to give you the chance to put your side before we publish anything.'

'What sort of information would that be?'

'It's about two controversial cases – ongoing cases – that involve your centre.'

'Ahh. You know I don't discuss specific cases.'

'I know. But in this case the family side of things is such that it would look bad if I can only say The Pemberton declined to comment.'

'Can you elaborate?'

'Well, one is about the twins – one black, one coffee-coloured. And the other's the parents who want a baby to save the life of their little boy.'

'And how did you come by this "information", may I ask?'

'Oh now, *please*, Dr Blaydon-Green. You know we always protect our informants.'

'Indeed I do! And you know that I protect my patients.'

'But surely it would be better for you to say *something* – whatever seems right without compromising your professional integrity.'

Silence.

'Is there somebody else I could talk to, maybe?' she persisted.

'No, I'll see you myself. But only because I don't want you

publishing a story that will be harmful to vulnerable families.'

'Thank you.'

'How are you fixed later today?'

'What time would suit you?'

'6.30? Can you manage that?'

Natalie could hardly believe what she was hearing. Her hand was actually shaking as she jotted down time and place.

She amused herself watching the many comings and goings outside the Sheraton Hotel while she waited, imagining the lives and loves of all these unknowns. The angular young man humping an ancient bicycle up the steps at 6.35 looked so totally out of place Natalie couldn't resist a second look. The man gave a half smile in response. But this clearly wasn't Dr Blaydon-Green so her interest was peripheral.

The cyclist hesitated. 'Hi. Would you be Natalie Wyatt?'

She sighed inwardly. That was the price you paid for being in the media world. If someone recognised you, you had no idea whether their recollections were good, bad or ugly.

'I'm afraid I would be, but please don't believe all you've heard. I'm harmless and I didn't do it.'

He grinned.

She glanced around. Still no sign of Blaydon-Green. That would be a medical 6.30 then.

'Well, hi again. I'm Scott Martindale. Dr Blaydon-Green sends his apologies. One of his daughters had an accident at school today, broke something or other, so he's at the hospital and couldn't get away. Sent me instead.'

'A sacrificial lamb to the slaughter, huh?'

'Something like that.'

They stood awkwardly.

'Why don't we pop in here, and I'll shout you an orange juice or a coffee or whatever you drink when you're driving a bike through the traffic,' she said lightly.

'Sounds good to me. But first let me chain this thing up somewhere. It may look like a rust bucket to the average onlooker, but it gets me from A to B faster than the sleekest car, and it's far kinder to this old world we ought to be hanging on to. So I'd like it still to be there in ten minutes' time.'

Ten minutes. Hmm. Now there was a challenge.

It was dim inside the foyer of the Sheraton but Natalie led the way to a corner table with a confidence that came from familiarity.

'What can I get you?'

'Coffee sounds perfect.'

She summonsed a waiter with an imperious gesture which made Scott's eyes narrow, but he said nothing until she'd placed their order and wriggled back in her armchair with a smile.

'So, Scott Martindale, tell me about you. What's a guy with a rusty bicycle and a fabulous Highland – or is it island? – accent doing in a fertility centre in the great metropolis?'

'I'm an embryologist. And there isn't much call for my particular esoteric skills in the wild wastes of the north.'

'Heart still back up there, huh? I'm not surprised. I'd say the Highlands – the real Highlands, I mean – are one of the most beautiful places on earth – bar the midges and the rain and the wind and the cold and the long dark nights.'

He laughed with her.

'So, what does an embryologist do when he's at home?'

'Since you're in work mode, I take it you mean home as in the hospital, not home as in where I keep my slippers.'

'Sorry. Poor choice of words.'

Aaron Leishman's voice reverberated: *And just you make damn sure you don't bugger it up!*

The arrival of coffee gave her space to think through her list. Black, two sugars. She made a mental note.

'So tell me, what exactly would an embryologist do in a procedure like IVF?'

'Maybe we should stick to what exactly you set this meeting up for.' All guards were up. Careful as you go, Natalie.

'How much did Dr Blaydon-Green tell you?'

'That you'd heard some stuff about cases in our centre and

wanted our side of the story.'

'And no doubt he told you to keep your mouth zipped, and just head me off. Well, since you look like a man who thinks for himself, I'll put my cards on the table.'

'But first tell me, where did you got the stories from?'

'Let's just say, a reputable source – a source as close to the actual families as you can get. You'll understand that I can't break confidences any more than you can. Our rules are much the same.'

'And what does your reputable source tell you?'

'Well, that black couple having IVF at your centre, the ones with twins – I heard that that was a minor miracle in itself. Your success rates are impressive, right?'

Scott grinned. 'You can print that bit, sure! It's true. Our success rate is now in the top ten in the whole of the UK.'

'Since you came, would that be?' It was a long shot.

'Since I came.'

'So one of your jobs as an embryologist is to help infertile women have kids. And you study the embryos and do things with them too, yes?'

'Aye.'

'So let's keep it theoretical. Say you've got a black couple. They have IVF. They have twins. But one of those twins is a different colour from the parents. That would tell you what?'

'Theoretically?'

'Theoretically.'

'It *might* tell me that that mother wasn't playing fair by her husband or partner.'

'Mm.'

'It might tell me that there was white blood somewhere in their family background – maybe they didn't know about.'

'Mm.'

'Or somebody somewhere made a mistake.'

'And in this particular case, would you be able to give me an idea which of the three possibilities it was most likely to be?'

'Nope.'

'So going back to theoretical, how could you tell?'

'DNA check.'

'But presumably you'd need parental consent for that.'

'Definitely.'

'So, supposing the DNA test tells you that the couple aren't both the kiddie's parents, where do you go from there? Theoretically, of course. This isn't about crucifying anybody. It's about telling it like it is. You're all really busy people, and I guess it's *technically* possible for a mistake to happen. What precautions do you take? Where could things go wrong? What d'you do next? That kind of thing. I think it'd help to reassure people, the fact that you take all this care.'

Scott took several sips of coffee before setting down his cup and looking at her.

'And is it OK if I take notes?' she rushed on. 'You're on a different plane from me here, I doubt I'd report accurately from memory.'

He nodded and waited while she took out her notebook. As she scribbled Natalie was grateful that he wouldn't be able to read her shorthand.

When he finished she let out a low whistle. 'I had no idea it was so tightly regulated.'

'Every fertility centre in the UK is bound by the same licences and regulations.'

'But even though all these precautions are in place, you still have to do a thorough inquiry, yeah?'

He nodded, his lips set.

'That must be frustrating.' It was another shot in the dark.

'That's putting it mildly. Whatever the reason for this kid being a different colour, she is. We can't change that. But the more time we waste on this case that we can't change, the less time we have for all the rest of the work where we could make a real difference.'

'You sound passionate.'

'I am. It's what drives us. Wanting to make a difference. Relieve some of the suffering in the world. Yuck, that sounds so sanctimonious. Don't quote me on that!'

She smiled. 'Fair enough. You mentioned all the rest of the work, are you able to tell me about some of these other things you do as well? To give a sense of how important it all is. So the public can sympathise with your frustration. That kind of thing.'

He picked his words with precision as well as thought.

Natalie whistled. 'Twenty-four hours doesn't sound a long enough day for that little lot.'

'It isn't.'

'So which things suffer if you get sidetracked by stuff you didn't factor in to your schedule?'

'Research,' he answered without hesitation. 'It's always the research that suffers. The clinical stuff *has* to happen. You've got these desperate couples sitting there, clocks ticking; you've got embryos that have to be used by a certain day; you can't put any of that on hold.'

'And that must be so frustrating too when all you're trying to do through your research is help people have babies, or cure horrible diseases, or whatever.'

'Exactly.'

Natalie refilled his cup, dropping in the two lumps of sugar without comment. Just as he took his first sip she said casually, 'And the other case? Can you tell me anything about that?'

'What d'you know? Remember, I can't discuss the specifics.'

'Of course not. I'm not looking for confidential information. But as I understand it, this couple are wanting to have a baby to save its older brother who's got a terminal illness.'

'Speaking theoretically again, huh?'

'Yes. I've read about the high profile cases in the press: Charlie Whitaker, Joshua Fletcher, Molly Nash, Zain Hashmi and Charlotte something.'

'You've done your homework,' She liked the look that lingered over her. 'Charlotte Mariethos was the name you're trying to remember. That was 2006. And I believe there's been another attempt more recently.'

'And *you* do that procedure? In your centre, I mean.'

'Well, let's just say we have the *capacity* to do it.'

'Fair enough. And *how* do you do it?'

'You're talking about a fairly rare procedure here. And the fact that you can list the cases tells you it's uncommon.'

'Right.'

'It involves creating a donor child who's the same tissue type as the sick kiddie, so it can provide matching stem cells, or bone marrow, or whatever, that hopefully won't be rejected.'

She took a couple of sips of her milky coffee, pressing her lips to the napkin before laying it down beside her cup, a perfect pink kiss imprinted on the white fabric.

'And can you talk me through *how* you do it? In words of two syllables. This is way beyond my O-grade science.'

'Well, it's basically the same procedure as IVF, but once you've created embryos in the lab, you examine them to check for compatibility with the sick kiddie. And you'd only implant the ones that are a match.'

'Seems fair enough. So why the big stooshie? Why do you have to go through so many hoops on this one?'

'How long have you got?'

'*I've* got as long as it takes, but what about you? Is there somebody burning the Yorkshire pud while you sit here talking to me?' It was an outright gamble.

'No. If you're sure you're interested.'

'You're kidding! This is absolutely fascinating. I got really hooked on it when I read up all these cases that've been in the papers, but it's even better listening to somebody who actually *does* this kind of thing.'

'Well...' Scott looked at his watch.

'What about going down to Brown's in George Street and having a bite of supper while we talk. If you're sure you haven't got anything planned. There's nobody cooking *my* tea, that's for sure! So we might as well eat while we chat.'

He looked hesitant.

'It's on me. You'll be doing me a favour rescuing me from

complete ignorance, and I'll be able to write something more accurate, so it's legit.'

Quite how much had been her undisguised admiration he couldn't decide. Perhaps it was more a matter of pique with Justin. Annoyance had been building ever since the Opakanjo birth had blown a hole in his schedule. Whatever the cause, as Scott lay in a hot bath that night, reflecting on how out of character his behaviour had been, his thoughts were uneasy. Not only had Natalie Wyatt kept him away from his work all evening, but she'd winkled family information out of him he'd divulged to no one since he'd left the Highlands. Information he would definitely not want broadcast.

She'd promised the rest of the evening was off-record. But what value could you place on a *reporter's* discretion?

What a fool! Damn the woman. She was too good at her job. He'd need to buy the *Evening News* every night until her story ran.

This was a warning shot. He mustn't lose perspective. He mustn't become vulnerable. He must not.

# 25

KARIM LOOKED UP from composing exam papers. Yasmeen was ironing baby clothes.

'How's Candice?'

'Tons better. She even let the dreaded mother-in-law take Orlando for a walk this week. Only Orlando, mind – Aurora wouldn't be seen out with Destiny, poor little mite.'

'Good.'

'The Pemberton people have been good, too. Candice and Samuel attended the clinic for so long the staff are like friends to them, so she's chuffed that they're still taking an interest. Dr Blaydon-Green rang her once when I was there. And Josephine – the counsellor, d'you remember? – she's been out to visit.'

'Presumably they're all still involved anyway – because of the business with Destiny?'

'Well, yes, but that's different. I'm talking about them caring how Candice is coping with being a mum.'

A pause.

'So will you be able to get some more rest now?'

'I'm fine.'

'You're not, Yasmeen. You're shattered, and I'm worried about you.'

'It's just, when Samuel's away on the rigs... it's tough for Candice. The sleepless nights and extra work. On her own.'

'How d'you think we'll cope with all that? At our age.'

'Quite a thought, eh? Starting that again.'

Karim watched her carefully for some time before he spoke. 'What's going on in that pretty head of yours?'

'Just something Samuel said yesterday when I called round with those pies.'

'Which was?'

'Would I mind if he used Sebastian as a kind of lever to encourage Candice to agree to a DNA test.'

Karim stared at Yasmeen.

'And you said?'

The conversation had been more disturbing than she cared to admit.

After the confidences Candice had shared, Yasmeen was guarded when speaking to Samuel. She had intended to simply hand over the casseroles she'd made, but he'd been insistent. It seemed churlish to refuse.

Indoors he seemed even more imposing. His presence dominated the room and it was strange to have him making drinks, producing biscuits, while she sat perched like a guest on the edge of the armchair in the very room where she had so often whirled around dusting, vacuuming, tidying. She noticed for the first time his absurdly long eyelashes, the chip off his front tooth, the muscles straining against the black T-shirt, the strength in his long fingers.

She smiled inwardly at the cup and saucer he handed her – visitor treatment, Candice called it. He took a seat opposite her and leaned back with a small sigh.

'Yasmeen, I don't know how Candice would have survived without you. You've been a real friend to her.'

'Your babies are gorgeous. You must see a big change every time you come home.'

'I can't believe how fast they grow – especially Orlando.'

'It must be very draining for Candice.'

'Does she ever talk to you about Destiny?' he asked suddenly. 'I mean, about her not being properly ours?'

'Sometimes. But not in those kinds of words. Candice sees her... I mean, don't you think Candice sees her as hers? Yours?'

'She says so.'

Yasmeen felt at a loss. This wasn't a bit like listening to Candice pouring out her confidences.

'It doesn't seem right to me,' Samuel said so quietly she wondered if he was speaking to her at all. 'Doing nothing.'

'What do *you* think should happen?'

The intensity of his look made a shiver run down her spine.

'I think we should get Destiny tested. Then, once we know who the real parents are, they ought to be told.'

'Oh.'

'It doesn't feel right, somebody who's been through IVF, not even *knowing*.'

'But how would anyone react to a bombshell like this?'

He shrugged. 'Well, for me, it's about not wanting to take something without permission. I mean, maybe Destiny doesn't belong to either of us. Or maybe she's Candice's anyway, and that gives us a right to keep her. Or maybe she's mine. But she must belong to at least one other person, and they deserve some information about her. An opportunity to stay in touch if they want to. That kind of thing.'

'And what would that do to you and Candice – having a third party involved?'

'She says it would be bad for Destiny. Bad for us as a family.'

'And you don't agree?'

'I can't see how it would be any worse than what we have now. The uncertainty itself is bad for us.' He broke off as if he'd already said too much.

Yasmeen leaned forward. 'It must be so hard for both of you.'

'It's a mess. But it's helped Candice having you to confide in.'

'But what about *you*? Do you have somebody to talk to?'

'Oh, it's different for me. It's a bloke thing. You just don't.'

Another wave of unease washed over Yasmeen. It didn't feel right being alone with this man about whom she knew too much. She drained her cup. But his next question caught her off guard.

'How's your little boy?'

'He's a bit better right now. Thank you.'

There was naked appeal in Samuel's eyes.

'It's because you're going through all that,' he blurted out as if he must speak before his courage deserted him, 'that I wanted to ask you something. I hope this isn't taking liberties.'

This was it then, the hidden agenda. Yasmeen spread her hands in a gesture that left the decision to him.

'If we don't find out who Destiny is – you know, her genetic background – what if she got something like your little boy has?'

'I see what you're saying.'

'If she got ill, we might not be able to save her.'

Yasmeen felt a surge of irritation.

'Well, there are no guarantees in our case either. We might not be able to save Sebastian. It's a complicated business, no easy answers, no certainties, even when you *know* the genetic background.'

'Sorry. I didn't mean to imply…'

She shook her head. 'No, *I'm* sorry. People don't understand how hard these decisions are, that's all.'

'D'you mind me asking? I don't know who else to talk to.'

'No. It's fine. I don't mind.' She paused to consider his original question. 'I guess your case is different. Of course, until it happens you don't know what you'd do if you were in the kind of situation Karim and I are in with our son. Nobody does. But then nobody would imagine being in your situation either. All any of us can do is make the best decision for our family at the time, and try not to be influenced or hurt by the things other people say. And that's not easy. It's not easy deciding, and it's not easy being criticised.'

'You seem so strong.'

Little did he know how hard she worked at always being upbeat around them, or what it cost her.

'Only because we have to be. We've done our share of weeping and doubting too, believe me. But at the end of the day, nobody else can decide for you. And what it boils down to for us is, we'd do anything for our children. And this is the one thing we *can* do to give Sebastian a chance, and *for us* it feels right. We think we can live with it. Not everybody could. I guess you have to decide what's right for you.'

'The trouble is, Candice and I don't agree. So I was thinking, maybe if you could talk to her about your decision, explain, persuade her.'

Yasmeen felt herself physically recoil. She shook her head, her hands up to ward off anything further.

'I *can't*. I can't take sides here. You must see that. I don't take Candice's side either. I simply listen. You have to work it out for yourselves. You're the ones who have to live with the consequences, not me.'

Samuel looked so crestfallen that Yasmeen touched his arm briefly.

'Look, please don't think I'm unsympathetic. But please, *please*, don't ask me to do it for you. I can't. I just *can't*.' Her voice cracked on the last sentence. She busied herself with brushing crumbs from her lap onto her saucer.

'I'm so sorry. That was completely out of order. And after all you've done for us.' He was on his knees beside her chair.

It was a shock finding her emotions so near the surface. Confused emotions. She didn't trust herself to speak. Her hand was suddenly seized in his enormous ones.

'Please forgive me. I didn't mean to upset you.'

Yasmeen brushed her free hand across her eyes, but the first thing she saw through the haze was Candice standing motionless in the doorway. She snatched her other hand back and darted around Samuel to pick up her bag. By the time she reached the door, Candice had vanished.

'Please, you'll explain… tell Candice.' she implored.

Samuel wore an expression she couldn't fathom.

Sleep was a long time coming to her that night.

Why was she so disturbed? What was *really* in the air during that exchange? What had she imagined was going on?

Beside her, Karim breathed evenly. She watched him, her thoughts chaotic. They had shared so much. Even through the years since Sebastian's diagnosis they had always been able to discuss the most painful subjects, their differences no barrier to their closeness. This man, who had been chosen for her, had been a rock in her storms.

She knew that if they were given permission to create a sibling for Sebastian, Karim would support her through every stage. The technological interventions, the calculated efforts, the selection – it wouldn't be like her other pregnancies. But at least this new child would share their chromosomes, hers and Karim's, mysteriously intertwined. Once she was pregnant, there'd be the same wonder and anticipation. With an added layer of hope for Sebastian.

She shivered. Today she had peered inside a chasm which scared her. She'd seen how an artificially assisted conception had driven a wedge between two people who had once been so close. Until today she'd always seen the disintegrating relationship through Candice's eyes. But now she'd seen *Samuel's* despair. *His* loneliness. A depth of need that had driven a proud, self-contained man to his knees pleading for his cause.

And she had turned away. Away... from what?

She pulled the duvet tight around her shoulders.

## 26

HELEN HAD ALREADY breakfasted when Justin put in an appearance. She was elegant in deep forest green, a shade that suited her colouring, turning her eyes almost navy.

'Wow! You look terrific. Remind me where you're off to today?'

'Conference at the Royal Society. *Medicine and the Humanities*.'

'You're presenting?'

She shook her head. 'Chairing.'

He grimaced. 'My pet hate.'

'Oh, I don't mind it, and it should be good today. Internationally recognised speakers. *And* I'm being paid to listen to them. It'll help foot the bill for Lexie's trombone lessons!'

'Well, rather you than me. Having to think up erudite questions, *and* field incoherent ones from the audience, *and* keep everyone to time, *and* remember to thank all the right people. Don't knock it.'

She moved over to kiss him goodbye, her sudden softness at odds with the professional façade.

'It's your big meeting about the saviour sibling case, isn't it?' she said.

'It is indeed. Wish me luck.'

'You don't need luck. If anyone can persuade them it's you, Dr Silver-tongue.'

'Maybe I've got too much riding on this one.'

'You've persuaded *me*.'

'You might be said to have a conflict of interests,' he laughed, releasing her.

She left a scent of Chanel and a promise of her support lingering in the air.

The girls drifted into the kitchen one at a time in various stages of wakefulness. Kate was first, as befitted a budding teenager who had yet to discover for herself that natural exuberance was 'so-last-year'. She had her mother's colouring and was neat in every detail, regulation navy uniform, polished shoes, covered books, labelled gym kit.

She threw him a broad grin as she helped herself to a bowl of four mixed cereals.

'Morning, Pops. Gee, I'm starving.'

'So it would appear. Good for you, Katey Kitten. That should see you through the first forty-five minutes at least.'

She spluttered over the first mouthful. 'Da-aad! You'll make me spill it, and then I'll need to go and change, and keep you waiting.'

'Nobody keeps me waiting today, my girl. I'm out of here on the dot this morning. So be there or be square.'

The 'Huh' that greets this ancient cliché came from Lexie, oozing through the door and straight for the fridge. Fruit juice, according to her, was undrinkable unless it froze the fillings out of your head. She yawned as she shuffled onto the stool beside Kate and reached for the toast. With the comfort of a lifetime's acquaintance they chewed without the need for conversation.

Lexie had a pleasing plumpness which distinguished her from her sisters, and she remained untroubled by either the extra inches or the niceties of dress codes. Her shirt-sleeves looked as if she'd slept in them, her pleats looked more like gathers, and her hair looked suspiciously as if she'd brushed only the parts she could see in the mirror. Her curls saved her from complete disaster but outwardly she was not the girl to showcase the expensive education she'd received for the past ten years. The school however remained remarkably tolerant, firm in the belief that Lexie would eventually bring glory to its name. 'Alexis *combines a fine mind with admirable diligence and if she continues to apply herself, she could go far,'* her last report concluded. '*She could have the pick of the universities if she realises her present promise.'* Sad to say Justin all too often heard the veiled rebuke for the way his elder daughter had chosen to go, rather than the genuine tributes to Lexie.

He rapped on Bobby's door.

'This is the last and final call for passengers on the BMW 404G to Edinburgh city. Would all those intending to travel on this flight please proceed to door number 3, where this plane is preparing to depart.'

He listened for signs of habitation. Hearing none he opened the door an unrevealing crack.

'We're leaving in twenty minutes, Bobby. I can't be late today, so get a wriggle on.'

Time was when he'd have built this kind of situation into a battle of wills. Not any more. Be there or not. She was old enough to take the consequences of her own actions. Nevertheless the tension still simmered beneath the surface.

When she lurched into the kitchen with six minutes to spare, he let out an inaudible breath. How this rebel managed not to get expelled remained a mystery to him. This was not the thoughtless dishevelment Lexie exhibited. This was calculated. The row of silver hoops in one ear hardly came into the category of 'single gold sleeper' the regulations grudgingly countenanced. The abbreviated skirt mocked the requirement for 'modesty'. The navy and white twist somewhere far south of her top button did constitute an emblematic nod in the direction of conformity, but hardly demonstrated the dignity demanded of pupils in his day. He remembered being caned for wearing his blazer with two of its three buttons undone one extremely hot June day.

He sometimes imagined the conversation in the staff room.

'*Robyn Blaydon-Green? Isn't she the kid who drove poor old Doncaster into the madhouse with her everlasting social challenges? What kind of parents let a sixteen-year-old girl wander around looking like a cross between a tart and a new age suffragette?'*

'Oh, don't you know her parents? I was at school with her old man. Justin Blaydon-Green. In the year above me. Bit of a swot. Made a name for himself in medicine.'

'They both come to parents' evenings. Seem like the caring sort actually.'

'Too busy with their careers to notice the kid going off the rails, if you ask me.'

He couldn't repress a shudder. Let *them* try moulding a girl made of steel and dynamite, always one fuse away from complete anarchy.

'Lex, any chance I could borrow your tennis racquet?' Bobby drawled, stretching her arms and bending her back, revealing in the process the sparkle of silver in her umbilicus. Justin looked away.

'Yep. Help yourself.'

'Where's yours?' he dared.

'Lent it to Marianna, on Monday. Hasn't given it back.'

'But you'll ask for it back?'

'I'm not a *dawk*, Dad!'

Justin had no idea how this translated.

'Breakfast?' he asked, adopting the essential approach to language necessary for early morning.

'Cereal bar in my bag.' She was already off to the hall to search for the said racquet. Lexie and Kate ate in silence for a further minute, then they locked eyes, smacked right hands, and leapt to their feet as if their stools were suddenly connected to a live socket. A herd of rhinos thundered up the stairs and across the landing before the bathroom door crashed open and Lexie gave vent to an ear-splitting whoop of triumph.

All three were safely in the car bang on the dot of 8.05. If he'd dared he'd have hugged them for their compliance on this difficult day. But in the teenage book of etiquette parental displays of affection of this nature were forbidden for anything less than the loss of a significant member of the family or imminent emigration to Australia.

The Clinical Ethics Committee was in full assembly when he arrived but an awkward air of secrecy lurked in the room, as if their private consultation hovered somewhere near the ceiling, just out of his line of vision.

Justin gave himself a mental shake. This committee had convened to help him analyse the issues and make a wise decision; they weren't the enemy. He smiled at the chairman, a consultant orthopaedic surgeon.

'Justin. Good morning,' Ian Hollinghurst boomed. 'I think you know everyone around the table?'

Justin indicated a Japanese lady, sitting upright on the edge of her chair with all the hauteur of a chrysanthemum monarch. 'I don't think...'

'Koto Tin. Embryologist from King's,' piped a thin voice. He felt a surge of merriment rise in his throat; it sounded so much like 'cocoa tin'. How Kate would love it!

'This is a tricky one,' Hollinghurst continued. 'So let's go round the table, shall we? Margaret, perhaps you'd like to kick off.'

Justin hadn't known Margaret Beuly in her heyday, but he'd seen enough of her in action as Emeritus-Professor to know she spoke an archaic language that required complete concentration. Now in her seventies, she'd shrunk inside her wrinkles, but she could still spot a hole in an ethical argument at forty paces. She was worth the effort. Her contribution to this case focused on justice.

'Thank you, Professor Beuly,' Justin said. 'You're quite right. We do need to distribute our limited resources fairly. However, it's highly unlikely that we shall have parents flocking to our doors for this particular procedure. I think we can safely assume this case can be considered on its merits alone.'

'I beg to differ.'

Jennifer Ruskin! Who else? A sharp-featured nurse with attitude, who was rumoured to have been co-opted onto this committee to stop her everlasting whinging.

'Don't you think this is a classic case of the slippery slope?

We should be very wary of taking even this first tentative step onto it,' she said. 'Don't get me wrong, I feel for this poor family, I really do. But where will it all end?' She paused for dramatic effect, her steel grey eyes boring into Justin. 'First it's selection for a serious life-threatening condition. Then it's for medical conditions that aren't life-threatening. Then it's for conditions the prospective parents simply don't like. And before you know it, you're heading for Nazi Germany!'

'There is,' Justin replied, 'as you suggest, always a potential for technology to be exploited or abused. But I think many factors provide safeguards against a scenario such as you describe developing.' He raised his hand and ticked them off on his fingers. 'The expense involved. Stringent regulations. The integrity of the staff. The unpleasantness of the procedure. The scarcity of people with expertise in this area.'

A murmur of assent went round. Hollinghurst nodded. 'Any other points you want to bring up, Jennifer?'

'How would you assess the chances for *this couple*?'

Justin referred her to page eight of the proposal where he'd spelled out all the statistics she could possibly think of asking about.

'Yes, I've read the papers, but what I'm asking for is *your personal assessment* for this particular couple. We don't know them, so, on the basis of what you know about them, how would you rate them?'

Justin outlined the facts about Yasmeen and Karim.

'And the boy?'

'Sebastian is four years old, and in the care of the haematology people at the Sick Children's Hospital. They're maintaining him on the usual regimen for Diamond Blackfan's, and are reasonably satisfied with his response so far, although no-one can predict how long this will continue. His treatment involves regular blood transfusions and plasmapheresis, and a battery of drugs, particularly high-dose corticosteroids. I'm sure I don't need to tell you about the side effects of all of these therapies. Even the transfusions, when they're this frequent, run the risk of damaging various organs. I understand there's been some talk of starting him on Interleukin therapy, but while he remains responsive to the steroids this has been shelved meantime. All in all, not an easy life for an active four-year-old boy.'

Several of them nodded.

'So would you say this family are strong enough, and sufficiently motivated, to cope with the uncertainties of pre-implantation genetic diagnosis and IVF?' the chairman asked.

'The psychological assessments suggest they would be. And I think so too.'

'And with the potential adverse publicity?' the Reverend Alex Steinbrook chipped in. It was more comfortable shifting gaze to this man. He'd walked through some hard times himself. No sharp edges, no territory. He was an ally to any clinician doing his best to tread the moral tightrope fairly.

'I believe so. They're very confident, and well-informed, and highly articulate. Not to mention incredibly good-looking. If you were seeking a test family to plead this case, you'd be hard put to find a more eloquent one than this.'

'But?'

'Well, I must admit, I'm cynical enough to fear it'll take more than that to keep the bigots and pro-lifers from rising up in outrage.'

'So you think they'd be in for a hard time,' Hollinghurst said slowly. 'If everyone gives this the go-ahead?'

'They could well be. It depends how much of the story gets out and who reports it. They're sure to attract criticism, but they're expecting that. I'm not sure how far it's appropriate to anticipate the more high profile attacks. If things are handled carefully it *could* possibly go by unnoticed by the militant elements.'

'I appreciate your honesty, Justin,' Hollinghurst was more sombre than he was wont to be on these occasions.

'You say they're nominally Christian.' The Reverend was back defending his own patch. 'Are they aware of the strong feeling amongst Christians about the sanctity of life? D'you think they might suffer from feelings of guilt about the destruction of life that goes alongside this procedure?'

'The mother is certainly aware of the implications – both of selecting an embryo and disposing of surplus embryos. Intellectually she accepts the rationale for both, but on an emotional level she finds the ideas difficult. Her line is to balance the destruction of a few cells against the life of her son; to throw *that* away would be the greater evil.'

'And the father?' Ray Brookes knew the burden of illness on fathers first-hand. His third son had been severely injured in a car accident and was now quadriplegic. The strain had told on Ray's marriage and in the end his wife had gone off with the two older boys. Ray had been forced to put his dependent son into an institution.

Justin held his gaze. 'He leaves most of the talking to his wife, in my experience. But he always insists he's fully supportive of this course of action.'

The silence that followed was full of thinking.

Jennifer Ruskin snapped it with a change of tack. 'How confident are you that you'll get enough stem cells from the umbilicus to treat this boy, or is this going to be a case of one donation after another?'

'Sadly, no one can answer that question – neither the obstetric staff nor the team looking after the Diamond Blackfan's side of things. Only time will tell.'

'That leads into the next question I'd like to ask,' Margaret Beuly interjected. 'What about the best interests of the donor child? What about the effect on him or her of being created to serve the interests of someone else?'

'As I understand it, there's very little empirical evidence regarding the balance of benefits and burdens for the donor child. On the plus side they have the satisfaction of having done something to help a sibling, and they're the recipients of the gratitude of the rest of the family. On the negative side, if they grow up knowing they were created for a purpose, not primarily for themselves, there's the possibility of them feeling a failure if their donation doesn't effect a cure. And as Mrs Ruskin has rightly pointed out, more might be asked of them at a later date.'

Professor Beuly nodded.

'Barbara? I think you wanted to say something?' Hollinghurst said.

Barbara Down was the lay person on the committee. A publishing editor and no intellectual slouch, she still managed to sound as if she'd like to snatch her words back as soon as she'd uttered them. 'Isn't that a big worry? Not knowing what the donor child will feel?'

'We can't, of course, know how any such child will feel about the reason for his existence, or the demands that may be made on him. But children are conceived for far less worthy motives and don't seem to be harmed in any significant way by that knowledge. And I think we know enough about families to know that most siblings would do anything in their power to help a brother or sister who needs help. Is that fair, Ray?'

The paediatrician had been sitting with his chin propped on his linked hands, elbows on the table, watching each person speak, occasionally scribbling a word or two and resuming his pose.

'I'd agree with that. Kids are remarkably willing to protect their siblings – even when it involves unpleasant experiences for them. It's usually a matter of how you tell them. And in this case, there might be very few demands made of this kiddie. It might just be giving cord blood. He won't even feel it; he certainly won't remember it. The older boy gets better. They're a normal happy family with three children instead of two.'

Justin nodded with him. He had a lot of time for Ray, but the paediatrician took him by surprise with his next point.

'I'd like to turn to one of the risks to the Trust, if I may. Any chance this couple might succumb to the wiles of the cheque-book journalists?'

'A good question, Ray. Well, I've only recently met them, but they don't strike me as the mercenary kind.'

*Although she might talk for the cause!* They didn't need to know that. Not at this stage.

'Dr Tin,' Hollinghurst said, 'we invited you along today because of your expertise in this field. Would you like to say anything at this stage?'

Koto Tin's questions were scientific, revolving around the available expertise to carry out the pre-implantation diagnosis and selection, and Justin felt well able to respond, thanks to all the discussions he'd had with his own team of scientists.

'Listening to all this, I'm getting increasingly uneasy about the selection process,' Janet Ruskin said with that edge that annoyed the doctors who worked with her. 'We're talking about discriminating against perfect embryos as well as those with Diamond Blackfan's Anaemia, aren't we? You're going to keep creating embryos until you find one that matches this little boy, and then presumably get rid of all the rest of them?'

'Put baldly, yes, but the whole point of the exercise is to create a matched donor. These embryos wouldn't have existed at all were it not for this child's need.'

'And the family's need too,' Barbara chipped in.

'Exactly.' Justin smiled at her. 'The needs and interests of each individual, and those of the family as a whole, are inextricably linked. The whole family faces the burden of caring for Sebastian throughout his life, and the prospect of losing this precious child. The whole family will be affected by any decision they make on his behalf.'

'Besides, if we were to leave it to this couple to try to have a match naturally, who knows how many kids they would either have or abort to get to that point? – if they ever did,' Ray added.

'Precisely so,' Justin agreed. 'Nature herself is incredibly profligate. And we don't go into mourning for all the babies conceived naturally who never come to birth, do we? Which reminds me, Mrs Zair has had a miscarriage so she knows the pain of that loss.'

Hollinghurst scanned the faces around him.

'Anyone anything more?'

'If I may?' Barbara Down hesitated. 'I don't know if it's a fair question but ... you needn't answer if it's inappropriate to ask. Would you personally, Dr Blaydon-Green – would *you* have a saviour sibling in these circumstances?'

'I would.' No hesitation. 'And it's a fair question. Thank you for asking it.'

'Me too,' Ray said. 'I've seen kids with DBA and I've seen what these illnesses do to parents, to families. Pretty much any parent would save the life of such a kid if they could. Sorry, Ian, I'm probably way out of line here.'

The Chair simply shrugged.

## 27

JACK LEANED BACK on the new leather sofa and fidgeted until he was moderately comfortable. It was a constant source of vexation these days; after only two years in residence, his girlfriend had got rid of the old settee that over the better part of his adult life had sunk to fit his shape so perfectly.

Ten minutes later the sound of high heels clacking on the wooden floor woke him. Patsy sashayed into the room, a vision in buttercup yellow.

'Off out?' he ventured.

'Yeah. Cucumber lotion's run out.'

'Would that be edible, cosmetic or medicinal?'

'For me eyes, silly. Maybe you could use some yourself, the hours you keep these days.'

Jack shot upright. 'You wouldn't! I'd never live it down. Please, please, *please*,' – he slid to his knees raising clenched hands in supplication – 'I'll do anything. I'll clean the loo for a week; I'll put out the bin for a year; I'll weed underneath that rose that's taken over the bottom border – anything, *anything* but cucumber on my eyes! I'm *begging* you!'

'Idiot.' She grinned at him. 'You should get out more. Look at you! Men take a pride in their appearance these days, y'know. They have their eyebrows plucked, they get their chests waxed, all that kind of thing.'

Jack covered his ears. 'Spare me. If I want to look like a woman I'll take hormones.'

'Shut up, and go back to your snoozing. I don't know what's got into you lately. You're permanently in second gear.'

'Well, I'm with my friend, Oscar, on this one: *I have always been of the opinion that hard work is simply the refuge of people who have nothing whatever to do... the root of all ugliness.*'

'It's no joke. You're becoming an old man overnight.'

'It's the struggle of keeping up with a much younger woman with voracious appetites.'

'I'm warning you, Jack Fitzpatrick. One of these days you'll drive me that bit too far.' She glared at him. 'And for goodness' sake, smarten yourself up. Look at you!' And out she stalked.

Jack closed his eyes, but sleep was far from his mind. He had a strategy to devise.

By the time Patsy returned with a bag crammed with cosmetics in exotic-looking packaging, he was a changed man. His all-over navy ensemble took inches off his waistline and added an illusion of height; the dark shoes instead of tatty trainers gave him the air of a man on the edge of action; the hint of after-shave made Patsy sniff the air appreciatively.

'Well, *that's* an improvement!' she breathed. 'You can be quite passable when you try. Pity you don't try more often.'

'We aim to please.'

Patsy wriggled out of her jacket, kicked off her shoes, and lifted one foot to massage it vigorously.

Jack didn't need the distraction of all that leg. Not right now. He dragged his eyes past layers of temptation up to her face. The hazel eyes were watchful.

'Cup of tea? And one of your favourites?' he suggested.

'Yeah, that'd be nice. Me feet are killing me.'

'Hardly to be wondered at in those straps that call themselves shoes half a mile off the pavement.'

'Philistine!' she shot at his departing back, but the tone was promising.

They drank in companionable silence for several minutes and Patsy crunched into her chocolate hobnob before Jack fired his first shot.

'How would you fancy moving somewhere different?'

'If you mean upstairs then forget it, Jack. I'm not in the mood, and I've got Tricia and Hetty coming this afternoon. I want to get me eyes done before they see me looking like an old hag.'

'Well, it's gratifying to see your mind working in such an altogether delightful direction. And if you weren't so busy with cucumber, chocolate biscuits and girlfriends, I assure you I'd avail myself of the suggestion with alacrity.'

'Oh, shut up, you, and get on with whatever it is you're trying to say,' she pouted. 'And you can cut all the clever stuff.'

'Right. How would you feel about moving away from here and pitching a tent somewhere else altogether?' His casual tone belied the tension in his stomach.

'Moving? From this house? Since when were you wanting to move *anywhere*? Good grief, it took eleven months to get you to book a blinking summer holiday!'

'Well, times change. And maybe a move would do us good. Get us out of this rut. You know.'

'Speak for yourself! *I'm* not in a rut...' Confusion, fear, caution, mingled together. 'Is this one of your idiotic wind-ups? Or... are you trying to dump me?'

'Nothing is further from my thoughts. If I *were* to move, I'd definitely want you to come with me. No question. In spite of your cucumber eye packs and your ridiculous sandals, not to mention your hatred of my particular muse.'

'So what *are* you saying? Come on, spit it out in plain English.'

Jack took a gulp of his camomile tea.

'Well, you know things have been, um, fraught at work, lately? With the inquiry and everything.'

'Ye-ah.'

'Well, I'm thinking – only *thinking* – of blowing the whistle on somebody. Thought you ought to know first, just in case you don't want to stay saddled to trouble with a capital T.'

She stared at him open-mouthed.

'See,' Jack went on in a conversational tone, 'I haven't got enough *proof* yet, but I'm working on it – anyway, I'm suspicious about one of the guys I work beside. I'm pretty sure he's doing things that he shouldn't. And if he is, I don't think I can sit back and do nothing.'

'What kind of things?'

'Oh, this and that. Bending the rules. I can't be more specific till I've got more evidence.'

'So what's this got to do with us moving?'

'Well, seems to me, once you clype on a colleague, it'd be kind of tricky working in the same place. Everybody'd suspect you were snooping around looking for more trouble. Stuff like that. It'd be uncomfortable for them, uncomfortable for me, too, I guess. '

'I thought you got on well with your lot.'

'I do. Everybody nearly. But there's the odd one that gets right up my nose.'

'So, we'd only have to leave if you *do* tell on this guy, yeah? If you don't, we won't.'

'Well, yes, probably.'

'D'you think you *will* find anything?'

'I'm pretty sure I will, or somebody else will if I point them in the right direction.'

'And if you do, that's us off and away?'

'I think it might be.'

'And does anybody else know about this guy, apart from you?'

'The boss *might* have an idea. I think he knows I'm suspicious, anyway. But he hasn't said anything. Well, quite the reverse actually. He as good as warned me not to rattle any of the cages of the senior people.'

'This is somebody *senior*?'

'It could be. But listen, Patsy, don't breathe a word of this. It might all fizzle out. And I don't want to move if I don't have to. And if I *do* have to go, I want to get a half-decent reference. You wouldn't want me coming home smelling of garbage after a day emptying other people's bins, now would you?'

'Has this got something to do with those twins?' she said, watching him like an owl observing a dormouse.

'I can't talk about specifics, Pats. You know that.'

'They came into the surgery last week. Did I tell you that? They're drop-dead gorgeous, like something off an Anne Geddes calendar, y'know? And the mum is brilliant with them. I don't think I could ever handle two at once.'

'That's good. That she's coping, I mean.'

'So that's it? That's all I get to know. There's something murky going on in your lab, you can't tell me what it's about, or who's doing it, but I have to start looking at properties in Timbuktu.'

'Timbuktu's a real place, you know. It's in Africa, founded in the 12th century by the Tuareg nomads. It's all sandy and…'

'For goodness' sake, shut *up*! You and your infernal facts. You drive me crazy!'

Jack hung his head in mock apology, but watched her sharply beneath his brows. 'OK, I wasn't thinking that far away. I was thinking maybe… well, Cornwall? You loved Cornwall. Remember?'

'For *holiday*! In the *summer*! Yeah! But to *stay*? What about the shops? All me friends? The night life? *Everything*.'

'Last time I looked, civilisation had arrived, albeit reluctantly, in the West Country.'

'But it wouldn't be the *same*!'

'No. True. But seriously, Patsy, where would you *like* to live?'

'I don't *know*,' she wailed. 'I haven't even *thought* about moving anywhere. I thought we were OK here.'

'And so we are. Fret not. We aren't going anywhere yet, maybe not ever. Just give it some thought, though. And if you come up with anywhere you fancy, we'll have a wee look to see if there's any biggish hospital where I might be able to eke out a meagre living. OK?'

She threw him a tragic look.

'Hey, come here,' he said, reaching across to her.

The next time she spoke her lips were so close to his neck he could feel the whisper of her breath down his collar. 'Are people safe – y'know – going to your place?'

He thought quickly. 'Depends how you define safe. But don't you worry, big bad Fitzpatrick's on the case.'

'Couldn't you just tell Dr Blaydon-Green, then *you* can leave it alone and maybe we wouldn't need to go anywhere?'

'I'll tell him as soon as I can. Promise.'

She snuggled up to him and he stroked the soft hair draping his shoulder.

'Want to hear what Wilde thought of women?'

'No, but I guess you're going to tell me anyway. Hey!' – she sat bolt upright – 'wasn't he gay?'

Jack laughed. 'Bisexual actually. But that's neither here nor there. What he said was: *Women are meant to be loved, not to be understood.*'

She dug her elbow into his side. 'Fine one you are to talk. I doubt I've understood half of what you've been on about this morning.'

'Half's pretty good!' He pulled her close again. 'Your usual complaint is that you don't understand a *word* of what I say.'

The next time Jack saw Justin the doctor was in full evening dress, beckoning him through the window of the lab.

He slid the last two bottles he was holding onto the shelf, put the remaining petrie dish into the fridge, and opened the door.

'Wow. Is it Holyrood Palace or Bute House tonight, then, Boss?'

'Neither, sad to say. Merely a College dinner. I called in to collect my notes.'

'Hmm. As Oscar would say: *The only way to atone for being occasionally a little over-dressed is by being always over-educated.* So I guess you're safe there, with all your degrees and distinctions.'

Justin laughed. 'Beats me how you retain all that Oscar Wilde stuff, Jack. But I guess you couldn't make it up. You're working late.'

'Got behind with some of the routine stuff, what with one

thing and another.'

'Everything all right?'

'So so.'

'Care to talk about it?'

'Not sure.'

'Well, it looked to me as if you were having a good old natter to yourself before I knocked on the window. Not a good sign that, Jack. Men have been locked up for less.'

Jack threw him a mischievous look. 'Well, *I like hearing myself talk. It is one of my greatest pleasures. I often have long conversations all by myself, and I am so clever that sometimes I don't understand a single word of what I am saying.*'

Justin gave a full-throated laugh. 'Apposite, I'll say that for it.'

'It's the way you tell 'em.'

'Indeed.'

'Which brings me to: *Whenever people agree with me, I always feel I must be wrong.*'

'You're serious?'

'Yep, he really said it. In *Lady Windermere's Fan.*'

'How come you know all this stuff, Jack?'

'Used to be in an amateur dramatic society. The lady who ran it loved Wilde. And boy, was she thorough! By the time she had us licked into shape I knew every line of everybody's part. Kind of grew on me. Maybe I'm a cynic at heart myself.'

'Whatever. I'm full of admiration. Damned if I can remember a single line of poetry or any play I ever studied. Wish I could.'

'More important stuff to store in *your* brain.'

Justin shrugged. Then he gave Jack a hard look. 'Chat? Thursday, maybe?'

'Maybe.'

'Say 11.30, my office?'

'Maybe.'

'I went to see Emma.' Justin raised one eyebrow. 'I guess you'd be interested in how she is?'

'Sure thing,' Jack said. 'Thursday morning it is.'

'Thursday morning. Now, you hop off home and get a good night's sleep. You're looking a shade knackered these days, if I might say so.'

'That's what Patsy says.'

'Must be right then. Bye for now. I'll see you in the morning.'

'Enjoy your evening.'

'I'll do my best.'

## 28

'DAAAD! *DAAAAD!!*'

The shrieks reverberated up the stairwell. Justin raced to the door of the bedroom.

'Bobby! Unless somebody's being burned alive...'

'Quick, Dad! Hurry!'

He took the stairs two at a time.

'In the kitchen. Come on!'

He entered in a rush, bracing himself for the calamity ahead.

'Listen!' She held up a quietening finger, her ear cocked to the radio where a bland voice stated, '*The Chancellor declined to comment.*'

Justin opened his mouth to protest but Bobby flapped her hand.

'*News has just emerged,*' the newsreader intoned, '*of a controversial procedure being debated in one of Scotland's leading fertility centres. The case involves a young boy of four with a blood disorder known as Diamond Blackfan's Anaemia.*'

Justin froze.

'*With a limited life expectancy this child is being kept alive with a gruelling schedule of blood transfusions and steroid drugs. His best hope is to have stem cells from an unaffected sibling who is the same tissue type. His only sister is not a match, so his parents have applied for permission to have a child created expressly for the purpose of supplying matched stem cells.*'

Justin clenched his teeth. No prizes for guessing where this came from!

'*This is not the first case of its kind in the UK...*'

They'd done their homework. The cases were all listed, the ones who'd had to go abroad, the ones who'd applied after the embargo was lifted. The ones who'd been successful. But fair enough; a quick trawl of the internet would give them the basic facts. He listened, alert for any distortion. The facts were technically accurate but there was nothing about the risks these people took travelling to more permissive countries. And the commentator's reference to 'reproductive tourism' grated. She made it sound like a holiday trip.

Science correspondent, Timothy Davenport, took up the story.

'*All of us will feel sympathy for a family facing such a tragic situation. A child of four is fighting a potentially fatal illness; his parents want to help him. But opinion is divided on the morality of the proposed procedure designed to create a baby who matches him in terms of the cells he needs to treat his blood disorder.*

'*In-vitro fertilisation is now commonplace, with success rates varying from centre to centre, but The Pemberton ranks in the top ten in the UK. A spokesperson*' – Justin held his breath – '*said that this is only one small step on from the basic method of carrying out IVF.*

'*The procedure would be exactly the same up to the stage where the best embryos are chosen, three days after fertilisation. At that point a further test would be undertaken to establish the tissue type of the embryos. This involves scientists taking one, or perhaps two, cells from these very early embryos, and only those that match the little boy would be implanted. The spokesperson described the furore surrounding such cases as "a storm in a teacup," and said that the Human Fertilisation and Embryology Authority were running scared simply because of a vocal minority.*

'*However, opponents disagree. Cardinal Quentin Fothering-ham, a prominent Roman Catholic in the South East, was quick to condemn the practice.*

'"*This particular procedure involves the deliberate destruction of perfectly healthy embryos simply because they don't match the sick child. It's a form of murder masquerading as a compassionate response to human tragedy.*"'

'Well, *he* would, wouldn't he,' hissed Bobby.

It was Justin's turn to lift a finger to silence her.

'*And Rebekkah Eisenholm, spokesperson for the pressure group,* Comment on Reproductive Ethics, *told us that, "This is another step along the slippery slope towards designer babies and children being created as a source of spare parts. Discarding embryos in this cavalier fashion is barbaric. It smacks of the Nazi programme of exterminating those who didn't conform to their ideas of perfection."*

'*The seriousness of this matter is perhaps captured by the necessity for each case to be approved and licensed by the Human Fertilisation and Embryology Authority. The HFEA recently changed its own position, making it legally allowable for doctors to offer this procedure in the UK. No decision in this latest case has yet been made.*

'*The long-running dispute between contestants in the reality show…*'

Bobby snapped off the radio.

'I take it you didn't say those things to the press,' she ventured.

'Too right I did not.'

'But Dad, why's it matter? The media could convince people it's the right thing to do.'

'You don't know the media,' Justin retorted, then held out a hand to her. 'I'm sorry, love. You're right in principle, of course. And I'm not mad at you. Only it sickens me that this family are now going to be condemned by people who have no idea of the agonies they're going through. I wanted to protect them, at least until we know whether they're going to be allowed to have this done. I don't want to stifle healthy debate, but there's a time and a place for it. And I'd rather it concerned the general and not the particular. These are real people with feelings and sensitivities

– a wee kid of *four*, for goodness' sake!'

'But you can see where they're coming from, can't you? *I* wouldn't want to be born to be spare parts for somebody else.'

Justin was suddenly arrested. 'You wouldn't?'

'No. Why should I?'

'You wouldn't think it was good to be able to save the life of Lexie or Kate, if you could?'

'That's not what I'm saying.'

'So tell me.'

'Well, Lexie and Kate are my *sisters*. Right? I love them. Well, most of the time I do, anyway.' She shot him a lop-sided grin. 'And if either one of them got sick, I'd be front of the queue to give them bits of me. But that's not like being made in the first place just for that purpose. I mean, if you only exist for something specific then what happens if they don't need you any more? It's like... well, guys buy wrecked cars to get the hub-caps or the engine out of them. Then they chuck the carcass onto the scrapheap. They don't want the car for *itself*, only for its bits. *I* wouldn't want to be like that.'

'But these families don't think of the child as a collection of spare parts. They love it for itself as part of their family. The fact that it can also help another of their children makes it *doubly* precious.'

'Yes, but what if it doesn't work out, eh? What if the older kid dies anyway? How does that make the spare-part kid feel? And what do the parents feel about that kid that let them down?'

'Well, that's one of the things we have to assess when we talk to the parents.'

'Well, I hope *I* don't *ever* have to decide something like that!'

'I hope you don't, too, sweetheart.'

A long silence fell.

'D'you agree with designer babies?' Bobby asked.

'Depends what you mean by that. I don't personally like the term, and it's certainly not something we say in the trade. It has definite echoes of slippery slopes in it. You start off with boys rather than girls. You proceed to no red-heads or kids who are tone deaf. Before you know where you are you're choosing kids with an aptitude for Latin, or American quilting, or riding a unicycle.'

Bobby grinned at him. 'Atta boy!'

'Is that meant to signify approval or disapproval?'

She threw her hands in the air in mock despair. 'You've got to get real, Pops.'

'Well, I guess the only safe course of action is to return to your question. Do I approve of designer babies? If the preference relates to selfish interests, vanity, ambition, greed, frivolous values, then certainly not. Children are to be valued for who they are, as they are.'

'Don't tell me you wouldn't rather've had a sweet little girl who did exactly what you said, never got into strife at school, rather than me.' She cast him a sidelong look.

'Who never went on animal rights demonstrations, never made me have to go to see the Head to plead insanity on her behalf, who never made me late for work, you mean? Well, now, that's a different matter,' he said, laughing with her. 'But seriously, Bobby, parents love kids for themselves. They sometimes give you a hard time, but that's part of testing boundaries, deciding their own values and beliefs. Not just being clones of their parents.'

'God forbid!' she said cheekily.

'Yes, and you've got nothing to fret about on that score, young lady! I've got my faults too, I'm well aware of that. And my parents probably despaired of me at times and wondered how I'd turn out. But one thing's for sure. They loved me. Just as your mum and I love you, navel-stud, dyed hair, lazy streak and all!'

'And you reckon it'd be like that if you had a kid specially for one of us if we got sick, yeah?'

'I honestly think it would, although none of us can say for sure until we're in that situation.'

'So, d'you think this family – the one on the news – should have a kid like that?'

'Strictly twixt thee and me? Yes. Yes, I do.'

'What d'you do if these committees say you can't do it, then?'

'Keep fighting.'

'And will the folk out there in the real world that say you shouldn't, come after you?'

'Some will. Undoubtedly. But as long as they stick to verbal discussion, and gun for me and not the family, I'm game for that. This is serious stuff with massive consequences, it raises huge questions, so it's only right there should be debate about the ethics. It's the other stuff, the things you and I talked about the other day, when Dan Cruse and his pal – what was he called? – Reuben something – got you roped into their seedy little activities – then I start to get angry. People who're prepared to do damage to others to further their own opinions.'

'But maybe *they'd* argue *you're* the one doing the damage. Forging ahead because you've got the technology and the knowledge and it's what you do. They might think that's you damaging other folk just to get *your* way.'

'They probably do. So what d'you suggest? Do nothing until everybody agrees? We wouldn't help infertile couples at all in that case.'

'Well, maybe we shouldn't. Maybe that's their bodies trying to tell them something. I mean, seems to me, from what I've read, lots of these folk who can't have kids normally, well, they have all this stuff done to them, jiggering up their systems and everything, making loads of eggs and stuff, but then they have several kids at once and they're born too little, or they have things wrong with them and they die, or they have awful lives. Maybe these folk would be better not to have any kids. Maybe nature knows best.'

Justin sighed. 'Oh Bobby, who knows? I've seen things go right; I've seen things go wrong. We never know which way they'll go. I wish I *could* tell. We can only try. Who am I, with three healthy daughters, to deny others that fulfilment?'

She tipped her head on one side and surveyed him quizzically.

'Why *did* you choose infertility, Dad?'

'It chose me, I think. A vacancy came up; I applied, got it, and before I realised it, I got sucked into the excitement and the satisfaction that comes when you pit your wits against nature and win. I guess.'

Bobby stood picking her cuticle before she spoke again.

'Did you and Mum want a boy?'

The question took him by surprise.

'Actually we weren't bothered either way. I suppose it'd have been nice for me to have an ally, instead of being ganged up on by four women, but no, we were quite happy with you three girls. Why?'

'Well, I was thinking, if you could've, would you have done things to make sure you had a boy? If you'd really wanted one, I mean.'

'No, I can honestly say I wouldn't. Even back then, there were all sorts of ideas of what things to do – as in, ordinary, non-invasive, everyday things – to make it more likely that you have one or the other gender, but we didn't even try any of those things. We were quite happy to take what we were given.'

'In the beginning, anyway,' she added with a grimace.

He laughed.

'But say you knew,' she persisted, 'we might be born with some horrible illness, one of those things that runs in families. I mean, before we were born, before we were conceived, would you have tried to stop that?'

'Yes, I probably would. For the sake of the child as well as for us.'

'And is *that* fair, d'you think?'

'Fair? I'm not sure if it's fair or not. Depends what balance you weigh it in, I guess. But at a micro level, if I could spare a child suffering a disproportionate burden of pain or suffering, and give the chance of a happy, healthy life to another one instead, then yes, I'd say that's fair.'

'But if I was a kid with that same thing wrong with me, you know what? I'd think it was pretty naff if you chucked another me in the bin because you didn't like the thought of having a kid like me. I mean, it sort of devalues the life of somebody who's got a disability, doesn't it? I think it kind of stinks. We've got this girl in our year – Elspeth McGregor – in a wheelchair and she talks all twisted, and can't do sports and stuff, and she has to get helped to the toilet. I'd *really* hate that. I don't hate *her*, but I feel sorry for her, and I guess you shouldn't do that either. But you can't help it.'

'Actually, Bobby, I think there's a distinction between valuing an existing disabled person, and not wanting to bring more suffering and pain like theirs into the world. If there's a choice.'

She twirled one of her ear studs as she thought about this. Justin watched, wondering where she would go next.

'I'm glad you're my dad. You're so... *sane*!"

It was so unexpected, so uncharacteristic, that Justin was robbed of words. But before he could recover, Kate erupted into the room, all legs and excitement, and threw herself onto his back.

'Guess what, Pops,' she said in his ear, her arms draped around his neck in a suffocating embrace.

'You're planning to throttle me and take your inheritance and run,' he said, loosening her hold but retaining a grip on her wrists.

She gurgled in response. 'No. Better than that! I got chosen for the netball team for our big match next Saturday.'

'Brilliant. Well done, Katey Kitten.'

'Ace, eh? *And* I got to miss English with the dreaded Ms Townsend. I *hate* English!'

'Since when?' he enquired, swinging her gently from side to side.

'Since last week when she made us start reading *King Lear*. I *mean*! *Dire*! I wish I never had to read another book as long as I live.'

'*The man who does not read good books has no advantage over the man who cannot read them,*' quoted Justin, but with a twinkle she didn't miss.

'Was that the guy your technician's always going on about?'

'Oscar Wilde, you mean? No, darling, that was Mark Twain. Author of *The Adventures of Huckleberry Finn*? *Tom Sawyer*? Oh well, never mind.'

'Well, anyway, it's rubbish. Give me a netball or a hockey stick any day. Or even *maths*!'

Kate let go of him and slid across the floor on her stockinged feet to the fridge where she helped herself to a large glass of pineapple juice and downed it in one.

'Want one?'

'No, thanks.'

'Where'd Bobby go?'

'I was wondering that same thing myself,' Justin said.

'Did I interrupt something? Were you in the middle of giving her a rocket or something?'

'Not at all. We were in the middle of a very special father-and-daughter moment.'

'Aw, sorry, Dad.'

'No worries. You've just given me another one.'

She blew a kiss to him and skipped out of the kitchen singing, '*I'm going on a summer holiday*', at the top of her voice as she leaped up the stairs to her room.

Justin relaxed against the back of his chair and closed his eyes.

His thoughts returned to the news broadcast. Thanks to Lexie's accident, falling down the stone staircase in one of the turrets at school, he'd missed the interview with Natalie Wyatt. There had been no question: if the girls needed him, he'd be there. But in Bobby's words, was it fair? He'd potentially jeopardised the comfort of Yasmeen and Karim Zair for what turned out to be a relatively trivial family matter, a hairline fracture that would soon mend. He sighed again. That was life. You made choices.

Sometimes you couldn't get it right.

OK, maybe Scott Martindale hadn't observed the rules for deputising. Maybe he'd overstepped the line of discretion. But given the situation all over again, Justin would have done the same. And maybe it wasn't Scott who'd leaked the details; Natalie Wyatt had clearly heard things already by the time she phoned.

He stood up, arching his back, and went in search of Lexie to see what kind of a day she'd had. A blast of her trombone from behind the closed door stopped him. No point in disturbing her until practice was over.

Helen's return instantly brightened his mood. He enveloped her in an embrace.

'What's prompted *that*?' she said, eying him with suspicion.

'Have I told you lately that you are rearing some rather fine young women?'

'No, and if you did, I'd start to think you were having an affair, or Alzheimer's was setting in.'

'Charming!'

'What happened to, "D'you think we could hibernate until they've all passed the age of twenty-five?" Or have I been asleep for a decade?'

'Even the worst offenders have their moments.'

'If you say so. But hey, look at the time? Have you forgotten you're taking me to the Usher Hall tonight? And I refuse to go out with anyone wearing a red tie with a blue shirt.'

'I have *not* forgotten, but my time was better spent being a parent than titivating before a mirror.' He moved towards the door as he spoke. 'Actually, my dear, I can tell you a thing or two about our wayward daughters that might surprise you, but I'll leave that until we're in the car.'

## 29

SCOTT KEPT HIS face expressionless.

'No, I didn't listen to the news last night. I was working late. Why?'

'Well, it seems our little lady reporter might have sold her story on beyond the *Evening News*. I'd like to hear your side of things, to establish exactly what you *did* tell Ms Wyatt.'

This was one of those times when Scott wanted that unruffled exterior to crack – not wide open; just enough to see what Justin was really thinking.

'I told her we were one of the top centres in the UK. And how the pre-implantation genetic diagnosis test is done. That's about it really. Oh, and she wanted to know what an embryologist did.'

Justin threw him a look that seemed to say, *You sucker*.

'How long did she spend talking to you?'

'Well, she was hungry, so we went to get something to eat, so I guess… about three hours. Something like that.'

'An investigative reporter spends three hours talking to an expert at the cutting edge of controversial practices, and all you said was, we have a high success rate and what PGD involves?'

Scott shrugged.

'If you don't mind me asking, who paid for this meal?'

It rankled.

'She did actually. Insisted. Said it went on expenses.'

'So *she* saw it as work-related.'

'It was. She knew it was sensitive and she wanted to do her homework properly. She'd looked up past cases but she didn't know the first thing about the science. She didn't want to make a fool of herself, or upset people by getting it wrong.'

'So you didn't tell her anything about the Zairs?'

'I did not, and with respect, Justin, I take umbrage at the suggestion.'

'Fair enough, and I apologise for the question. But this woman got a lot of personal stuff from somewhere.'

'From a source close to the family, she told me.'

Justin was staring at him with a look on his face that shrieked, *Why the hell didn't you tell me that in the first place?*

'So, let me get this straight. She knew all about the Zair case already before she talked to you?'

'She did.'

'So, what was she asking from you?'

'How it would be done.'

'In theory.'

'Well, *I* said it would only be in theory.'

'Right. And who brought up the subject of the Opakanjos?'

'She did. Well, not by name, but her description meant it had to be them.'

'And how much did she know?'

'She said the story was already out there in the public domain – which was true. She wanted to know, in theory, where mistakes could happen. It gave me a chance to tell her how tightly it's all sewn up in our place.'

'I don't understand. Why would she spend three hours and a chunk of her hospitality budget when she could get most of that on the net for nothing?'

Scott felt a flush of something he couldn't name creep up his neck.

'She said it made more sense coming from somebody who actually did this sort of thing.'

'And she could legitimately claim to have the words of a spokesman from the hospital at the centre of the controversy – perhaps even the person doing the procedure.'

'Maybe. I remember she said it wouldn't look good if they

used what they had from the family side but nothing from us.'

'So your comment was?'

'Just what I told you.'

'So you didn't say the whole furore over PGD was a "storm in a teacup"?'

Something lurched in Scott's gut. 'I tried to downplay it as a little bit extra tagged onto IVF, which is a tried and tested procedure that everyone accepts.'

'How about the "HFEA is running scared" because of "a vocal minority"? Ring any bells?'

Scott shrugged.

'Does that mean you might have said that?' Now there was a sharpness in Justin's tone Scott hadn't heard before.

'I might have done. I daresay an odd opinion slipped in. But there was nothing about our actual cases. And in fairness, she didn't try to get any details. In fact, she said, if she was one of our patients she'd want us to respect her privacy and confidences.'

'I bet she would,' Justin responded dryly. 'But she *isn't* a patient, she's a journalist!'

No comment.

'Did you know she was selling it on?'

'No.'

Poor thanks for stepping in at short notice, sacrificing three hours of research time.

'Is there anything else I should know about, Scott?'

He hesitated. Then plunged.

'Since you ask, there is. I wasn't going to say anything, but if we're being frank here, I want it on record that I have serious reservations about one of the technicians. Jack Fitzpatrick. He's becoming a liability. If you're looking for leaky sieves you might do worse than look in his direction. His partner works in the surgery where the Opakanjos are patients. Pillow talk and all that.'

'You're seriously accusing Jack of...?'

*Now* the ears were pricked. Scott took heart.

'I don't like the way he's always sneaking around, in the lab all hours, on his own. And I'm not at all convinced his lab practices are all they should be either.'

'Since when have you noticed this change in his behaviour?'

'Difficult to pinpoint, but I'd say, since that mixup with the twins.'

'Are you suggesting…?

'There's nothing concrete, but I have my suspicions. He has the opportunity. And if he had made a mistake, he's bright enough to know what to do to cover it up.'

'You interviewed him, I take it?'

'Aye.'

'And did you feel then that he knew anything about the mix-up?'

'Well, he burbled on about how busy we were that day, a whole load of stuff about no time to clean things properly, and how maybe standards weren't as high as they should be, *because* we were so busy. I got the impression he was awfully anxious to make sure it was lab procedures that were suspect, rather than any individual. He wasn't comfortable. That's all I can say.'

'So when did you start to suspect he might be the weak link?'

'Well, it's… his manner. He has a kind of insolence lately. Like he's cock of the walk.'

'I'm surprised you haven't mentioned this before. Nothing came out of the formal inquiry. But I'll certainly have a word with him. I'm not prepared to tolerate insubordination or sloppy practice.' Justin frowned. 'Strange. I would personally have said he was one of our most reliable colleagues.'

'In the past, maybe. But I will say this, he's an Angus McCormack man. He's resented any changes we've made since Angus died. I know that for a fact.'

'I see. Well, thank you for that. And go canny with the media if you happen to bump into them again, Scott. In fact, say nothing.'

Nothing of this conversation leaked into the evening Scott spent with Natalie Wyatt later that same day.

He'd surprised himself by the invitation. It had been a long time since he'd asked any girl to take him away from his research. But there was something about this one. Was it her knack of making him feel valued? Was it that hint of ruthlessness? The way she listened to him, as if there was no place she'd rather be? The ash-blonde hair that made him want to run his fingers through it? Or those eyes?

Whatever the attraction, she was undoubtedly good company. And he couldn't remember the last time he'd had anyone remotely interested in the minutiae of his life.

This time he'd insisted: the meal was on him. She'd succumbed with a yielding gesture of her hands that had somehow lightened his heart. And this time there was no rusty bicycle, no sweat stains on his shirt, no rucksack.

They talked of holiday destinations, childhood memories, favourite composers, books they'd loved, disastrous meals they'd cooked. And the subject of work was off-limits by tacit agreement. Quite when she'd steered the conversation towards his research he didn't afterwards remember. But she was lying curled up on his settee, her head resting against his shoulder, her fingers weaving patterns on his forearm.

'What's the biggest passion in your life?' she asked him, not lifting her face.

'My research.' It was unhesitating. 'And yours?'

'My terriers.'

'Tell me about them.'

Both mongrels rescued from the local dog and cat home, Shaquita and Tyfany, 'all attitude and no breeding'. Her kind of creatures! Had to be housed in different rooms unless she was there to keep the peace. But there for her when she went home to an otherwise empty flat.

'And what about *your* great love? Tell me about your research.' She snuggled in closer as she said it, lacing her fingers through his.

'You don't want to know. It's not all romantic and personal

like your dogs. It's boring old science to anybody else.'

'Come on! I'm sure it's not *boring* whatever else it is. Not if it's anything like your other work. It's fascinating. Convince me it's a worthwhile thing to do and you'd be much better being there right now than here.'

'Not at all. I hope you aren't getting that impression. I've had a great evening.'

'And it ain't over yet,' she said in a sultry voice.

A smile softened his face.

'My research? Why do I do it?' He paused. 'Because I want to eradicate diseases that destroy human beings.'

'Well, that sounds about Nobel Prize level for ambition. Can you give me a clue what it means in real terms?'

'At the moment, I'm doing something that nobody's ever tried before. If it works – *if* it works – we should end up with the ability to take a person with a degenerative disease – Huntington's, Muscular Dystrophy, Parkinson's, that sort of thing – and regenerate the damaged tissue. Give them back a life. And hopefully, in time, eliminate that disease altogether.'

'You're kidding me.' She leaned back at arms length the better to check his expression.

He shook his head. 'No, that's the aim.'

She gave a low whistle. 'Reaching for the sky, then! And how far away from utopia would you say you are now?'

'Ten, maybe twenty years, from it being available in clinical practice to real live people. Before then it would have to be *tested* – with selected humans.' He stopped abruptly.

'So. A cure for horrendous diseases. And you thought I'd find it *boring*?'

He threw her a sheepish look. 'You'd be bored by the science.'

'Out of my depth anyway, that's for sure. Wow! A cure!'

'That's the *theory*, anyway. And I'm convinced it *can* be done. But there's a way to go yet. More trials. Bigger samples.'

'And when you say it's your passion, you mean it.' She was looking at him with an expression in her eyes that made something melt somewhere deep inside.

'Sorry! Nerd. Geek. Saddo. That's me.'

'You're kidding. There's nothing remotely nerdish about what you're doing. But what made you go down this particular route?'

His face closed down. 'It's personal.'

'Sorry. I didn't mean to pry. Forget I asked.'

But the apology didn't repair the rift.

She sat up, uncurled her legs and started to put her shoes on.

'You're not going?' His voice sounded like a schoolboy's.

'I think I might just have outstayed my welcome,' she said, with a rueful half-smile.

'No, please. It wasn't you. It's… delicate. I'll explain. How about another drink?'

By the time he'd poured and brought the glasses back to the sofa, he was in control again. He sat down close enough to feel her leg against his, the silky fabric of her skirt…

Scott slid his arm around her, drawing her head under his chin, where she couldn't watch his expression. She laid a tentative hand on his thigh and waited.

'It's my brother, Lochlain. He's two years younger than me. My parents had him at home until he was twenty-five, but then my dad had a stroke and my mother, well, she couldn't deal with both of them. So Lochlain went into sheltered accommodation. He's in a wheelchair now. He just about copes; folk come in several times a day to give him a hand. During the bad times he needs round-the-clock care. But one day he'll need residential care – unless I get my cure out before then.'

'And what's wrong with him?'

'Multiple sclerosis. It's unusually rapid in his case. With pretty much no remission.'

'Oh, Scott. How awful. How truly awful. For you as well as for him.' She wrapped both arms around him and held him tight.

He couldn't speak. But she must have felt him trembling.

'And d'you get to see him?'

'Whenever I can. But he's up in Thurso. I wanted to transfer him closer to me, but my mother – well, she isn't too keen on me taking him away from them.'

'It must be devastating for them. No wonder you're passionate about finding a cure. What a driving force!'

'Actually,' he said into her hair, 'I'd be grateful if you didn't mention this to anybody else. I don't talk about it. It's personal.'

'Don't worry, I *wouldn't*. But thanks for sharing it with me. D'you have any other brothers or sisters?'

'Nope. Only Lochlain. And you?'

'Three sisters and one brother. I'm the eldest and the rest of them all live in the Kent and Sussex area. I blame their aberrations on the horrible water down there!'

She'd lightened the mood and they were back in his comfort zone again.

It was a novel experience for Scott asking a girl if she'd care to stay the night. He did a mental tally of which towels he'd used in the bathroom, where his underwear was, what reading material lay beside his bed. But for once his own excessive orderliness and his predecessor's latest gadgetry were an asset not a default position.

When she accepted he felt a surge of gratitude; when he woke to her hair in his mouth he smiled; when she offered to cook him breakfast he allowed himself his first late arrival at work. Ever.

## 30

YASMEEN'S HEART WAS THUDDING as she entered The Pemberton Centre.

Two women had accosted her at the gate, their faces too close as they hissed, 'These people are playing God. Don't let them mess with your life.'

She'd almost grabbed their leaflet and walked on.

'Babies are a gift from God. He wouldn't want you to tinker with nature,' came after her.

She'd stuffed their leaflet into her bag. One look was enough. She told herself, they didn't know who she was; it wasn't personal. But it was a relief to get inside. To find Karim waiting for her.

'You OK, honey?'

'Nervous,' she said, 'but better now you're here.'

The waiting room was mercifully empty. Lily-May was her usual friendly self, asking about the children, listening, genuinely concerned.

All morning Yasmeen had been steeling herself for rejection; now she clung to this last thirty minutes of hope. Twenty minutes... sixteen... ten... nine... She hunched her cashmere jacket closer around her. She picked up a magazine, letting her eyes roam idly over the stick-thin models, celebrity weddings, true-life stories. The kind of drivel she would never normally look at, let alone buy.

A headline arrested her attention: *Mother Reunited With Baby She Thought She'd Lost For Good.* Her thoughts leapt to Destiny.

But this was a toddler who'd been snatched in a supermarket. Ten months – *ten months!* – the police, the family, the entire neighbourhood, searched. Nothing. Then for no apparent reason the abductor gave herself up; a middle-aged woman with an unfulfilled craving for a child. She'd cosseted the girl, dressed her in designer clothes, fed her all her favourite foods. The child skipped into the police-station hand-in-hand with her kidnapper, happy and confident. She was carried out two hours later, screaming and kicking. She felt betrayed and abandoned, the psychologists said. It took weeks of careful work by experts to forge again the bonds that had been severed.

For Destiny Opakanjo there would be no memory, no link to at least one of her natural parents.

'Mr and Mrs Zair, would you like to come this way?'

Yasmeen reached across to Karim; his hand closed firmly round hers, the pulse pounding in his wrist.

The warmth of Justin Blaydon-Green's smile was heartening, the strength of his handshake encouraging. But Yasmeen knew a sinking feeling. *He was being extra kind; the news was bad.*

'How's Sebastian?' 'And you?' Normal, unexceptional questions. *Just say it! Say it! Get it over.*

He took his time. *He doesn't want to tell us.*

'Of course, I realise the possibility of having a saviour sibling has been haunting you for a long time now. It must be hard to take a break from thinking about it. But have you, by any chance, had any change of heart? Are there any doubts, any questions, you want to talk about?' *Maybe he'll still fight for us even though it hasn't gone our way so far.*

Yasmeen vaguely heard Karim's solid conviction. She watched the doctor lean towards them, his eyes flicking from one to the other. Kind eyes. Smiling eyes.

His voice seemed to come from a long way away. 'Well, since your minds are made up, and I have no doubt as to your understanding of what's involved, I can tell you' – he paused – 'we have been granted permission to carry out this procedure for you.' Then, seeing Yasmeen's expression, he added with a twinkle, 'I take it you weren't expecting this?'

'I was sure you… were trying to prepare us for rejection,' she said shakily.

Karim released her hand and turned his own to show the nail marks in his skin.

'So it seems!'

Both men were smiling at her.

'Thank you, thank you so-o-o much!' she breathed.

'Yes, thank you, Dr Blaydon-Green.' Karim reached across to grasp his hand. 'We know this has involved a lot of work on your part.'

The rest of the conversation was lost on her. Over and over she told herself: We can do it! This is for Sebastian. We *will* do it! When could they start? She wanted to get away, tell her mother, Pia, Sebastian himself. Candice. Oh, *everyone*!

For some reason she didn't analyse too closely, Yasmeen decided not to phone Candice. She'd go round in person the following afternoon once Karim was home from school to care for Sebastian and Shahira.

It was Samuel who let her in; Candice was in the living room playing with the twins. Yasmeen's attention was arrested. They hadn't known she was coming but Candice's hair was neatly braided and threaded with rainbow coloured beads, her blouse was stain-free, her trousers smartly pressed. Her smile was wide and warm.

Samuel turned towards the door, but Yasmeen said, 'Do stay, if you can spare a few minutes. I won't be long. I wanted to come and tell you in person because you've both been so kind about Sebastian. We've been given the go-ahead! We can try to have a baby – a match for Sebastian.'

'Oh, Yasmeen!' Candice cried out, startling Destiny whose bottom lip quivered. 'Oh, if anyone deserves this, you do.'

'I'm not sure about deserving, but we're thrilled. At last! I can hardly believe it myself.'

'That's brilliant news,' Samuel said quietly. 'I hope it all works out.'

'Thanks. All we can do is try, and if it's meant to be it'll happen.'

She declined their offer of a drink and ten minutes later left them with their insistence ringing in her ears.

'No more cooking or ironing for us. You need to keep all your energy for this new baby, and take care of *yourself* for a change. But you will stay in touch? I shall want a blow-by-blow account of how everything's going. And when your baby's born perhaps we can start a mother-and-baby group, eh?'

Karim was playing a game of Hedgehog with Shahira and Sebastian and for once she felt no resentment for the untidy floor, the sticky rings on the worktop. Their happiness, their safety, was far more important than her pernickety standards.

She stood watching the three glossy dark heads bent over the board, absorbed in the competition. They'd been a family of four for so long now, how would everyone respond to a new addition? Four made for natural pairing – for games, for trips to the toilets at motorway stations, for sharing seats on fun rides, for twin beds, for ferrying them around, for assisting with homework.

It was weird, this detachment. Now the initial euphoria was passing, her inner mood felt hollow. What if...?

Not until the children were safely in bed did she share anything of her conflict. Karim held her close and listened to her stream of doubts. Was she too old? What if none of the embryos matched? What if they were too late for stem cells to work? What if...?

'You know your trouble?' he said lightly. 'You've spent the last umpteen weeks reminding yourself of all the good things about staying just as we are, and now you've got to start telling yourself *this* is the best news.'

Before she could reply the phone rang.

Karim wore a strange expression as he held the phone out to her. 'It's Samuel Opakanjo. Wants to speak to you.' He covered the mouthpiece and whispered, 'Remember you've *got* to rest now – for Bassy's sake.'

She took the receiver.

'Hi, Samuel. Something wrong?'

'No. Quite the opposite actually, and I wanted you to be the first to know.'

'Oh.'

'After you'd gone this afternoon, Candice and I had a really good talk. She was in such a good mood about your news that I thought there probably wouldn't be a better opportunity to mention what I said to you.'

'And?'

'She said the thought had occurred to her too, and maybe we should get Destiny tested. No way is she giving her up – and fair enough, I don't want her to. But at least we'll have the information. And, hopefully, we'll come to some agreement about what we do with it. Now we're properly talking again I think we will.'

'Oh, I'm so glad. That *is* good news. A red-letter day all round.'

It was well after midnight when Yasmeen and Karim stood looking down at Shahira spread-eagled across the bed, her hair like a dark waterfall hanging down to the floor.

'She's going to be a beauty, like her mum,' Karim whispered in the darkness.

'So mature in many ways, still a babe in others,' Yasmeen's voice was a caress.

Out on the landing they lingered in a long kiss before sneaking into Sebastian's room.

The little ghost light beside his bed was enough to show that the bed was empty.

He was lying on the floor.

In a stride Yasmeen was at his side, feeling his forehead, checking his breathing.

'Phone for an ambulance, Karim. *Now!*'

The paramedics took one look at the child and instantly began preparations to transfer him. Perdita arrived seconds behind them and Yasmeen gave her a rapid update before racing out to the car. Karim had the engine already running for the dash to the Sick Children's Hospital in the wake of the screaming ambulance.

'I *hate* leaving Shahira without preparing her,' Yasmeen said through her shivering. She hadn't stopped even for a coat; it had been so hot beside Sebastian's fever.

'Can't be helped. No point waking her, she'd only be exhausted for school. She'll understand. As long as Bassy's OK, she'll cope.'

'Poor kid, taking second place so often. All the broken promises, plans changed at the last minute. It's a wonder she trusts us at all.'

The rest of the night passed in a whirl of confusion. The gravity of the doctors, the silence around Sebastian, the palor that replaced his feverish flush, spoke for themselves.

Yasmeen and Karim spoke little, huddling together for comfort, the joy of yesterday's promise eclipsed by tonight's dread.

'What if we'd already started on another pregnancy?' Yasmeen whispered, when yet another doctor had shaken his head and gone away.

'Don't even go there. He's a fighter, our Sebastian.'

# 31

IN SPITE OF TREPIDATION about his appointment with Justin, Jack was in buoyant mood when he arrived for work that Thursday morning. Patsy had actually started looking at jobs in various places and seemed much more upbeat about the possibility of moving.

'Best not to say anything, remember,' he'd had to caution her.

'You're not the only one that can keep secrets,' she retorted, with a toss of her head that set her earrings jangling.

'I hope you're not going to be disappointed if this thing fizzles out.'

'What d'you take me for?'

'A snazzy little number who lights my match every time.'

'Huh! I never know if you mean it or not.'

'Come on! You know you do.'

'I'm not sure I even know what you're on about,' she said huffily.

'Sometimes I hardly know myself,' he said in an affected drawl. 'No, but don't you feel even a tinsy bit excited at the prospect of your man maybe blowing a scandal that could hit the 6 o'clock news? "*Sleuth technician exposes hospital disgrace.*" Pretty good headline, don't you think?'

'If I thought for one minute you had the balls, I might start to get a bit excited, but since when did Jack anything-for-a-quiet-life Fitzpatrick stick his neck out? Nope. You wouldn't.'

'So what did you think I was on about when I asked you whether you'd follow me to the ends of the earth if I blew the whistle?'

'Well, you haven't, have you?' she said tartly.

'Not yet, no.'

'There you go.'

'I've been waiting for the right moment, that's all. Actually, today might just be the day I *do* say something.'

'"Today" as in Thursday?'

'Yes.'

'Before the sun goes down tonight?'

'The very same.'

'Is this another of your wind-ups, Jack?'

'Nope. On my honour as a wimp and a procrastinator. The boss has called me in for a meeting this morning, and if it feels like the right time, I might spill the beans. Depends. But I might.'

'*Depends*. You *might*. See what I mean?'

'Well, I don't know what he wants me for. Maybe he's promoting me to second-in-command. I mean, you wouldn't want me to risk turning down a million a year now, would you? See, that's one example of a not-quite-right moment.'

'There you go again. Can't you just be sensible for two minutes?'

'Sure. Synchronise watches! Two minutes coming up!' And with a flourish Jack swung his wrist round to lie alongside hers.

She wrenched her arm from his grasp and hissed through her teeth, 'You know something, Jack, I'm seriously wondering about whether I want to come with you if this is the way you're going to carry on. For goodness' sake, *grow up!*'

'Ah, now, growing up. That's something I *did* want to pass by you when the mood was right. Say I was to make a mighty effort and take a flying leap past the adolescent phase, I was wondering if you and I might start to think about adding to the Fitzpatrick/Graham household.'

'What on *earth* are you whiffling on about?'

'Babies. Or at least, a baby, singular. Unless you fancy twins or triplets or more. But one would do for starters. Practice run.

How would you fancy trying to make a littl'un for our personal use and pleasure?'

Patsy's face was a study in incredulity. 'Are you *serious?*'

'Yes.'

'You want... *us* to have... a *baby*?'

'Well, I kind of laboured under the delusion that you wouldn't be too keen on me breezing up to some other dame and asking her to do it for me instead.'

Right in front of him two tears rolled down her cheeks, leaving twin tracks in her impeccable make-up. Jack was instantly contrite; Patsy wasn't the weeping kind. He held her against his shoulder, rocking them both to and fro.

'I'm sorry, sweetheart. Really I am. I didn't mean to make you cry. But you know me; not good at the touchy-feely stuff. If you hate the idea I'll never mention it again. Promise. Heck! *I* wouldn't choose me to father my babies either! Forget I even spoke. Me and my nonsense.'

Suddenly he was absolutely unable to rattle on any more. His mouth was clamped to Patsy's, and she was robbing him of any thought but the armful of womanhood pressed against the length of his body at this precise moment.

When she finally moved far enough away for him to see her, he could only stand open-mouthed and – for once – silent.

'Yes, you crazy loon. Yes, I'll have your babies. You drive me insane, but I love you. Heaven knows why, but I do.'

'You will? You do?'

'Yes.' Her eyes were sparkling through the tears. Jack kissed first one, then the other, with a tenderness that brought a fresh flood.

'Maybe there's hope for you yet,' she wept, running her hand down his cheek.

'On which happy thought I'd better stir my stumps and get to work. We'll talk more tonight, yeah?'

'We'll do more than talk.'

He laughed. 'Now that's a promise I like the sound of.'

'How about we go out for a meal, instead of me cooking?'

'Hey, you don't get to put your feet up till you've done the work! And by then you'll be feeling too sick for a gourmet meal.'

Another long kiss made him smug as well as late. But her parting shot brought reality coursing through his veins.

'If you tell the boss today, will you be out on your ear tonight?'

'Doesn't work like that. Besides, Doc B-G may be the biggest giant in the outfit, but he sure is a friendly one.'

'Now you're talking! If you can quote Roald Dahl instead of that Oscar Wilde I'll be a happy woman.'

'In case it's escaped your notice, I haven't quoted my friend once this morning. There's restraint for you!' And with a jaunty wave he pedalled off down the road.

Twice that morning Scott asked him tetchily to stop sizzing. If he was surprised by Jack's compliance he said nothing. But Jack derived inner satisfaction from being able to deny him other requests.

'Can you get that lot checked and catalogued by lunchtime?' Scott said, waving his arm in the direction of a new delivery of stock.

'Not possible, I'm afraid,' Jack said, concentrating on dripping liquid into a petrie dish.

'I beg your pardon?' Scott's words emerged like king-sized porcupines.

'I can't. Sorry,' Jack threw over his shoulder, moving to the fridge with a smirk on his averted face.

'Now you listen to me, Fitzpatrick,' Scott hissed in his ear the second Jack closed the door. 'I've pretty much had enough of your bloody insolence. When I ask you to do something, you damn well do it, you hear?'

'I hear perfectly well, but Dr Blaydon-Green's prior instruction makes it impossible for me to comply with your demand.'

'What instruction?'

'To be in his office 11.30 sharp.'

'For what?'

'I have no idea.'

'You're lying.'

Jack swung round to stare straight into the glowering eyes. His voice was icily polite. 'I object to that accusation.'

'I don't give a damn about your objections. If I say you check the stock, you'll bloody well check the stock. And I'll be speaking to Justin about this, mark my words.'

Justin's door was closed when Jack arrived two minutes ahead of schedule. At precisely 11.30 he rapped twice.

'Ah, Jack. Come in. Coffee?'

'Are you...?'

'Yes, I'm having one and I'd like your opinion on this blend – I'm still trying to decide if I like it or not. It's Brazilian medium roast. A smoother richer taste, it says on the packet.'

It wouldn't occur to him that until Patsy came on the scene Jack had never bothered with anything other than instant from a jar. While the coffee gurgled its way through the machine, Justin leaned back in his chair, steepled his fingers, and started on his agenda.

'So, as I said the other day, I've been to see Emma.'

'And how is she?'

'A bit sore about the way things panned out, naturally enough, but appreciative of your support. She's got a couple of interviews lined up and I'd say she's in with a good chance with one of them. She gave me permission to pass that on. Our loss, of course.'

Jack opened his mouth to ask about the reason she'd left but closed it again.

'Right, Jack, let's not beat about the bush. Emma's the tip of the iceberg. We both know that. Things are not good in the lab these days, and I've been getting complaints from various quarters. How about you fill me in on your version of things.'

'When you say complaints, d'you mean about *me*?'

'One complaint was about you, yes.'

'From Dr Martindale, I presume?'

'You presume correctly.'

Jack looked at Justin, unsure how to respond.

'Am I allowed to know what he accused me of?'

'Sloppy practice. An agenda of your own. "Insolence" was, I think, the word he used. How's that for starters?'

'"Sloppy practice"! Where's *that* coming from? The only thing that's sloppy round here... well, never mind. But "insolence" – well, I guess I knew that was coming.'

'And is it justified?'

'Not from where I'm standing, no.'

'So why d'you think Scott said that?'

Jack swallowed hard. 'Do I have to say? Seems like schoolboy stuff when you repeat it. And it doesn't feel right – telling.'

'I'd appreciate your version, if you could. Seems to me this has gone a bit beyond playground banter.'

Justin got up and poured the coffee.

Jack took advantage of his back view. 'Well, the thing is, I object to being called a liar. It's one thing that sticks in my throat. Goes back to... Well, anyway, I reckon we need to be able to trust each other in this job, and once you get a reputation for lying, I don't see how you can work in a team like this one.'

'Fair comment. And what were you supposed to be lying about?'

'What you wanted to see me about.'

'Now you've lost me. Roll back to the beginning.'

'Scott asked me to do some cataloguing and stuff before lunchtime. I said, sorry, I couldn't – politely. He said if he told me to do something I'd better do it – or else.'

'Not so politely, huh?' Justin interrupted with a shrewd look.

Jack offered nothing more on that topic.

'Anyway, I told him I couldn't because you'd asked me to be here. He said, what for? I said I didn't know. He called me a liar. I took exception. You didn't tell me, did you?'

'No.'

'And that was it. He said he'd report me. So I guess I knew this was coming.'

'Except that he hasn't been to see me this morning.' Justin paused. Jack's tension mounted exponentially. 'His complaint was actually some days ago. And it was about your attitude in general. He feels you have no respect for him and that you resent the changes he's made since he came. He sees you as a McCormack man. And I guess at heart that's true, eh?'

Only when he was certain his voice was under control did Jack venture a response.

'He was a good man, Doc McCormack. Salt of the earth. Knew his team. And he'd pitch in and work alongside you. You knew where you were with him.'

'I know. And I agree. He was an excellent team leader. So is there more to this than Scott not being Angus?'

Justin sat back waiting and Jack knew it was now or never.

'Look, this is hard for me. But there are some things I think you ought to know. Only now it looks as if I'm just trying to get my own back. But I'm not. I've been thinking about this for ages, and trying to find out for sure before I said anything.'

'OK. In your own time, Jack.'

'Well, d'you remember when you thought you saw somebody on my bike at 2 in the morning?'

Justin nodded.

'Well, it was *me*. And I've been in other times too when nobody was here.'

'Why would that be?'

'Because I *know* something's not right. Something went wrong for those twins, and I'm pretty sure I know what it was. And I know other things too. But it sounds so far-fetched I didn't think anybody'd believe me. Besides, I'm not keen on accusing folk of things. Specially not people who work hard and get things done.'

'And what do you suspect, Jack?'

'Well, I was double-checking that time. The Opakanjos, I mean. Only Scott cleaned the sperm before I came in, and I only checked the fertilisation. That's one of the changes, see. When Angus was here he reckoned you needed two of you all the time. For everything. It was no hassle. Everybody knew why. Everybody did it. No exceptions. But Scott wanted his own space. He didn't want folk breathing down his neck twenty-four seven, he said. He was too busy for all this doubling up. So he'd do bits of it himself.'

Jack broke off, darting looks at Justin, gauging the temperature.

'And to be fair, Jack, we have been busier than we've ever been. We're in competition with other centres of excellence. And since Scott came our success rate has rocketed.'

'Ah well, that's another thing,' Jack said through set teeth. 'Success rates. But I'll come to that in a minute.' There! Now he'd *have* to say it all. Timbuktu here we come!

Justin was studying him intently. The end result seemed like a foregone conclusion: this was a big hungry cat stalking a gazelle – he might as well go down with a clear conscience.

'The day of the Opakanjo fertilisation, like I said, I'm doing the checking. When I come in, there are these two pipettes lying on the bench and it looks to me like one of them's been used and one's new. So Scott gets out the eggs and we check them. Then the sperm. And it's all OK, names, numbers, everything. And then he picks up this pipette to draw up the sperm. Only I say, "I think that's been used." And, well... let's just say, he isn't best pleased, reckons I should stick to what I know and leave the real stuff to my "superiors". Anyway, he just goes right ahead and uses that pipette and seems to me, looking back, now we know about that coffee baby, well, stands to reason there could've been white sperm mixed in with those black ones quite easy.'

When he eventually spoke, it seemed to cost Justin something to keep his voice low and still. Thunderclouds were gathering in the eerie stillness before the storm.

'And you didn't see fit to tell me all this when the inquiry started?'

'I didn't have proof. Nothing concrete, only what I saw. It

was just my hunch. Scott was the senior, and I *had* questioned what he was doing at the time – it wasn't like I never said anything. And even so he went ahead. And after the twins, when I had to go and see him – you know, for those interviews – well, I mentioned it again then, but he just rubbished it. Seems to me you'd have said, "Well, he must have been sure." I mean, why else would he just ignore a direct challenge? Unless…'

'Unless?'

'Unless he was doing something deliberately. Or maybe he just resented me seeming to criticise him. Anyway I thought you'd take his word over mine.'

'*His* word is that you were the one who made the mistake.'

'He… said… that?'

'He did. Only he doesn't have proof either.'

Jack felt a wave of nausea.

'You said there was something else, Jack. About the success rates?'

'Well, you're not going to like this, either. But I hope you'll still see your way to giving me a reference.'

'Who said anything about you leaving?'

'Well, Scott, as it happens, but it's not because of him saying it. It's because I don't see how you can blow the whistle on your colleague and still stay put. Not in this job. We have to be a team. We have to trust each other. And, well, I can't – trust him, I mean. And now it looks like it's his word against mine. So that means one of us has to go, and that means it'll most likely have to be me.'

'I don't quite follow – why's Scott saying you'll have to go?'

'Because he reckons I'm insolent and a liar.'

'I see.' It was crushing. Jack felt suddenly very alone.

Justin drained his coffee cup before saying, 'Which leaves the matter of the success rates since Scott took over from Angus. What about those?'

There was nothing left to lose. At least Patsy couldn't say he'd chickened out this time. It fell out in a rush.

'I think somebody ought to test some of the embryos. The

ones where the quality of the sperm was poor. I reckon there's something fishy going on.'

The look on Justin's face made Jack falter to a stop.

'And this is based on?'

'Absences. Unmarked containers. Signatures. Behaviour. Sudden increase in rates.'

Silence.

'Could you elaborate?' Every word came out as if stunned.

'I'd rather not, Boss.'

After an age, Justin responded. 'If I get your drift, this is an extremely serious accusation.'

'I know.'

'This isn't retaliation, is it, Jack? For Scott accusing you.'

'No. Besides he's hinted the same to Emma, and Nina, and Zubin – to my certain knowledge. It's like he's trying to make everybody doubt themselves. Folk are getting pretty scunnered, and it wouldn't surprise me if more don't leave if it goes on like this. It's not a happy place any more, Boss. Not like it was...'

'In Angus McCormack's day.' Justin finished for him.

'Well, it's not, and that's a fact.'

Silence fell again.

When Justin next spoke his voice sounded different, like he'd stretched it tight over a drum and he couldn't get any variation in pitch. It took a few goes to get the elasticity back.

'I must confess, I had no idea this was coming, and at this precise moment I'm not exactly sure how best to proceed. Obviously I can't ignore your suspicions. If your hunch has any substance, the HFEA will have to be involved. They have the clout to remove anything, test anything, so you'd get your proof if it exists. But this would have huge ramifications. You do realise that, don't you, Jack? Not only for the team, but for patients.'

Jack cringed. How many lives would be devastated by his accusation? Would it have been better to let everyone carry on in ignorance?

But Justin was still speaking.

'...and I realise this puts you personally in a very difficult position. If your hunch turns out to be unfounded then, of course, your place here will have to be reviewed. If your theory proves to have some foundation in fact then, well, frankly, God help us all.'

Jack nodded.

'D'you think you can continue working in the lab as before, until such time as I talk to you again about this?'

'I'll give it a go anyway.'

'Knowing that your suspicions are being taken seriously enough to investigate. Which means you can stop being detective yourself.'

Jack nodded again.

'It's in everyone's best interests to keep the work going as normally as possible.'

Jack hesitated. 'Can I ask you something else? – something that's bothering me big time.'

'Certainly.'

'*You'll* be all right, won't you? I mean, last thing I want is for *you* to be in the firing line.'

'Hard to say. Depends what comes out of this. But if it's as you suspect and I knew nothing about it, then I'm not legally accountable.'

'And The Pemberton itself? They wouldn't close us down or anything, would they?'

'Well, they have the *power* to withdraw our licence, as you know. But they wouldn't do that if the problem was confined to one individual doing his own thing. But if their concerns are more widespread – then they might.'

'See, that's what I was afraid of. I don't want *you* to get it in the neck. And I don't want to be the one to close down the whole shebang. If you think they might do that, then maybe I need to think again.'

'Too late for that. No, you were right to tell me, and I'm grateful you found the courage. Leave it with me now.'

Justin stood up. Jack followed suit.

'Thank you, Jack. I'll be as discreet as I can be. And I trust you will be too. We both know the damage this could do if it gets out.'

'My lips are sealed.'

Jack's legs were shaking so badly it took a huge effort to walk from the room.

## 32

IT HAD BEEN a very, *very* long day. Yasmeen laid down her crocheting, her eyelids drooping. Sebastian had taken hours to settle after a fractious afternoon. There was only so far a mother could go with inventing games, offering distraction; some days the patient was miserably consumed by his illness, and no amount of cajolery or threat could win him round. It was a relief when sleep finally claimed him.

She hardly dared to move lest she disturb him.

Within Sebastian's cubicle life held its breath; outside it a hustle of activity continued. Through the glass partitions she watched the nurses darting from room to room. She knew them all. She heard the low keening of a child too weak to cry lustily, the occasional jubilant shout of an older patient winning at an electronic game, the distant chatter of a television. During snatched breaks she'd met most of the other parents and knew their stories. It was a curious consolation knowing that others inhabited a world much like their own, tiptoeing through the antiseptic environment, isolated from normality, in daily dread of a crisis which would prove to be the last, carrying a constant burden of guilt for the sorrows and deprivations imposed on the rest of the family, taking nothing for granted, not even the next breath.

Karim had wanted to share the week's vigil, but she'd urged him to go on the fourth-years' field trip as arranged. 'Mum and Pia will be there for me. Sebastian's definitely over the worst. You can't penalise twenty-four youngsters who're simply trying to get good grades in their biology exams.' Nonetheless it was proving a heavy load to shoulder alone. Yasmeen dreaded the phone ringing when she wasn't at the hospital; she shrank from the sight of the consultant's approach when she was. But at least while she was with Sebastian she knew he was still alive, he had a fighting chance. Leaving him at night was like tearing her heart into pieces. Without Karim's steadying influence and the busyness of normal everyday life, her imagination took her into scary realms.

When Yasmeen eventually let herself into the house, Perdita was dozing in the chair, purple shadows ringing her eyes, her body slumped.

'Mum, you look tired out. You need a break from Shahira tomorrow.'

'Nonsense. She's been as good as gold. Wait till you see what she made for you after school today. I think you have a budding Delia Smith on your hands.'

'Pia says she'll take a turn. Why don't I ring her and see if she's free tomorrow? You have a complete day off.'

'No, really. It's only a few hours in the afternoon. It's something I *can* do.'

'Well, if you're sure. Shahira loves having you all to herself.'

'I love having *her* all to myself, too! How's Sebastian today?'

'Apart from being a little monkey, you mean? Well, they seem to have got the infection under control at last. His blood counts are improving. Drip's down. He's drinking well and he's even started eating more. And complaining! You know how he hates hospital food, but he loved the little boxes you packed up for him. All his favourites.'

'So is he really out of danger now?'

'This time around, yes. He should be home by the weekend.'

Perdita fished behind her for a scrap of paper she'd torn off an envelope.

'There was one phone call. From somebody called Cicely Felton? A BBC reporter. Wanting to talk to you about having a baby for Bassy.'

'That was all?'

'She left her number, and she said she'd ring back another time.'

'Right.'

Perdita was watching her daughter closely. '*Do* you want to talk about it?'

'If it helps society to accept the need for these procedures, yes. All these months of waiting for a decision – well, we could have had the baby by now, and Sebastian could be leading a normal life instead of yo-yoing back and forth to hospital, fighting for his life.'

But it wasn't that number she rang after her mother had gone.

'Karim?'

'Meena. How are things?'

It helped, talking the decision through with him. After all, he would be every bit as much in the firing line as she would. And the safety and privacy of Shahira and Sebastian were his responsibility too.

'D'you want me to ask this reporter to wait till you get home?' Yasmeen asked.

'If you want moral support. But I trust you to go it alone too. It's up to you.'

'I'll be glad when you get home. I've missed you. It's been a long week.'

'Me too.'

In the event the decision was made for her. At 9.30 that evening the phone rang again.

'Is it possible to speak to Mrs Yasmeen Zair, please?'

'Speaking.'

'Oh, Mrs Zair, I rang earlier. My name's Cicely Felton from the BBC. I'm so sorry to ring you at this hour, but I understand you aren't available during the day.'

'My little boy's in hospital, I'm spending most of the day there.'

'This would be your little boy with Diamond Blackfan's Anaemia?'

'Yes. Sebastian. He's only four so he needs someone familiar with him.'

'And how is he?'

'Improving, thank you.'

'It must be so worrying for you.'

Yasmeen choked back the sudden restriction in her throat.

'I realise this is a very personal and agonising experience for you and your family. I don't want to add to your troubles, but I was wondering if you would be willing to share your story with us? We'd very much like to draw attention to the need for these controversial treatments, to help the public see that sometimes every choice is a hard choice.'

'May I ask, is this for a short news item, or a longer piece discussing the issues, or a documentary, or what?'

'Just a shortish news item – at the moment anyway. With one or two experts giving the facts. But it carries so much more weight when the people most concerned tell their side of the story.'

'What d'you need to know?'

'Well, would it be possible for me to come round and ask you a few questions? Maybe bring a camera.'

'I'm at the hospital every day. And I'm very anxious not to have any information disclosed that would lead people to our home. We have to protect the children.'

'Of course. We'll respect that.'

'Could we perhaps talk on the phone, now?'

'I'd be happy to, if that suits you. Is it all right if I record this conversation – to be sure I get it right?'

'I think so. Yes.' Yasmeen took a deep breath. 'I gather from what you say, that you know quite a lot about us already. Could you tell me how you came by this information?'

'Well, most of it has come from other reporters. There was a clip on the radio and a short item in the *Evening News*. Did you see or hear either of them?'

'Someone showed me the *Evening News* piece.'

'That's what alerted us to the story in the first place. But they just reported the bare bones. I presume from your question that the story didn't come from you, then?'

'We haven't spoken to anybody about this.'

'And yet you're the people most nearly concerned. That doesn't seem fair to us. You ought to have the opportunity to tell your side of the story.'

'Thank you.'

'Perhaps I could tell you what we have already, and if anything isn't right you can correct it?'

'Fine.'

Her early facts were easily corroborated – names, ages, Sebastian's diagnosis.

'And you're seeking permission to have another baby who's a match.'

'We *were*.'

'I'm sorry. I thought…'

'We've now been given permission to go ahead.'

'You have? That's brilliant.'

Yasmeen warmed towards her questioner.

'I know there are no guarantees with this procedure, but could you tell me something about the problems, as *you* the family see them?'

'Well, number one: the success rate even for normal IVF is low. And number two, in our case, even if we do get embryos that are viable, we need a specific one – a match for Sebastian. Number three, the longer it takes, the older Sebastian gets, the lower the chances of the stem cells working for him.'

'Ohh.'

'And four, the older *I* get too, the lower the chances of IVF working.'

'I see. What was it that clinched the decision to go for a saviour sibling?'

'There wasn't much of a choice really. As I said, this is the only real cure for our son's condition.'

The questions segued into what if the next baby had the same condition? What did Yasmeen think about eliminating serious disorders? And slippery slopes to designer babies? And babies as commodities? What would she say to critics who condemned what she was doing?

Nothing she hadn't thought through a million times before. Yasmeen answered everything with honesty, emphasising that this was her view, what was right for her family.

'Mrs Zair, you've been wonderful. And it is so refreshing to get the family perspective articulated with such warmth and clarity. I hope this all works out for you and Sebastian.'

'Thank you. That's kind.'

'Now, I know you weren't keen on me bringing a camera, but do you perhaps have a photo we could use of you and your family? Or we could meet somewhere and take one ourselves if you'd rather. It's just that a picture – especially one of your little boy perhaps – would touch people at a different level.'

'I'd need to check with my husband. Could I maybe call you back?'

'By all means. Then I could come by tomorrow first thing if that would suit you.'

'Or maybe come to the hospital. I could meet you outside.'

'Perfect.'

Cicely Felton held the professional photograph in her hands like a priceless illustrated manuscript.

'Wow!' she breathed. 'A real heart-breaker! And he looks so happy.'

'He is,' Yasmeen said proudly. 'He isn't responsible for his looks, but he can take credit for his personality. He's very kind-hearted. I think his illness has made him more thoughtful than children normally are at that age.'

'He sounds gorgeous. And thank you so much for letting me borrow this photo of the four of you. I'll take great care of it.'

'You'll understand, it's rather precious.' Yasmeen's voice lingered softly over the thought.

Karim arrived home earlier than expected. Yasmeen had her back to him, stirring cheese into sauce for a lasagne – one of Sebastian's favourite dishes – and he watched her unseen for several minutes. The sparkle of tears on her lashes surprised him.

'I'm so sorry you've had all this to cope with in my absence.'

'Things will settle down again now Bassy's home.'

'A quiet weekend calls.'

'That would be good,' she said, layering the pasta and sauces. 'And you're back in time to watch the report about us this evening.'

'So as soon as my back is turned, my wife becomes a TV celebrity, eh?'

'I only hope I said the right things. Cicely seemed really nice, anyway, not like that woman from the *News*. She understands about protecting the children.'

'I'm sure you did everything you could.'

'But you never know what it'll sound like when they pick and choose bits of what you say.'

'And how is our little fighter?'

'Tired. A bit aggrieved that he missed out on all the activities Granny Dita did with Shahira. Bless her, she's promised to do similar things with him while Shahira's at school. But now Bassy's home we must make sure she gets some rest. Can't have her cracking up.'

'Or you.'

'So, tell me about your field trip. What mischief did the kids get up to this time?'

Yasmeen watched his animated face as he described the antics of the week. For a short time he lost the drawn look, and she saw again the man she'd married before Sebastian aged them both.

# 33

MAKING THE CALL to the HFEA was going to be tough. Admitting to mistakes was never comfortable, but identifying something more deliberate... Justin shuddered. Even as he rehearsed the issues a small voice mocked the credibility of such a story.

He'd agonised over how much he could alert Scott himself to the reason for this new and more stringent inspection. What *was* appropriate in such circumstances? But Scott gave no indication of having heard the oblique warning, not even about computers being removed, embryos being biopsied – things anyone in his position would normally – indeed *should* – have baulked at. With one eye on the clock and barely suppressed annoyance at the unscheduled delay, he seemed more preoccupied with catching his plane to Manchester, and the paper he was due to present at a conference the next day.

'I so have *not* got time for this,' he said. 'There are things I *have* to do before I leave. Clinical stuff. I can't let the patients down just because the HFEA have got their knickers in a twist over some piddling little thing. They'll just have to take us as they find us.'

By the time Justin got home from work and sat down to watch the news with Helen he had convinced himself his appearance in it would represent disaster number three.

He had mixed feelings about watching the programme with his daughters but Bobby, Lexie and Kate were already in front row seats. A preview would have been good. Had he expressed himself as well as he'd like? Had they distorted his words with their editing? Had they been sympathetic to the Zairs? It was uncomfortable having so little control.

But underlying this was a much more personal anxiety. Any publicity threatened his family. Since birth the girls had been shielded from the dangers attached to his job, but the perils were different now that they were moving outside his protective ambit. They were old enough to form their own opinions, go their own ways, select their own friends. They were at risk from the likes of Reuben Fox.

He leaned back in his chair and surveyed them one by one.

Bobby looked like a Hallowe'en spook. Black-clad and draped at right angles across the armchair, her bottom lost in the cushions, her knees angled over the broad arm, heels flicking against each other rhythmically, fingers twirling the hoops in her ears, she exuded a sense of latent energy, too pent up for rest.

Lexie lounged opposite her sister. Her navy-blue tracksuit, one leg ripped along the seam, had become her habitual garb in the evenings now that her plaster-cast made jeans an impossibility. With her leg covered in scrawled signatures elevated on the footstool as instructed, she looked like an eager fan awaiting the pen of a celebrity. Sensing his scrutiny she turned, her smile at once innocent and genuine. 'All my classmates are going to be watching you, Dad.'

'Oh dear. Let's hope I don't disgrace you then. But... wait a minute. How did they know? We only got the message this afternoon, while you were at school, to say it'd be on the evening news.'

All three girls groaned.

'Da–ad! Have you never heard of *texting*?' Bobby said, in her most patronising voice. 'You know, on a mobile phone – P. H. O. N. E. – you press these little pads and the words appear on the screen of the person you're texting.'

'Or a whole string of people you want to know about it,' Lexie beamed.

'Sorry!' Justin shared a speaking look with Helen, who'd long ago resigned herself to being left behind in the technology stakes.

Kate, still in her school shirt but sporting frayed jeans, with a huge red scrunchy and bandana keeping her curls under control, unravelled herself from the floor at his feet and jumped up into his lap, squirming until she was comfortably nestled against him.

'Well, *I* think it's cool having a dad who comes on TV as an expert. Anybody can send a text; nobody else's dad knows all about this stuff.'

'Well, thank you for that vote of confidence, Katey Kitten.' Justin gave her a hug.

'Shhh. Here it comes,' Helen interrupted.

There was nothing new in the main report: '*A family living in Scotland has just been granted permission to undergo a controversial procedure...*'

The bare bones of the story told, the anchor newsreader handed over to their science correspondent, Felix Ireland.

The journalists had done their homework. The facts about the Zairs were accurate, the approach sensitive, unsensational. And surely this level of detail, both fact and opinion, had to have come from the family themselves as they claimed. Justin certainly hadn't divulged it.

'Wheeey! There you are, Pops!' Kate cried, bouncing up to peer at the screen.

Justin dodged around her, watching critically. First an outline of the basic procedures for creating a donor sibling. Hmmm. It was measured and clear. Next the arguments for granting the Zairs their wish. He sounded rational at least, which had to count for something.

'*The fusion of egg and sperm is part of a process – the end result is a person with a unique genetic identity; a unique DNA.*' – showed his reverence for life.

'*But the very early stages of development are a far cry from the picture of a little fetus with all its organs and limbs, sucking its thumb, which is often presented. At the stage we're making choices it's simply a small clump of cells. Nothing recognisably human at all.*' – defused the emotion.

The interviewer, Cicely Felton, chipped in, more quickly than he'd noticed at the time. *'But I thought you said the individual person is there – in rudimentary form.'*

*'That's right. The genetic building blocks are there in that early embryo, the foundation for the emergence of this unique person who goes on to have rights and interests. But simply because the potential is there for it to become that person, it doesn't follow that early cluster of undifferentiated cells, that blastocyst, is that person.'*

The reporter bounced back. *'Well, maybe it isn't exactly the same, but even at the moment of conception it's an earlier version of the person it will become, isn't it? Only that blastocyst, that embryo, will become Jenny. Only this other blastocyst, or embryo, will become Peter or Harry. Surely. It's simply at an earlier phase of development.'*

Justin held his breath.

*'At a certain point that becomes true. But at the very beginning of embryonic life, although the potential is there, it needs all sorts of external conditions to be optimal for the process to continue, for those cells to become a human being. It requires further artificial procedures to turn this pre-embryo, this in-vitro entity, into a proper embryo capable of developing into a real human being. The main reason I don't personally think the early blastocyst is as yet a human being is that it has no ability to think or reason or have any consciousness of anything. The primitive streak hasn't yet formed.'*

Kate fidgeted in his lap.

'We did about the primitive streak in biology,' she whispered.

'Jolly good.'

Cicely Felton started talking before he finished. *'You could argue that old people with severe mental problems, or patients in a persistent vegetative state, don't have a mental life either. But would you say they aren't human? That you can mess around with their lives? Cut off their potential?'*

*'No, I wouldn't. But they've already established themselves*

*as unique human beings, worthy of full rights to dignity and life, and all the other rights that attach to being human.'*

'*This distinction isn't as clear for everyone,*' Cicely said. It was filmed in a different place, looking directly at the audience. Her frank gaze seemed to be saying, Don't believe a word of it.

A wave of disappointment washed over him. They hadn't used most of what he'd said. He had to force his mind to refocus on the screen.

'*There are many who see experimentation on, and destruction of, the early embryo as the thin end of a wedge leading to infringement of other rights and laws.*'

The introduction of adults with limited capacity and mental competence hadn't been a helpful tack to take from his point of view but, Justin had to admit, it led nicely for her to the critics.

First up was a pro-life campaigner, Melody Turner. She churned out the usual arguments, completely divorced from real-life ethical choices that he'd heard countless times before; but to many watching the news today they'd come as a dash of cold water against the Zairs' claims, against his own arguments. He tried to banish his preconceptions and listen fairly.

'*This procedure, IVF with PGD, involves a form of eugenics.*' Ms Turner almost sneered as she said it. '*It's destructive more than therapeutic. Human lives are being deliberately created but, because they don't fulfil certain arbitrary criteria, they are disposed of. These are perfectly healthy, normal embryos, with souls, destroyed simply because they aren't wanted, or are surplus to requirements. This barbaric practice commodifies life. Like I say, it's a form of eugenics.*'

Justin saw her eyes dart towards the reporter who was just out of vision. Presumably she saw enough encouragement to continue.

'*The rules keep sliding further and further towards the rights of women, away from the rights of the child. First the HFEA allows for destruction of embryos with diseases like muscular dystrophy and cystic fibrosis; cases where the embryo definitely has the affected gene and the child will certainly develop the disease. Then they allow eradication of embryos which have a susceptibility to a disease – things like breast cancer; diseases which may or may not'* – an eloquent pause – *'develop later in life, and even if they do, might be successfully treated. Where will it all end?'*

Her early premise was fair comment; Justin himself felt there was too much emphasis on women's rights too. But this line of argument didn't help in the Zair case which was ultimately about helping to *save* the life of a child with a disease, not obliterate him.

It was a relief to move away from this disgruntled woman with her rigid beliefs, but the reporter continued to stray from the argument for Yasmeen. A disabled woman wheeled into the picture, her impairments so obvious she hardly needed to speak, save to say how much she valued her life. For some reason she kept her face averted and most of the time the camera showed her back view, with the reporter looking directly at her, holding the microphone towards the trembling figure. Justin wondered if the voice was dubbed to make her sound more articulate, or whether she feared to say these things in her own strength. No surname was given. 'Maggie' became the anonymous voice of disability everywhere.

From her perspective, emphasis on eradicating the carriers of disease meant less effort in curing or treating the illness. It put people like her at a disadvantage, implied her life was of less value because she wasn't the kind of child parents desired or society approved.

Justin felt his spirits sink. It was ever thus. As soon as these arguments and emotions were presented his work took on menacing overtones.

The reporter swung suddenly and surprisingly to a different tack as if she too found the disability argument uncomfortable and unfair.

*'The specific procedures associated with creating a donor sibling are one facet of a much bigger issue, as we've just heard,'* she said crisply. *'But how morally defensible is it to go down*

*this route of correcting nature's mistakes? Felix.'*

Felix Ireland came back on the screen.

'*We hear more and more about improving on nature, eliminating illnesses, changing the structure of embryos. First of all we need to ask the question: Is it even possible? How far are we from realising such a utopian dream?'*

Professor Harry Featherham looked every inch the expert, standing against a background of high tech equipment, his white coat pristine, his hair encased in a cloth cap, his eyes myopic as if his sight had shrunk through the prism of too many microscopes.

His voice was gravelly and slightly breathless. '*Well, I won't go into the morality question, but I can say that, even if we felt this was a desirable way to go, to try to eliminate every anomaly – and many, probably most of us, are far from sure it is – we're a very long way from realising such a dream. There are direct as well as indirect and as-yet-unknown consequences from tinkering with the early development of embryos. It's a bit like a child with a wind-up watch. He takes it all apart. If he's bright as well as inquisitive he might be able to assemble it again so that it works. But what if he decides to improve it? He wants to add – let's say, a bigger face and hands so he can see the time more easily. Or he wants to make it luminous or waterproof. But the bigger hands and the coatings slow down the mechanism. Now it doesn't keep time – its main purpose. He can see there's something wrong, but he doesn't necessarily understand the scientific explanation, or the precise engineering calculations that are needed to keep perfect time, the tension in the springs, the interaction of the gears, etc, and once he's made those changes he can't necessarily reverse it.'*

Justin was impressed. This professor might be top of his elevated tree but he could reach ordinary people. He made a mental note of the name; a congratulatory email would establish contact.

'*As scientists we have to be very sure we understand the intricate mechanism we're tinkering with, before we attempt to make changes, particularly those which will be passed on to future generations.'* Professor Featherham's voice held an authority and caution there was no denying. The world was safe in his hands. He'd thought of everything.

'*Where you make fundamental changes to the inherited material which are then irrevocably passed on, you mean?*' the correspondent clarified. Good man. Now you're going somewhere.

'*Exactly. Making changes which affect one single individual is one thing, and even there we need to think long and hard about why we want to change anything, and what the consequences might be from a moral as well as a scientific perspective. But making changes which affect not only that one individual, but also all of his or her descendants, is a much bigger and more serious matter. And if you get it wrong, then what do you do about it? Short of eradicating the line it's difficult to see how you could undo the harm caused.*'

Felix Ireland faced the camera squarely. They had an unfair advantage these reporters; they could manipulate pictures and words to suit their own purposes.

'*This might seem to be taking us away from the question of whether the Edinburgh family are right to have a child as a donor for their little boy whose life expectancy and quality of life are seriously impaired by his illness. But opponents of these procedures worry about the slippery slope. Until recently the HFEA were against the creation of saviour siblings in this country. Now they've changed their stance and approved the practice in certain clearly-defined circumstances. We return now to Dr Justin Blaydon-Green, the doctor treating the family.*'

Ahh. A second bite at the cherry.

Cicely's voice off-camera posed the question. '*Dr Blaydon-Green, do you see the HFEA's changed stance as opening the gates to a more and more liberal interpretation of the laws governing reproductive medicine?*'

Justin saw himself think for a moment before replying.

'*The whole area of reproductive medicine is governed by*

*some of the strictest regulations of any branch of medicine. The role of the HFEA is to ensure an appropriate level of caution is exercised as we creep forward in our understanding of the human genome, which genes influence which areas of development, what happens if we try to modify genes in order to prevent or correct anomalies. These are all immensely complicated questions in terms of both the science and morality. We have to ask ourselves not just,* Can *we do this? but also,* Should *we be trying to do it? And for every case we have to study all the circumstances, and consult many experts, in order to establish how far it's appropriate and desirable and permissible to go.'*

*'Can you elaborate on that?'*

*'Every family is different. We need to consider the opinions, values, beliefs and wishes of each member. But we also have to think of what's in the best interests of any future child – a difficult thing to do, given that we know nothing about this potential child. So we undertake extensive investigations to try to ascertain, as far as we're able, that the motives and wishes of the parents are conducive to the wellbeing of the children.'*

*'Does this mean that you might deny this treatment to some couples who, in your estimation, wouldn't care for and love the child in the way that you think a child should be cared for?'*

Justin's mind flew to Jesus Christ on trial for his life, aware of the loaded questions thrown at him. Damned if he did; damned if he didn't. Yes, he wanted to say, Desirée Wanless wouldn't get my vote; Yasmeen Zair does. So what's so terrible about that?

*'Well, of course,'* he said calmly, *'we don't impose our own personal standard of morality on our patients.'* Heaven forfend! *'But we do measure the likely happiness of any children against the standards set by society in general. And the various bodies and committees which examine each case help us do that, because they're made up of a representation of society's views, so it's as close as we can get to being fair and impartial.'* So pick holes in that level of scrutiny if you can!

It was as good an answer as he could have given to a difficult question. Helen shot him an approving smile.

Professor Benjamin Norton filled the screen. Justin did a double take. Ben had been a real ally over many years – ever since Justin had come to the Fertility Centre, in fact. Now Professor of Law and Medical Ethics at Edinburgh University, he combined a logical mind with a real understanding of human diversity. And he'd always been a safe pair of hands – rather too safe perhaps, because he was rarely interviewed. The media liked spiky characters with polarised opinions who could provoke strong feelings. By his own admission Ben was too moderate, too even-handed, too sympathetic to all sides.

On screen he looked so avuncular, he was an instantly reassuring presence, but what would he say? Justin knew Ben had an uncomfortable knack of homing in on weaknesses in your argument: valuable at a personal level, not so helpful when you were needing to plead your case to a largely lay audience. He leaned forward, dislodging Kate from his shoulder. She squirmed.

'Da-ad!'

He pulled her closer without taking his eyes off the television.

'*Professor Norton, we've heard that The Pemberton Centre has received permission to provide the treatment necessary to help this little boy with a serious blood disorder. Many people are anxious about this relaxation of the laws governing what's permissible in this country. How do you weigh up the rights and wishes of individuals against the wishes of society in general?*'

'*Well,*' – the South African accent was mellow but somehow authoritative – '*anxieties in themselves don't justify extensive regulation. The personal preferences of individuals command respect. Serious moral claims require the greatest respect, and if you're going to deny a person what they want in those cases you would need to have a very weighty reason to justify such a denial. One can't get much more serious than a claim which amounts to saving the life of a beloved child. So the burden of proof lies with society and individuals who would curtail this liberty. These parents have very, very good reasons for choosing this path. There's nothing frivolous or selfish in it. It's difficult to see how, in the specific case you're talking about, anyone else who's outside of this tragedy could legitimately and fairly deny this little boy a chance of life, and such a case must be judged on its own merits and specifics. Using it as a thin-end-of-the-wedge gate to larger issues, hypothetical developments, or future possibilities or embargos, should be reserved for the debating chamber. At the point of clinical decision making, it's the merits and demerits of creating a particular embryo specifically to save Sebastian Zair's life, that's at issue.'*

Bravo, Ben! Off the fence on this one at least.

And the professor had the last word. The screen returned to the London studio.

*'The debate about this case will continue but for now at least, Yasmeen and Karim Zair can pursue their wish to have a child to act as a donor for their little boy, Sebastian. There are many hurdles between the granting of permission to proceed and a potential cure, but time is running out for this family. The stem-cell treatment is less effective the older Sebastian gets. The chances of IVF being successful for his parents also diminish with age. And on top of the low success rates for the IVF procedure, very specific embryos are required which are the same tissue type as Sebastian. The end result is by no means a foregone conclusion.'*

The news moved on. Bobby flicked the remote control and turned to her father.

'So, Pops. What d'you think? That last Professor was best, wasn't he? I reckon he's right. The people who say you can't do it, have to prove it.' Bobby sounded fierce. His thoughts flew to her brief skirmish with the demonstrators at his clinic. Had she learned her lesson?

'Ben Norton's a good chap,' Justin said quietly. 'He cares. He doesn't just say things for effect, he thinks them through, and then says what's right. And he doesn't live in an ivory tower, as some of these ethics people do. He's out there in the real world getting his hands dirty. I have a lot of time for Ben.'

'Did you all know who else was being interviewed?' Lexie asked, poking her mother's knitting needle down the side of her plaster-cast and scratching without inhibition.

'Well, I certainly didn't.'

'Interesting,' Helen said. 'I rather liked the bit about the watch.'

'Could any of that po-faced lot stop you doing it?' Bobby asked, tipping herself right way up out of the chair and leaping back in, with her skinny legs curled under her like a cat.

'Not in principle. We've got permission from the HFEA. That means it's legal and approved by the top authority. But these people have the power to make the whole thing so fraught that a couple might back out, to avoid the hassle. It's tough for them.'

'What a beautiful woman that mother is,' Helen said, looking at the blank screen as if Yasmeen's face was etched into it. 'She reminds me of that woman who married the Shah – Farah something. The Empress of Persia or Iran or whatever it's called.'

'I know what you mean,' Justin said. 'She's her own best advocate. Almost fearless in her conviction.'

'So, what if it takes too long?' Kate asked, twisting around to look up at her father. 'Y'know, like that woman said at the end.'

'If it's too late for a successful stem cell infusion, they might have to think about a bone marrow transplant. But that's much more invasive, much more risky. And thankfully not my department.'

'Hey, won't it be on the Scottish news as well?' Bobby interrupted suddenly, waving the remote. She turned the volume down until the Zair story came on.

Now he'd seen the main report Justin felt easier about seeing it again. OK, he hadn't performed brilliantly but he hadn't disgraced himself – or his daughters – either.

The local news followed much the same pattern minus the disabled lady. It was the summary at the end that caught Justin unawares.

*'This is a fillip for Scotland, once again at the forefront of medical advances. But concern has been raised in some quarters about the wisdom of granting permission for such a controversial procedure to a reproductive centre already the subject of an enquiry.*

*'Earlier this year twins were born to a Nigerian couple, one of whom was clearly not the rightful offspring of both parents. Close examination of all practices in this centre is currently ongoing. If errors are uncovered it seems likely that this new case will be transferred to an alternative centre.'*

A stunned silence fell in the room. Bobby switched off the television and turned to stare at her father.

'Is that right?'

'It's right that we're under investigation,' he replied evenly, 'but we're continuing to practise as normal. And that's the first I've heard of anyone being transferred elsewhere.'

'Could they close you down?' It was Lexie's turn to look aghast.

'Well, if they found evidence of malpractice they could.'

'And would you be out of a job, seeing as you're the top man?' Lexie pursued.

'Well, I'm the PR, the person with responsibility for everything done under our licence, so the buck stops with me.'

'Would we have to move away?' Kate's voice came from a hollow place.

'Hey. It hasn't come to that yet. And I'm not expecting it to do so. I'll let you know if it becomes a possibility.'

'Like you let us know you were under investigation, you mean?' Bobby said sharply.

'Your father was only trying to save you unnecessary anxiety,' Helen said. 'There's absolutely no need for you to pack your bags just yet.'

'And whilst on this theme,' Justin tucked in quickly, 'it would be best if you say nothing to anybody – texting or otherwise – meantime.' Justin threw a warning look at Lexie. 'If you know nothing, you can say nothing. And that goes for the saviour sibling case too. And you know about all the rules for your own safety, be *extra* vigilant now. Let your mother or me know where you are, who you're with. Don't speak to strangers. Don't take any unnecessary risks. Now scram, you lot. Homework!'

# 34

'YOU CAME ACROSS well, Justin,' Helen offered.

'Thanks. Sounded rather ponderous, I thought.'

'Just serious. How's morale in your team?'

'Not good. And things are about to get a whole lot worse.'

'Oh?'

'Another investigation. The only consolation is we'd already applied for ISO creditation – the next level of excellence – before all this blew up. So everyone knew there'd be extra auditing. Hopefully most of them will think this coming inspection is part of that process.'

'But it's not?'

Justin went to the door and checked outside. No sign of the girls. He sat down close to her and kept his voice low.

'Jack came to see me yesterday with an astonishing claim. Reckons Scott's been up to no good.'

'Scott Martindale?'

'He reckons it was Scott who fouled up the twin fertilisation. And worse.'

Helen raised an eyebrow.

Justin hesitated a moment before leaning closer and whispering in her ear.

She recoiled. 'You have to be joking!'

'I wish! The HFEA are about to descend. This time from a great height.'

'But *why*? Why would he want to do something like that?'

'No idea.'

'So d'you think he's guilty?'

'I'm trying to keep an open mind. But one of the HFEA guys reckoned he'd been pretty difficult about the previous audit, so I dread to think how he'll take more probing. I spoke to him briefly before he went off to Manchester.'

'And how did he seem?'

'Well, I didn't specify exactly what they were looking for, just that they'd need access to his computer and all the embryos, etcetera. But, no, he seemed quite offhand about it.'

'D'you think Manchester's genuine? Could he have run off?'

'The thought never entered my head.'

'So, will this affect patients?'

'Could do. If they find anything untoward when they test embryos.'

'You mean...?' – he nodded – 'Doesn't bear thinking of.'

'Quite so,' he said grimly. 'Hopefully, he'd cooperate, minimise the fallout. Presumably he kept some kind of records. But then we'd have to contact the couples involved, give them a chance to say what they want us to do.'

'And what *could* you do?'

'Many of them wouldn't want anything done. Some are so desperate to have a family they'd just want to let sleeping dogs lie. For the ones who want confirmation, we could offer tests. Blood tests for existing children, biopsies for embryos – that'd give us limited information, anyway. But in some cases it might mean destroying the embryos.'

'But why would he do something like that?'

'Who knows? Presumably there's a mental problem. *If* he's done anything. And I hope to God he hasn't.'

'What would happen to the centre?'

'There'd be a major enquiry. The last one I heard about, the staff had to go to London, there was a big fat report spelling out what they'd found, and a list of things they had to do to be worthy of their licence from there on in. It's not always negative though; sometimes the recommendations are positive – more staff, more support, better facilities. But in our case – well, it's hard to see what they could do, except get rid of Scott.'

'You poor dear. What a ghastly thing to have hanging over your department.'

He grimaced eloquently.

'Is it only Jack who's suspicious?'

'As far as I'm aware, but, of course, I can't go round asking. I know from several quarters that Scott's been rubbing people up the wrong way, insinuating that they might have been responsible for the twin error, but Jack's is the only suggestion of malpractice. But then Jack'd be the first one to be alerted to something not quite right.'

'How so?'

'He's in the lab. He's the guy who checks fertilisation procedures with Scott and Nina. Besides it's easier for him to blow the whistle than some of the others. He's popular with the rest of the staff; he's got a good reputation as an honest, reliable colleague who helps everybody out, goes the extra mile. And he's also got less to lose.'

'But even Jack doesn't have any proof?'

'No. Short of doing DNA testing – which, as a technician, he has no power to authorise – he couldn't get it, after the event. By the time he suspected the pipette in the twins' case, Scott had long since dealt with it.'

'The atmosphere between them must be pretty much intolerable, I'd have thought.'

'I'm not in the lab so I don't know what it's like in there. But in the staff room, and at meetings, they both seem to be operating much as usual. And as far as I know, Scott has no idea that Jack's brought this accusation to me.'

'But Jack knows about Scott's accusation against him?'

'Well, yes. I told him.'

'Which suggests to me that you believe Jack.'

'I believe he genuinely suspects Scott. That's not to say his suspicion is correct.'

'So, if these inspectors find something, what happens next?'

'Well, it'd finish Scott, of course. It might even mean a custodial sentence, and difficult as he can be, I wouldn't wish that on him. He's a committed scientist. Works hard. And he's forging new lines of enquiry with his research, by all accounts. I don't know exactly what it's all about – the lab side of things isn't my area, and certainly the basic science is way outside my league! – but he's got a pretty good track record with publications in reputable journals, and you don't get that from mucking about.'

'And you? Where would it leave you?'

'I don't know, Helen. I've taken advice, I've initiated all the right steps. It looks as if I can't be held accountable for the malpractice of one of the team if I knew nothing about it. But you could argue I *should* have known.'

Helen took his hand in both hers. 'You don't deserve this, darling.'

The door burst open suddenly and Justin braced himself.

'Pops, are you busy? Have you got half an hour to help me?'

'Depends what you're asking for, Kate.'

'My biology homework. It's a genetics thingy. And I don't get it. Only if I hand in some garbage, Mrs McFarlane'll write something withering about expecting more of me because of who *you* are.'

'Seems rather unfair.'

'It is! As if I can be expected to know it just because you do. I mean! This stuff isn't in you when you're born, is it? You don't inherit it in your genes. Even *you* had to learn it in the dark ages, didn't you, Dad?'

'Indeed I did, Kitten.'

'So will you?'

'With pleasure. I only hope I can live up to Mrs McFarlane's high expectations.'

'Pph-hh! You know *stacks* more than *her*! I mean, nobody gets *her* on TV to tell everybody how these things work.'

He threw Helen a laughing look and allowed his youngest daughter to drag him off to her room.

# 35

JACK WOKE WITH A START. The luminous dial reproached his wakefulness. Only 6am. He flopped back on the pillow and closed his eyes again.

'You awake?' Patsy whispered.

'Half.'

'How d'you fancy Australia?'

'Wow! You can't get much farther away than that.'

'Do they have your kind of hospitals over there?'

'Sure do.'

'So you wouldn't miss out or anything?'

'Shouldn't think so. I'd have to dig around a bit, see what's out there. And get a good reference.'

'Dr Blaydon-Green'd give you one, wouldn't he?'

'Think so. Depends what comes out of this inquiry.'

'You know what? I'm proud of you, Jack. I never thought you'd go through with it. But this time you really did stand up and be counted.' She propped herself up on her elbows and looked down at him admiringly.

Jack let his gaze wander over this new perspective before replying. 'Well, I guess it was all that talk about being a dad. No kid wants his dad to be a wimp, huh?'

'Straight up?' Patsy's eyes were wide and solemn.

'"Straight up" as in, do I mean it that I'm ready to be a dad? Or that no kid wants his dad to be a wimp? Or as in how you'd like me to make love to you this very minute?'

'Jack!' she giggled.

'Well, we'd better start practising, don't you think?' He

wriggled across to slide underneath her, but then stopped suddenly. 'Although if it's *Australia* you've got your heart set on, I guess we ought to start calculating when'd be the right time to go for it. You'll not want to be on the point of popping when you fly round the world.'

'They don't let you fly when you're that far gone.'

'Right enough. So,' – he ticked off on his fingers – 'can't be when you're due, or when you've got a brand spanking, squeaky new sprogget, or when you're vomiting and peeing every five minutes.'

'Are you trying to chicken out, Jack?'

'Me? As if!'

'What *are* you saying, then?'

'Just that we need to work this out. Seems like we both want to have kids. But if we're moving – *if* we're moving, best we do it when you're in good fettle. So, how about we see what this inquiry throws up? If we have to vanish, we can scarper – wherever, and then start trying properly. If we *don't* have to disappear, we can get going soon as you like. If that's still what you want.'

Her eyes bored into him as if she was seeking entry into his brain through his pupils. It was unnerving.

'I don't get it. Why now? You've never mentioned having kids before.'

It was a question he'd been asking himself.

'Guess this business at the lab has made me take stock. Like you've said often enough, I've been in a rut for ages. Then suddenly I have to choose. When your world starts to unravel, you realise what you most want to hang on to.'

'Which is?'

'You, Pats. And family life. My work's all to do with folk who can't have kids. I don't want us to leave it too late.'

'It mightn't happen for us as well.' It was a fraction above a scared whisper.

'We'll sure give it a good go though, eh?'

She stared into his eyes. 'Would you go for treatment? If we couldn't do it ourselves, I mean?'

'Yeah, I would. Being in that world, I'd be able to choose the right guys, but mostly they're a good bunch. Hearts in the right place.'

'Just not this one you're suspicious of.'

'Excepting him. Right.'

She snuggled close and Jack forgot about work.

By the time he reached the hospital grounds he was whistling a Dolly Parton number at the top of his lungs. He clattered across the pavement setts, the chatter of his teeth temporarily distorting the melody. Then it was down the other side and a swift cornering to avoid the Jaguar gliding towards him. He free-wheeled down the hill, singing the only line he knew, and lapsed into sizzing the rest as he swung his bicycle round into the staff parking area.

The hooded figure came out of nowhere. His wheel hit flesh with a sickening sound. The bicycle and Jack were thrown sideways and the creature slumped to the ground. In an instant Jack was on his feet, racing towards the motionless heap of cloth. He knelt and wrenched off the death mask. He stopped dead. He was looking into the face of a schoolgirl.

The eyes were closed, the lips pale with a blue tinge. He drew up one arm and leg to put her into the recovery position, and felt for a pulse. Regular. Strong. Good.

The sky seemed to darken. He looked up to find a circle of uniform black figures surrounding him, all peering at the girl on the ground.

'What've you done to her?' one growled, grey-green eyes flashing through holes in the head of a skeleton.

'She stepped right out into my path.'

'Typical. No respect for life,' someone spat out.

'One of you, go for medical help,' Jack said urgently, pulling the chin of the girl higher, watching her breathing.

The tiniest pause.

'Number six, you go,' the growler ordered.

The balaclava nodded and the floor-length cape, gold chain

clasp glinting at its neck, backed out and loped off in the direction of the hospital building, like some portent of evil.

'Please don't crowd her. Give her some space.' Jack flapped his arms at them. The girl was just starting to come to.

'Hello. Hello. I'm Jack. Can you tell me your name?'

'No names!' someone barked.

Jack snorted. 'This isn't a game. I'm trying to find out if she's hurt.'

'You don't need names for that.'

'OK young lady, where does it hurt?'

She pressed a hand to her pelvis. Jack's heart sank.

'Try not to move. Someone'll be here soon.'

By the time two paramedics came running towards them with a trolley, the girl was fully conscious, the colour returning to her face.

Jack gave them the basics, she mumbled a few words, and suddenly they were off towards Accident and Emergency, a pale child surrounded by the symbols of death. Jack followed in their wake, guilt chaining him to this embryonic demonstrator.

Once in the Emergency Department the trolley was swallowed up by swing doors, and Jack was left with six unknowns staring at the notice: *Authorised entry only.*

'Can someone give me some particulars?' the clerk called. 'Hello. Someone? Anyone?' She peered over her half-moon spectacles at the anonymous faces and seemed on the verge of coming out to personally unmask them, when the growler disengaged himself and moved in her direction. It was clear the woman wasn't happy with his responses but Jack kept his distance. No point in getting involved any deeper than he was already.

'Look,' Jack said to the shape closest to him. 'I'm going to go and report in for work, but I'll be back to see how she is. They'll probably do X-rays and things. It'll take time. I'll be back. Promise.'

Without waiting for a reply he left.

Justin was in his office and blinked when he saw Jack's

dishevelled state. But his reaction to the unravelling story was even more unexpected.

'This girl, Jack, describe her.'

'Slim, about five eight, I should think. Short dark hair. Pale skin.'

'Let's go!'

They flew down the corridors, slammed through the swing doors, thundered through rooms where patients were congregating for early appointments.

The clerk frowned at their approach.

'I'm *Dr* Blaydon-Green, here to see the girl who was knocked down in the car park outside my department.'

'Which department would that be, Doctor?'

'The Pemberton.'

'Did someone ask for you?'

'No. But I have reason to believe I might know this girl.'

Jack stared at Justin. Know her?

'One moment, Dr Green,' the clerk said, appraising him. 'I'll just check for you.'

Justin swung round and his eyes fell on the six black figures huddled in a corner. In three strides he was confronting them.

'The girl – the one who was knocked down – who is she?'

'No names,' someone hissed.

'No names,' several chorused together.

'Well, well, well. If it isn't Dr High-and-Mighty himself!' Jack recognised the voice of the growler, but now it sounded lighter, mocking.

Justin turned, his eyes narrowing.

'Ahh. Mr Fox.'

'No names,' they chorused.

'Not content with killing babies, you're hiring people to kill off their defenders, now,' the growler sneered.

'Don't be a fool. The girl, d'you know her?'

'More to the point, do *you* know her? Why else would you be here? Or are you beginning to see the harm your meddling with life does?'

The 'authorised' doors swung open and a doctor in blue scrubs emerged.

'Dr Blaydon-Green?'

'Yes.'

'Hi. Sandy Kennedy. A & E consultant. You might know this girl?'

'It's possible.'

'Well, we can't get any joy out of this bunch, and the lady's not for speaking, no identification on her, so maybe you could take a look for us. We need her next of kin.'

They vanished and Jack slumped into a seat at one side. The spectres seemed curiously deflated, but still managed to exude a menace despite their ridiculous attire. He raked through the past twenty minutes. Had he given his name? Did this growler know who he was? He'd certainly known Justin. And what's more, Justin had known him.

It was a relief when Justin barged out of the doors.

'Let's go.'

Back at The Pemberton he beckoned Jack into his office.

'The girl's fine. Bit bruised and shaken, but no breakages, no internal injuries. And she's accepting full blame for the accident.'

'She appeared out of nowhere. *Did* you know her, Boss?' Jack asked cautiously.

'Yes, actually. She's a friend of my eldest daughter. Her brother's got mixed up with that crowd, and for some reason she decided to join them today. But I rather suspect she'll think twice about doing it again once her mother's finished with her!'

'Oh.'

'But how about *you*, Jack. Want me to give you the once-over?'

'I'm fine, Doc. Small graze on my knee, bruise or two, but otherwise everything intact. But thanks for asking.'

'Right. So I suggest you go and clean up and grab a coffee. I'll phone the girl's mother, and then get the police to remove those idiots.'

Jack shut the door behind him very quietly, feeling suddenly shaky. He bent down until the dizziness passed.

'Mrs Cruse? This is Bobby Blaydon-Green's father. I'm afraid Melanie's been involv—'

Jack moved out of earshot.

From the staffroom window he watched the black caravan move down the road to the main gates, looking like ancient nomads in search of a promised land.

'Jack. Are you OK? Justin's just told me what happened.'

He swung round.

'Hi, Nina. A tad shook up, but this'll put me right.' He raised his mug.

'Fine. Take your time, but when you're ready I could do with you to witness in the lab. Scott's still not in. And I want to keep things moving if I can.'

'I'm on my way!' Jack said, pouring the rest of his coffee down the sink with a flourish.

Looking back over the day, Jack found it hard to analyse.

There was no police visit, no irate parent to face, no summons to account for his bicycle being abandoned in the car park. He'd slipped out at lunchtime to secure his machine, grateful to find it intact. The skid marks were impressive but the soft ground had saved the metal from anything more than a scratch on the crossbar and a crushed front light. He surveyed the scene.

Why had the girl suddenly popped up? He'd been making enough racket. She *must* have heard him coming.

Fragments of a conversation drifted towards him from a few cars away.

'I was like, "Can they really do that? Can they make this kid special to save his brother?" And she goes, "Aye. It's legal and everything". And I go, "But they don't let you choose what kind of kid you have normally – when you have IVF, I mean." And she goes, "It's different when it's medical, like." But I still can't see it. I mean, my pal, Kirsty, she had three kids one after the other, something wrong with all of them. And they never said *she* could get one with no problems. Postcode lottery, that's what it is.'

'Maybe with Kirsty it wasn't something you could find on genes like with this wee boy.'

'Well, I don't know. But I tell you what, *I* wouldn't go through all that.'

'All what?'

'All that IVF stuff. This woman down our street's had it, and she says you get loads of pain, you feel sick all the time, you go right off sex, and you have to stick needles into your belly. No thanks!'

'Well, it's a good thing you've been able to have yours naturally then. How many's this now?

'This one's number four. And this is it. I told my Davey. "No more," I says. "It's the snip for you."'

Jack ambled away, his knee throbbing, lost in thought. So this was the currency of the street, was it? He wasn't sure which was worse, what he'd just heard, or the anarchists who probably knew every statistic. Did working in this rarefied atmosphere dull your senses to the cost of infertility treatment? Not for the first time, he hoped he'd never have to find out the hard way.

The afternoon whirled by. Scott's unexplained absence created a heavier workload, but that was offset by a reduction in tension. Nina seemed to relax into the increased responsibility. Banter soon peppered the atmosphere.

Jack had started to pack up to go home when Justin reappeared.

'How're you faring, Jack? That was a nasty experience this morning.'

'I'm fine, thanks. I blame the journalists.'

'Oh?' There was a knowing twinkle in Justin's eye. 'Why do I smell a Wilde moment coming up?'

'Well, they have a lot to answer for, don't you reckon? And it's them that brought the campaigners and that kid out this morning.'

'I agree in principle, of course, but actually I thought they handled the Zair case quite responsibly this time.'

'Didn't see it myself, I'm afraid. Out jogging. But Patsy reckoned you came across well.'

'Professor Norton was better.' Justin said quickly. 'So, tell me, what gems did Wilde pen for journalists?'

'My all-time favourite is: *In centuries before ours the public nailed the ears of journalists to the pump. That was quite hideous. In this century journalists have nailed their own ears to the keyhole. That is much worse.*'

Justin's face broke into a smile. 'Excellent.' It was the first time they'd laughed together since Jack's accusations.

'Or there's: *Lying for the sake of a monthly salary is of course well-known in Fleet Street.*'

It was too close to the bone to amuse either of them as it otherwise might.

# 36

EVERYTHING WAS WATERTIGHT. Why this sense of dread every time his mobile rang? Scott glanced down at the screen. *Justin again!* Fourth time today. Damn the man!

Moving to the Travelodge had been a spur of the moment thing. It had given him breathing space. But – and it was a colossal 'but' – he was now hamstrung. Fair enough, his animal experiments were finished; but how would he complete his analysis in time for that conference in Montreal?

He felt anchorless. Without focus.

The sight of the HFEA official sitting in *his* chair, staring at *his* screen, had been enough. He felt violated. He'd left the building without speaking to a soul.

Without him there to guide the inquiry, who knew what they'd conclude?

His phone rang again. Natalie Wyatt!

'Hi, Scott here.'

'Hi. How're things?' He could hear the smile in her voice.

'Fine. And you?'

'Bored. Looking for distraction. Interested?'

'Could be. What d'you have in mind?'

Even as he spoke second thoughts were drowning his eagerness. This was no time for *anyone* to creep under his guard. Least of all a reporter!

'Fancy a takeaway and a video?' So normal.

'I'm not really a video person.' Idiot.

'Are you an eating person? How about I bring over a bottle of plonk?'

Scott did a rapid calculation. 'I'll be home in half an hour. Give me time to put the heating on.'

He'd just placed three low candles on the dining room table when the bell rang. Natalie stood there holding up a bottle of wine in one hand, a gateau straight out of Marks and Spencers in the other.

'Behold! I am the bearer of good cheer.' Her eyes narrowed. 'Hey, you look knackered. If this isn't a good time.'

'No. Come in. Please. It's just... I've not been sleeping too well. A lot on my mind.'

'Have you eaten already?'

'No. I wasn't hungry.'

'Well, *I'm* ravenous, but I hate eating alone, so how about we order a takeaway? Then pitch into this totally decadent pud. And if you want me to leave, just say. I know what a bad day feels like. Have them every month myself!'

'A takeaway sounds great.' He handed her a sheaf of menus. 'What kind d'you fancy? Italian, Indian, Chinese, Thai, Turkish?'

'Let's go for Chinese.'

It gave him a strange feeling ticking her choices – loved cashews and mushrooms with everything, bamboo shoots, seafood – the bigger the better. Hated black bean sauce, spare ribs. Ambivalent about sweet and sour. Cautious about the hot stuff – the kind he'd become addicted to of late, the stuff that made you forget trivia.

She teased him for setting the table with serviettes in the glasses, chopsticks, warm plates. 'Wow! For an impromptu meal you sure have style!'

'I just don't like slimy food or sticky fingers, I guess.' It was true. Even on his own he avoided mess.

She didn't comment on the candlelight. But it felt right, protective rather than intimate.

She wasn't adept with chopsticks and he liked the feel of her hand under his as he showed her how to place her fingers. He lingered behind her chair until she got the hang of it, inhaling musk. When she held out the last jumbo prawn for him on perfectly balanced sticks, her eyes held his as she said, 'My last Rolo!' He took a small bite and passed the remainder back to her with a challenging look. 'My last half-Rolo.' She let her own teeth close around the mark of his and slid the prawn into her mouth. He watched her chew it slowly.

'Dare you to finish off the Szechuan chicken,' tipping the dish towards her. 'No rice. No noodles. No water.'

'You're on!'

By the time she'd finished her eyes were watering and her face was flushed. She eased off her jacket and fanned herself with the serviette, before gulping down a whole tumbler of water.

'You've got guts, I'll say that for you,' he said. 'That stuff's lethal.' He dropped extra ice into a second glass of water. 'Here, you've earned this.'

What was it about this girl? How did she manage to…?

She panted in an exaggerated fashion. 'I need a break after that. How about we save the gateau for later?'

'Fine by me.'

She leaned on the table. 'The photo in your hallway. Tell me about it.'

It was a magnificent stag dappled by light filtering through pine trees north of Achnasheen. He'd lurked for hours to capture that shot, and it had won top prize in a BBC competition that year. He found himself showing Natalie his three cameras, and photographs he'd been pleased with, including two other shots that had won awards.

'You could go professional,' she said, her eyes on a black and white photograph of a blasted tree reflected in muddy water.

'You never know, I might have to!' He instantly regretted the comment.

She didn't react. 'I wish *I* had a skill like this to fall back on.'

She continued to study his work, giving him time. He focused on the soft sheen of her skin, the curve of her neck, the delicate way she touched his pictures.

'D'you fancy coming out to take a couple of shots in the evening light?' he asked suddenly.

'I'd love to.' She turned to him with sparkling eyes. 'You could teach me some tricks.'

'And we can make some space for the gateau,' he said lightly.

He took three photos. A homeless man curled up against railings; a tortoiseshell cat padding towards a dilapidated house; Natalie herself, framed against the dark silhouette of a city preparing for the night.

'I'll give you a copy of that if it comes out OK,' Scott said.

Before she could reply he had gone, striding towards a disabled man wheeling himself laboriously up the hill towards them.

'Hi. Want a hand? It's pretty steep up this last bit, but the view's worth it.'

'Thanks. Appreciate it,' the man managed through his breathlessness.

Scott manoeuvred the chair across to a vantage point, touched a shoulder lightly, before returning to Natalie.

'You made that, I don't know, not at all patronising,' she said quietly.

Scott shrugged, taking back the camera he'd thrust into her hand. 'Lochlain showed me all that. I got it wrong more times than I got it right. At first.'

'Tell me about your brother. Does he look like you? Were you close when you were kids?'

'I thought as reporters you were taught to ask one question at a time.'

'But I'm not a reporter now. Not with you.' She spoke so softly he had to move closer to hear. 'I just want to know more about you, about your family. How you tick.'

Don't let your guard down, he told himself. But there was something...

He started walking without giving her any warning.

'Lochlain?' It sounded detached, impersonal. 'He's got the same colouring, same skinniness, same nose. We were pals when we were kids, but he was the bookworm, I was the one with the scabs on my knees, my arm in a sling.'

'I didn't have you down as the boisterous kind.'

'It was a long time ago.'

'So what turned you into a workaholic?'

'Lochlain.'

They walked in complete silence for so long Scott went miles into an imaginary conversation and back again.

'Want to talk about it?' He wasn't sure if she'd actually spoken.

'He was only in his teens when it started. At first my mother thought he was faking it, dodging games, looking for a day off school.'

She slid a hand through his elbow and squeezed his arm. When he didn't respond she removed it again.

'My dad didn't believe it when they told us what it was. A kid couldn't get that, he said, not a kid of Lochlain's age. He'd get specialists. But the next guy said the same thing. And they didn't give him long, not with the speed it took hold. But they bargained without my mother. Once she knew for sure, she just did everything anybody could do to give that kid a life. Talk about single-minded. Her whole world centred around Lochlain.'

'Leaving you...?'

'Me? I wasn't important. Everything we did was for him. I'd cut off my own legs if it'd help him. And that's when I decided.'

'Decided?'

'Decided to find a cure.'

'Hence your research.'

'It's what drives me. To get there – before it's too late.'

'But I thought you said you're decades off testing it with people.' He felt his teeth clench. 'D'you think Lochlain will still be… it'll still be possible?'

The pause went on and on. In the end she gave up waiting.

'Your mother sounds like a very special person.'

'Aye. She is. Hey, look at that.'

'What? What am I supposed to be looking at?'

'See that street lamp? See how the light softens the stonework on that building, silhouettes the ironwork? Now there's a picture crying out to be taken.'

He angled the camera to include the edge of a grimy curtain flapping outside an open window.

'D'you always think pictures when you're out and about?'

'Not always, but this evening the light's brilliant. Aye, I guess I do. Sorry. It must be a real bore.'

'Don't say that. I'd never have noticed the things you're showing me. Makes me want to have a go myself.'

'Feel free,' he said, pushing the camera into her hands. 'Go on. Have a go.'

'You're serious?'

'Sure. Why not?'

She darted glances everywhere, and then started walking. Watching.

The girl appeared out of nowhere. A skimpily clad figure, standing half in the doorway, the light from her cigarette lighter flickering in one hand, an eerie reflection cast onto her shadowed face. Natalie snapped her just before the cigarette ignited. The girl pocketed the lighter and was off, leaving a spiral of smoke hovering in the air.

'Quick thinking,' he said.

'I'll call it, *The lady of the night*.'

'Let's hope she doesn't ever see the caption then, eh?'

Natalie laughed with him, handing back the camera. 'Thanks. That was fun.'

'Ready for that gateau now?'

'I sure am. But this has been great. Thanks for sparing the time.'

'Thank you for persisting. Sorry about earlier.'

'I always find it easier to talk outside tramping along. Don't know why it is. But it's true.'

'Aye. It's true.'

'And everybody's allowed to have off-days.'

'I know. But not to bark at the wrong people.'

'I didn't take it personally.'

'Good. It wasn't personal.'

'I'm sorry you're having such a hard time. But remember if you want to talk… I can be discreet you know. Especially when I care.'

He wanted to believe it. He couldn't forget her trade.

She made a ceremony of cutting the gateau. The cherries and cream oozed out as soon as she lowered the knife. The meringue splintered and shed white crumbs over the cloth onto the carpet. Scott bit his lip.

He was pouring hot coffee, not seeing her expression, when the question came out. 'How d'you deal with the seamy side of your job?'

'"Seamy"?' Her voice sounded odd. 'How d'you mean?' The air between them was holding its breath.

'Like talking to somebody who's just seen a fatal accident. Interviewing a mother the minute her son's been killed in Afghanistan. Folk that are traumatised.'

'I like to think I'm sympathetic,' she said carefully. 'It's my job to find things out, report the story, add the human interest. But I try not to trample on people's feelings.'

He didn't respond. He couldn't even look at her.

'Why?'

'I wondered, that's all. In our work we have to tell people bad news. You learn to deal with it, but on bad days it's hard to leave it behind. I wondered how *you* separate out what you have to do, from what you don't think you should do.'

'Well, I guess I'm not so personally involved as you. I don't really know these people. I'm the story-teller not the therapist. What about you? How d'you decide how far to go?'

'My role's clear. I'm here to facilitate patients getting the treatment they need. If we do sail close to the wind, it's to help them.'

'Whereas they'd get by much better without folk like me steam-rollering over their lives,' she said. But the smile was back in her voice.

He shrugged. 'Somebody has to bring these things to the public's attention. We need healthy debate. I accept that. But sometimes...'

'Sometimes?'

'Well, take what the press did with that post-mortem story a while back; wheeling out those parents whose babies were buried without various organs. Relatives stopped giving permission for autopsies after that.'

'But there were bad things going on behind the scenes. Surely the media had a duty to expose that?'

'There are one or two mavericks, maybe. But pretty much everything we know in medicine has been built on the bones of the dead. And now loads of exciting work has been stymied because researchers can't get the organs or tissue to examine.'

'Well, from my vantage point, knowing next to zilch about the medicine,' she grinned, 'I'd say that reporters have a responsibility to present a balanced case. Yes, the tearful personal accounts grab the attention, but you need the careful science too.'

'I wish more of you would present a balanced picture for the things we do.'

There was a long pause.

'You know,' Natalie said, 'I'd have a hard time reconciling what *you're* doing with my conscience.'

'Like what?'

'Tinkering with nature. You can't possibly know what long-term consequences there might be from some of your work, can you? It'll take years to show up. And it's people's *children* you're messing with.'

'Every move is tested and re-tested. Every step is scrutinised.

It's very careful and incremental.'

'But it's still scary stuff. I guess it's down to each individual to make sure they're squeaky clean.' She suddenly reached across and rubbed a finger against his hand. 'Do you squeak, Scott Martindale?'

'Do you, Natalie Wyatt?' he countered.

'I'm not proud of everything I've done, I admit.'

'Ditto.'

'But for what it's worth, I've been scrupulous where you're concerned. Nothing you've said in private has gone any further. I give you my word on that. I hope you believe it.'

'Thanks for that.'

'How's the research going?'

'It's not. That's the problem.'

'How come?'

'Too much else going on.'

'No wonder you're despondent.'

He shrugged.

'Have you still got those inspectors in?' It sounded casual.

'Aye. Swarming everywhere. And *they* don't understand what we do either. Them and their rules and regulations, their tight little boxes. Life isn't like that. You can't force people into rigid moulds and shut the lid on them. Every case is different. And sometimes you need to walk in the wavy grey area in order to reach a goal you know is right.'

'Well, they'll soon be gone and you can get back to normal. At least you can tell yourself you've nothing to hide, so you've nothing to fear.'

That clinched it. He mumbled something about pressure of work, an early start, papers still to be read, but inside himself he knew. His defences had already been breached too far, he couldn't trust himself to let her creep any closer to his centre. He had things to do tonight – urgent things.

If she was disappointed not to be staying the night, she gave no sign of it. He insisted she took the rest of the gateau.

She left in good spirits and a black cab he'd already paid for.

# 37

YASMEEN STOOD BACK to survey the flower arrangement. One stem of lilies was a shade too long on the right. Her fingers had just closed on the offending flower when Sebastian screamed and the phone rang simultaneously. The entire delicate edifice collapsed onto the table, scattering pollen, petals and water in a wide arc.

She swore under her breath and threw a towel in the direction of the seeping water as she flew into the sitting room. Sebastian's eyes were screwed shut, his mouth open in an ear-splitting shriek, blood running through his teeth and forming a drooling pattern on his clean white T-shirt. Instantly the terminal stages of his form of anaemia raced through her mind. She gathered him close, heedless of the effect on her blouse.

It took time for her to register the broken plastic bubble-maker. She grabbed his head and pressed the edge of his shirt against the blood and froth. Yes, there it was; a clean cut embedded inside his lower lip, already noticeably swollen. Relief washed over her with such force that, for a few seconds, the world spun.

As soon as he had her full attention and sympathy, Sebastian's cries subsided to a thin wail. He meekly accepted the bag of ice cubes she placed on his cut lip along with a promise of ice-cream for lunch, if he was big and brave. In no time he was lying back on the settee absorbed in his favourite cartoon DVD. Checking on him twenty minutes later Yasmeen found him fast asleep, a trickle of bloody saliva oozing round his thumb, his other hand clutching the stained but long-suffering Humphrey. She stood for a long while simply watching him. How many times could you say goodbye to your son?

It was an effort to drag herself back to the kitchen. She stopped on the way to see who had rung. Candice: she'd ring back another time. Yasmeen felt her eyelids pricking. She just wanted to be left alone. Why couldn't they see that? What was it with people wanting to get in on the act all the time?

Down on her knees mopping the floor, the first tears mingled with the flower solution. The fragility of her emotions appalled her. She had survived so many emergencies with Sebastian; she had weathered crises with Shahira and her parents; now it only took a spilled drink or a chance word to throw her into despair.

She felt Karim's constant concern. After his first instinctive response – 'I feel as if my wife's gone away and left this stranger I don't understand in her place!' – he knew better than to say anything, but the tension was there nonetheless. And she resented it. Her mother had come right out with it. 'Yasmeen. You must ease up. You'll be in no fit state for a pregnancy if you go on like this. Let us help. Your father and I. And Pia. Let us have the children.'

'I'm all right. It's the hormones. I'll be all right.'

'But you're *not* all right. You know you're not. Come on. Don't let your need to be in control all the time ruin your chances of success with this treatment.'

It was hard hearing it; harder still because she knew her mother was right. But they'd come so far, fought so hard for this, it would be foolish to jeopardise their chances for nothing more than hurt pride.

The leaflets told her that everything she was experiencing was within the to-be-expected parameters, but this irritability, this total preoccupation with her fertility, wasn't within her own personal boundaries. There was no getting away from that. Compromises would have to be made. Especially if she became pregnant. If? *If?* When! She *had* to keep faith. For Sebastian's sake. The alternative was too grim to contemplate.

But even motherhood seemed overwhelming these days. It had taken Sebastian a long time to recover from his latest bout of infection. Yasmeen had stared for hours at his wan face as he struggled for breath in the endless watches, night after night. She'd bathed his fevered skin with infinite gentleness but had still made him wince. She'd read and re-read the literature on steroid treatment, searching for a kinder explanation for his symptoms. She'd coaxed him through extra blood transfusions with promises she feared might never be fulfilled. What if...?

And Shahira seemed daily more unmanageable, driving her closer to breaking point. Torn by her own internal conflicts, Yasmeen abandoned her customary firm discipline, and tried indulgence, adding further to her daughter's insecurity and her own sense of rushing headlong to ruin.

And it was all her fault.

But the habit of a lifetime got the better of her present melancholy, and she was soon setting herself impossible targets to be accomplished before Sebastian awoke, before lunch-time, by the time Shahira had to be collected, before Karim came home.

The tall arrangement of flowers became a circular wreath of ivy and hebe with the remaining undamaged lilies and sprigs of gypsophila popped in at intervals. The kitchen floor was not only mopped but polished. The assorted left-over vegetables in the fridge were transformed into a nutritious soup. Shahira's ballet dress was repaired, washed and hung out to drip dry. Appointments were made with the optician and the dentist. The front path was swept, the water feature re-filled, the dead heads removed from the roses.

By the time Karim came home that evening, Yasmeen had ticked everything off on her job-list and re-established her priorities. The pasta she'd cooked for the children had been a huge success. The butterscotch meringue pie had been a lever for extra co-operation. Shahira had completed her homework and piano practice without complaint before beating her mother at Chinese Checkers. Both children had cuddled up to her for three whole chapters from their favourite *Fairy Tales and Other Fantastic Stories*. Life appeared to have returned to the old order of things.

Karim oversaw bath-time and Yasmeen used the opportunity to finish off their meal, adding candles and wine to the table, resolutely turning her back on the detritus in the kitchen.

'How was your day?' Karim ventured as they lingered over the cheese board.

'Mixed. But it improved as it went on.'

He hesitated. 'Is this a good moment for a surprise?'

'I'm sorry. I know I'm unreasonable these days.'

'It's not your fault. But I must confess I'll be relieved to get my steady, controlled Meena back again!'

'*I'll* be glad to get my control back again too!' she flashed.

He covered her hand with his. 'It must be a hundred times worse for you, caught on the inside of all this.'

'It does make me wonder.'

He waited.

'We *are* doing the right thing, aren't we, Karim?'

'We are, sweetheart. We have no choice. It's Sebastian's only chance.'

'I know,' she sighed, her finger tracing the outline of a diamond in the damask cloth. 'It all seemed so straightforward back then when we decided. When it was only a possibility.'

'It'll get better. Once you come off the hormones. They said that, didn't they?'

'It had better!'

'I'm sure it will.'

'Well, let's just hope it works first go. I'm not sure I could take a repeat.'

'Why don't you have more help in the house?'

'No. But thanks. I get so wound up by... people! If I'm on my own just getting on, I'm fine. But as soon as someone gets in my way...' She mimed an explosion. 'As you know only too well!'

'My mother wants to help. Is there anything she could do – apart from stay away?'

'Well, if this thing drags on over the summer – God forbid! – perhaps Shahira could have a holiday with her. Maybe. If the little minx can be trusted to behave herself.'

'Has she been playing up again?'

'No, she was really good this afternoon. But you know what she's like these days.'

'Perhaps it'd do her good to be away from us,' Karim suggested. 'I guess the poor kid needs to be made to feel special.'

'I know she does. But then, what about when she has to play second fiddle to a new baby? I mean, she knows Bassy's ill and why his needs have to take precedence – even if she rebels sometimes. But a new baby?'

'She's old enough to do things with it. She'll love it.'

'If she's talking to me at all by that stage!'

'Sounds like practice for the teenage years,' Karim said with a rueful smile.

'I'm sorry. You get tantrums and moods enough at school. You don't need anarchy at home as well.'

'Oh, it's completely different. The kids at school are simply students. If they throw wobblies or disobey it doesn't affect me in the way that Shahira's nonsense does.'

'Even so. I feel bad that I don't have her more in control.' She gave a deep sigh. 'I used to pride myself on her being the kind of girl you could take anywhere, always sunshiny and obedient. Not any more! She's a perfect hooligan at times. Maybe that's what's upsetting me. Feeling a failure.' She swallowed hard.

'Whatever else you are, Meena, you are not a failure!' Karim said emphatically. 'You just expect too much of yourself.'

'Well, I'm not the woman I was six months ago, but don't let's go on about it any more. What was it you were saying about a surprise?'

He surveyed her for a long moment with an expression she couldn't read. Then, as if plunging from a higher board than he'd attempted before, he suddenly blurted it out. 'How would you fancy a weekend away? Just the two of us.'

'But the children...'

'Your mum's offered to take Bassy. And Pia wants to take Shahira to stay with her. She's already planning trips to the safari park, and the beach, and a ceramic painting place, and goodness knows what else. You know Pia!'

'But what if Bassy...?'

'We can be back in a couple of hours. And you can ring your mum to check whenever you feel like it.'

'Where? Where are you proposing we go?'

'The Trossachs. It's so lovely and peaceful up there. Remember when we went before?'

'Before we had the children. Before...'

'I know. But we loved it, didn't we?'

'It was lovely.'

'I know it's nowhere exotic, but I didn't think you'd want to be too far away.'

'I wouldn't.'

'The break would do you good. Do us both good. Before the next stage of this treatment.'

'When were you thinking of?'

'A week tomorrow?'

'A *week*!'

'It's half term. I can be off on the Friday and the Monday. Shahira too. And Bassy hasn't any treatments scheduled for those four days.'

'Four days. I don't think...'

The tears simply streamed from her eyes, no sobbing, no warning. Karim held her close, stroking her head, saying nothing until the floodgates closed again.

'That settles it. You, Yasmeen Zair, are desperately in need of a holiday.'

A whole weekend. Far away from everyone who knew what they were doing. From the comments, the advice, the looks. From all the pressures of family life at it was nowadays. Yes. A few days just with Karim.

It sounded like heaven.

# 38

JUSTIN SAT IN his consulting room drumming his fingers on the desk. His eyes strayed to the clock. 10.20. Samuel and Candice were due at 10.30. He was in no hurry to bring this meeting forward by so much as a nanosecond.

He'd rehearsed the conversation so often it sounded contrived in his head. Was he being too dismissive of the significance of this latest discovery? Was he opening the way to a lawsuit?

Once upon a time Samuel had had a fine sense of humour. Once upon a time Candice had been a brilliant athlete; giving it all up to become a mother. Once upon a time they'd seemed to be a close, united couple. And then this shadow had fallen over their lives. Who knew what effect today's news would have?

Lily-May popped her head round his door. 'Mr and Mrs Opakanjo are here. Shall I send them in?'

'Please.'

They came in smiling and shook his hand warmly.

'And how are those beautiful twins of yours?'

'Doing fine, thanks,' Samuel said. 'Just fine. Orlando looks like he's heading for wrestling, or the rugby scrum, I'd say. Putting on the beef at a rate of knots!'

They laughed, and Justin indicated the two seats placed close together.

'And Destiny?'

'More ladylike. But a fine eater all the same.'

'Excellent. You didn't bring them with you?'

'Oh, we did. But the lady at the reception desk said she'd keep an eye on them. They're both fast asleep.'

'Good. I must say, Candice, you're looking terrific.'

'Well, it makes a huge difference getting a night's sleep. I think I only realised how much it took out of me when the night feeds stopped. I was like a zombie – all the time.'

Justin shuffled the papers on his desk before turning back to them.

'I asked you to come in because we have some results from our investigation. We now know what happened. I want to give you a chance to ask any questions, and talk about how you want to proceed.'

Samuel's hand slid across to Candice's. She didn't move away.

'On the day of your fertilisation we were extremely busy. I'm not offering that as an excuse, but trying to fill in the pieces of the jigsaw. We always have two people checking the eggs and sperm, and the embryos, at every critical point, to make sure we have the correct ones. And they both sign to say they've done it. It's a rule laid down by the licensing authority for all centres like ours, and we always do follow it. Without exception. Of course, everything is carefully labelled, but we still double-check. And that did happen in your case. Two lab staff signed to say so, and it was all done by the book. But unfortunately the instrument used to bring the sperm and eggs together got mixed up with another one that had already been used for the fertilisation before yours.'

He gave them time to assimilate this information.

'It was a genuine error.'

Still they said nothing.

'Thanks to you giving us permission to check Destiny's DNA, we do know something about the other genes Destiny carries. I'm sure you'll understand I can't name names, but I assure you there's nothing to give you any cause for alarm. No inherited diseases or anything at all detrimental to her welfare.'

'So was it… white genes? Or what?' Samuel's voice sounded steady but Justin saw his free hand was clenched.

'Yes. White.'

'And was it the father... or the mother?

Justin paused. 'I understand why you ask that question. But I want to suggest that you think again about that point. It might be better for you as a family, if you could see this as a case of both your gametes being used – which they were – for both babies, but this extra bit was introduced from someone else. Samuel's sperm were drawn up and mixed with your eggs, Candice, for both babies. In Orlando's case your own sperm and eggs actually created him. In Destiny's case a third set of gametes got mixed in. It seems to me that's better than one of you feeling that you aren't the real parent.'

Their unblinking gaze was disconcerting. What were they thinking?

'You probably need time to talk this through. You have a right to the truth, of course, and I will tell you more if you're both sure you want that information. Once you know, there's no going back.'

Samuel was nodding. 'I can see that. It makes sense.'

Justin turned to Candice.

'I need to think about it.'

'And the real mother or father? Don't they have a right to know?' Samuel said. 'That's something that's been bugging me right from the start.'

'The biological parent, you mean?' Justin corrected gently. 'Well, we have told the other couple about the mistake, of course. Like you, they've been through all the trauma of infertility treatment, so they're sympathetic. But happily for them, they now have all the family they want. They even have spare embryos frozen if they change their minds in the future. And they feel that it would be best to leave things as they are. They asked me to pass on their best wishes to you.'

'They don't want Destiny?' The edges of her words were ragged.

'No, Candice, they don't. They know she's a beautiful baby, in a good home, with a family who love her, and they're content to leave it at that.'

'Thank you. Thank you so much.'

'No, please, don't thank me. The original error was ours, and we deeply regret it.'

'But what if Destiny wants to know? In the future.' Samuel's tone was level, but Justin saw Candice flinch.

'It will be up to you how much you tell her. But she does have a legal right to know when she gets to an age of discernment. Information will be stored that would enable her to find out for herself if she decides that's what she wants. On the other hand, it could very well be that a simple explanation will suffice. By that time she'll have all the security of years of being a much-loved part of your family. Eighteen, twenty, thirty years from now, things will feel very different for everyone.'

'So what if, say, she got sick, or needed a transplant, or anything?' Candice was leaning forward, rocking herself with her arms tightly round herself. Her full breasts strained at the flimsy fabric of her dress, and Justin noticed the beginning of a stain of excess milk. He looked away quickly. What he saw in her wide dark eyes made him want to reach across to her pain, but he resisted the temptation. Samuel was there.

'That's something we can deal with in a very straightforward way. But I'm impressed by your clear thinking.'

'Thanks to Yasmeen Zair,' Samuel said.

'I'm sorry?' What had Sebastian's mother to do with all this?

'She's had to make decisions for her little boy, and we thought, well, if something like that happened to Destiny, we wouldn't be able to help her if we didn't know where she came from.'

'Ah. I didn't know you two knew each other,' Justin said. Where was all this going?

'We met in the clinic and now we're friends. It was Yasmeen who got me back on my feet.'

'I see,' Justin said. 'Well, to answer your question, now we have the necessary information about Destiny, it will be held in our archives. If at any stage Destiny herself, or you and her doctors, need to know more about her genetic inheritance, then it's there. Does that sound reasonable?'

'It could be donkey's years before she needs it. What happens if the hospital closes down, or none of us are around?'

'That's a good point. Perhaps a note of how to access these data could be kept with your solicitor. Just the basic contact details. Oh dear, this is sounding very Harry Potterish! I'm not meaning to be secretive, but this is sensitive, and it wouldn't be understandable to the average layperson. It would require expert interpretation.'

'Yes. I can see that,' Samuel said. Candice nodded.

'I'm happy to answer any questions you have right now, but I also think it would be sensible for me to see you again in a week or so. Give you time to mull this over. Shall we leave it that you phone Lily-May when you're ready to talk more and we'll meet again then?'

Samuel nodded for both of them.

Justin followed them down the corridor, noting how closely they walked together, hands clasped. He smiled.

The two children were still asleep, Orlando breathing heavily through a slightly blocked nose, Destiny half invisible under the embroidered cover. Lily-May was behind her desk. She looked up as they approached.

'Oh, have you finished already? I was hoping they'd wake so I could get a cuddle, but they haven't stirred.'

Candice bent to unfasten Destiny's belt and handed the baby to her. Lily-May lit up.

'She's gorgeous,' Justin said softly, bending to look into the little face.

Orlando woke at the sound of voices and Samuel lifted him up. Justin held out his hands. 'May I?'

Both parents looked on with obvious pride.

As he watched the family walk away it struck Justin: Samuel always carried Orlando. He made a mental note to talk to Josephine.

Having written his report of the Opakanjo meeting, Justin

leaned back in his chair. So far so good.

But the ripples caused by Destiny still washed over the wider Pemberton sands. Just how many castles would they threaten? His eyes fell on the photographs of their successes but his mind ranged over current patients.

The Harrisons – would they continue to seek to bank HLA-typed frozen embryos as a source of stem cells for their children in the future if they knew what had been going on in his department?

Ashley Turner – would she stop pursuing her dream? Poor Ashley. She was only twenty-two when they found the cancer. Back then, for Ashley and Carl, it was a simple choice: frozen embryos versus no child of their own, *ever*. But the endless treatment, the tears, the fears, took their toll. Carl disappeared. It had never occurred to Ashley he'd renege. She fought. All the way to Strasbourg. But the courts were adamant; *both* parents had to agree. End of story. And Carl now had three lovely kids of his own with Tamsin, as nature intended; he didn't want any more.

Justin still saw Ashley sometimes. She had this peculiar notion that he was the gatekeeper guarding her embryos. She talked of them as if they were babies in cradles, pink and blue ribbons, smelling of Johnson's soap. More than once Justin had thought it'd be easier if they were destroyed; then she could grieve and get on with life.

She'd asked him once – on a day when he was running late: 'Would you ever consider cloning a human being?'

'Absolutely not,' he'd said, before his brain was in gear. 'I believe it would be criminally irresponsible to do so.'

Her look told him he'd been too brutal.

'Why not?'

'There are huge scientific and moral problems associated with cloning. Every responsible practitioner agrees on that point.'

'Such as?' she persisted.

'Well, it's only been tried in the animal world up to now. But the success rate is frighteningly low. It's a really, really inefficient procedure. For every birth of a cloned animal there's a litter of death, disability and pain in its wake. Even those fetuses that survive to birth have a limited lifespan. And they're prone to all sorts of congenital anomalies and diseases. Some scientists in the business of cloning animals have even said they wonder if there is such a thing as a normal clone. And that's before I start on the psychological effects on the child.'

'This wouldn't have anything to do with finance, resources, stuff like that, would it?' She was game, he had to concede that.

'Definitely not. If we had millions to spare I doubt you'd find a single consultant in this country who'd go down the cloning route.'

She'd backed off then, but Justin lived in dread of her resurfacing with some other hair-brained idea. Maybe if she heard about the mistake she'd quit.

Who else was he currently concerned about? Ahh yes. Ilona and Adrás Domokos? Scottish by birth, Hungarian by blood. Lovely couple. But what tragedy they'd known; five pregnancies, every one abnormal. All to do with a failure of fusion of the neural plate. Ilona herself had had a hare-lip and cleft palate – beautifully repaired, but you could only alter the appearance not the fact. The babies' abnormalities had been far more serious – all incompatible with life; the last one so badly hydrocephalic it had to have its head collapsed in order to get it through the birth canal. And still they wanted children! Would *they* keep attending his clinic if they knew the full story?

Justin gave himself a mental shake. He must stop this. He had a clinic to attend. He must concentrate on the positive good he could do today; let tomorrow take care of itself.

The phone jerked him back to the present.

'Yes, Lily-May?'

'Carol and Roy Nicholson have arrived. They came early because her mother's been taken into hospital, and they really want to make it for visiting time. I was wondering if there was any possibility you could see them earlier than the appointment?'

'I'm on my way.'

For some inexplicable reason one of Jack's Wilde quotes came into his mind as he strode down the corridor: *There is only one thing in the world worse than being talked about, and that is not being talked about.* At this moment he'd give a king's ransom not be talked about for a very long time!

But in reality his world was probably on the very brink of imploding. Everyone would soon be talking about it.

# 39

THE WARDEN WAS vague. 'Your uncle? I think he said Uncle Cameron. Or Campbell. Or Calhoun, would it be? Strong accent. Tall. Thin. Looks a lot like you. Shall I let him in?'

'Might... as well.' Lochlain said.

There was no mistaking the kinship. The visitor had the lanky height of all the Martindale men, a bit stooped with age, but the same loping stride as if his feet had grown too fast for his walking skills. Aunt Dorothy once said they were a throw back to kangaroos, pushing off from their extremities – it was part of a diatribe against her soon-to-be-ex-husband, Donald Martindale, and it didn't sound cuddly.

Wisps of grey hair straggled from beneath a worn trilby, and the tinted lenses in his round spectacles gave him the air of a mole emerging into sunlight after a very long excavation underground. His Harris tweed jacket had seen better days, but the cut was unmistakably authentic, though it looked (and smelt) as if it had hung around in charity shops for a few years.

He advanced in staccato strides, both bony hands outstretched.

'Lochlain! How *are* ye, son?' The Highland burr extended the last word long enough to bring the visitor to the wheelchair where he clearly knew all about the younger man's inability to shake hands. He placed his own on both Lochlain's shoulders.

'Good to see ye, laddie.'

'Come away... in... will you,' Lochlain slurred. 'Thanks... Maggie... I'll be fine.'

The warden backed away, closing the door behind her.

The world reduced to the one main living area of Lochlain's flat, the old man flung off his coat and hat.

'What … in the… world?' Lochlain managed, staring at the apparition.

'Whisssht. Make sure she's gone. I'll explain.'

The two men sat in silence listening.

'Now then…' Lochlain began but was instantly interrupted.

'I needed to speak to you but if anyone asks, you haven't seen me, huh? Only Uncle Campbell frae Inverkirkaig' – the voice lilted over the names – 'north o' Enard Bay, ye ken? The warden'll back you up.'

They grinned at each other. How they'd loved mimicking the Highland accent when they were lads.

'Why the… secrecy?' Lochlain said, the words grinding out harshly.

'It's a long story. Are you sitting comfortably?' Lochlain nodded. 'Then I'll begin.'

Except that he didn't. Suddenly he couldn't.

Lochlain watched his brother's struggle in silence. The surprise of the visit was enough to deal with, without expending his dwindling energy on talking.

Eventually Scott found his voice. 'Remember I promised I'd find a cure? Well, I'm onto something. I'm certain it'll take me to what I need. Only there's been a bit of a hiccup. I'm going to lie low for a bit, maybe go abroad. Don't know yet. But I don't want a trail. And definitely not one that leads to *your* door. So remember, you never saw me, right?'

The pause seemed to go on way past its sell-by date.

'I'm going to leave this with you.' Scott fished in his pocket and held out a memory stick. 'It's a promise: I'll be back. I'll find a way. And just you be there waiting. I mean it! OK?'

It took Lochlain time to summon, 'What's… happened?'

'It started with a slip-up in the lab. One little mistake. But it's brought the heavies out of the woodwork. They're turning up stuff – stuff nobody knew about.'

'What… have you… done?'

Scott dragged his chair closer. He sank down with his elbows on his thighs and leaned forward, his spidery hands hanging down as if the strings of a puppet had been unexpectedly dropped.

'Best you don't know, Loch. Not that I don't trust you. But what you don't know you can't talk about.'

With a great effort Lochlain shook his head. 'You h-have... to tell me... how... far you've... got.'

'I don't want you mixed up in this.'

'I *am*... mixed up... in it. It's... *for* me... But I... can't keep... hanging... on. Not... unless...' Suddenly his face contorted and his whole body seemed to go into spasm. Scott held him, massaging, supporting, until the paroxysm passed.

'Co... ffee?' Lochlain managed.

'You be all right if I go and make it?'

'I'm... OK... Just need... to get... my... brea... th.'

It was a good thirty minutes later that Lochlain managed, 'Right... Tell... me.'

Scott pursed his thin lips, a frown creasing his brow, as he looked at his brother struggling for every syllable.

'You sure?'

The ferocious look in Lochlain's eyes dared his brother to deny him this request.

'You lie back there and rest then. Don't try to talk. I'll tell you but remember, this is *my* mess. I'll get out of it. You know me. Mr Ingenuity. I will, Loch, I promise.'

As if fulfilling his side of the bargain, Lochlain leaned back against the pillows in his chair and closed his eyes.

'There's two bits to my job, right? The clinical work with infertile couples, and my research. And you know me, I can't stand mediocre – never could. So, since I went there, I've put a bloody great bomb under The Pemberton Centre. Our success rates have shot up. I'll tell you more about that in a minute.

'Anyway, I made a mistake. A while back we had this Nigerian couple. Nine months later they have twins. Only one's black and one's coffee-coloured.' Scott sketched out his spat with Jack. 'It had to be that damn pipette. But then the HFEA come barrelling in. I knew they wouldn't find out, no way they could. Except...'

Scott shot a furtive look at his brother lying back, no colour in his face. Lochlain opened his eyes, briefly, but it seemed too much effort to hold them open and listen. Scott ran his tongue over dry lips.

'The thing is, Loch, I've got several strings to my bow, just in case. And one of those sidelines means we get good results – results that put a smile on the face of the Chief Exec, and the director, *and* the HFEA. Keep the money coming in, and keep me in a place where I can work on *our* stuff. I've been, how can I put it? – creative! Upping the success rates for our IVF programme. See, over the years, male fertility's been decreasing, we know that. I won't go into why. Lots of the guys we see have deficient sperm: not enough, poor swimmers, funny looking. Not up to doing the business. So every now and then, I give them a wee helping hand. The men feel good, the hospital looks good, we get more trade, and nobody's hurt.'

He stopped suddenly, checking. Yes, the pulse in Lochlain's neck was throbbing visibly.

'I don't want to boast or anything, but I know my sperm are A1. Checked them myself. So a wee dash of them mixed in with the dad's, leave them to take pot luck, and bingo! Only I didn't do it for this black couple; I *know* I didn't. His specimen was borderline admittedly, and I did wonder about giving him a helping hand, but I know I remembered in time he was black. Besides it was her really. She's one of these big black women, solid muscle. Used to be a top athlete. They don't know what kind of damage it does to their bodies, all that training, all the strain of extreme physical exertion. Anyway, it was a genuine mix-up. Some other bloke's sperm left in the pipette. They've checked the DNA and it definitely wasn't mine.

'It kills me that I slipped up over a genuine mistake. If it had been anybody else but that bloody Fitzpatrick I'd have listened.'

Scott fell silent, tasting the bitterness of this truth.

'Only now the inspectors are poking their noses into everything. The official line is it's for our new licence. I'm not meant to know, but this guy in the DNA testing outfit is a mate, and he phoned, wanting to know what was up, with all these weird orders he was getting. So I had to get out before they came knocking on my door.

'But, don't you worry, bro. I've got it all sewn up. If they shut down that bit of my work, I've still got other things on the boiler. There's my mouse stuff. Those results – wow! They blew me away. So that's the procedures sorted. Next step, I needed the right material.' He leaned closer and his voice sank to conspiracy level. 'I can tell *you*, Loch – and nobody else in the world knows this – I've got these chimeras – part animal, part human. Perfect for the job. Nothing wrong if it's *my* semen, is there? Not hurting anybody else. And again, great results.

'Of course, the damned inspectors might just go stampeding all over the labs too, and if they find them, they might destroy them. But even if they do, I've got it covered. I've copied all my data onto this stick that I'm leaving with you. And I've got spare embryos in the lab – human embryos made with my sperm that the couples don't need. Frozen. Waiting till I can use them. And I can't see they'll destroy those. Not when they belong to real patients.

'Besides even if they did, there are still actual *kids* out there who've got my genes and nobody – *nobody* – is going to dispose of real live human children!'

Lochlain lay motionless. Scott sat for a long time looking at the distorted limbs, the deformed rib cage, the emaciated frame. Waves of pain washed over him. For the millionth time he knew the guilt of being a survivor. Why did this evil thing have to strike his brother? Why couldn't it have chosen him instead?

He'd done the only thing he could do: turned his own health to Lochlain's advantage, pursuing a career that took him towards a cure. And he'd uncovered a trump card that nobody could have predicted: they were the same tissue type. That fact alone had opened up undreamed-of possibilities. On the long, lonely nights he'd spent poring over his work, it had been some comfort that, though he got up to Thurso infrequently now, his whole life was devoted to Lochlain's cause. Once he'd found that cure, then they'd make up for lost time. They'd cycle round the coast to Duncansby Head together, watch sunsets from Scrabster, finish climbing the rest of the Munros they'd started ticking off in their teens.

He let his shoulders relax. Revealing his secrets had been cathartic. But what would it do to Lochlain? Would he understand? Scott smiled, remembering. How, when they were children, he'd read the prohibitions against 'lying with' animals in the Bible, in the days when their parents had dragged them to the Sunday School every week. He'd sniggered with Lochlain, imagining their mother sneaking off on a Saturday night to 'lie with' their cousins' Limousin bull or their own golden retriever, Cadbury. Leviticus seemed to say the surrounding nations did it, it was only the Israelites who were forbidden to practise it. Their minds conjured up plenty of amusement but they never for one moment believed it happened.

As an adult he recoiled from the idea of mixing human gametes with those of lower animals. It was nothing to do with religion, he'd left that behind along with adolescence. It just seemed intuitively wrong. Dangerous even. Imagine being responsible for viruses or other pathogens crossing species. And only an idiot would risk ten years behind bars for something they were uneasy about doing in the first place.

But then concern for Lochlain began to erode the borders of his scruples. The balance swung. What was his personal risk against the life of his beloved brother?

Besides, the potency and quality of human sperm had been tested on hamsters for ages. How many people knew that? And if they did, how many would object? It served a purpose.

So why not use animal eggs in research? It was an undisputed fact: there was a desperate shortage of human material. The current state of knowledge and technology meant they were using hundreds of eggs from young women to generate a single embryonic stem cell line. If you wanted to study specific diseases – MND, Huntington's, Alzheimer's, Parkinson's, whatever – you needed cell lines carrying the specific defect. Surely it made sense, economic as well as practical, ethical as well as scientific, to use animal eggs as a surrogate until the scientists had improved the efficiency of the whole process. Demonstrate that it works first, *then* you could move on to use human gametes further down the track, when you were more efficient and less wasteful.

And more than that, if you decided you needed to keep these embryos alive beyond the approved limit of fourteen days, it'd be a lot less repugnant to destroy them, than if they'd been wholly human.

The scientists, waiting for the right moment, passed on the whisper: hybrid embryos; 99.9% human, only 0.1% rabbit or goat or cow or whatever; they were the route to cracking conditions everybody dreaded. Including multiple sclerosis. An insignificant shift for a potentially vote-winning result. In 2007, four years after Scott started breaking the rules, the authorities finally got around to rubber-stamping the creation of chimeras.

But the moral indignation of the masses persisted: *'abhorrent', 'obscene', 'grotesque', 'undermining the essential distinction between species and the separateness of human beings.'* The new permission remained hedged about with provisos: the hybrid embryos could never get out of the lab; they had to be destroyed within fourteen days when they were no bigger than a pinhead. Same old narrow boxes, clipping the wings of the visionaries. Guaranteed to slow everything down. It would take years to hobble out of the lab.

And years was what Lochlain didn't have.

It had never been the Martindales' style to go down under the sheer weight of adversity. A problem presented, there had to be some route round it. What the moral guardians didn't know wouldn't harm them. Scott had lived up to his heritage. He'd been creative and dogged. Damn that bloody pipette.

When Scott woke himself it was to find Lochlain had slumped forward in his chair. He eased his brother back into a more comfortable position and wrapped a blanket around his withered legs. His hand lingered.

'Farewell, Loch. I'll be back.'

'Uncle Campbell' slipped away without a single witness.

# 40

QUESTIONS AND DOUBTS flickered around in her mind as Yasmeen looked down at her sleeping son. Little did he know the sacrifices they'd made for him.

She sighed. Life as a successful lawyer seemed so long ago, and even if this special child saved Sebastian, she'd still be needed at home caring for a new baby. Would she have the energy in her forties to juggle a demanding outside job with the broken nights, the endless domestic chores, the stream of minor ailments?

She'd been shocked at the toll this whole process was taking, in spite of her almost superstitious attention to detail. Each stage was etched on her memory, rehearsed again and again.

Harvesting the eggs had been a day for the turquoise outfit she'd worn to bring baby Shahira home from hospital, calm but momentous. Even so, she'd wept in the car going to the hospital. She'd wept for Sebastian left with his grandmother – again. For the prospect of no viable eggs. For the hopelessness of her son's future. Karim did his best to comfort; her sorrow was beyond rational argument.

But those tears were ruthlessly suppressed as soon as she stepped out of the car at the hospital, as if a giant windscreen wiper had engraved a smile on the entire surface of the world. No one else should know about the sick emptiness in the pit of her stomach, the sudden weight of her sandals. That, too, became part of the memory.

She chatted to the staff as they draped her and swung her legs up into the lithotomy poles. She laughed at Justin's jokes as he probed and extracted – even the jokes about eggs. She dismissed all suggestions that this was an emotional day; they'd had months to prepare for it, she said, studiously avoiding Karim's puzzled stare.

Nina, perched on a high stool somewhere out of sight, sent her verdicts through to the team at the sharp end: one good egg... two... three...

Yasmeen's jubilation when they harvested eight healthy eggs was genuine, the unpleasant effects of ovarian hyper-stimulation were forgiven. She clutched Justin's still-gloved hand and thanked him as if he had conjured this bounty out of nowhere. The nursing staff congratulated her. Karim ordered the largest bouquet of roses he had ever given her. 'Four for every potential baby!'

Only alone in the dark of that first night afterwards did she peep into the future prospect of none of those eggs being suitable for purpose. One glimpse, then she turned her back on disloyal thoughts. The first hurdle had been cleared with a wide margin.

Waiting for news of the fertilisation, there was absolutely nothing she could do but pray.

Karim's edginess was a new development, and Yasmeen realised for the first time how much she had come to depend on his calm confidence and support. It was her turn to reassure. Hadn't he successfully fathered two lovely children? Men's fertility was more durable than women's. Even if it didn't work this time he had plenty more where that came from; *he* had no need for artificial boosting, *he* wouldn't need injections.

She found herself tensing every time the phone rang, willing the conversation over, to leave the line free. All plans became tentative. Enquiries from the family, the children's naïve questions, every comment, began to irritate. Trepidation became her constant night companion and she began to push back her bedtime, preferring mindless tasks and tedium to insistent doubt.

The call came at 3.27. She was wearing a red maxi-dress, her nails painted to match. She was ironing a dress of Shahira's, listening to a play on the radio, a play about a heroin addict who befriended an elderly widow who… She missed the ending.

'Hello, Yasmeen. This is Astrid from the clinic.'

The world stopped.

Of course, Astrid was the ideal choice. An ectopic pregnancy in Sweden, followed by a miscarriage, and ten years of infertility; she knew all about bad news.

The sensation of moving in slow motion, of speaking from another planet, in a foreign language, became part of the memory.

'Yasmeen? Are you there?'

'I'm here. I'm just steeling myself.'

Astrid's voice smiled. 'I know exactly what you mean, but it is good news. Are you ready?'

'As ready as I'll ever be.'

'You gave us eight good eggs, remember?' As if she could ever forget! 'Five have fertilised, so we now have five embryos to test for Sebastian.'

'Five.' Yasmeen heard herself as if from a vast distance.

'Yes, five. This is a very good result. You should be happy.'

'Astrid, I shan't be happy until I'm holding Sebastian's brother or sister in my arms and he's had the stem cells. Successfully.'

'I understand. But we are over the *second* hurdle. We have embryos at least. Sometimes it is not so. And for you we have *five*. Five good ones.'

'I'll keep telling myself that.'

'We will let you know when they are tested.'

Eight down to five. Where next?

Karim was too positive and optimistic. Her mother was too silent. Pia was too anxious. Shahira was too persistent. Steering a course through this minefield was like hovering between a wedding and a funeral.

The inside of a pomegranate would forever remind Yasmeen of the third hurdle.

Sebastian had become a pernickety eater during hospital stays and indulging him during his illnesses had exacerbated the problem. Grilled grapefruit and fresh pomegranate had become unlikely favourites, and Shahira loved to retrieve the juicy seeds for him. She managed to smother everything in her range with the sticky red droplets, but her concentrated enjoyment made it all worthwhile.

On this occasion Shahira was standing on a chair beside her mother, wearing one of Karim's shirts to cover her from chin to ankle, bobbing up and down in her anticipation of the task ahead. Yasmeen had just washed her hair and it had started to slide out of the restraining grip, but her hands were already too sticky to touch it.

Her hands were what she remembered most vividly. They held the two halves of the pomegranate, the fruit packed in so tightly it seemed about to burst from the tough skin she'd just sliced. Like two ovaries packed with ripe follicles.

The shrill ring of the phone startled her out of her reverie. 4.24 precisely.

'Now go carefully, sweetheart. Try to keep all the juice in the dish too. Use this spoon. Don't touch the knives while I'm out of the room, will you? I'll just answer that and I'll be right back.'

Shahira delved into the succulent flesh with more enthusiasm than finesse, her tongue held between her teeth exactly like her father. Yasmeen threw one last look over her shoulder and moved into the hall. Strange how the sight of one drooping flower in the arrangement on the stairs held her attention. She wanted to stop the world while she removed it, start again with everything in order.

'Hello, Yasmeen. This is Astrid from the clinic. How are you?"

'Fine.'

'Is Karim with you?'

'No, he's still at work.'

'Ahh.'

'It's bad news then.'

'No. I only thought he might like to hear it with you.'

The pause was painful in its intensity.

'He won't be home till late tonight, I'm afraid,' Yasmeen said. 'They've got some performance coming up at school and it's the last full rehearsal.'

'Well, never mind. You will be able to tell him yourself. You remember you had five lovely healthy embryos? But we need only the same tissue-type as Sebastian, yes?'

'Yes.' It came out as a cracked whisper. If only they knew the sharpness of the sword that pierced her heart when they emphasised the healthiness of those unwanted embryos.

'And we only need one, yes?'

'Well, only one baby. But...'

'We have one!' she let it crow through the space between them. 'One good healthy embryo that matches. Well done. I am so pleased for you.'

Yasmeen crumpled down onto the floor, cradling the receiver against her ear, rocking herself back and forth.

'Yasmeen? Are you still there?'

'Yes,' she whispered.

'Are you all right?'

'Right this minute I don't know what I am, Astrid. Can you repeat that, please?'

'You have one healthy embryo that is a match for Sebastian.'

'Thank you. We have one embryo. We have an embryo. A match.'

'That's right. It is good news.'

'Good news.' Yasmeen heard her robotic voice coming from miles away. 'It *is* good news. What happens now?'

'We arrange for you to come in to have the embryo implanted. I will ring you again when you have had time to let this sink in, yes?'

'Yes. I need to talk to Karim.'

'Of course. I will speak to you soon.'

Yasmeen replaced the phone gently as if the click might splinter the fragile hold she had on sanity.

One chance. All their hopes pinned on one single embryo implanting successfully. Otherwise it was back to the starting post. It was like a board game with fortunes lost and found on a throw of the dice. She knew a moment of sympathy for Shahira's despair when, after successfully climbing ladder after ladder she bypassed all the competition, was within touching distance of the finishing line, only to land on a snake's head, plummeting down to square three on the board. She too wanted to shriek and stamp her feet.

*Shahira*!

She leapt to her feet and opened the kitchen door. Shahira looked up with an expression of unalloyed pleasure on her face. In front of her was a flat plate with an intricate pattern of red pomegranate seeds woven across it.

'This is for Bassy when he wakes up. See, this is his garden. And there's me. And there's you. And there's Daddy. And there's the new baby. And there's all the carrots and everything.'

'And Bassy? Where's he?' Something refused to dislodge itself from her throat. It had all the power of a prophetic omen.

'I'm doing him now. Only you came back too soon. He's going right in the middle. Cos it's his plate, and he can eat us all up, and then there'll just be him.'

Yasmeen hugged her sticky daughter.

'Thank you, darling. Bassy will love it. And I love you for doing all this for your little brother. And for being good while I was on the phone.'

Shahira was concentrating much too hard to reply.

'Can I leave you to finish off your picture while I phone Daddy?'

She nodded.

Merely telling Karim was all it took to open the tear ducts wide.

'I'll come home,' he said.

'No, don't. I'll be all right. I just needed you to know. It's all the emotion. I'll be fine in a minute. And Shahira's being a real sweetheart.'

'You sure? You're more important than a silly show.'

'I'm sure. And it's not a silly show. There's the self-esteem of thirty kids to worry about.'

'Bless you, Meena. I'll be home as soon as I can get away. Love you. And hang onto this: we're still in there with a chance.'

And Karim remained positive even in the face of her own doubt and despair. It irritated her, it annoyed her, it drove her to sharp retorts. But she needed him to keep the candle burning for both of them. She had an absurd sense that hope alone was keeping their dream alive.

For some unknown reason the memory of that gypsy woman predicting dark clouds swam into her mind. Only her love could save Sebastian. And Karim's strength would keep that love from faltering.

On the day of the implantation, events conspired to make it unforgettable in several ways.

The door-bell rang at 9.05 in the morning. Yasmeen was just back from taking Shahira to school and Sebastian was curled up on the settee watching CBeebies.

Arthur Frobisher had been to their house before but this time he stood on the bottom step empty-handed.

'Morning, Mrs Zair. And how are we today?'

'Fine, thank you.' Yasmeen glanced around for enlightenment.

'I was checking, like. In case you was out. No point lugging them flowers all the way up your path and then finding you was out.'

'Oh. You have flowers for me?'

'Indeed I do, ma'am. Not one, not two, but *three* lots and, if I may say so, our Ruthie's done you fair proud this time.'

Apparently each arrangement warranted a separate trip, and Yasmeen marvelled at the inefficiency of this aging delivery-man who clearly felt his mission was to bring sunshine and chatter to anyone who had the misfortune to be in their homes during working hours.

'Is it your birthday then?'

'No.'

'Something special though?'

'Yes.'

'Well, whatever it is, I hope you have a happy day.'

'Thank you very much.' What would he say if she told him? 'Pleasure to deliver flowers to a lovely lady like yourself.'

'Ruthie' had indeed surpassed herself. Yasmeen buried her nose in Karim's gift. The lilies in it were gorgeous, but their heady perfume might induce a headache if Sebastian inhaled them constantly. They were consigned to the hallway. She would still pass them countless times a day herself.

Her sister's orchids in ornamental grasses and reeds were dramatic but less overwhelming, and they tucked in nicely on the shelf beside the television, an artistic reminder of Pia's promise of support.

The third arrangement of chrysanthemums and roses, alstroemeria and carnations carried an unusual card. It looked as if it had been written at home and given to the florist to attach. '*Holding my breath and crossing my fingers for you today. Nobody deserves success more than you. Love and thanks, Candice.*'

Not every morning began with such affirmation, and Yasmeen found herself smiling as she worked surrounded by so much positive energy.

Karim had elected to go to work in the morning but be home in time to escort her to the clinic for 2.30, so Yasmeen had space to think and practise all her relaxing techniques.

At 12.15 the phone rang.

'Yasmeen. How are you, dear?'

'I'm fine, Mother. What about you?'

'I'm fine too, but I'm afraid Dad isn't. He's had very bad diarrhoea and vomiting this morning. The doctor's advised water only, but he's feeling very poorly.'

'Then, of course, you must stay with him. We'll be fine. Karim will take care of the children. Give my love to Dad. I hope he's soon better.'

'I feel really badly about letting you down today of all days, but I daren't come near Bassy until we know what this is. The last thing *he* needs is a tummy upset.'

'Absolutely. You take care of yourself too. The last thing *we* need is you ill as well!'

Yasmeen felt perfectly calm about the change in plans until Karim arrived home.

'You can't go for this on your own, Meena.'

'Course I can. Don't be silly. As long as I know the children are all right, I'll be fine.'

'But you need someone there with you. Shall I ring Pia?'

'No! I don't want to disrupt her plans at this late hour. Besides, she'd only fuss. The staff are old friends, and they'll be there for me. It can't be helped. Let's make the most of it.'

'Well, I'm not happy about it.'

Karim stomped off to the kitchen leaving Yasmeen willing herself to stay calm. I'm perfectly OK on my own. It'll happen if it's meant to happen. As long as the children are all right. The double meaning of 'the children' hit her foursquare. This embryo was also one of 'the children'. Their children. Hers and Karim's. And this one had a special pass in its pocket, a priority ticket to happiness.

She stood in the shower letting the warm water soothe and massage her. At the last minute she changed her mind, abandoned the plain navy trouser suit and chose a pale lilac shirt and straight black skirt that made her seem even taller than usual. It had no association with motherhood at all. She looked like a professional going to the office. She added an ornate silver bangle Karim had given her on their third anniversary. It suddenly mattered that she had something of him circling her.

With only minutes to go before the taxi arrived, saying goodbye took all her courage.

'This feels terrible,' he said into her hair.

'Well, gee, thanks. And I washed it only this morning.'

He gave her a half-hearted smile.

'I intend to treat you like egg-shell for the next nine months.'

Yasmeen saw the lines etched into his face and realised that today his was the harder role. At least in the centre of this particular drama she could play an active part.

'I'll be fine. And I'm not at all sure that I like the sound of egg-shell. But all our eggs are in this one basket, so fingers crossed, eh? '

'Thanks, Meena, for everything. You're fantastic.'

She kissed him quickly.

'Now, don't hurry back. Make sure you rest for as long as you can afterwards.'

It was a relief to hear the tooting of the horn.

'Pray for us, Karim,' she whispered, and was gone. She didn't dare look back but waved in his general direction with what she could only hope was a jaunty gesture.

'Where to, hen?' the taxi driver muttered vaguely, preoccupied with twiddling dials to turn off the crackling interference.

'The Infirmary. The Pemberton Centre, please.'

Whether it was the impossibility of knowing what to say to a lady going to the fertility centre, or because he was naturally taciturn, he drove in silence, occasionally picking at a spot on his neck, twice waving to a fellow cabbie.

The first person she saw was Astrid who strode forward to meet her, her face wreathed in smiles.

'I'm so pleased you're here,' Yasmeen said.

'I wanted to be here. And Dr Blaydon-Green wanted me to be here for you, because I have been your main contact. It is nice having the continuity.' Yasmeen felt a pang of disappointment. Connection, affection, special interest – something warm and emotional, please, not continuity. But Swedes weren't known for their effusiveness, the clipped precision of Astrid's speech was only a feature of her origins. As long as there was a friendly face, someone on her side. What nonsense! They were *all* on her side. Hadn't they fought for this moment? Hadn't they gone out on a limb for her? Yes. Everyone here was willing it to work.

One embryo; one chance. She had to give it all she could. She willed herself to conjure up a picture of Sebastian; her beautiful little boy. Four years of age. Wanting to live long enough to experience adolescence, manhood, old age. This was his lifeline.

She was already gowned and on the couch, relaxed in the dim light, when Justin Blaydon-Green entered the room, pristine, as if he'd just donned freshly laundered scrubs for a photo-shoot. He took her hand in both his, hands that held her destiny. Inexplicably she noticed the white mark where his watch usually sat, the prominence of the veins in the back of his hand, the moons on his thumbnails, absent from his fingers.

'Everything looks as good as it could be,' he said quietly. 'You've done really well. And we're all rooting for you.'

'Thank you so...' She couldn't continue. Closing her eyes, she felt him squeeze her hand, but remained perfectly still.

Padded footsteps moved in the background, murmured voices reached into the room. Astrid stayed close enough for Yasmeen to smell her perfume. Christian Dior's *Poison*. Justin talked her through the procedure.

'There. That's it, safely in position.'

3.42 precisely. Engraved on her memory.

He stood up, pushing the stool back, unravelling from a head to a giant in seconds. 'Now, I'd like you to remain like this for at least half an hour. Astrid will stay with you. She'll go over the precautions you should take when you get home, but otherwise that's it. Best of luck and we'll hope for good news when we next meet.'

Yasmeen tried to speak but nothing came out. Justin patted her arm. He knew.

Astrid kept her talking for far longer than the prescribed thirty minutes, and even then made the transition to sitting up a leisurely business. This was a precious embryo for them too.

Yasmeen lingered in the café, staring out at a lone rabbit grazing on the grassy bank, glancing at couples coming in the door at intervals – couples who slunk in, couples whose eyes darted, couples who clung close, couples who swaggered. Even two young women on their own. All with their own story to tell. All searching for a miracle.

Her mind strayed to Karim trying to occupy the children, his thoughts wandering the ten miles to the clinic. Should she ring him? No. She wanted to escape this place with dignity and composure. Time enough for emotion later.

Her mother would be living each second with her. But she must wait until Karim knew.

The taxi driver was a woman this time. She came right into the reception area and looked around her. As soon as she saw Yasmeen she moved forward.

'Mrs Zair?'

'Yes.'

'I'm ready when you are. Take your time.'

She walked alongside as if waiting for any sign of weakness, matching her stride to Yasmeen's. A hand under her elbow made Yasmeen feel protected as if this stranger shared her enormous secret by virtue of her womanhood.

She drove with great care and spoke only twice. 'You OK back there?' and 'I'll go this way – less bumpy.'

As soon as they drew up outside the house, Karim was at the door assisting her.

The driver smiled. 'You take care now.'

Memorable days every one.

But none harder than the Thursday she was due at the clinic to hear if she was pregnant. This time Karim insisted; he *had* to be there. Shahira would be at school, Pia would stay with Sebastian.

Yasmeen had no expectations. There were no outward signs; she felt exactly as she'd done before the implantation. Karim seemed to be shielding her from any outside stress: attending to

Shahira himself, taking her to school, playing with Sebastian until Pia arrived, despatching her to have a long soak in a scented bath.

She stood looking at the row of colours in her wardrobe. Something with good vibes. Something soft and caressing. The soft blue silk tunic with embroidered neckline and sleeves, yes. Matching trousers. Brand new, no associations, good or bad. She moved to the full-length mirror. Straight on. Sideways. She placed her hand gently on her flat abdomen. Chaotic thoughts chased one another through her mind. She moved abruptly to choose jewellery – silver – plain silver, to complement the blue.

Karim whistled. His appraisal, the look in his eyes, became part of the memory. He was wearing a black shirt, black trousers, standing very upright as if someone was about to measure his height for posterity. Funereal. It seemed to Yasmeen he drove as though reluctant to arrive.

The Pemberton looked exactly as it had done every other time she'd come here. No banners, no balloons. No hushed music. Nothing to declare this an auspicious day.

Only one other couple sat in the waiting area. Chinese, nervous, unknown. It felt like a luxury to be greeted warmly by four familiar faces, nurses who knew their story and had accompanied them on the journey.

Astrid detached herself from the group.

'Oh, you've had your hair cut! It suits you, Astrid. Very pretty.'

'Thank you. It is easy to care for so. I don't know how you manage to have yours so immaculate always – so thick, so shiny, so long.'

'I'm often tempted to chop it off, I can assure you!'

'And I won't let her,' Karim said quickly.

They all laughed before Astrid led the way down the corridor.

'How are you feeling?' Astrid asked.

'Fine, thanks.'

'Good. Take a seat. You are a little bit early but we will try not to keep you waiting. Dr Blaydon-Green wants to see you himself, of course.'

*Wants to see you himself.* So he expected bad news.

But Astrid would be there in case... No, *Karim* was there in case. So many safety nets.

Each second stretched to an hour. Karim kept sneaking glances at her out of the corner of his eye. She gritted her teeth.

Astrid reappeared. 'Would you like to come with me now?'

9.44.

Karim's hand clenched like a vice.

The room seemed bathed in light and Yasmeen had to shade her eyes to see the doctor against the window.

'So, how have you been since we last saw you?' The fact that he had been crouched between her legs, running catheters into her, last time they'd met seemed like an irrelevance.

'Fine, thank you. A little nervous, perhaps. But fine.'

Karim had the grace to say nothing.

'Any problems? Any spotting? Any symptoms of any sort?'

She shook her head to each query.

'OK. We're going to take a little blood, and then we'll know exactly where we are with this.'

Waiting in that clinical setting on their own made all the previous delays pale into insignificance. Karim held her in an enveloping hug, but they sprang apart when the door handle turned.

9.59.

With what seemed like great deliberation the two members of staff entered the room, their faces neutral, and took their seats. Yasmeen felt her heart pounding in her throat. Her eyes darted from one to the other. It was Justin who lent towards them.

'Congratulations. You are pregnant.'

The silence was deafening.

10.02. Two minutes past ten. Precisely.

Yasmeen closed her eyes fighting the burning sensation in her eyes, her throat, her chest. Karim was clutching her hand, waiting for her reaction before relaxing his own guard. When she opened them, the room swam through tears.

'Thank you. Thank you so, so much,' she whispered. And to her own astonishment she stood up and kissed first Justin, then Astrid, in turn. They smiled indulgently. It must often happen.

'We are all so thrilled for you,' Justin said, holding her hand in both his own, before releasing it and shaking Karim's. 'You don't need me to tell you how precious this little person is; you're the ones who've been through the mill to get to this point. So take very good care of yourself, Yasmeen, for the next nine months, and don't hesitate to get in touch if you have any questions, any problems. The obstetric team will keep us posted, but if you feel like dropping by any time we'd love to see you. And you can be sure Astrid and I will both want to see you once this little one arrives.'

'I'll make sure she takes care.' Karim was smiling broadly at her as he said it, but not until they were alone, cocooned in the car, did they really let themselves accept the reality.

'We've done it. We're going to have a baby.' Yasmeen said, her hand on her abdomen. 'A baby for Sebastian. I really didn't think I could be pregnant. I don't *feel* pregnant.'

'Well done, darling. Well done.'

Their kiss was a seal on all the promises made during the long painful months of waiting and fearing.

It was left to Shahira to change their emotion to laughter.

'...so we want you to be extra good and help Mummy so she doesn't get too tired,' Karim explained.

Shahira swung one leg and twirled the edge of her skirt, looking at her mother with a slight frown on her face. 'But I can still be naughty for Aunty Pia.'

'No. Of course you can't.'

'She'll still play with me, and she won't tell me off.'

'Have you been giving Aunty Pia a hard time, Shahira?' Yasmeen said sharply.

'No. I haven't. *Really, truly. I haven't.*'

'So how do you know she isn't cross when you're naughty?'

'Cos she told Granny Dita. I heard her. She said she couldn't be cross with me cos I was a poor little thing.'

Both her parents stared at her.

'I am,' she pronounced indignantly. 'I counted it. There's only three pounds and five p in my piggy bank. And I asked Granny Dita if you were poor if you only had three pounds and five p in the whole world and she said, yes. So Aunty Pia won't be cross.'

Yasmeen was still chuckling over this as they prepared for bed. Her moods changed like quicksilver these days, but it was disconcerting to feel the blast of cold air on her peace of mind so soon.

'There's one other thing, Karim – the press. They'll want to interview us. But I can't. Not now.'

'Fair enough. Don't.'

'My emotions are all over the place. And I refuse to break down in public. And what if things don't work out in the end? I can't. I can't face those people who say we're murderers.'

She buried her face in his shoulder. He held her tight.

'And you needn't. That's the least of your concerns. You're a life-giver. Your priority is to stay calm and healthy, and give this pregnancy – and Bassy – the best chance possible. No mum can do more than that.'

'But what if they find out?'

'We'll have a chat with Dr Blaydon-Green about it. I'm sure somebody in his team could field any questions the press might want answered. We have a right to privacy and so do the children. All three of them.'

'But I did agree before.'

'That was different. You weren't all hormonal then! And before it actually happened it was simply a theoretical possibility.'

'Which was an entirely different thing from the lived reality. Strange that. But it was. Now it's a baby. A real live baby. Our baby. It's not a means to an end. It's a person. A special person. Does that seem crazy?'

'Not to me. I'm in this too, you know. These are my children. And you're all my number one priority. We're not campaigners fighting for the right to have a donor sibling any more. We fought when we had to – well, *you* did! You helped move thinking on. Now we're the family of that donor sibling, its protectors, fighting for it to be born well and strong, and in a position to save its brother's life. Pretty high octane stuff, eh?'

'What would I do without you?'

'You're not about to find out.'

# 41

JACK SLID FURTHER along the hated leather sofa and wedged one foot against the arm to hold himself in position more securely. He fidgeted for several minutes, propped his book open on his chest, and settled down to read. What bliss! A whole Saturday morning of uninterrupted peace with Douglas Kennedy's latest novel.

'Jack. Jack! Wake up!'

The sight of Patsy's startling eyelash-extensions at close quarters was disorientating. Jack's mind shot to Gulliver. He moved one arm a millimetre. No, he wasn't pegged down.

'Uhhhh?'

'For goodness' sake! *Wake up!*' she hissed.

He shook himself, and adopted his best Dalek impersonation. 'I have now re-entered the land of the living. I have relinquished all prospect of a peaceful morning. I am entirely at your disposal, Mistress.'

Patsy leaned forward and prodded his chest with her long nails.

'Shut *up*, Jack, and listen. Dr Blaydon-Green's been on the phone.'

Jack shot bolt upright, smoothing his hair, pushing his feet into his shoes. 'Why didn't you get me?'

'Because he said to leave you sleeping, that's why.'

'You *didn't* tell him I was dozing.' His appalled expression made her grin.

'No, I told him you were so sound asleep I *couldn't* wake you!'

'I was *not*!'

'You were too.'

'Well, anyway, what did he say?'

'He wants you to ring him, once you've had your sleep.'

'Did he say what it's about?'

'Nope.'

'Didn't you ask?'

'Nope.'

'Did he leave a number?'

'Yep.'

Jack listened to Justin's news in complete silence.

'Thanks, Boss. Good of you to phone... Will do... See you Monday. Bye.'

As he walked back into the living room, Patsy backed away.

'What? What is it?'

Jack stared at her. 'This goes no further, OK?'

She nodded, her tongue slipping out to wet her lip.

'Remember Scott? The guy in our lab.'

'Yeah.'

'Well, they've got him. They caught him this morning. The boss has just been told. Thought I'd want to know.'

'That was good of him. Phoning you.'

'He's a good bloke, Dr B-G.'

'What else did he say?'

'Seems Great Scott was about to slip out of the country.'

'You don't sound exactly pleased or anything.'

'That's because I've just seen the time, that's why. Ten past one! Where's the morning gone, that's what I want to know?'

'Don't try to change the subject, Jack. You know where it went. Why aren't you pleased?'

'I don't know.' He was thinking on his feet here. 'Must be something wrong with a clever fellow that goes off the rails like that. I guess, well, he deserves a bit of privacy. He probably needs treatment. Who knows?'

'Well, blow me down! This is the guy that bullied you. That tried to get you chucked out of your job. The guy that's been guffing up stuff. And you think...' She spread her hands in despair. 'Sometimes I can't fathom you, Jack.'

'Well…'

'Don't you *dare!*' Her ferocity took him by surprise. Her hand came down over his mouth; he smelt Nivea handcream. 'You quote one single word of Oscar flaming Wilde and you're dead meat.'

He let his eyes appeal for him.

'Promise?'

'Promise,' he said against her palm, dropping a kiss behind the word to seal it.

She moved away cautiously, keeping him in her sights.

'Well, well, well. So, Mr Clever Clogs will…' he said softly, more to himself than to her.

'What'll happen now?'

'I haven't the foggiest notion. Depends why he did it, I guess. The boss thinks probably psychiatric help.'

'But they wouldn't take him back up at your place, would they?'

'Nah. They couldn't. And I seriously doubt anybody'd employ him as an embryologist ever again.' A long pause. 'Pity that.'

'How come?'

'He was hard working. Knew his stuff, got results. And by all accounts an exceptionally good researcher.'

'Good? I don't call it good mucking around with babies. Giving people mixed-up twins, babies that aren't properly theirs.'

'No, course not. I didn't mean good as in morally good. Good as in clever. Good as in internationally recognised.'

'He very nearly sent us off to Australia!' Patsy bridled indignantly at the very memory.

'Aw, now, come on, Pats, be fair. Australia was your idea.'

'Only because you said we had to get away.'

'Anyway, we didn't go. Here we are in our own wee nest, same old useless sofa, same old antiquated me, same old, same old. So tell me, are you happy here? D'you want to stay put, or d'you want to spread your wings and try some place else? It's up to you.' He sat down and pulled her onto his knee.

She draped her arms around his neck and searched his face.

'You know what, Jack? I want to hear what *you* want.'

'Me, I'm an old stick-in-the-mud, me, as you know only too well. As long as I've got a roof over my head, a few creature comforts, a job I enjoy, my books, I reckon I could be happy pretty much anywhere. So you choose.'

'You're something else, you know. But what I *do* know is that you're a different man nowadays. Since that Scott person scarpered. And I kind of like having the old Jack back; sizzing, Oscar, hairy ears – the lot. So if you're happy, I'm happy.'

'And the other thing?'

'You mean...?'

'Yep. Babies.'

'I'd really like that, Jack,' she said softly, tracing his cheek with one thumb.

'Good show.'

'I'll even come up to your place if we need it – now that guy's gone. Seems to me you lot do a pretty cool job, all things being equal. Those twins came in for their injections this week, and they are so-o scrummy.'

'Now steady on! *You* might be OK with coming into the shop, but what about *me*?' He strummed his chest for emphasis. '*I* have to look these guys in the eye on a daily basis, remember.'

'So you'd better do your stuff properly here then, hadn't you?'

He grinned at her.

'Just say the word, Mistress.' The Dalek monotone covered his awkwardness.

Much later he propped himself up on one elbow and stared down at her.

'You know what, Patsy? When you're cooped up at home with a bunch of squalling kids you could write those books we talked about. And you've already got the plot for the first one. There's this clinic with all sorts of skulduggery going on. Getting things all mixed up. And when it becomes a bestseller and you're on the telly, I can talk about my partner, Patsy Graham, the novelist.'

'Write it yourself! You're the one with your nose everlastingly in books, not me.'

'Ah, my friend was on the button as usual. *Good novelists are much rarer than good sons.*'

But Patsy was right on one thing. Work was once again a happy place to be.

The new embryologist, Dr Heather Maxwell, was a friendly Glaswegian. She came, not with a hugely impressive CV, or an all-consuming passion for high-powered research, but with yards of compassion and a real team spirit.

Jack whistled as he cycled to work. He was the first in, the last out many a day. Ease and trust returned. In spite of the stringent regulations, they joked as they worked. They developed a cheerful rivalry over who handled the most cases in a week. And Heather became a worthy sparring partner; she traded facts, one-liners and insults alike.

Jack was listening to her and Justin expounding on the latest technique for retrieving eggs when he dared his first sideswipe.

'*Learned conversation is either the affectation of the ignorant or the profession of the mentally unemployed.*'

'That lets you off the hook then!' she'd quipped.

Jack was her slave from that moment.

In her second week he recounted a bizarre experience where he'd received a substantial parcel of unsolicited books.

'Sounds to me as if you need another parcel of books on the proper use of English,' she taunted.

'Meaning?'

'Your use of the present perfect tense distorts the whole sense of what you're trying to convey.'

'*I am sick to death of cleverness,*' Jack flashed back. '*Everybody is clever nowadays. You can't go anywhere without meeting clever people. The thing has become an absolute public nuisance.*'

'Brilliant,' she responded, eyes dancing. 'I wish I had your facility with these quotes.'

'How about you teach me to speak Queen's English in return for me teaching you a few Wilde quotes? If you mean it.'

'Oh, I mean it. But a) I doubt my own grasp of English grammar would get us very far. And b) I doubt I could remember your quotes well enough to get them exactly right.'

'Course you could. Brain like yours.'

'Right then. Give me a try.'

'Well, say two people are arguing and you're wanting a bit of peace. There's: *It is only the intellectually lost who ever argue.* But, of course, you need to know the people in question have a sense of humour. Your predecessor was a one for arguing, but he sure was behind the door when the Almighty was giving out a sense of humour.'

'Hmm. So I don't have to be a bona fide comedienne to get brownie points there then.'

He grinned. 'What was that quote I just gave you?'

'*It is only the intellectually lost... It is only the intellectually lost who ever argue.* Yes?'

'See. Easy, isn't it?'

'Next?'

'How about one that'd make a good placard for your desk?'

'Try me.'

'Apparently some place like a club or a hotel or somewhere, I don't remember the details, but anyway they had a notice over the piano: *Please do not shoot the pianist. He is doing his best.*'

Heather grinned. 'And you think I could adapt it to: *Please don't shoot the embryologist. She's doing her best.*'

'You're quick, I'll say that for you, Doc.'

'A few more months stuck in these four walls with you and I'll be quicker still – out of the door!'

Jack laughed.

'D'you know anybody that bores on a bit about something or other?'

'Yeah. You!' she retorted.

'OK then. Here's one to sling at me: I'm *bored by the tedious and improving conversation of those who have neither the wit to exaggerate nor the genius to romance...*'

Some weeks later Astrid bounced into the staff room in the middle of one such lively exchange.

'Yasmeen Zair is here. Jack, you have met her; the saviour sibling case, remember? She has brought her little boy to see us. You know, the one with Diamond Blackfan's. He is so-oo beautiful.'

It was such a rare experience to see the Swedish nurse animated that both Heather and Jack jumped to their feet.

Yasmeen was looking fabulous. Dressed entirely in black, her blue-black hair gleaming, touches of gold at her neck, her ears, her wrists, her feet, she looked like someone straight off the catwalk.

'Hi,' Jack said, crouching low towards the child standing close beside her. 'You must be Sebastian. We've heard lots about you. My name's Jack. Like Jack and the Beanstalk. Little Jack Horner. Jack fell down and broke his crown.'

'Jack be nimble, Jack be quick,' Sebastian said with a darting look.

Jack hopped smartly round the clinic. The boy nodded, following his antics. The smile grew across his face.

'And this is Heather,' Jack said. 'She's new here but...' – he put his hand up as if to tell a secret – 'she's a really cool lady.'

'Hiya, Sebastian. And how old are you?' Heather said.

'Four. But I'll be five in December.'

'*December?* What date? Christmas Day?'

'No! That's *Jesus'* birthday.'

'When's your birthday then, when you'll be a big five?'

'The second.'

'Second of December. Wow. My little boy's birthday's the second of January. The next month to yours.'

'How old's he?'

'He'll be seven.'

'My big sister's seven in three weeks.'

'That's big.'

'But we're going to have another brother or sister next year.'

'Are you now? How cool is that?'

Heather stood up and smiled at Yasmeen. 'I'm so pleased for you. How're you keeping?'

'Tired, but otherwise fine, thanks.'

'You look amazing, but I know that doesn't help when you feel lousy.'

Yasmeen looked down at Sebastian. 'But Bassy, you came here to say something very special, didn't you?'

All eyes focused.

'Remember? What do you want to say to all these kind people who're helping you get better?'

'Thank you,' the child said, his eyes solemnly surveying each in turn as if his scrutiny would winkle out any imposters.

'Well, d'you know something, Sebastian?' Jack said, crouching down again. 'I've been here the longest of everybody in this room, and that's the first time we've ever had a wee boy who's four, going to be five on the second of December, come in to say thank you. I think that deserves a big clap, yes?'

They all applauded, and another smile broke across the child's face.

'I've just been to see the consultant obstetrician but I wondered if Dr Blaydon-Green was available,' Yasmeen said.

'Hang on a sec,' Jack said, 'I'll go and check.'

Justin needed no persuasion.

As soon as he entered the waiting area the rest of the team melted away.

Jack beckoned to Sebastian. 'Want to come and see what we keep behind the door over there?'

Sebastian advanced with caution and Jack gave him space, but shuffled comically over to the corner where the toys were to be found. In no time the two were building a track for the ancient wooden train. Keeping the engine on the ragged tracks required concentration, but fragments of the adult conversation filtered across the room as if from a child's homemade walkie-talkie set.

'The paediatricians... building him up... prophylactic antibiotics... as well as possible... stem cells... thanks to...

He had only just ironed out the wrinkles in their design when Yasmeen approached and they took their leave.

Justin and Jack watched them walk out of the building.

'You wouldn't know there was anything serious wrong with him seeing him like that, would you?' Jack said pensively. 'Lovely kid.'

'No. The cruelty of nature, huh? Beautiful family, ugly disease.'

'Well, as my friend would say: *Nature has good intentions of course, but, as Aristotle once said, she cannot carry them out.*'

'Ahh now, that's a different kettle of fish. Aristotle has a certain something Wilde lacks.'

'Antiquity? Gravitas?'

'Something along those lines.'

'Feels good giving nature a wee bit of a nudge in the right direction for such a family, though, eh?'

'It does, Jack. It certainly does. Mind you, this is a year I certainly don't want to repeat. Ever!'

'I don't know. We got Heather because of it.'

'True.'

'And the Opakanjos didn't sue us.'

'True again.'

'And if Mrs Zair has that baby you fought for, and it can save the life of that cute little fellow – I'd call that a success and a half.'

'Our first saviour sibling. You could be right, Jack.'

'And I'm still here to pester you, Boss.'

'Don't push your luck!'

# POSTSCRIPT

AS A PRECAUTION Justin was chairing this last session of the reproductive medicine conference himself, on hand to intervene if things threatened to get out of control.

'Ladies and gentlemen, it's an enormous privilege for me to introduce our last speaker of the day, a lady whose courage, whose integrity, whose charm, inspired the whole team at The Pemberton Centre where I'm based. She's a successful lawyer and an accomplished musician, as well as a member of a Clinical Ethics Committee. And she's here to tell her own story. Please welcome Mrs Yasmeen Zair.'

The audience responded politely.

Yasmeen, impeccably groomed, looked every inch the professional. And bewitching. Her voice was low and even, no theatrics, no gimmicks; the unvarnished truth was enough. The atmosphere throughout her talk was electric. Justin, watching the rows of faces in front of him, saw every eye riveted. But she ended her comments with her own bombshell.

'And now I should like to introduce the real stars: my children. Without them there would be no story to tell. But they specially asked that they be allowed to add their perspective.'

Two children walked onto the platform to utter silence.

Shahira began. She had grown from an engaging youngster to a beautiful young woman, the image of her mother, with a poise and elegance to match.

'I just want to say a big thank you to Dr Blaydon-Green and his team for having the courage to fight for our family. During the years my brother was so ill we lived every day afraid. I can still remember watching him being carted off to hospital terribly sick, every time dreading he would never come home again. Then Vashti Armani was born, and our whole lives changed. Her birth saved Sebastian's life. It also gave us security. Now, when my parents say they'll be at my end-of-year ceremony at school, or sports day, or my graduation, or my wedding, I believe them. My only regret is that they didn't have another donor sibling for *me* as an investment for *my* future.'

A ripple of amusement, followed by strong applause.

Sebastian stepped forward. At fifteen he was tall for his age and he looked out at the hundreds of unknown faces fearlessly.

'I'm the cause of all the trouble.' He hesitated as they tittered. 'And I have to be grateful to everyone: my parents for caring enough to fight for me; Shahira for putting up with all the broken appointments, the chaotic childhood; Dr Blaydon-Green and his team for helping my kid sister to come into existence; and Vashti Armani for saving my life. *My* only regret is that she wasn't a boy. I can't say I'm keen on having female cells circulating in my body.'

Clapping and laughter greeted this admission and a grin lit up Sebastian's face.

There was a pause, then Karim stood up from the audience and began to push a wheelchair towards the platform. It was as if a solid door had shut out every sound in the auditorium.

Vashti Armani was small and slight and somehow lost in her chair. She hesitated and reached a hand back to Shahira for reassurance. Karim, standing to one side, took a hesitating step forward, but then stopped as Shahira bent to adjust the microphone for her sister's reduced height, and crouched beside her, whispering reassurance.

'I'm nine, nearly ten. I expect you're wondering why I'm in this wheelchair. I got meningitis when I was two and they had to take off both my legs and four of my fingers. Usually I can walk with my prostheses, but right now I need new ones because I've just had a growth spurt and the old ones rub, so it's not as bad as it looks. Anyway, I know that I wouldn't have been born at all if my brother hadn't been ill. I'm glad I was, though, because I have a great life. My family all love me and I love them, and if

I get sick I get first claim on Bassy's organs! Only trouble is, his legs are too long for me!'

Shahira stepped back and the entire audience rose to their feet. The applause was thunderous. Yasmeen moved across to stand behind her children for a few seconds, and then shepherded them off the platform, this time wheeling the chair herself. Karim was openly wiping his eyes.

Justin walked forward still clapping until they were safely seated.

'If there is a single person in this conference hall without a lump in their throat or a tear in their eye, let me tell you something; you're in the wrong job!'

A murmur of assent went up.

'Thank you hugely from all of us, Yasmeen, Shahira, Sebastian and Vashti Armani. Your voice is one we too seldom hear. It's my personal privilege to know you all. And it's the privilege of everyone here today to have been moved by your eloquence, your courage and your insights. Not one person who attended this conference will forget your contribution. I didn't know that you young people were actually going to say anything, but there can be no more appropriate endorsement for what the rest of us do than to hear from your own lips what this experience has meant to you and your family. Sebastian, I hope that in time you'll mind less about the female stem cells. Who knows, perhaps it'll help you to be more in touch with your feminine side, and more sensitive to what makes women tick!'

Sebastian grinned, Shahira nodded vigorously, the audience chuckled.

Justin kept the concluding remarks brief. His eye caught that of Natalie Wyatt seated two rows from the back.

'May I again remind anyone from the press that, as we said at the beginning of the proceedings this morning, nothing from this conference should be reported without prior sight of the conference organisers. These are sensitive issues and a chance word taken out of context can damage lives.'

He made it his personal responsibility to shadow the Zairs to ensure they received the praise of the majority without being exposed to intrusion or criticism.

Not until they were in the car park did he relax his guard. Then just as Karim was about to drive away, Sebastian leaned out of the window.

'Dr Blaydon-Green.'

'Yes, Sebastian?'

'What's the one new thing you hope nobody gives you for your birthday?'

'Tell me.'

'Pneumonia.'

They were all laughing as they drove away.

# Discussion Points for Bookclubs

Q. Could you summarise in no more than four adjectives the main characteristics of Justin, Scott, Jack, Candice, Yasmeen, and Natalie? How true to form is their behaviour as the plot unfolds?

Q. Who is your favourite character in the story and why?

Q. Justin is the pivotal character around whom all the different strands of the book twine. How satisfied were you with this structure given that it's the Opakanjos and Zairs whose stories form the strongest narrative threads?

Q. If you were the parents of the twins would you wish to know which one of you was not biologically related to Destiny? Does Justin's argument for not knowing (Chapter 38) persuade you?

Q. At what points did your own suspicions about what happened in the lab change? What influenced your thinking?

Q. The relationship between Candice and Samuel changes dramatically. How much is this a feature of becoming parents, or the circumstances leading to Destiny's conception, or their basic personalities? Could the problems have been circumvented?

Q. All the Zair family suffer in various ways because of Sebastian's illness. Whose burden is greatest, would you say? Without the benefit of hindsight the nurse in the prologue believes Sebastian should be spared years of suffering and allowed to die peacefully. Do you agree?

Q. Have your views on a) fertility treatment and b) saviour siblings changed as a result of reading this book?

Q. Professor Ben Norton in Chapter 33 says that society and individuals need to have a weighty reason to deny the Zairs the opportunity to save the life of their son. Could you give a weighty enough reason?

Q. Bobby suggests (Chapter 28) that a) infertility treatment might not be in the interests of would-be parents and b) selection of embryos devalues the life of disabled people. Do you agree with her arguments?

Q. If you were the consultant approached by the Zairs would you have supported their cause?

Q. The destruction of healthy embryos involved in IVF with PGD is a major stumbling block for Yasmeen. Would it be for you?

Q. What do you think about the creation of embryos that are part human, part animal? Have your opinions changed after reading this story?

Q. Jennifer Ruskin, on the ethics committee, wheels out the old argument about slippery slopes (Chapter 26). Melody Turner, the pro-life campaigner, picks up the same theme (Chapter 33). To what extent do you agree with them? Would you be persuaded by Justin's defence? Are you influenced by the personalities of the individuals?

Q. The radio (Chapter 28) and TV (Chapter 33) news reports summarise the debate about saviour siblings. Whose arguments are most persuasive in your judgement?

Q. Scott's moral boundaries changed over time and with circumstances. Did your sympathies change with more knowledge of what drives him? At what point do you feel he overstepped an acceptable limit? Were his motivations sufficient reason to go beyond the legally allowable? When he revealed all to his brother in Chapter 39 what was your overriding response?

Q. Natalie is under pressure to deliver a newsworthy story. How far do you think her tactics are justified? She promises Scott their conversations in private are confidential. Would you trust her?

Q. How far is it legitimate for protesters to go in *defending the rights of innocent creatures*? Justin asks Dan Cruse, *'Is violence ever justified?'* Is it?

Q. Karim acquired information about the Opakanjos' address in the course of his professional work. Was he right to divulge it to his wife?

Q. What part do you think Jack's sense of humour plays in the story? Why do you think it took so long for him to share his suspicions with Justin?

If you are interested in further information about medical ethics or this series of books, visit the author's website and weekly blog. The website provides further discussion questions for students and teachers of medical ethics; an author profile; details of her books and the ethical topics covered in them; and links to related websites.

www.hazelmchaffie.com
www.VelvetEthics.com

## Right to Die
Hazel McHaffie
ISBN 1 906307 21 0 PBK £12.99

## Remember Remember
Hazel McHaffie
ISBN 978 1906817 78 7 PBK £7.99

Naomi is haunted by a troubling secret. Struggling to come to terms with her husband's death, her biggest dread is finding out that Adam knew of her betrayal. He left behind an intimate diary – but dare she read it? Will it set her mind at rest – or will it destroy the fragile control she has over her grief?

Caught by the unfolding story, Naomi discovers more than she bargained for. Adam writes of his feelings for her, his challenging career, his burning ambition. How one by one his dreams evaporate when he is diagnosed with a degenerative condition, Motor Neurone Disease. How he resolves to mastermind his own exit at a time of his choice... but time is one luxury he can't afford. Soon he won't be able to do it alone. Can he ask a friend, or even a relative, to commit murder?

A startlingly clear-sighted and courageous story, this novel explores the collision between uncompromising laws, complex loyalties and human compassion.

*Lively and intensely readable...*
ALEXANDER McCALL SMITH

The secret has been safely kept for 60 years, but now it's on the edge of exposure.

Doris Mannering once made a choice that changed the course of her family's life. The secret was safely buried, but now with the onset of Alzheimer's her mind is wandering. She is haunted by the feeling that she must find the papers before it's too late, but she just can't remember...

Jessica is driven to despair by her mother's endless searching. But it's not until lives are in jeopardy that she consents to Doris going into a residential home. As Jessica begins clearing the family home, bittersweet memories and unexpected discoveries await her. But these pale into insignificance against the bombshell her lawyer lover, Aaron, hands her.

*It provides an amazing insight into the thought process of someone with dementia, as well as being a gripping and heartfelt narrative.*
JOURNAL OF DEMENTIA CARE

**An Experiment in Compassion**
Des Dillon
ISBN 978 1906817 73 2 PBK £8.99

**My Epileptic Lurcher**
Des Dillon
ISBN 978 1906307 74 5 HBK £12.99

Stevie's just out of jail. Newly sober and building a relationship with his son, he's taking control of his own life. But what about his younger brother, Danny?

In this touching and darkly funny story of retribution and forgiveness, Stevie battles against the influences that broke him before, while Danny and his girlfriend spiral further into self-destruction. Can the bond between the two brothers be enough to give them both a fresh start?

Cycles of alcohol abuse affect individuals, families and communities. For each person who tries to break away, there are innumerable pressures forcing them back into familiar patterns. And for those that can't escape, that are fated to make the same choices again and again – can we still feel compassion?

*...amongst the violence and paranoia, lies hope, love and a great deal of wit. And it is this that Dillon captures so truthfully: the backstory behind the Buckfast.*
THE LIST

The incredible story of Bailey, the dog who walked on the ceiling; and Manny, the guy who got kicked out of Alcoholics Anonymous for swearing.

Manny is newly married, with a puppy, a flat by the sea, and the BBC on the verge of greenlighting one of his projects. Everything sounds perfect. But Manny has always been an anger management casualty, and the idyllic village life is turning out to be more *League of Gentlemen* than *The Good Life*. As his marriage suffers under the strain of his constant rages, a strange connection begins to emerge between Manny's temper and the health of his beloved Lurcher.

*...it's one of the most effortlessly charming books I've read in a long time.*
SCOTTISH REVIEW OF BOOKS

## A Snail's Broken Shell
Ann Kelley
ISBN 978 1906817 40 4 PBK £8.99

*What if I had been born with a normal heart and normal everything else? Would I be the same person or has my heart condition made me who I am?*

For the first time in years Gussie can run, climb and jump. Every breath she takes is easier now, and every step more confident, but Gussie can't help wondering about her donor. Was she young? Had she been very sick or was there an accident?

And with her new life comes a whole new set of problems. She is going back to school at last – but she doesn't know anyone her own age. With school not meeting up to her expectations, Gussie turns to her old pastimes of birdwatching and photography, but troubling news awaits her there too...

*A Snail's Broken Shell* is the fourth book in the the Gussie series. The first in the series, *The Bower Bird*, won the Costa Children's Award and the UK Literacy Association Book Award.

## Archie and the North Wind
Angus Peter Campbell
ISBN 978 1906817 38 1 PBK £8.99

The old story has it that Archie, tired of the north wind, sought to extinguish it.

Archie genuinely believes the old legends he was told as a child. Growing up on a small island off the Scottish coast and sheltered from the rest of the world, despite all the knowledge he gains as an adult, he still believes in the underlying truth of these stories. To escape his mundane life, Archie leaves home to find the hole where the North Wind originates, to stop it blowing so harshly in winter.

Funny, original and very moving, *Archie and the North Wind* demonstrates the raw power of storytelling.

*The tale is complex, but told in confident style. Although every page is marked with some unquiet reflection, these are off-set by amusing observations which give the novel a sparkle.*
SCOTTISH REVIEW OF BOOKS

## Da Happie Laand
Robert Alan Jamieson
ISBN 978 1906817 86 2 PBK £9.99

In the summer of the year of the Millennium, a barefoot stranger comes to the door of the manse for help. But three days later he disappears without trace, leaving a bundle of papers behind.

*Da Happie Laand* weaves the old minister's attempt to make sense of the mysteries left behind by his 'lost sheep' – the strange tale of a search for his missing father at midsummer – with an older story relating the fate of a Zetlandic community across the centuries, the tales of those people who emigrated to New Zetland in the South Pacific, and those who stayed behind.

*Jamieson's strange masterpiece Da* Happie Laand *haunts dreams and waking hours, as it takes my adopted home of Shetland, twisting it and the archipelago's history into the most disturbing, amazing, slyly funny shapes.*
TOM MORTON, THE SUNDAY HERALD

## This Road is Red
Alison Irvine
ISBN 978 1906817 81 7 PBK £7.99

It is 1964. Red Road is rising out of the fields. To the families who move in, it is a dream and a shining future.

It is 2010. The Red Road Flats are scheduled for demolition. Inhabited only by intrepid asylum seekers and a few stubborn locals, the once vibrant scheme is tired and out of time.

Between these dates are the people who filled the flats with laughter, life and drama. Their stories are linked by the buildings; the sway and buffet of the tower blocks in the wind, the creaky lifts, the views and the vertigo. *This Road is Red* is a riveting and subtle novel of Glasgow.

*…one of the most important books about Glasgow and urban life I've read in a very long time. It offers an insight into city life that few Scottish novels can emulate.*
PROFESSOR WILLY MALEY

## **Luath** Press Limited

*committed to publishing well written books worth reading*

LUATH PRESS takes its name from Robert Burns, whose little collie Luath (*Gael.*, swift or nimble) tripped up Jean Armour at a wedding and gave him the chance to speak to the woman who was to be his wife and the abiding love of his life. Burns called one of the 'Twa Dogs' Luath after Cuchullin's hunting dog in Ossian's *Fingal*. Luath Press was established in 1981 in the heart of Burns country, and is now based a few steps up the road from Burns' first lodgings on Edinburgh's Royal Mile. Luath offers you distinctive writing with a hint of unexpected pleasures.

Most bookshops in the UK, the US, Canada, Australia, New Zealand and parts of Europe, either carry our books in stock or can order them for you. To order direct from us, please send a £sterling cheque, postal order, international money order or your credit card details (number, address of cardholder and expiry date) to us at the address below. Please add post and packing as follows: UK – £1.00 per delivery address; overseas surface mail – £2.50 per delivery address; overseas airmail – £3.50 for the first book to each delivery address, plus £1.00 for each additional book by airmail to the same address. If your order is a gift, we will happily enclose your card or message at no extra charge.

**Luath** Press Limited
543/2 Castlehill
The Royal Mile
Edinburgh EH1 2ND
Scotland
Telephone: +44 (0)131 225 4326 (24 hours)
Fax: +44 (0)131 225 4324
email: sales@luath.co.uk
Website: www.luath.co.uk